# Prisoners of Beliefs

To Sean,
Thank you for everything
you do for everyone.
Sept. 2022

## Richard Roe

(died, sadly, 12.1.23

First published in the UK in 2022



ISBN (PB) 978-1-7391622-0-7

ISBN (E) 978-1-7391622-1-4



A CIP catalogue record for this book is available from the British Library.

To all the people who have shared the challenges of their lives and helped me on the journey to write this book.

# Part One

# The Arrivals

## 2019, Africa, Karrle

Was the cold shudder shooting down his spine the future warning the present? Everything he understood about life had ended. Karrle suddenly realised that he was utterly alone for the first time in his life.

In short, he had become a migrant.

## 2022, London, Charles and Karrle

Charles's delight cannot be concealed as he returns to his Rolls Royce. Karrle sits in the front passenger seat. Sharing his joy, Charles opens the conversation. 'How did you know they could not meet the delivery schedule? That's not what they said!'

'Observing animal behaviour. You've never stalked an animal for food, have you?'

Rather pompously Charles retorts, 'It has not been necessary in my supermarket.'

'Whilst you listened to the words, I studied the language of the body. Every time delivery was mentioned, their hands blocked direct eye contact and they fidgeted nervously. Your purchase order was huge for them. They feared that the tight deadline might endanger the launch of the new product and damage your reputation in the market, and be a catastrophe for them.'

Charles looks at his employee like pupil to master. Karrle continues. 'You are a businessman, trained to follow logic, but their bodies betrayed their words. Delaying the launch one month, and dual sourcing for twelve, avoided failure and was their best chance to keep the contract.'

An inward smile radiates through Charles; he cannot resist reflecting on his good fortune at discovering his new friend, and in the strangest of circumstances, as if nature's plan were unfolding in a pre-ordained ever-brighter future.

The limousine seamlessly joins the motorway and both men retreat into their thoughts, detached from time and location. Charles focuses on his ambitions and Karrle relives the day that changed his life forever.

........................

Sitting at home, drinking tea with his mother, stampeding feet burst through the front door. An intruder spat a message so urgently that the occupants were stunned. 'Karrle, they're coming. You have to get out, NOW!'

Gathering her senses first, Mother asked, 'Who?'

'The militia.'

'How long?'

'Seconds. They're right behind me. You must get far away.'

Scrambled thoughts paralyse comprehension.

The old lady was the first to move. Ignoring arthritic joints, she scurried across the floor, opens a cupboard and removes the family pot. She thrusts all the notes into her bewildered son's hand. He could not know that this would be his last image of her, or the last words he would ever hear his mother say.

'Go! Take my dreams with you.'

Events prevent reflection. Escaping through the rear door into a world of crops, Karrle is instantly hidden from view but not sound of rat-a-tat questions machine-gunning the defenceless occupants. Flight rules guilt as his pounding feet and heart separate him from everything he has ever known and loved. Distance will deliver ignorance but no comfort; survivors' guilt would allow plenty of time for remorse.

Hiding in the fields until nightfall, he walks forty kilometres to a friend's house, avoiding all the villages along the way.

'I can give you some money and clothes, but you must leave the country. They know this address and none of us will be safe if you stay.

Go north to Agadez. Nobody knows anybody there, and you can stay hidden. But be careful. Very bad things happen in Agadez.'

His friend drives him two hundred kilometres north to a remote bus station and buys him a ticket. Karrle, acknowledging the debt he owes his friend, struggles for words. 'Thank you. How can I ever repay you?'

'If we both stay alive, we might meet again.'

'If we don't, know that wherever I am, you will forever be in my heart. Goodbye, dear friend.'

Turning abruptly, car and rescuer are gone. Gazing at the sky, Karrle captures the last few precious moments of the only country he has ever known. Wispy clouds stroking heaven dance across the sky, waving their farewells; like him, they are drifting to unknowable destinations. Sunlight touched the walls, busy bees work in harmony, and birds sing their playful melodies to celebrate the joys of life. He drinks the tender warm air as whispering winds kissed his face goodbye and drift into the tunnels of his mind.

How could radiant perfection be the setting for such unthinkable horrors? What tentacles of evil could conspire to perpetrate the infectious madness that converts neighbours into a mob of pretend soldiers, their swelling ranks attracting malicious inadequates and gullible adolescents; children lacking wisdom, experience or alternatives who are as vulnerable as their victims, demonising others with the mantra that attack was the *only* defence. These ethnic militia become killers with the promise of martyrdom and rewards in the afterlife. He would never escape the flashbacks of screaming, bewildered innocents drowning in chaos.

A tired, neglected bus lumbered into the station. Stepping onto the vehicle, Karrle could not know that this would be the last time his feet would touch the land of his birth. He was setting out on the most dangerous journey of his life. In one step he unwittingly enters a wormhole, joining the invisible society of the anonymous, sacrificing identity and human rights to be tossed about by forces he cannot control with outcomes that cannot be known and barely imagined.

Agadez awaits him.

## 2017, Coventry, Three Strangers on a Train

The train pulls out of Coventry station as a newly boarded passenger searches for a vacant seat.

'Is this seat taken?'

'No, mate. The invisible man just got off.' Alex laughs inviting a response.

Rose apologises as she moves her bag that is taking up the seat. 'Sorry. I'm going to London to do some shopping.'

Alex announces with obvious pride, 'Yeah, I'm down the Smoke (local expression for London). Never miss a game,' he proudly announces with unnecessary emphasis.

Charles's impeccable attire and polished manner articulate his importance as he graciously acknowledges Rose. 'Thank you.'

The British custom of travelling in silence is observed until a ticket inspector slowly moves down the carriage. The inspector is a handsome, middle-aged man with a gentle, courteous manner. He is also black. Peering at Charles's newspaper Alex spots a headline *Conflict Spreads*, and cannot resist voicing his opinion. 'It won't be long before they bring it over here.' Glancing down the aisle he adds, 'There's another one taking our jobs.'

The inspector is barely three seats away and probably within earshot. Charles feels compelled to respond. 'Many do the jobs that the British don't want to do.'

Rose, whose accumulating years have treated her kindly, searches for something positive to disperse the unpleasantness. 'We were all immigrants once.'

Alex's snaps back, 'Not me. My family have lived here forever.'

'Everyone has to live somewhere,' she offers apologetically.

Unmoved, Alex stands his ground. 'Yeah, in their own country. They're not welcome 'ere!'

This cannot be left as the last word. Charles folds his newspaper and responds authoritatively, 'The British colonised territory all over the world.'

Rose, looking to build on her positivity, adds, 'And we brought them Christianity.'

Alex's response is instant and fiery. 'Yeah, and look how they repay us. Fucking wars all over the place.'

Charles, whose formal education included British history, pronounces, ‘The British did not gain an empire without fighting. We were not always saints.’

In no mood to retreat, Alex’s face displays rising anger. ‘That was a long time ago. It don’t make it right for them to come ’ere now.’

The sharp-suited businessman displays a measured sense of exasperation. ‘I can’t get British workers. I have to employ some foreigners. Many are excellent.’

Drawing from a deep well of resentment, Alex loads up. ‘Not in my book, they ain’t. It’s people like you inviting these buggers over that’s destroying our community. My kid feels like a foreigner in ’is own school. You can’t see a bleedin’ doctor any more, and all these bloody churches… My wages haven’t gone up in ten years. You…’’ glaring directly at Charles, ‘you cream off the money, live in a posh house and don’t give a shit about the country. Unlike politicians and you businessmen, I’ve joined a group that takes direct action to defend my culture.’

This outburst is greeted with frozen silence, which fails to mask deep mutual disapproval. Nobody wants to pursue this conversation. All three are from the same white British society, and yet their diverse opinions are based on personal experience and understanding, all interpreted differently to support their beliefs.

Alex goes to his football match, Charles attends a business conference and Rose goes shopping with a friend. They never meet again.

## 2018, Vishnu, Assam India

Vishnu enters the house. His posture instantly signals to Chaaya that her husband's struggles continue unrewarded. She does not want to add to his woes but she has no choice. 'Charvi has not eaten for two days. I took her to the medical centre but they have no medicine, and the nurse has gone to England and not been replaced. She must see a doctor.'

'You know that is impossible. There is hardly enough seed for next year's harvest. How we are going to get through the winter, I do not know.'

'Charvi will not get through the winter. That will save some food.'

They both know that winter without their nine-month-old daughter is inconceivable. The next day Vishnu borrows money from a cousin for the doctor's fees and takes her to the hospital. The bus journey is more than thirty miles, and the untamed terrain conspires to defeat travellers. Just over half way there, the struggling bus succumbs to the mud trenches in the road gifted by the rains. A relief bus may take hours.

Vishnu resolves to take charge of events and walk. If a relief bus comes and there is space, he can still board with his ticket. Stopping neither for rest nor refreshment, his wrapped bundle nestles passively on his back. Striding triumphantly into the hospital, he unwraps his treasure to discover the baby is dead. There is nothing to do but return the lifeless package and bear the unbearable.

Vishnu learns that Charvi's condition is common. Although treatment is cheap and widely available in the West, the hospital has no supplies and there is no information about future deliveries.

His family have lived in the same village for longer than anyone can remember and never contemplated a time when that would not be so, but recent crop failures are pushing survival beyond known limits. Some say it is global warming. Vishnu does not know but, as head of the household, it is his duty to protect the family. Facing the unthinkable, he must make a decision that will transform all their lives to leave the community and abandon the land of their ancestors.

Against every fibre in his being, Vishnu announces that they will go to Coventry, England, where his cousin owns a restaurant and he can work in the kitchens. Reyansh, his eldest, can get a job to support the family, and his daughter, Mohini, will start at the local school. The family will have access to the National Health Service and they will be safe. Vishnu states that this is the best solution to protect the family and their traditions.

With no invitation for discussion, the family's thoughts remain private. Questioning the head of the family would be disrespectful, and sharing worries would only burden others who are powerless to change what will be.

## 2019, Lodz Poland. Lech

His mind is not on shopping, but what could he say after his wife had left their two children with a neighbour to go and help her mother rescue her father, who had fallen over again? Wearily pushing the empty trolley, Lech selects two fresh cabbages, sauerkraut, mushrooms and sour cream to make lazanki, a cheap and sustainable meal for the family.

Life is conspiring to crush his dreams, leaving only burning anger and frustration. Their damp rented flat is affecting their children's health. Plans to move were unfolding handsomely until the largest factory in the town closed and Lech was forced to take a low-paid job. After his father-in-law's coal mining accident, he felt honour bound to support his in-laws as well, necessitating taking on cash-in-hand, black-market employment, but even that is insufficient. They are eating into their hard-earned savings.

As misfortune and despair become daily bedfellows, they try to shield the children from the growing tension in the house with diminishing success. Dark clouds foretell that even this joyless existence cannot be sustained or endured much longer.

Something has to be done, and urgently, but there are no good jobs in the town and he knows his wife will never desert her parents. Lech will miss his family and friends, but he has to look for work abroad.

As he leaves, his wife's stoical face conceals her inner pain, though not from her husband.

## 2019, Agadez,

Using a series of buses zig-zagging across Western Africa, it takes ten days before Karrle completes the nerve-racking 2,000-kilometres journey to Agadez. Giddy and thirsty, he descends from the bus to be greeted by a swirling blanket of dry, choking sand.

Surveying his temporary new home, he is struck by all the low, clay, single-storey buildings, the focal point being a twenty-seven-metre-high minaret and a single defiant tree with miraculous green leaves. The buildings, originally constructed of hard, red-mud bricks, are like the people: faceless, cheerless and uninviting. The desert is master of everything.

Stories he has heard about Agadez being a trading post for fake goods, hashish, cocaine, heroin and human trafficking do not do it justice. To continue his escape across the Sahara Desert he will have to depend on the locals to whom he is now a commodity, to be traded at the whim of unknown strangers.

How to survive in this environment is foremost in his mind and immediately answered. Unobserved, and without introduction, a stranger appears through swirling dust, like Clint Eastwood in a spaghetti western. But this is not Clint Eastwood. The man points to the north and utters one word 'Libya?'

Karrle nods and confirms verbally, 'Yes.'

With an uncoordinated gesture, the stranger disappears into a side street as quickly as he appeared. With no alternative but considerable trepidation, Karrle glances in several directions before entering the long, narrow passageway. As he trails his guide, there is no invitation for conversation, making language skills unnecessary.

His escort is small, undernourished, with a furtive manner and pronounced limp; indeed, with all the appearance of a pathetic wretch. Reflecting on their respective situations, it is an inescapable fact that the escort is doing a job and his trained eye has easily recognised the visitor's need. Maybe, like Karrle, he is just trying to survive as best he knows how. This produces an unexpected, almost kindred spirit with his new companion and Karrle can't help warming to this odd little man and wishing him well, however pointless and unknowing his good intent.

The guide takes a series of turns down ever-narrower backstreets. Karrle is completely disorientated in this maze, and fears that he may be walking into a trap. To his relief, they eventually arrive at a large, tumbledown building which might once have belonged to somebody important. Later Karrle learns that this is a 'connection house' where arrangements are made with 'connection man' for the 3,000-kilometre journey across the Sahara.

'Connection Man' is clearly the boss, but any air of authority is undermined by his manner, which is agitated, suspicious and impatient. Sweaty fear pervades the atmosphere, suggesting danger might leap out from any wall at any moment. Wearing the worries of the world on his face, his leathery skin looked as old as the Sahara. Maybe he had a youth bypass and was born old. Muttering a few private words to Connection Man, Karrle's guide disappears. Without ceremony or introduction, the terms of business are dictated without any invitation to negotiate.

'It will cost you 180,000 West African francs for a truck to Libya; 60,000 for the police before you enter the desert; 12,000 to the gendarmes at Tourayat; 25,000 for the police and the republican guard at Seguedine; 30,000 at Dao Timmi to the military and transit police, and 15,000 at Madama. That is as far as I can take you. When you get to Libya, you are on your own. Have you got the money?'

These demands will take most of his funds, with no opportunity for replenishment. Despite the undertone of hostility, Karrle feels he has to discuss the prices. 'Why so expensive?'

Connection Man fails to conceal his irritation at being questioned by someone in no position to negotiate, and can hardly be bothered to reply. 'Look, my friend, you need to understand that you are the one who wants us to risk our lives taking you across the desert, where you are always close to death. If the bandits don't kill you, the desert will try. We are not criminals. We offer a people transport service.'

This strikes Karrle as a beautiful euphemistic misrepresentation of the cruelty and exploitation that is meted out throughout the 'people transport service'.

Observing the hesitancy on his client's face, Connection Man continues. 'Do I live like a king? No! I have many people to support, including all my family.' Clearly, whatever wealth he may have is not on display.

'But what about the bribes on the journey?'

Connection Man feels obliged to expose the ignorance of this transient and enlighten him on the new realities of his life. 'The police on the borders are often not paid anything by the government. Corrupt officials usually steal the money before it is delivered, especially in

Niger. The security forces have their own families. Everyone in the community benefits from the police, from the town council to the children. Without these payments they would starve, there would be no security at all, and things would be even worse.'

Karrle feels he needs clarity on the dangers he may face. 'Why are bandits such a danger?'

'You need to thank the countries you are trying to get to and ask them. For a thousand years, Agadez has been a trading centre. Before the West killed Gaddafi and Libya descended into chaos, Agadez had tourists. When the tourists disappeared, the people became desperate. Normal life collapsed and survival depended on opportunists who were prepared to do anything for money. Now transporting people is the biggest business, but it mixed with the drug trade, military weapons and other underground businesses. Ignorance and desperation are exploited by many different groups. The trafficked people are lied to and the West pretends it is not their problem.'

These are concepts that Karrle has no understanding of. 'How is it the West's problem?'

Connection Man is becoming annoyed by the persistent questions and grudgingly decides to sacrifice more time. 'European imperialists drew straight lines on a map to protect the resources they controlled, ignoring the people who had lived here for hundreds of years. Nomads crossing these meaningless borders came into conflict with the local governments supported by the West. The black Africans were in the majority and often slaughtered cattle, destroying our traditional way of life and threatening the existence of nomadic tribes like mine, the Toureg and the Toubou. When Gaddafi was killed, many weapons depots were raided and arms sold to insurgent groups in neighbouring countries. Lines drawn in pencil are now being redrawn in blood.'

Karrle is intrigued to understand and risks another question. 'What can the West do?' The conversation almost interests Connection Man, who indulges him a little bit more.

'Not what it thinks. Angela Merkel came to Niger to try and stop the flow of migrants. They arrested many people like me. Did it stop desperate people trying to escape? No!' A muscle twitches as his jaw tightens. 'The price doubled! If you destroy our livelihoods, you will recruit young men into Boko Harem, Al Qaeda and many other groups. Do you know how big the Sahara Desert is?'

'Big?' Karrle replies, having no idea.

Connection Man laughs indignantly. 'Big? It is 9,200,000 square kilometres, twice the size of Europe. Weak governments in West Africa cannot control this area – the only ones who can are us. The West must give us alternatives to trafficking. They take our resources, pollute the land and destroy our traditional way of life. Nomadic tribesmen have no benefit or power. In Nigeria, oil flows freely into rivers, polluting the land for fishing and agriculture. In Niger, the French company, Areva, extracts uranium, contaminating the air and water.

'When there was an oil embargo in Iraq, there were hundreds of lorries queuing on the Turkish border selling oil. The Americans could see this with their satellites. Everyone knew. Why did they not bomb them and stop the trade? Because it would have destroyed the economy that millions depend on, and more people would have tried to get to Europe. They say one thing and do another. Things will not get better until the West gives practical support to the people.'

The conversation is terminated and a minder takes Karrle to a compound. Reflecting on their exchange, Karrle is struck by the similarities with his own country. Here is another civilisation that has collapsed, and Connection Man seems to blame the West. Both men are victims of circumstance, attempting to survive by avoiding the wrath of the powerful and the deadly embrace of the Sahara. The difference is that Connection Man is dancing with death on home territory, defending what he knows and with 'connections,' whereas Karrle is an isolated itinerant leaping blindly in search of sanctuary.

## Hell Seeking Hope

The compound holds maybe a hundred men and a few women. They are protected by guards armed with daggers and swords. This is not to stop the men leaving – they have nowhere to go – it is to stop other gangs kidnapping tradeable assets. They all sleep on the floor.

Rice and water are delivered once every two days at 600 francs per day. With no way of knowing how long he will have to endure Agadez, Karrle is deeply concerned that his money might run out.

'There is no confidence to equal ignorance,' Orson Wells.

Agadez is a honey trap: easy to enter but escape depends on strangers with very different agendas. Observing the hordes of hopefuls, Karrle cannot fail to admire the tenacity of the hundreds of innocents who, denied a future in their homeland, pour in every week, like him, sustained by dreams of destinations none of them have seen.

For some, chancing life on unknown risks is perceived as noble, even heroic, but this imaginative leap provides the town's main source of income whilst obscuring terrifying realities. Once arrived, this little pocket of hell only becomes evident as you witness the daily humiliations waiting for something better.

Under the thin veil of righting past wrongs, tribal frictions are enflamed by the selective retelling of historic atrocities. Dehumanising victims justifies exploitation and merciless brutality. Dissenters are driven into the desert and abandoned to face certain death. In their dispersed, chaotic splinter groups, such practices are accepted as 'normal.'

It will be much later, when Karrle is in Europe, that he will fully understand the impact of the West's refusal to acknowledge the reality of life for economic migrants and the West's contribution to the grinding poverty of their lives. The only relief from this weary struggle against fate is a pointless death, ignoring the effect on the human spirit and the abandonment of everything that elevates humanity.

Even the 'lucky' few that achieve their dream of entering Europe will be classified merely as 'economic migrants', with diminished entitlement to human rights from the state and local population. Karrle hopes that the threat to his life from his own countrymen will qualify him as an asylum seeker; a tragedy turned to opportunity - how twisted an aspiration?

Walled by hostility and the crushing boredom of enforced inactivity, the only escape from uninterrupted fear is an occasional conversation with a fellow prisoner. Abidugun is from Nigeria. He tells Karrle his name means 'born before the war'.

'I could not support my wife and children so I sold the family house and land for $4,000, gave $1,000 to my wife and decided to travel to Europe. I cannot go back. Better to die trying.'

Yusuff is from Sierra Leone. He has fallen into debt and become the property of his Connection Man, labouring in the hope of paying for the next stage of his journey. If you cannot pay, you might be beaten, sold or killed. When he was unable to work, he was thrashed and nearly died, surviving only because other detainees shared their food. He has run out of life's reserves of  money, body fat, energy or friends that can change his circumstances. Yusuff has not seen his family for eighteen months and does not know if he will see them again.

'I have to go to Europe and get a job,'' he says. ''I am the eldest. It is my duty. All my family think I am in Europe. I cannot tell them I have failed. I am ashamed.'

For the women it is worse. Beatings are common and those without money have to become sex workers or slaves. Even with money, they are frequently raped by the guards. One woman who refused sex was gang raped and beaten to death.

Women may have to work as sex workers at every stage of their journey; they earn $3 per day, most of which goes to the madam. There are no timescales for paying the debt and many never get beyond Agadez. Eighty per cent of the Nigerian women are sexually abused on their trek to Europe, and a significant number of those who make it to Libya are already pregnant.

If you come from Benin, a forgotten powerless country neighbouring Nigeria, all parties now expect this treatment and are complicit. It is a girl's duty to run this gauntlet to earn money to support her family. Everyone in the supply chain understands this, from the families sending their children, to the recruiters in Nigeria, to the traffickers crossing the Sahara, to those providing the boats to cross the Mediterranean. And in this foul network, yet more waiting for them on the shores of Italy to work in brothels before they are moved to other countries.

The most vulnerable are the unaccompanied minors. They have to trust somebody, which makes them defenceless against gangs that often abuse and torture them. The lucky ones find older travellers, but it is chance whether they are protected or merely prey for the depraved.

Becoming sick is very bad news; no-one will transport or employ you, and the expected outcome is a lingering death. In Europe, the illusion is that everyone wants to cross the Mediterranean, but twice as many cross the Sahara from Agadez than the Mediterranean from Libya and the death rate is higher. Washed-up bodies on the shores of Europe, like three-year-old Alan Kurdi, might be a reminder of the unfolding tragedy and a challenge to the West's moral declarations, but the desert has far more secrets and is more efficient at hiding them. This vast continent has millions fleeing their homelands, of whom 94% never try to enter Europe.

Every Monday the town bursts into activity when drivers, appear from nowhere, race to the ghetto compounds loaded with water and fuel to pack about thirty people onto a Toyota Hilux open truck. Wooden handles are attached to the frame to grip during the bumpy ride, which can last three days or an eternity if the shifting sand dunes misdirect the drivers.

In their reckless attempt to cross the Sahara, every Monday up to 5,000 desperate souls form a convoy to reduce the risk of attacks by bandits. Karrle's place is booked, and he is elated as unleashed energy he did not know existed surges through his body. The procession passes the derelict airport, now only a memorial to the forgotten tourist trade. The police are bribed and the convoy turns left and is off.

Any enthusiasm for the journey evaporates within the first few hours as bumping, jostling and heat extinguish the joy of leaving Agadez. Breaks are only permitted to swap drivers and refuel. Sleep would be a blessed relief, but the fear of falling off a truck makes certain death a waking nightmare.

One racing trailer hit a sand dune and overturned; a man from Eritrea was fatally wounded and several others injured. His friend could hear him calling his name as the traffickers shovel sand over the evidence.

Occasional abandoned vehicles decorate the roadside, a few with passengers who have completed their final journey. Stiff-limbed and contorted, their slumped bodies burnt black by the sun, they are half-covered or uncovered by drifting sands. Accusing empty eye sockets have a message that no passing itinerant wants to hear, their shattered dreams lost forever in a universe of uncompromising rock and dust. Their only legacy is the pain of those they had known, but who have yet to join them. Dehydration mocks vomiting as an empty gesture; the remorseless journey overwhelms all senses morphing into a delirious blur of competing nightmares. Maybe the only peace is death.

## 2020, Libya

Crossing the Sahara Desert leaves the survivors dehydrated and exhausted. Reaching Libya, Karrle is taken to Sabha, a modern town of stark white buildings and wide streets surrounded by older settlements of mud-walled dwellings and covered alleyways.

Any illusion that escape has been achieved is immediately dashed as they witness confirmation of the rumours that the route is plagued by bandits who hate black Africans. They rob and beat them, hold captive for ransom, enslave and sell them. Competing gangs, known as 'Asma boys', transfer the latest consignment of humanity where more bribes are extracted. Marshalled into a large 'safe house,' which was probably once a public building and is now a makeshift prison, the captives are escorted to a room which is then locked and guarded as they start the interminable wait for transport to Tripoli.

Sleeping, waking and eating in the same room provides ample opportunity to occupy vacant hours with anyone willing to talk. Joy, a girl in her early twenties from Senegal, is a sex worker. Her minders use her for free. Karrle asks why she is on this perilous journey. Her answer is disheartening. 'I had a boyfriend who I thought loved me, but he used me and sold me. That is what broke me. The only way to escape was to borrow money and leave my country, family and friends.'

Like many, before she left she swore a juju oath to repay the people who funded her journey. She believes that if it is not repaid, the curse will kill her and her family.

Her friend, Hope, is a delicate, fleshless, fine-featured teenager. Being penniless and vulnerable, prostitution is her only meal ticket. Sitting next to Hope, Karrle is instinctively drawn to her eyes; they are lost in the hopelessness of attempting to survive the remorseless daily abuse pillaging her youth.

Their early words are circumspect, but small talk gradually establishes a connection revealing glimpses of innate kindness in a gentle soul with a beautiful smile, much in need of protection-. The two travellers exchange stories and dreams, evoking in Hope occasional, spontaneous, light-hearted laughter like the pitter-patter of angel feet dancing on a pond. It is a precious moment in a desert of torment.

Yet the stark uncertainties of both their futures cannot be excluded from the conversation. Hope is traumatised by the shocking reality of crossing the Sahara, and oblivious to the dangers that lie ahead.

She did not know that Libya was a war zone and thought the boat trip to Italy was thirty-five kilometres, not 350, if fuel, waves and navigation skills permit.

Karrle's attentive manner and natural gentleness allows her to share a few inner confidences hidden from the world. With unvarnished openness Hope explains, 'I want to go to Germany because my friend told me it is nice. I want to study to be a nurse. It is my dream.'

Her naked, clueless innocence is simultaneously heart-warming and heart-breaking. Once in Europe, she believes that she will be welcomed. A broken, submissive smile pleads for confirmation that there are alternatives to this chaotic nightmare. Hell cannot last forever otherwise the universe makes no sense, so Europe must be better, right?

Karrle looks at her pure, beautiful, minimalist, black face. What can he say? All he can think of is, 'If that is your dream, I will pray for you.'

With disarming simplicity Hope replies, 'When we talk, it reminds me of my family. Please remember me. I will remember you with respect and affection.'

Her delicate humanity touches his heart. After wishing her well, he does not see her again but often recalls their conversations. He does not want to know what becomes of her.

Joy has not earned enough money for the madam, who phones Joy's mother and says that if she does not pay 200,000 West African francs (about £260) her daughter will be forced to work as a prostitute. The girl is put on the phone to confirm her situation, but does not tell her mother she is already renting her body.

The mother cannot pay. She tells the village council, which lends her the money at exorbitant rates. It is paid by a MoneyGram exchange service. Once it has been paid, Joy is allowed to continue her journey. Armed men put her on a truck covered in sacks of maize to conceal her from rival traffickers and take her to a disused warehouse holding sometimes eighty drifting itinerants. She remains there for several months. Beatings and rape are part of daily life, barely meriting comment by the victims or the perpetrators. The basest instincts of individuals can inflict enormous cruelty.

Each week brings fresh waves of shattered innocents worn down like the drifting desert sands into anonymous fragments of humanity hollowed out by life's experiences. In one Libyan prison, guards kill five men every Friday to make room for new inmates. One Gambian boy,

Ousmane, is selected but an older man steps forward and volunteers. 'Kill me instead.' He turns to the boy and requests, 'When you go to The Gambia, go to my village and tell them I am dead.'

Karrle meets Gainde, who is returning to Mauritania where he was born. Karrle asks him why. 'When you start out, you have so many illusions, but my experiences helped me decide that the risks were not worth the possible rewards. If I can get to Gao in Mali, there is a place called The House of Migrants. It is a refugee centre that helps migrants travelling in either direction. Once there, they will arrange the rest of my journey home[1].'

'Why do the guards let you return home?' asks Karrle.

'Because my brother sent one of the leaders some money.'

Karrle reflects on the huge gap between the hopes that this venture will improve these transients' futures and the absence of any experience to realise those hopes. Their heroic naivety is deeply disturbing, such a waste of humanity, and for what purpose? Their only transgression was leaving a place they knew in search of places they did not know, and for this sin the punishment is exploitation.

Their vulnerability is instantly recognisable and visible to all. Exposed and defenceless, they are victim to an indescribable variety of abuse, violence and exploitation by anyone with such a mind, with no escape or recourse to justice. All believe that the perpetrators are immune from the consequences of their actions; the absence of social norms offering no restraint or protection. Observing sporadic brutality without warning or reason plays on the imagination, conjuring visions of danger skulking in every corner, every second. Pointless terror without relief is exhausting.

It will be much later that Karrle understands that, given the right conditions, all humans are capable of exacting the same destructive outcomes that were responsible for his own flight and fate. The consequences go far beyond the comprehension of the countries receiving these unfortunates, whose lack of understanding will infect future generations. What he does know is that many of these rootless souls will never reach their promised lands. What he *cannot* know is that those lucky enough to complete their escape face years of remorseless struggle, isolation and loneliness before any form of bearable normality returns to their lives. Their final, protracted punishment of life's journey will be the

[1] Aljazeera, *Witness*, broadcast 16/06/2022)

damage inflicted and retained by memories that deny them inner peace until the relief of death or old age offers some philosophical acceptance. What they cannot know is that this burden will never be lifted from their shoulders. It will be their children who grow up in new pastures, hearing but not understanding the trials of their parents. Free from injury, their children will have the same lack of experience as their new host populations. These desperate migrants cannot know that they are travelling not for themselves but for their unborn children.

## England Welcomes Lech

Lech borrows money from Uncle Franciszek and takes the coach to England, arriving in London at Victoria Coach Station. He is immediately dismayed by the cost and scarcity of barely habitable accommodation. With no income and dwindling savings, he takes the advice of a local estate agent and moves to Coventry where his manufacturing skills are more likely to command a living wage.

Another coach trip brings him to Pool Meadow Coach Station. When he registers with numerous agencies, all offer warm words and positivity but no interviews. Repeat experiences leave the impression that he is added to an anonymous list, or maybe his CV is discarded immediately he leaves the agency. In desperation he makes enquiries with several Polish shops and is surprised and delighted how quickly he is offered employment and accommodation.

Holding an address scrawled on a ripped piece of A4 paper, he seeks out the lodgings, which take some finding. The house is a mid-terraced, Victorian property located in an obscure back street at the end of a labyrinthian housing estate only known to refuse collectors, debt collectors and social services. The accommodation consists of three bedrooms and two living rooms, all occupied, plus a cramped kitchen. It is home to eight Polish, one Latvian and one Ukrainian, all male. The bathroom needs a wash and the toilet is a health hazard. In winter, the high ceilings conspire with the inadequate boiler to retain all the heat above head height, offering the stark choice of stale or cold air.

Lech is in the biggest bedroom but has to share with two others. There is just enough room to push his suitcase under the uncompromising single bed. The stains on the mattress do not invite enquiry as to their origin. This is worse than Poland.

The only resident pleased to see him is the local cat, nicknamed Bungle by the housemates. He inspects all new arrivals for any gastronomic delights that might be exchanged for momentary affection before continuing his tour of other neighbourhood benefactors. Polish food is not to Bungle's liking, apart from *bigos* (hunters' stew).

One day, to the surprise of all the housemates who thought Bungle was a male, the cat gives birth to four kittens in the garden shed.

Each night Lech hides from the rest of humanity to sit with them for a moment of mutual affection. Their little fluffy bodies crawling onto his lap for warmth and attention evoke memories of his children.

Being part of a small team at a carwash, the accommodation is dependent on retaining his job. The hours are punishing: twelve hours a day, six days a week for £3 an hour. This is well below the national minimum wage, but he pays no tax, has no legal rights and his employer knows he is in no position to negotiate. The rent is £60 a week. After food and Tyskie (Polish lager), Lech sends as much money as he can to his wife, usually around £70 a week.

The work is tedious and draining, and his face quickly becomes thin, gaunt and hollow eyed. His clothes, like his body, display a shabby tiredness; in short, he looks rough. These diminished circumstances, along with his accent, puncture his confidence and broadcast his status as 'disadvantaged migrant.'

Social interaction is limited to shops and the street, where people are courteous but defensive and unwelcoming, closing down conversations at the first opportunity. Strangers eye him warily, and pedestrians stare at the ground as if to hide their eyes, unwilling to reveal their innate hostility. Adjusting to his environment, Lech cultivates his own dark emotions which he does not want to share. To be treated like this is a new experience, as is the constant stress.

In Poland he was known and respected in the community, but in England he has joined the underclass where identity is the entitlement of the privileged. Nowhere is welcoming, his only retreats being the bottom of a can of Tyskie and the kittens. The absence of family is deeply dispiriting. He ruminates on what he is missing back home, what they are doing at this moment and whether they miss him as much as he misses them. His greatest dread is that they are learning to live without him.

Maybe tomorrow will be better.

## Escaping To Freedom

A rumour spreads that a boat is leaving Libya for Europe that night, maybe to Italy. Karrle eventually hunts down the organiser and, after a harrowing negotiation, offers all the money he has to book a space.

He is told not to mention his departure to anyone, no goodbyes, nothing. He must assemble on the beach at 4am. It is imperative that they are out of sight of the coast before dawn. The only illumination is from the stars and a few distant street lights. An assortment of the terrified and diminished assemble at the water's edge, not knowing if the shadowy figures are other victims or the authorities and all is lost. A few exchange secretive whispers of recognition. One heartless trafficker is heard saying that if they drown it is 'God's will'. Using God's name to justify sending people on perilous journeys with inadequate equipment all in the name of profit is deeply offensive, but Karrle cannot say anything.

In the blindness of the night, another life is sacrificed to the god of pointlessness as a woman gives birth on the beach. Her exhausted body, released from life, is even denied sight of her child. In minutes she bleeds to death, leaving her traumatised husband to abandon his wife's warm carcass and collect the tiny stranger, trailing the dispossessed infant's severed and knotted umbilical cord across his forearm.

Not understanding its loss, and rejecting this hostile new world, the baby bellows its objections in the only language it knows. Together with the wailing of the wretched father, their discordant chorus drifts across the cold night waters before drowning in silence as if the moment had never been, but the indelible scar engraved on the petrified souls of every witness reminds them all of their own desperation and possible fate. Later, on the inflatable craft, the new father explains the pitiless irony that his wife had insisted they go to Europe as soon as she learned that she was pregnant. She did not want her child to witness the atrocities in their homeland.

At precisely 4am, a tightly inflated rubber dinghy arrives. Protecting personal space is the last dignity and immediately abandoned. Wading waist deep into cold, numbing water, most scramble on board, fearful that they might be left behind. A few hesitate, fearing that the black liquid sea monster's beguiling invitation is but a trick, the true destination being a watery grave and whatever lies beyond death. Like wildebeest spotting crocodiles salivating at the river's edge, desperate decisions are hurriedly made as herd instinct persuades all to board until the dinghy is almost submerged.

The lifeboat must be lightened. Removing women and children might spark a mob, and although the gang have weapons they are heavily outnumbered. Secretly, they all want the same outcome. Countless, silent eyes, gripped by fear, witness events unfold as those least able to protest are hurled back into the shallow night waters to be returned to the safety of the land and the treachery of the land owners.

A sinewy old man with surprising strength grips a handle with all his might, but the audience is deaf to his cries for assistance. His victory in that battle could be fatal for all. The onlookers remain motionless, watching as the traffickers do their dirty work for them. The victim's only reward is a smashed hand, delivered with a gun butt. As the delicate craft slowly enters the unseen, his audience is deaf to his pitiable cursing. All observe an oppressive silence, broken only by the mosquito whine of the underpowered engine and tiny waves licking the sides of the vessel as they are caressed ever deeper into the mouth of the sea monster. The black liquid of the deep becomes as one with the darkness of the night.

Karrle's eyes are now redundant, heightening his other senses. He feels the gentle rocking of the boat and the bodies of fellow escapees crushed against his limbs. This new world is disorientating, timeless, and just as threatening as the one they are trying to escape from. Imperceptibly, universal black morphs into universal blue. The land has magically disappeared and there is no visible means of return.

Karrle surveys their plight as far as mobility allows. Phone numbers of loved ones are written on several bodies in case the sea monster disgorges their remains. There are few life jackets, little food and only enough fuel to strand them in the Mediterranean.

Later, furtive, barely audible whisperings are muttered as if fearful of disturbing their host. Isolation is reinforced by the multitude of tribal languages. As Karrle observes the diversity of nationalities and ethnicities in this sad collection of seafarers, he realises that this is not a homogenous migration but a series of flights from terror and despair, evicted from countless homes over months and years, converging in Libya all with stories that most will never tell. From the few that speak

English, Karrle learns that his travelling companions include escapees from Syria, Iraq and Afghanistan, amongst others. Meandering thoughts surmise that Libya is a strange route to Europe, but these drift away in waves of exhaustion.

'We are already dead,' says a mystery voice to anyone who can understand. Karrle cannot identify the owner as he is pinned by a wide backside between his legs and cannot move. The lady's bottom forces an intimacy that he never wants to repeat, and he wonders if he will ever walk again. Comfort is unattainable. Any expectation that a passing ship might find them is slowly displaced by numbing fear and a desire that these moments pass, whatever the outcome.

And then, the miracle of imagination. Somebody has a mobile phone *and* the number of the Italian coastguard. Within an hour, the horizon gives birth to a tiny speck that slowly inflates into a glorious Italian naval ship. Fear evaporates and all are consumed by ubiquitous celebration at the anticipation of rescue and a new life in Europe to be rapidly displaced by boredom, frustration and more exhaustion upon the realisation their superhuman efforts to get to Europe have only achieved a new condition of powerlessness as fresh unknowns crystallise into an endless stream of obstacles to happiness.

## Mohini's First Day

The teacher calls the class to attention. 'Quiet please, everyone. We have a new classmate joining us today. I'd like you to welcome Mohini. She is from India and this is her first day at school. I expect you all to help her settle in.'

A sea of faces stare at the new girl, who fails to become invisible.

'Right, Mohini, if you would take a seat. How about over there next to...Andy? Andy, look after Mohini, please, and show her where things are.'

'Yes, miss.'

Mohini crosses the room to the vacant chair with only a flash of eye contact with the boy who says, 'Hi.' To her relief, the attention of the class moves on. Now she can observe her surroundings unobserved.

Andy is delighted that he has been chosen to look after the new girl. She is very pretty and seems nice, though shy. After the lesson he shows her around the school. He is well mannered and attentive but uncertain how to behave, which puts the new girl at ease. As he describes the layout of the school, it creates a context for conversation that avoids any direct personal questions.

Mohini thinks the teacher has made a good choice. Andy has a warm friendly smile. Although unsure what to say, he is polite, allowing her to fill the gaps as they chat. She loves the experience of a personal chaperone without her parent's controlling influence.

Sitting next to each other in every lesson, Mohini orbits Andy's social circle and listens to others converse, indirectly introducing her to new schoolmates. Through casual chit-chat, they gradually share more information about themselves. Explaining their lives to somebody from a different background broadens the discussions, and with understanding comes a growing attraction drawing them closer together. Andy thinks she is beautiful and Mohini can investigate in the safety of Andy.

This is the first positive interaction that any of the migrants have had with locals – and it is fun.

## Crossing Europe

The Italian coastguards deliver their human cargo to a designated port, where the migrants disembark before being registered and taken to a holding camp. It is huge, chaotic, filthy and intimidating, run by the mafia who take money directly from the EU. The services are minimal and the profits huge; it is a 'legitimate' racket financed by the authorities.

Food is basic, 'foreign' and unpalatable. Snatched sleep barely differentiates the waking hour. Reliable information is very limited and swamped by ubiquitous rumour and dubious advice. Nobody knows anybody, nobody trusts anybody, everyone tries to avoid strangers and many do whatever they can get away with.

New arrivals are gripped by an overwhelming sense of abandonment, disorientation and apprehension. Rescue from the sea has been exchanged for deprivation and harassment, with no visible sanctuary. Any residual faith that they have arrived in a civilised society that respects their human rights is frequently and cruelly exploited. Everyone knows that these desperate, rootless transitioners are easy prey and a magnet for predators.

Fear and intimidation are constant companions where nothing inside or outside the camp is welcoming. Many migrants drift off to continue their exodus or are collected by pimps, traffickers and opportunists. There is neither the space nor the budget to do more, and opposition from the resident voters is already inflamed. The local authorities are complicit in this process, to make room for the next delivery of humans.

Slowly and warily, Karrle inches northwards across Europe, usually on foot, sometimes with occasional free lifts from benevolent travellers. He rests in camps before continuing his journey. Opportunities to eat are sporadic, with occasional meals from a hotchpotch of caring strangers and charities, but his primary preoccupation is avoiding migrant gangs and hostile inhabitants.

Most migrants seem surprisingly healthy, apart from scabies and lice which are common. Arriving in France, Karrle becomes ill. Not being pregnant or a child, he is not a priority for the overstretched medical services and he recovers in a few days. For an educated man, this is an education he never wanted.

In Southern France, a kind camp official allows him to use his mobile phone to call a trusted neighbour in his home town. The crackling line delivers a message that shatters everything. His friend's mutilated body has been found in a ditch by local children shortly after Karrle's narrow escape. The warning that Karrle was wanted by the militia has cost his dear, noble friend his life. Overwhelmed and drained of strength and will, Karrle's debilitated body collapses to the floor. He wishes his heart would stop beating to kill the pain. Standing up against injustice had brought him to the attention of a local warlord, but this was a price he never wanted to pay. It was not HIS to offer. Did his actions directly cause the death of his friend? What could he have done differently?

There is no comfort in knowing that he has been spared at the cost of a life freely offered, and Karrle's childhood memories will forever be tainted by this single event. He recalls the day his friend was born, wrapped in a white shawl, cradled in his mother's brown arms, a tiny bundle with a profusion of tight curly hair. Free from pain, Karrle's friend is now wrapped in the warm, brown arms of Mother Earth.

Karrle can never go back home, any more than he could turn back the clock. His friend's gift is a mountain and now a burden on Karrle's shoulders. He must continue the struggle to give meaning to his friend's sacrifice.

To sustain him through 'the slings and arrows of outrageous misfortune,'[1] Karrle recalls his mother's last words : 'Take my dreams with you.'

Six months later, he arrives at his intended destination.

England.

---

[1] *Hamlet,* William Shakespeare

## Business As Usual

Charles's pursuit of profit started when he was at school, buying and selling anything that his schoolmates would pay money for. Now he is a self-made, multi-millionaire and the proud owner of several businesses. Making money keeps him very busy, and he is always making plans to make more. Before he goes to bed at night, he thinks about how he is going to structure the following day to maximise his time. When he wakes up in the morning, he knows all the targets he must hit that day.

The responsibilities are enormous: providing work for so many employees; satisfying the demands of his customers; selecting the right suppliers and constantly negotiating products, price, delivery and quality; whilst always trying to stay on the right side of the government and the regulatory authorities; avoiding bad publicity and still making a profit; planning strategy for the future; balancing the endless calculation of risk versus reward and always risking his own money.

Although sales are increasing, he complains bitterly about the impact of the rising minimum wage on the profitability of his businesses. Challenges are everywhere and his competitors are always looking for something new and better, so he needs to look even harder and is always eager to find anything that will give him a competitive advantage.

This endless success is irrefutable evidence that he is 'a good citizen.' Charles always has statistics to hand on the benefits his activities bring to the rest of society, the wealth he creates, the numbers employed and taxes paid.

He is highly respected and a glorious example of how the capitalist system is good for the individual and society. His own wealth is confirmation of his achievements, and the effortless accumulation of accolades is further affirmation of society's approval. Any indulgences he enjoys are richly deserved. What possible reason is there to change anything when everything is working so well?

There aren't any!

# England – At Last

Karrle is homeless, penniless and friendless, a worn shadow of the man who escaped nearly two years earlier. He immediately applies to the Home Office for asylum and is allocated a room in a shared house crammed with other migrant hopefuls of various nationalities, all with unknown experiences, problems and aspirations. Not knowing who to trust, the residents do not mix. Far from gravitating towards people from his own region, Karrle feels especially wary in case he becomes the target of retribution. Completely alone, relying on the remnants of his inner strength, he has only his thoughts for company.

Surveying the room, he wonders what freak of time travel has brought this cacophony of furniture to the same location. Like him, it has clearly suffered greatly from the journey. The wardrobe door sings in its own language every time it's contents are displayed. The warped drawer, jammed half open, refuses all other positions however hard it is rattled. The bed in too much pain to support a human and complains to everyone who tries to join it; its' only wish is to be left alone. The absence of a chair correctly assumes that friends are unobtainable in such an environment.

The realisation slowly dawns on Karrle that these four walls are not for his protection but to protect society from him. He has the keys to his own prison but no invitations to visit other people's. Occasional outbursts from residents disturb long periods of oppressive silence, creating a tension that discourages conversation. Sweet pungent smells in communal areas suggest private, non-tax paying pleasures are normal. This is a place to survive in the hope of finding other normals, but there are no timescales. Too long in this environment and a resident will become like the bed: shunning company and opportunity.

In Africa, he knew he was poor but he never felt impoverished until he came to England. Back home there were always friends, family, fresh food and space to move around. This new environment will take some getting used to.

Karrle had always believed that all life is precious and unique, but fragile. Right now he feels of no value to himself or anybody else. Haunted by memories and plagued by loneliness, there is no comfort or escape. Remembering the struggle to get here, he obsesses on the pointlessness of all human endeavour and muses that all effort comes to nothing in the end; the only tragedy is if it does so during your own lifetime.

Meandering thoughts keep returning to his dead friend. Has he found peace at last? And what of his own fate? Is his destiny to be condemned to perpetual torment until the release of death? For a young man, this is a sentence his spirit cannot bear.

Flailing desperately for hope, he explores the thought that he is in England. There must be opportunities – but even they will not extinguish the reliving of past pain or the knowledge of the continued suffering of those dearest to him. But he is already 'saved' compared with those that had created the world he has now deserted…

Creeping nightfall slowly hides the room in a curtain of darkness but fails to conceal these realities or the blackness of his thoughts. Even his own shadow has deserted him. Switching on the light would change nothing. Yet he *is* safe and has choices. The lone candle of hope must not be extinguished. However remote, he might be their only possibility of rescue. If he is saved and gives up, how can he expect more from those he left behind?

Time will not diminish this reality. Focusing intently on the bulb, he slowly rises from his bed, crosses the room and switches the light on.

The one thing he does have in abundance is time. Time to think – and he has a lot of thinking to do.

# Rose is Bored

Since she was a little girl, Rose's life has been mapped out by other's expectations : parents, school, husband, housewife, children. Her world of stability and comfort has successfully avoided most of life's dramas, which is a blessing, but as she gets older she feels strangely unlived. Is this all there is?

Some people seem to have extraordinary existences, most of which she is grateful not to have knowledge of. But is that really it? When she dies, will she be tidied away and instantly forgotten? Will her epitaph be: 'Born… Died… Respectable? Didn't do much wrong!'

Surely she could do something worthwhile without risking her reputation. But reputation with whom? Her unchallenged life has reduced her circle of friends and family to a small nucleus and they all seem self-sufficient without her. What is there to risk? Only her sanity if she does nothing? She decides to broach the subject with a long-standing friend.

'Why don't you volunteer in a charity shop?'' the friend asks. ''They raise money for wonderful causes. I've seen a programme about it. There's one in the village where the old baker's shop used to be.'

Rose ponders the possibilities. It can't do any harm. She decides to give it a try.

The ladies are nice, and she is recycling things for the needy that might otherwise be thrown away. This *is* good!

# The Green Folder

Home Office rules prevent Karrle from working until asylum is granted, but that is not certain and timescales are unknown. With no money, friends or occupation, even the therapy of employment is denied him. He has been handed a clock with no hands, a diary with no entries and an instruction manual with one instruction: do not leave the waiting room. Abandoned, forgotten and totally isolated, Karrle's only emotion is despair. All he can do is look through the window at other lives passing him by.

To find his sanity, he must escape this room and make contact with people, but there is nowhere to go. Barricaded in his cell, the barriers that deny him human contact are invisible and insurmountable. Suspended in a timeless zone, minutes have no beginning or end. Loneliness wins.

The powerful tormentors of solitary confinement, enforced inactivity and frustration, are fermenting an acidic, corrosive concoction. Karrle is a hostage, forced to witness his own destruction, condemned to death by decay. Each day he feels a little more anonymous, more disconnected from the world as if his soul is evaporating. He wonders how much of himself will be left when he is challenged to grasp an opportunity or resist destruction? This insanity must be endured if he is to preserve his own.

As the winter's afternoon slowly steals the light, Karrle is alerted to creaking floorboards accompanied by shuffling outside his second-floor room. A moment's silence is immediately followed by the wheezing of punctured bellows and a purposeful knock on the door. 'Come in, it's not locked,' he instructs the unknown visitor.

The handle turns and the door leisurely swings open to reveal a shape nearly as wide as the door but considerably shorter, indeed almost a square. The naked landing light is directly above the head of a male of advancing age. Is this a celestial gift from the heavens – in which case this fallen angel has landed too abruptly resulting in severe compression? But no, the wheezing, now subsiding, offers a simpler explanation: an earthly ascent from someone enduring unaccustomed activity.

'Good afternoon, Room Number 6. I presume you are Carl.'

'Karrle, it is African not British. And yes, I am.'

'Apologises. Pleased to meet you. I am Graham, your support worker. May I come in?'

Karrle's fingers reluctantly unfurl and with an understated movement of his arm he gestures for the man to enter. The large, obviously English heap shuffles into the room. With no chairs, he slumps unceremoniously onto the bed, which utters a graunching plea for mercy.

'Oops, sorry! I hope I have not broken it.'

'Don't worry. It was already broken.'

With the well-practiced art of starting idle banter, Graham opens the conversation.

'I've really put on some weight.' Silence. 'You know, I used to be seven pounds!' he continues.

He smiles invitingly at the lean stony face below the tight-coiled hair, but his audience remains unmoved. The support worker moves into his well-practiced explanation of his role as his client listens in silence. Coming to the end of his standard patter and talking generalities, Graham tries to find a point of human contact. His new client speaks good English, which is always an advantage, but his motionless face and wasted frame show no desire to interact. The troubles he fled from and the trauma of the journey have left him bereft of effort.

Turning to the blandest subject he can think of, Graham observes 'It's getting nippy out there but winter's nearly over and the summer will be here soon.'

Karrle rejects such optimism. 'I have only experienced two seasons in this country, August and winter.'

Graham laughs; maybe he is getting somewhere. Glancing around the desolate room there is nothing to invite conversation without emphasising the stark reality of his client's plight. His eyes alight on a lonely carrier bag with one handle ripped and a tear at the bottom. It is clearly no longer serviceable. Its final suicidal act would be to disgorge its contents at the first opportunity. 'What's in the bag?'

The remoteness of Karrle's monotone voice confirms his sense of complete isolation. 'Er.... some letters, Home Office registration forms, doctor's address, your letter. My identity as a human.'

Graham tries to give this unshaven shadow a sense of self-worth and bounces back. 'What's your favourite colour?'

'What?' Such a fucking infantile question is wasting his time and only re-affirms his sense of isolation. In no mood to be entertained or entertaining, Karrle knows that his future partly depends on this man who will write reports to unknown officials who will make decisions impacting the rest of his life.

Receiving no answer, Graham repeats the question. 'What's your favourite colour?'

If the game must be played then Karrle had better jump through the required hoops. 'Er, not blue. I saw enough of that in the Med. Green?'

He responds without interest or conviction, but then fleetingly reminisces. 'It reminds me of the forests back home … space … noises … smells.' For the first time his face flickers a response.

Triumphantly Graham awards the prize. 'Good. I'll get you a green folder to keep your papers in. That will make things better.'

The client remains motionless. The conversation ends with Graham explaining the asylum process.

Once outside, Graham mulls over their first meeting. Slow start, another poor soul carrying the world. He has seen so many over the years, and although he is worldly wise he is also worldly weary. Some pull through, some don't. He will do what he can.

The solitude of the room offers no competition for Karrle's inner thoughts and his visitor is instantly forgotten. Searching for comfort, his mind drifts back to those blissful early days of his childhood in Africa, tinged with guilt at his frustrated yearning for adventure that was later crushed by his success at finding it. Only now does he understand how hard his mother had worked to keep food on the table and a home together after his father died, whilst requiring so little effort from him.

He had felt so safe, as if harm did not exist and danger was only an adventure from which you could return to safety at will. Would this present adventure ever allow him to regain the peace of mind he used to take for granted?

How desperately he yearns to be whisked back and tell his mother how much he loves her and regrets his thoughtless resentment at sharing even minor chores. Her lack of complaint only confirms how effortless the routines of his life were. Like a revelation, it is only in England that he has found the understanding and humbling respect for the mundane, forgettable life to which she had willingly volunteered. It was a gift given so freely, without a word of complaint, that it had appeared of no value and had passed unnoticed. How stupid he was! Stupid, foolish, ignorant boy. He is no better than the innocents he met crossing the Sahara, or the girl who thought that the Mediterranean was thirty-five kilometres wide. The difference is that now he has seen things fall apart with no possibility of repair.

Were these pockets of happiness based on innocence shielded by ignorance? If so, was his mother right to protect him from danger and leave him ill-prepared to deal with it when it could not be avoided? He does not know the answer, and may never have the opportunity to understand his mother's life and struggles, an important chapter in his life he may never read.

Thoughts reach his eyes as droplets amuse themselves by playing 'follow my leader' tracing the contours of his cheek, with a heart is so, so heavy that it might fall through his body. He feels gratitude for those good times, and knows with certainty that happiness is obtainable and worth striving for.

Karrle is lost in a forest of memories only inhibited by awareness of the hazards that lay beyond.

# Part Two

# The Search for Truth

## Confinement Is Not Freedom

Graham knocks on the door and waits to be invited in. 'Morning, Karrle. How are you today?'

'Fine!' The effort of pretending to be OK is exhausting.

'Another fortnightly visit. I'll stand, if that's OK. I don't want to vandalise your bed again. I have a few questions from the Home Office about your application to remain.'

'Not again! What do these people want? My dead body, to prove I'm in danger?'

Sensing the deep undercurrent of frustration, Graham offers explanation rather than comfort. 'That would help. They operate a safety-first policy. Not yours – theirs! The political pressure to reduce the number of migrants is so great that they search for any reason to reject applicants. The worse the war zone, the greater the fear of importing terrorists.'

Alarmed, Karrle asks, 'How long might it take for them to decide?'

The answer is as unwelcome as he feared. 'Don't hold your breath. I have clients who've waited years.'

Overwhelmed with despair, Karrle cannot hide the challenge to his sanity. With sagging shoulders he holds his head in his hands and eventually responds. 'OK. Let's get on with it.'

Answering the letter takes about thirty minutes, followed by some lighter conversation. Seeing his client is very down, Graham looks for something positive to say. 'But at least you are in the UK and free.'

His unthinking comment exposes his lack of understanding of the poverty of Karrle's situation and detonates a deep well of anger and frustration.

Losing control, his client stands and unloads. 'WOO, WOO, WOO, WOO, WOO! I AM NOT FREE! I am in England and have protection from persecution and limited financial support that your government allows whilst my case is being reviewed, but I am stuck in this room for an indefinite period. The possibility of becoming free is based on rules I hardly understand and seem to change like the wind. If my application is rejected, I may be deported back to the people who tried to kill me. In the meantime, I cannot move; get a job; form relationships; have independence; plan my future or live a normal life.''

He casts a contemptuous hand around the room. ‘‘THIS IS NOT FREEDOM.’’

This level of frankness could be dangerous, but Graham interprets it as it is meant: a compliment that he is trusted enough to be told what his client really thinks.

## Rose wants more

Rose works mornings Monday to Wednesday at the charity shop. The other ladies are good company and, as the weeks flow into months, she is fully accepted as a regular team member. She sorts, organises, presents and hangs the clothes in the shop, which is what she has done at home for decades – and it bored her to tears then.

Apart from a sense of duty this work is suffocating. Her quest for achievement is not fulfilled. Where does the money go and who are the people that benefit? Back to her friend for advice. 'Well, it did get you out of the house and you enjoyed it for a while.'

''I did. Maybe they do good things with the money, but I don't feel involved enough.''

'How much do they raise?'

Rose tries to remember what she has been told. 'On a good week, £1,000. After expenses we often have £600 surplus.'

'For some, people small sums can make a big difference.'

'I know.' Rose sighs.

Her friend sees that this logic is not enough. 'Have you looked for something else?'

'I can't think of anything. What do you suggest?'

'I don't know… How about volunteering at the hospital? You'll meet all sorts there.'

***

Rose, Lech and Karrle are all living in the same community, unaware of each other's existence or how widespread loneliness is. The Indian family do not feel isolated, but none of them are integrating with British society apart from Mohini, who becomes progressively aware of the divide between her family and the local community. Divided loyalties and a growing sense of confusion are becoming ever more inescapable.

## Casual Comment Opens a Door to the Mind

Limitless time fills the room. Rest delivers the gift of physical recovery, but without human contact or occupation of mind and body, constant stress is a festering ulcer. Fixating more on less and less, Karrle is sufficiently self-aware that this is an assault on his mental stability.

The door is closed.

Life fades away.

The only company is the sound of wind blowing through the warped window.

Isolation ferments a roaming imagination, unleashed.

He thinks and smiles and laughs at himself,

But every laugh is a pretence, a denial, a gasp for air.

Desperately trying not to drown, but there is no water,

Only in his mind.

And a spade digging an ever deeper hole in his heart,

A dark one, an empty one, a scary one.

One that must remain buried.

There is smoke. Through it seeing what cannot be said.

He wants to take a chance today.

The key on the table will set him free

But if he escapes, where to go? There are no adventures.

And once free, what will freedom mean.

His scars alone will tell the tale

And show the world what could not be said.

The door is closed and here he stays,

Sinking and hoping to find a way.

With nothing to hold on to,

But listen to the wind blow through the warped window.[1]

The journey into his mind is a long, long way away, safe, to hide, uninterrupted. In this infinite time zone external events are unwelcome intrusions, valueless and probably uneven. A loud knock on the door ejects Karrle from his imagination. Blinking, he is back in his cell. Graham is due to visit but what's the fucking point?

Detecting the heavy mood of his client, Graham fumbles for anything to sound cheery. 'I see you have put on a bit of weight. You look better for it.'

Starting a conversation is an effort not wholly welcome, but once underway the burden eases. 'My weight gain is because I don't walk anywhere. At home I used to walk everywhere, but here I have nowhere to go. I find the English food is not to my taste, and most African food seems to be Nigerian. At home we always ate with family and friends. It's not the same eating on your own.'

Graham uses a time-honoured technique of asking about happier times. 'What do you like to eat?'

''Succotash, the way my mother used to cook it! But I haven't found it here.''

Unusually, Graham is in a hurry today and interrupts his client even at the risk of serving an unwelcome dish. 'No news yet about your asylum application. It is still very early. The Home Office have to make enquiries through the British Embassy and they are well-practiced in the art of losing paperwork.'

'This inactivity is killing me. Every second is torture.'

'That's a good sign, because you expect better. Those who accept the present have given up. You're young and ambitious, you'll get through.'

The gayety of Graham's optimistic words are confirmation that he does not understand how lost Karrle is and the conversation is now only with himself. Unconvinced he replies, 'I hope so.'

Graham knows that if he allows Karrle to wallow in self-pity, his client may become too depressed for the battles ahead.

'Well look on the bright side we will have a lot longer to get to know each other. Oh, by the way, as the Home Office assemble your file

---

[1] Orphee Kinshala, adapted.

they will call you for an interview, probably in Liverpool. It’s vital that you attend and whatever you do, don’t be late.’

Listening without response, this may be reality but it is not what Karrle needs to hear. Changing the subject, Graham moves on. ‘You need to occupy your mind. Why don’t you go to the library and study whatever interests you?’

If this is a lifeline, it is a slender one with no immediate appeal, but in the absence of alternatives Karrle cannot think of an excuse to reject the suggestion. ‘It's a thought. I can't survive like this.’

## The Library

Graham's comments suggest that escape to the library may be Karrle's only refuge for some time. With no alternatives, he decides to follow his support worker's advice.

Now he has somewhere to go, the invigorating twenty-five-minute walk energises his thoughts. The library is in the precinct, almost camouflaged, in the middle of a row of shops. Arriving at the entrance, he takes the lift to the first floor which opens into a huge room offering a world of books and media. The staff are friendly, the environment warm, quiet and *safe*. People move at a gentle pace and talk in whispers, yet there seems to be plenty of time for everyone. Scattered chairs and tables create private zones that are respected by all.

This is the first time in England that Karrle feels at peace, with nothing to think about but investigating ideas. Aisles of shelving display a confusing array of choices and Karrle takes some time flicking through the contents of a variety of eye-catching covers. Never before has he had limitless time to explore a world of knowledge and although this is a distraction from painful memories, his own problems loom largest in his mind.

*Why is there so much injustice in the world?*

*Why am I forced to be unproductive when I have so many important things to do?*

He has not come to England to escape his homeland. England is a safe haven where he can develop his plans to improve the lives of his people.

*Why are societies as they are?*

*How can the library help?*

The more he ponders, the more certain he is that there are answers. He must be asking the wrong questions.

Thinking about his roots in Africa, his tribe have their own ways of doing things, but there are many other tribes each with their own rules and customs. Now he is in England in another tribe with different rules. Each tribe accept ancestral wisdoms handed down through the generations as pronouncements, sometimes elevated to absolute truths – but what is an absolute truth?

Karrle asks a librarian if he can use the computer and searches Google for 'absolute truth':

*'An absolute truth is something that is true at all times and in all places.'*

Many beliefs contradict each other, and therefore they cannot all be absolute truths. Some, maybe many, cannot be right, but where they work within a society they must contain some realities. So why do they have beliefs and what is it about the group that makes individuals willing to sacrifice their lives?

*The first question is why do people live in groups?*

History and sociology provide lots of relevant information. Humans, like many birds, fish, animals and insects, are safer living in groups where they hunt in packs, look out for predators and perform acts of mutual benefit, like preening and nurturing the young. Man has evolved to be inherently sociable, needing and enjoying the company of others. Humans, like insects, will often sacrifice their own lives to preserve their young or the group because it is the best way of preserving their lineage. Indeed, societies place so much importance on defending the group that they bestow highly prized honours on those who are prepared to risk everything.

*But why do small groups form into big groups?*

Early man was a hunter-gatherer and therefore moved from place to place. The development of agriculture provided a reliable source of food but shackled humans to the land. Bigger populations working together enabled the exchange of ideas and the formation of cities, but relying on fewer crop varieties departmentalised agriculture, making man more dependent and vulnerable to environmental changes. A bi-product of this process increasingly detached man from nature. Interestingly, the success of agriculture encouraged many ancestors to influence environmental outcomes by turning to religion and offering sacrifices. These early gods frequently took on aspects of nature, only later taking human form, e.g. Christianity.[1]

Studying economic, political and military history it becomes apparent that large groups living close together are better able to communicate, control tasks, create, process, transport, store and protect

[1] James Fox, *Nature and Us: A History Through Art.*

the output of their labours. Specialisation enables humans to focus on individual tasks, raising productivity so the total output of the society is greater than the sum of the individuals. Town dwellers are more productive than those in the country, and city populations are more productive than those in towns. The more productive a society is, the more people can be supported. This becomes a magnet for others to join the community, increasing the population still further. Paradoxically, it occurs to Karrle that although people all over the world gravitate into towns, cities and prosperous countries, without the village there would be no cities.

The structure of society will be determined by how they need to organise themselves to overcome the challenges they face in their particular environment. This requires a hierarchical society, whether rules emanate from a dictator like the country Karrle has just escaped from or a democratic process like the British Parliament.

*What is the impact on the individual of living in a society?*

Individuals sharing the product of their labours benefit enormously by their entitlement to receive the output of others. This must bring challenges, so what are the possible downsides?

An individual who focuses on one activity gains skills and knowledge, learning more and more about less and less (specialisation), but they sacrifice their independence by having to rely on others to supply the things they no longer provide for themselves. This inter-dependence makes them vulnerable to the risk that others may not fulfil their duties. The individual's only safeguards are the creation and enforcement of rules by the group on all members, administering both rewards and punishments.

*How did these rules evolve?*

The first societies would have been based around the family, with small tribes evolving into larger tribes. Humans living in different parts of the world have to survive in completely different environments, so the rules would evolve according to their knowledge, needs and opportunities, often with little awareness or contact with other groups.

Over thousands of years, humanity spread across all the continents. Attempting to interact across vast distances and terrains would have required tremendous effort, often resulting in more danger than reward, and was historically rare. Experiences would have been very similar *within* a group but very different *between* groups. Even within the same group, over time, if the environment changes so do the rules. The environment is not only physical, but also social organisation, e.g. the birth of philosophy, religion, political beliefs, customs, etc. The social structures needed to survive produced very different societies. Each society would pass down cultural norms through the generations, explaining the truths by which their society understands the world.

*How can different explanations all be complete and correct?*

Because groups throughout the world survive in wildly varied environments, their social structures and experiences will be particular to them. Credible justifications of the rules to ensure co-operation and compliance must be based on what they know, supported by inherited customs. Where they have limited understanding, plausible explanations must fill in the gaps.

*The truth is a mirror ... that fell and broke into pieces. Everybody took a piece of it, and they looked at it and thought they had the truth.*[1]

Leaders would justify, interpret, and dictate the rules according to the belief systems of the group. This offers intoxicating opportunities to manipulate the majority to achieve the personal ambitions of those in power.

Karrle spends many hours reading, sifting and thinking, and is surprised how much information is readily available. Isolated pieces start to fit together leading to bigger questions. Although only at the early stages of his research, he believes these are important steps in shedding light on his home country and may offer some insight into the turmoil, abuse and exploitation that have brought his life to this point. He finds this voyage of discovery fascinating and, although it offers no answers, he is confident that he is beginning to ask the right questions.

This research is surprisingly tiring, but Karrle is grateful that it fully occupies his mind. Who knows? It might lead to something – but not today.

[1]Mawlana Jalal-al-Din Rumi, thirteenth-century Persian poet.

## Unearthing Truth

When Graham next visits Karrle, his cliente has something to talk about. 'I took your advice and went to the library.'

'Excellent. And what did you do there?'

'I study the history of societies, how they form and why.'

'Wow! Heavy stuff. It must be doing you some good – your spirits have improved, despite the Home Office wrecking ball.'

'I do feel better. It is interesting and gives me insight into important questions.'

'And what are your conclusions?'

'None, as yet. They only lead to more questions. But it gives me a context to understand some of the events in my life. I want to learn how groups can protect or destroy lives. At least I am in a country that offers civil liberty and allows me to do my research.'

Reflecting on his education to date, Karrle realises that much of it has been a whitewash, accepting the re-telling of stories without comprehension. Understanding history is an essential part of identity, and as he learns more, he feels increasingly connected. Relishing his new project, for the first time in more than two years, he is gaining a sense of direction in his life.

## Home Office Interview

Karrle cannot have peace of mind until the Home Office grants his asylum application and he has not even had a date for the interview. Until then, planning the future is pointless. Fixating on a date for the interview consumes every idle moment; it becomes almost mythological, like a *Waiting For Godot*[1] event, where everyone talks about it but they secretly know it will never happen. Graham's explanation that 'due process' proceeds at its own pace in an overloaded system, with poorly trained staff, is of no comfort. Sleep or burying himself ever deeper into his studies is Karrle's only escape. It is the one thing in his life that is important that he can control and exhausting his mind makes sleep easier.

With no forewarning, a letter pops through the letterbox and is left on the shared table by the front door. It could have been there a couple of days, because Karrle never receives post and rarely checks. It is from the Home Office and could not have been more important if it had been delivered by the Queen of England.

The interview is in Liverpool and remembering Graham's warning that failure to be present at the appointed hour might be fatal to his aspirations, and having discovered the vagaries of public transport, Karrle sets off very early. The journey complete, he enters the timeless zone of Home Office officials and waits for hours.

The interview is in a magnificent eighteenth-century building, which he later learns was financed from the profits of the slave trade when the sun never set on the British Empire. Its grandeur is an enduring statement of power, giving the impression of impregnability to the conspiracies of mere mortals.

Migrants congregate like driftwood washed upon a foreign shore. Karrle is approached by two men. One looks like a general; he is strikingly tall with piercing eyes – suggesting X-ray vision. Sloping shoulders drooping from a thin frame fail to occupy the clothes which hang in loose, ungraceful folds. The other has the impressive appearance of a devotee of intense physical training, but his stare is unnerving and suggests obsession is his preference. He must be the foot soldier. Both are African.

---

[1] Samuel Becket 1953

[2] *Hamlet,* William Shakespeare

The General initiates the conversation. ‘Are you here for the Home Office interview?’

Karrle stares as both men before replying warily, ‘Yes.’

A few sentences quickly acknowledge common experiences. The Foot Soldier declares, ‘When they see the colour of your skin, they won’t believe a word you say. You are guilty until proven innocent, and they know innocence is impossible to prove so you have lost before you start.’

Their demeanour makes Karrle uneasy and suggests they have a mission, as yet undisclosed.

Eventually an assistant informs Karrle that the interviewers are ready to receive him. He is accompanied down a long corridor and into a huge room with elevated ceilings that catch and return every sound, but there are no sounds apart from the footsteps and conversations of those inside. Here is a world of serenity and certainty, where the mere mention of danger is unseemly and suggests the unwelcome are tracking in their own dirt.

Karrle’s chair is screwed to the floor, as is the interviewers’ desk, removing any possibility of moving or stealing anything. No refreshments or small talk are offered.

Two sharp-suited men, both under thirty, stare without welcome, at the new applicant. One dominates the conversation, his supercilious attitude implying that he is the representative of an inherently superior society, interviewing the national representative of an inherently inferior society; an imperfect hopeful pleading to enter their perfect world.

The quiet one appears shy, possibly even humble, until he speaks. As the interview progresses his comments reveal an appalling arrogance, which is both dumbly and doubly inappropriate as he fails to display anything to be arrogant about, apart from having the good fortune to be born socially advantaged. The game revolves around catching the interviewee out with probing questions to uncover unguarded reactions to discredit the applicant. Questions are probing and irrelevant, homing in on details that Karrle cannot remember or never knew.

‘You say you left Agadez. What date was that?’

‘It was over two years ago, around July, or maybe August, I think.’ He knew he could remember but pressure scrambles clarity, robbing the time to calculate the sequence of events he had been trying to forget.

‘Which was it, July or August?’

Karrle stumbles and hesitates. He does not want to give a wrong answer in case it later proves incorrect. The quiet interviewer can see a winning position and jumps in.

'We need to know NOW.' His demanding tone only multiples the difficulty. After several more seconds of indecision, the interrogators interpret the failure to offer the correct answer as a victory. Exchanging knowing glances and they write something down and move on.

'What was the address where you were held in Sebha?'

'I don't know. They do not tell you.'

The now not-shy second interrogator thinks of a question he must know the answer to.

'You say you were kept in a house in Tripoli. How many rooms were there?'

'I don't know. We were locked in one room and not allowed to roam. The house was quite big. There were many of us.'

The blessed amnesia that has protected Karrle from his most painful memories is now turned against him; truth feels like falsehood, conjured to manipulate an audience for dishonourable purposes. Shaken confidence proffers an apologetic delivery acknowledging the falsehood has been discovered.

Without refreshments throughout the three-hour interrogation, Karrle's voice becomes dry and croaky. Calm words spoken in an autoclaved institution mock his attempts to recount the terror inflicted by the depraved on a distant continent. This timeless sanctuary, built out of the pain and suffering of the vulnerable, is emotionally dead; it is incapable of recognising the fear these stories attempt to convey.

By the end of the ordeal Karrle is exhausted, utterly disempowered and now has another emotional trauma to manage on his own.

His support worker later explains that Home Office interviewers are rewarded with meal vouchers for every applicant they reject. Karrle surmises that they probably dine exceedingly well on the extended diet of suffering they dish out to the defenceless. He cannot avoid the thought that the building is a monument that glorifies the past, where white men are still deciding the fate of black men.

## The Revolutionaries

Interview ended, Karrle leaves the building, and is immediately greeted by the same two Africans, who suggest going for a coffee. The Foot Soldier asks, 'How did it go?'

Karrle is in no mood for conversation, but replies honestly, 'badly.'

With obvious glee the Foot Soldier rejoins, 'See, I told you they wouldn't believe a word you said.'

The conversation quickly darkens, becoming intense. One man has military training and talks about 'action' sprinkled with emotive words like 'imperialism,' 'western capitalism,' 'suppression' and 'revenge,' all linked by the inclusive hook 'brother.'

This is not familiar language to Karrle when conversing with strangers. 'Why do you call me brother?' and is quickly corrected by the Foot Soldier. 'We are all brothers.'

Refusing to be smothered, Karrle responds, 'We are not related, I have never met you before, and we are not even from the same country. We are just three men from the same continent who happen to be in England.'

Stepping in, The General directs the conversation. 'No! We are all here for the same reasons. We must unite to right the wrongs against our people. The white man has treated us as slaves for too long. Now is the time to teach him a lesson he will *never* forget.'

Karrle is too surprised to answer, but he must look unconvinced because The General slips into auto-pilot with a mantra of dogmatic pronouncements, filling his own consciousness and drowning the audience in a vitriolic monologue that leaves no space for alternatives or invitations for discussion.

Karrle waits for the machine gun to reload before replying. 'The wrong done against me and my people is being done by my own black countrymen. White men did not invent slavery. It was the Africans and Arabs who taught the whites how to make money from the trade. Africans had been trading slaves for hundreds of years before the white man appeared, and they still do today in failed states. It was the whites who abolished slavery, despite the money they were making, because of their belief in the right of men to be free.'

Supporting The General, the Foot Soldier rushes to the attack. 'The white man has abused my people, stolen what is not his, and pays money to corrupt leaders who are happy to sell my country to feed Western materialism for their own personal gain. We are suppressed and robbed of what is ours. Whites say what sounds civilised and do nothing. They have to experience the pain they cause others.'

This is going to places Karrle is not comfortable with, but he wants to bring these challenging statements to a conclusion. 'You left your country because of the actions of your countrymen. You bring your anger with you, and want to repeat the things you have learnt about war, hate and destruction to the country that offers you the freedom you want back home. You base this judgement on historical injustices, only some of which are true. Learn the lessons about what doesn't work, and use your freedom to change and improve your country, not spread the battlefield. You have personal experience that it does not work, but you refuse to see it. Win the argument, because you will never win the war.'

The failure to convert this misguided fool cannot suppress The General's frustration. Unable to conceal his mounting anger, an undercurrent of unmistakable aggression is delivered with disingenuous friendliness, falling back on the old language. 'Brother, brother, brother. You are safe now, but you have an obligation to help your own people.'

'Yes, I am safe now because I am in this country which gives me rights as a human being that are denied in my own country. Don't alienate many good people by talking about black and white as if that is the same as right and wrong. All life is precious, and you have no right to endanger other people's unless your own life is in danger. You are under no threat in England. Don't you see how misguided you are?'

The General spits his response, 'Not under any threat here? Have you been to a detention centre like Yarl's Wood?'

'No.'

Raising his voice, The General blasts back, 'Then your opinion is worthless. You have swallowed the white man's lies.'

Having witnessed revenge practised in his own country, Karrle is deeply opposed to their ideas. 'But you are not British and have come here uninvited. They have to check out who you are to be allowed to stay.'

The Foot Soldier speaks from the heart, recounting personal experience. 'In my country, if you go to the British Embassy and apply for asylum and the government finds out they will kill you. The British know this and leave us no choice but to come here illegally, whatever their international obligations. They make the process as difficult as possible to discourage others. If they put you in a detention centre, you have no rights. It is worse than prison – it is worse than death. In prison you know when you are going to come out, but in a detention centre you die slowly. Sometimes when you are ill they do not even call a doctor. People come out in boxes. There are people in detention centres awaiting deportation most of whom will never get deported. All are depressed, all are damaged. Nothing prepares you for that. Detention centres are Britain's Guantanamo Bay.'

Karrle does not know how to answer this. He sits in silence, which is interpreted as stubborn refusal to acknowledge the facts, further inflaming his opponents. The General makes a final appeal to his dignity as a man. 'How can you not support your brothers? Have you no honour?'

This is an issue Karrle has lived with for a long time and he pushes back with conviction. 'I have honour, and accept my obligation to help my people, but there is no honour in spreading the suffering. You come from one background, but you don't own all the events of the past. Don't be a prisoner of your past. Your spirit roams free and all experiences are open to everyone. Just because you are black does not give you a monopoly on injustice. If you keep it as an exclusive black entitlement, you isolate yourself from many others who might support you. You perpetuate the division, and then *you* become part of the problem and a barrier to solutions. Revenge breeds new victims. Only justice restores order.'

The General stares in disbelief at this spineless, white-loving coward who is selling his soul to his suppressors, devoid of honour, integrity or rights as a human being. Radiating fury, he leans forward. Karrle can see the thoughts behind his eyes. In synch, the Foot Soldier edges nearer, twitches and moves into hunting mode, a cat ready to pounce.

Chilly as a tomb, The General's upper lip slowly rises to reveal the veneer of a smile and release a hollow, mirthless laugh, like an echo from a dungeon, unworldly and devoid of humanity. 'I cannot believe you… You are one of us, but…' He stares at Karrle with incredulity. 'It's people like *you* who let the white supremacists get away with it! They have to understand the suffering they are causing by feeling it themselves.' Fingers puncture the air like spitting knives designed to kill. 'You have NO honour! YOU! …YOU … ARE <u>NOT</u> … A BROTHER!!!'

All three are coiled springs, locked and loaded. Rigid. Silent. Ready.

Raw bubbling anger cannot be contained any longer, but this is no place to explode. Exhaling, The General suddenly deflates and, in seething exasperation, tosses his hands in the air. The tension is broken. His dying words have concluded the confrontation and Karrle is dismissed from thought and deed.

In despair, the gang of two gather their scattered emotions and saunter off in pursuit of other converts: two righteous crusaders addicted to war porn, preparing to detonate. Imposing their beliefs on others, they paint squares and instruct others to stand in the square of their choosing; all in the name of freedom – whilst simultaneously denying the freedom of others.

Shaken but not stirred, Karrle is convinced that if this misguided pair succeed it will result in chaos. The power vacuum they create will allow other extremists to move in with their own agendas, denying the rights of the majority. Blood is the currency of war, and instability breeds instability that is gifted to future generations.

In his later studies, reflecting on this, he reads about the Russian revolution of October 1917 when the overthrow of the Czar was hijacked by Lenin. Once power was seized, he crushed all opposition, killing the democratic process. This tyranny still dominates the lives of Russians today. Vladimir Putin reminds Karrle of a man who has inherited a huge country mansion but can only afford to occupy the ground floor as the building falls apart. Reminiscing on a distorted interpretation of the past, Putin channels all his energy into restoring past glories, however expensive, misguided and ultimately damaging.

Just because one form of injustice is removed does not mean that it is replaced by something better, as half of Africa can bear witness. Karrle realises that his country, like many on the continent, has a long way to go. Whilst acknowledging many of the injustices, he believes that spreading understanding by focusing on what is true and building together is the best way to gain support for the changes that will be necessary.

He feels that his research is the best way that he can contribute to the lives of his countrymen. Indiscriminate smashing of all opposition will polarise groups into head-on conflict, and from his experience it is always the vulnerable who suffer most. As the West is more powerful, it is the Africans who would come off worst.

Eventually Karrle will come to understand how the West mistakenly equates radicalism with irrationality and fails to understand that these revolutionaries have merely chosen a different path to manage their power base. By believing that an alternative opinion is irrational, the West deludes itself that once its opponents rationalise the situation, they will agree with the West. This apparent logic will never solve today's problems and therefore never become a reality.

Rebuffed by the Home Office and rejected by his fellow migrants, Karrle abandons the Liverpool café to begin the long journey back to his singing wardrobe and complaining bed. Right now, solutions feel like daydreams without wings.

## Organisations

After the bruising encounters in Liverpool, Karrle needs to hang onto what remains of his sanity. The chasm in the attitudes between the Home Office officials and the revolutionaries only convinces him of the desperate need to establish common ground and the importance of his research. Doubling his efforts, he now spends more hours at the library than the staff.

Having looked at the evolution of societies, what strikes Karrle first, is how wonderfully adaptable humans are in their ability to survive in deserts, forests, mountains, oceans and frozen lands on every continent. These environments demand specific skills and extensive knowledge of how to find and process local resources and adapt them to satisfy their needs. Secondly, it is clear that no society is a single homogenous block. Every nation has many types of organisations, including political, military commercial and social. Each organisation normally has an individual leader, with tasks allocated within a hierarchy.

People are passionate about their culture, which is a powerful source of nationalism. The identity of the group also gives individuals a defined identity within the hierarchy. Rules created by the group do not hang in mid-air, they are anchored very firmly in the belief system used to justify the rules. These rules have to answer the challenges faced by the group and presented as complete, but they cannot know everything, so assumptions must be made in areas where information is limited or non-existent.

Surprisingly, when Karrle starts to look at things in this way he finds common threads in all organisations. Using the library computer, he Googles: 'Belief Systems meaning.'

*'Belief systems are stories we tell ourselves to define our personal sense of reality.'*

Yep, that's it. Next he types: 'Charismatic Leaders meaning'.

*their ability to inspire and motivate followers to perform at high levels, and to be committed to the organisation or the cause.*

Yep. Got it again. He is on the right track. Shared values must be based on the positives of mutual self-interest and at some level, emotional commitment: love. Individuals give to the group in the expectation of sharing the rewards provided by the group. Humans are not just economically better off in groups, they derive feelings of self-worth by their relationships with others, and these shared values are the glue that forms and maintains societies. If charismatic leaders can persuade group members to co-ordinate their actions, they make the group more successful. The acid test is that it works.

Scientific and medical evidence proves that people across the world are very similar in their biological and social makeup. One interesting fact Karrle uncovers is that there is more biological variation within Africa than in the rest of the world, invalidating the idea that there ever was an African 'type.' So if people are very similar whichever part of the world they come from, why do they see themselves as different? It is the organisations they join that emphasise the differences, not the similarities.

The groups that you join give you the values by which you judge others. Therefore, the rules must define who is in the group and who is not. These rules also determine how group and non-group members are treated. The Buddhist faith respects all life forms (human and non-human). The mafia show great loyalty to group members, often based around the family, but emotionally detach themselves from the suffering they cause others. Because the Mafia benefit from the exploitation of those outside their group, to empathise with non-group members would destroy their source of wealth and therefore the group. It is essential that they emphasise differences, real or imagined.

If you never meet people unlike yourself, and accept what you are told about them by group members, is it surprising that people form negative opinions about other groups? It is a natural desire to look for differences as proof that your group is better. The reality is that just because somebody is not in your group does not make them less of a human; but there are groups that can rob you of your humanity, destroying the foundations of civilisation.

People need to be very careful which groups they join, and also objective about which groups they were born into. When people tell you which belief system they belong to, they think they are telling you what sort of person they are, but frequently they are merely describing where they are from. Many an undiscovered personality is hidden in a group; they may not know who they are themselves! What is probably unsurprising is that personal experiences frequently find the similarities greater than the differences, contradicting the stories they have been told.

Societies prosper when individuals contribute to the group, whether it is an English nobleman winning a battle for his king, or goods or services provided to the society. The intention is to encourage behaviour that protects the society (e.g. the army) and makes the members more prosperous (e.g. merchants). Those that control the wealth creating mechanisms are hugely rewarded, and are often not the originators.

The distribution of wealth to individuals is a reward system to maintain the group. How those least advantaged are treated depends on society's values. Concentrated wealth concentrates power, dividing society, resulting in the disadvantaged being disregarded or exploited and abused. Class systems are a very useful method of structuring society where abuse of the disadvantaged is accepted and barely visible, even by those abused. Living permanently under one set of rules rarely generates the need, or the benefit in the rules being challenged, unless survival demands a re-assessment of their relevance. External threats expose the reality of mutual interdependence. Everyone joins together to repel a common enemy, before falling back on the old divisions once the danger has passed.

Whatever the social structures, empires (Chinese, Russian, Roman, British, etc.) were established by 'charismatic', often military, leaders who built huge power bases. They may have been conquering lands to increase their empire and wealth or just fighting oppression, but they always exploited opportunities to win control of the group for themselves and defeat opposition.

In terms of explaining the mighty organisations of the world, 'the pen is mightier than the sword' was written by a thinker with a pen not a sword. Where are the great writings of Putin, Napoleon, Genghis Khan, etc? They were brilliant strategists and administrators but not creative thinkers. Ruthless ambition, not original thinking, is the essential characteristic of all empire builders. The power hungry might use philosophy, but only in the same way that they manipulate the group using money, military might or the weakness of others. The mechanisms of power are seized with a sword and justified with a pen.

Many empires fade with the death of the leader unless they are succeeded by another charismatic leader. These leaders are not philanthropists but motivated by self-interest, greed and a lust for power, sprinkled with intellectual curiosity or a philosophy like communism, which is adopted and hijacked to justify their actions. To survive over generations empires become institutionalised, like the Roman Empire and the British monarchy, so that continuity is maintained by the establishment of rules which are then manipulated by the power hungry. Might is needed to seize power, but persuasion, deception and cunning are needed to maintain it.

Power is proportionate to the number of people who support the leader. Control can be maintained as long as the leader can continue to persuade others to do their bidding. Large organisations can create an inner world that is so seductive that it becomes the only focal point, obscuring the realities of their actions. The faithful blindly following the rules requires no understanding.

People with power determine the morality of their society. Criminality is more about breaking group rules than ethics. Rules are justified by the beliefs that societies adopt, elevated to moral judgements. Rule breakers are not just ignoring codes of behaviour; their actions are seen as damaging society and a blot on the character of the perpetrators. Society then administers punishments, detaching their emotions from the suffering of those punished.

Imposing values on others is an effective way to increase society's power. Historical events are often cited as evidence that others are different, often without understanding the circumstances. It is as if previous generations were all sinners and have now been exposed by the enlightened present. Isn't that merely perpetuating 'now' as the 'norm,' and the arrogance of self-belief?

Many groups believe that respecting all life is important and causing unnecessary suffering is uncivilised. However, all individuals and societies are capable of detaching their emotions by justifying their actions and inflicting the most appalling atrocities. People particularly lack empathy, becoming de-sensitised, when they don't believe that the misfortune of others could possibly happen to them. Examples include war, fishing (fish suffocate out of water) and factory farming. Killing for survival is normal, healthy and how life evolved. Humans are not responsible for evolution; this is the natural order of which mankind is only a tiny part. Not to recognise this is not to understand yourself.

Recent attention has focused on the appalling and disproportionate suffering caused by the European empire builders who expounded high principles regarding the defence of those that formed their powerbase, whilst ignoring the rights of those they targeted. This is how Hitler manipulated the Germans to persecute the Jews, Poles,

Gypsies and Russians. Hitler won 80% and 90+% of the votes in relatively free, but information manipulated, elections.

The same thinking was used by the Russians against the Germans, the Italians against the Ethiopians, the Japanese against the Chinese, the Belgians against the Congolese, and the conquistadors against the Aztecs. Sadly it is being used by Putin against Ukrainians today. It is easier to kill strangers if you can justify it with a philosophy. If you don't know them it is easier to accept stories you are told as justification. You might even be heralded a hero.

The techniques used by dictators to manipulate followers form a depressingly familiar pattern :

First, the group has to feel under threat. This is often real but can be manufactured.

Secondly, there must be a target enemy – Jews, Americans, Muslims, Tutsi, Rohingya, Arabs, white or black people, capitalists, Arabs, communists, British imperialists, whoever. It does not matter who they are as long as there is a perceived difference from the people whom the dictator purports to defend. The target can be moved to whatever the dictator desires, provided there is a plausible explanation and the power to carry out his wishes. This is very important in building empires. The real target is anyone who stands in the way.

Thirdly, this perceived difference must depict the target as sub-human so that emotions can be detached from their suffering. The dominant group often portray their actions as virtuous and heroic. Examples include Isis, Crusaders, Conquistadors, Ku Klux Klan, Boko Harem, Americans in Guantanamo Bay, al-Qaida, and all the European empire builders at some points (though not everyone all the time). This is the history of all societies.

*Not a single nation on earth has emerged without bloodshed.* Matthew Syed, The Sunday Times, 28th Feb 2021

Most nationalistic agendas are driven by those in charge harnessing the support of powerful sectors of society. Dictators need a mythology to justify their actions. Stories have always had a key role in the transfer of ideas but what is told can be deceptively selective. Facts have no loyalty so the dictator must control all sources of information (television, newspapers, radio, internet, movement of people, etc.). Instances include Putin and Lenin in Russia, Kim Jon-un in North Korea, Xi Jinping in China, Hitler in Germany and Saddam Hussein in Iraq. This blanks out alternatives and is a constant danger within all societies, including the West.

'For evil to flourish, it only requires good men to do nothing.'[i] Simon Wiesenthal, holocaust survivor.

Autocratic leaders gather supporters around them who are like-minded and can be trusted, i.e. they have compliant personalities and a keen sense of self-preservation. Citizens are treated like children as the dictator attempts to convince them that only he can prevent the country falling apart. Retaining control is essential, even attempting to pass on an entire country as an inheritable family asset.[1] Too often the victor writes history and is remembered. He also loves statues. As they say in Europe, 'might is right.'

Independent thinkers can be among the most dangerous opponents of dictators because they cannot be bought. Suppression of information advantages the dictator and diminishes society. Independent thought, open debate and academic research is vital to the stability of society and the advancement of understanding. Equitable rules enforced in law are vital in protecting minorities; we are all minorities in one way or another. Losing the right to use evidence exposes every citizen. Academic research, and archaeology in particular, has proven many a myth about the past to be incorrect. In the mid-nineteenth century a brilliant black American orator came to Britain and said to packed audiences,

'If one of us is not free, then none of us are free.'

There is no automatic right to freedom for the individual. The West breath it as if it were a law of nature, but it is a man-made concept based on ideas about how we should relate to each other. What is a law of nature is that diversity strengthens society. The broader the pool of talent that organisations can draw upon the stronger they are to optimise opportunity and adjust to change. People should celebrate their differences because it enables individuals to contribute to the group what others cannot. Uniformity suppresses individuality and reduces social flexibility.

[1] Al Jazeera, *The Arab Awakening*. 20th Feb 2012

[i] Simon Wiesenthal, holocaust survivor.

If competing groups usurp power, the collapse of civil order can unleash rampaging mobs that represent nobody. Mob hysteria can easily override intellectual processes and anyone can be their next target.

Karrle recognises that he has come from a country that is tearing itself apart. His research sheds important light on his experiences in Africa. Small groups hijacked legitimate complaints of injustice and persecution to grab the mechanisms of power and wealth creation. White Europeans were obvious and often justified targets.

Once power had been gained, the new rulers focused their energies on crushing all opposition and showed no empathy for the suffering of their own countrymen. They justified their actions by using plausible explanations that fitted some of the evidence, and was within the understanding of the group. The result was inequality and impoverishment, internal instability and a mass exodus of the people.

His country became vulnerable to external domination by foreign powers, either by invasion or bribing corrupt leaders to become strategic allies. This perpetuated the inequality, which made the rulers ever more dependent on external support to sustain their rule by suppression. To justify their actions, they sacrificed the truth, corrupting all the national institutions. Many turned to religion for comfort, forming small congregations, the organisers preaching and taking money from the poor.

Like a trainee reporter, Karrle tries to cross-reference everything two or three times; apart from an occasional disappointment, this only confirms the direction of travel. As he ploughs through vast quantities of information, many fragments of thought coalesce. They offer beguiling invitations to imagine bigger pictures. Like a jigsaw, ideas become less of a puzzle and offer glimpses, and maybe even a peek, at the whole.

Enough has been done today. The last to exit, even the library staff are waiting to lock up as Karrle retreats to the solitude of his room to rest.

## Friends Become Lovebirds

Being a female and the youngest in the family, Mohini has never been the centre of attention. Now she is learning how wonderful a relationship with a boy can be. Andy is so lovely that she feels treasured and safe. When they are together every minute is precious, and when they are apart she counts the minutes until they can be together again.

To this graceful and unassuming girl, every experience is fresh, every moment a delight. For Andy, explaining aspects of his life that have passed unnoticed opens discussions that are like revelations and fascinating to both of them. The world is a better place for Mohini being in it, and Andy is better for being in Mohini's world.

As conversations skip along, they touch on darker matters. Andy is apprehensive about mentioning his father, but it is a truth that cannot be hidden. He tells Mohini that it would be a problem if he took her home because his father is a member of the English Defence League and hates all foreigners.

To his considerable amazement and relief, Mohini immediately understands. She tells him that her family are devout Hindus, and partnerships outside of their religion are forbidden. Her father will choose her partner; she will have to live in her husband's household and do most of the housework for the whole family every day. She will not be fully accepted into the family until she gives birth to a son, and if her husband dies she will lose her status in the family. This time-honoured practice is accepted in India, but here in England it is inexplicable to Andy and appears increasingly odd to Mohini. Neither can understand why their relationship is a problem for their parents because it is not for them, but neither know how they can be together and open to the world. Their love for each other is drawing them closer together and separating them from their communities.

## The Missing Link

Karrle is sitting in his room. Again somebody in the shared kitchen has eaten his supper. He only has 49p left of his asylum seekers allowance of £40.85 per week for food, clothing and everything personal. Isolated and alone he does not move. There is no sound as if the world has stopped. The only escape is the library. All the staff acknowledge him, smile and look him in the eye when they say 'good morning.' The library is where he belongs. This room is uncaring, lifeless; the silence a punishment. With no time frames, feedback or guidance from the Home Office, emotion is suspended. Unable to plan anything beyond today, even that is not possible with 49p.

He re-runs the interview over and over in his mind, wondering what he could have said differently. What could they use against him? Will the police arrive unannounced and send him to Yarl's Wood Immigration Removal Centre? From what others have said, it is hell. You cannot move within the centre unless you are accompanied by guards.

The only thing Karrle can do is pour his energy into research at the library. This daily escape is becoming ever more vital to his mental wellbeing.

Graham provides the only relief from anxiety, and thankfully his fortnightly appointments are increasingly interspersed with social visits where relaxed conversation permits some unwinding and mental space. It makes the present bearable, and reminds Karrle that there is life beyond this suffocating bubble.

Chatting allows freedom of thought, but putting ideas into words that make sense to somebody else is surprisingly hard. Their free-flowing conversations highlight omissions, but also crystallise ideas as new realisations emerge that have previously only been half-explored.

The interludes between visits are opportunities to mull over previous conversations, generating fresh thoughts and momentum for their next meeting. Graham's throw-away comments are often a seed to investigate a wealth of information in preparation for their next discussion.

Although regular, these visits are too infrequent for Karrle to waste opportunities not talking about the latest developments in his thinking. Eventually, his visitor arrives.

'Hi, Karrle. How are you today?'

'I am good, thank you. Would you like to be the first visitor to sit on my chair?'

'Thank you. This is a pleasure. Life is getting better.'

'I was hoping it would be a bit quicker than this. I didn't come to England to sit on a chair.'

This gentle banter is no more than the pitter-patter of soft rain on leaves as each reaffirms that everything is OK, before Graham asks the question that Karrle has been waiting for: 'How's the studies?'

Karrle whisks through his thoughts on why and how all organisations function, Graham listens intently without interrupting. Concluding, Karrle waits for a response but his guest remains silent. Karrle refuses to break the silence.

Finally Graham says, 'You know what you have not looked at?'

Karrle is taken aback because he felt his analysis was thorough. 'No. What?'

'Religion!'

'What has that got to do with organisations?'

'Everything!' Graham answers with conviction before explaining. 'Religions have all of the characteristics that you are talking about: belief systems, shared values, leaders, rules and they are amongst the largest organisations in the world. As for conflict, how many religious wars have there been around the world over thousands of years, many of which continue today? And whilst you're at it, look at the history of how religions were formed.'

Karrle immediately responds with what he knows. 'Well, Christianity started with the birth of Jesus and the disciples spreading the word.'

'No, not the stories. Look at how the *organisations* were formed.'

Whatever can Graham mean? This is an intriguing challenge and sets tomorrow's task.

## Religious Organisations

The next day, Karrle is at the library before the doors are unlocked. His thoughts revolve around his Christian upbringing in Africa. He was familiar with, and had accepted, the teachings of the Church. He is surprised by his own ignorance regarding any objective historical understanding of how the Church has become the institution it is today, and what role the Bible has played in that process. He already knew that the Old and New Testaments were stories handed down over many generations, but assumed that somewhere there were original first-hand accounts of the birth, life or death of Jesus.

*'I did my very best to hold on to my faith that the Bible was the inspired word of God with no mistakes and that lasted for about two years... I realized that at the time we had over 5,000 manuscripts of the New Testament, and no two of them are exactly alike.'*[1]

*'The Gospels are full of discrepancies, were written decades after Jesus's death, by authors who had not witnessed any events in Jesus's life. They go on to say the Gospels were authored not by eyewitnesses who were contemporary with the events that they narrate but rather by people who did not know Jesus, see anything he did, or hear anything he taught, and that the authors did not even share a language with Jesus.'*[2]

The earliest stories in the Bible are Matthew, Mark, Luke and John, which were written fifty to seventy years after Jesus's death. There was no direct interaction between Jesus and any of the writers of the Bible.

Karrle is shocked, but this becomes less surprising when he understands the evolution of humans and Christianity. In the first, second and third centuries, Christianity spread in many directions and interpretations became increasingly diverse. Stories were retold countless times, some written down, many spread by word of mouth. Unsurprisingly, there were variations and obvious discrepancies between the stories, including amazing accounts of mythical creatures, God in the

[1] Bart D. Ehrman, Distinguished Professor of Religious Studies at North Carolina University, scholar and author. Wikipedia.
[2] Bart D. Ehrman/Robert Eisenman. Wikipedia.

sky, and hell being in the bowels of the earth. Some stories were so embellished as to be ridiculous, robbing them of credibility.

It became clear that there was a need to agree on one version that everybody could use. This did not happen until 397AD, and the committee was dominated by powerful and moneyed *men*. This version eventually became known as the King James Bible. Academics believe that the stories selected were more influenced by politics and economics than the search for truth, with more being excluded (called the Apocrypha) than included.

Having agreed the stories fashioned into a standard Bible, many of the Apocryphal stories were banned and destroyed. The Archbishop of Egypt decreed that it was heresy even to read these ancient manuscripts. Thousands of documents were hidden, buried behind walls and in the ground, anywhere to keep them safe.

Over hundreds of years, Apocrypha were discovered offering fascinating insights that sometimes contradict traditional teachings. Even today, fragments of ancient documents still turn up and are offered to the team at Timbuktu library every week.[1] This did not stop the Catholic Church from collecting and hiding Apocrypha themselves. Indeed, under the Vatican building in Rome there are five miles of shelving with ancient manuscripts and artefacts. The Roman Catholic Church concealed their very existence until the last few decades, and still refuse to allow open scholarship of these important historical documents.

The Bible, once defined, was used as a document of control to dictate what people were allowed to think, say and do. The Church determined what sin was, giving it the authority to reward those that conformed and punish those who did not. Indeed, no new work could be published without its permission, giving the Church enormous power over access to information.

For many years, William Tyndale was hunted by the Catholic Church to prevent him from translating the Bible from Latin into English. Commoners could not read Latin, so the interpretation of the Bible remained the preserve of the Church. When captured in Antwerp, the Church authorised his execution.

[1] Timbuktu Manuscripts, Wikipedia.

*'William Tyndale ... is well known for his translation of the Bible into English... In 1536, he was convicted of heresy and executed by strangulation' and then burned at the stake whilst still alive.'* [1]

William Tyndale had as much influence on the development of the English language as Shakespeare, and yet he is almost written out of history. He created phrases that are used in everyday language today: the Lord's Prayer 'Our Father, who art in heaven'; 'Fight the good fight'; 'Am I my brother's keeper?; 'The spirit is willing but the flesh is weak'; 'Salt of the earth' are but a few.

Once the translation became widely available, control had to be re-established. Within two years, it was officially adopted and formed the basis of the modern King James Bible. Maintaining power was the key; what you believed was relatively unimportant unless it challenged the power of the Church, in which case it could get you killed.

Galileo, 'the father of modern science,' built a telescope that proved that the Earth was not the centre of the universe, but this was in direct contradiction with the teachings of the Church and human observation. Standing on the ground and staring at the sky gives the sensation that the Earth is stationary and the sun, moon and stars are moving around it. Gravity demonstrates how everything falls to the ground, so the Earth must be the centre of the universe. Yet despite all these self-evident truths, Galileo persisted in contradicting the Church.

*'The matter was investigated by the Roman Inquisition in 1615, which concluded the idea ... 'was foolish, absurd, and heretical since it contradicted Holy Scripture'. Galileo.... alienated... the Pope. He was tried by the Inquisition, found "vehemently suspect of heresy", and forced to recant. He spent the rest of his life under house arrest.'* [2]

During the Middle Ages, the dominance of the Church was considerably strengthened by granting indulgences to sinners who offered the Church money or land for the forgiveness of sin, thereby enhancing their chances of going to heaven.

At its peak, one third of the land in Western Europe was owned by the Church. This institutionalisation of religion enabled the collection of the vast wealth needed to construct magnificent cathedrals and

---

[1] Wikipedia.

[2] Galileo Galilei, Wikipedia.

churches to glorify God, whilst simultaneously demonstrating wealth and bestowing worldly power on those in charge, all of whom were divinely blessed.

The Bible had a profound impact on the cultural evolution of the Christian church. Some historians believe that women contributed more than men to the spreading of Christianity in the first three centuries. After 397AD women were relegated to a subordinate role and the central characters in the stories were exclusively male. Christianity focused far more on the male image: God the Father, Jesus, Son of God, twelve disciples, all male.

Jesus's mother was sanitised as a virgin, and for 1,600 years Mary Magdalene was maligned as a prostitute; this was not corrected by the Pope until 1969, when the fabrication could no longer be sustained in the face of historical evidence. Some historians believe that she was the senior disciple, Jesus's confidante and girlfriend. Recent archaeological evidence suggests that God had a wife, Asherah. Undervaluing the contribution of women is historically inaccurate and still re-enforces sexual inequality in the Catholic and Protestant Churches today.

Some religious groups take every word in the Bible as the word of God, enshrining absolute, universal and eternal truths. They are so entrenched in the stories they want to believe that they are fearful of looking over the parapet at alternative possibilities for which there is plenty of evidence. They claim to have certain knowledge, but many have very limited understanding of events that challenge their own certainties.

There is nothing more threatening to an absolute truth than evidence. There is nothing that has ever been written that was not written by man, and nothing that cannot be changed or improved. The Bible was not written by God, and contains information based on logic applied to the evidence available to man at the time.

This reminds Karrle of the comments of young children who make delightful observations by applying logic to what they know, which adults often find amusing, whereas grown-ups, having lived longer, understand more about the world. The same observation can be made about many of the world's religions. Many assertions were wrong; if they were the word of God, he would never have offered such inaccurate information, or mentioned so little about the universe.

The organisational structure of the Church is similar to any government or military establishment. It is far removed from the stories describing the life of Jesus or the original followers of Christianity who, through self-denial, solitude and prayer, sacrificed comfort to have a closer relationship with God.

Once religions become institutionalised, their worldly position has to be defended and this restricts the search for truth. It is vital for all organisations or biological organisms to isolate and destroy anything perceived as a threat; the stories they want to tell must be preserved, unchanged and unchallenged. The easiest defence is to demonise critics, a tactic that is uncomfortably similar to that of dictators.

The creation of the Catholic Church as a powerful organisation spanning the world was the result of the tireless efforts of power seekers fuelled by 'ambition, violence and greed'[1]. The activities of the early popes included political intrigue, murder, rape, poisoning and other activities that were as heinous then as they are today and typical of every other empire in history. This need for control helped develop a secretive culture that has attempted to conceal the activities of those in the Church hierarchy throughout the ages, and is as virulent now as it has ever been.

The challenge to Church culture comes from the availability of information in open societies that is treasured, particularly in the West. Where the evidence is undeniable, apologising for malign actions as the 'failings of man' is a weak excuse; the Church blames the individuals, not the institution, despite the widespread evidence that many of these deeds were performed with the full knowledge and approval of the Church.

The actions of the Church were deliberate and planned by men with worldly ambitions in the full knowledge of their consequences, and completely against the teachings that were being extolled to everyone else. It was these calculated actions that built the rich and powerful organisation it is today. Their secret weapon was however bad things are on Earth, there is a better place in the afterlife if you obey the Church. This does not demonstrate the existence of a god of love; indeed, the Church's actions suggest its members do not truly believe their own teachings.

[1] *Saints and Sinners*, PBS America, 18th February 2020

## Sins of the Church

Christian beliefs gave the Church an over-arching moral authority above the rights of man. It could decide who were 'sinners' and administer punishments; this has led to religious persecution and the death of millions over the centuries. Even those within the Church were denied what today would be called their humans rights.

The heavy hands of the Church have successfully concealed many of its deeds. Evidence has only come to light recently that reveals practices which go back decades, even centuries. The power of the Church and the social norms it created were so pervasive that no-one felt able to challenge the institution. It hid widespread exploitation whilst a submissive society tolerated the abuse or rejected the evidence, leaving victims suffering in silence.

It was independent-minded individuals and organisations that documented evidence and placed it in the public domain. As society's attitude and tolerance of systemic abuse changed, particularly of vulnerable children, this begs the question: when did these practices start? Perhaps they have always taken place, and the secretive nature of the Church was the perfect breeding ground for them. The organisation knew what was happening, protected the perpetrators and concealed the evidence for hundreds of years in order to protect the institution and themselves.

In 2017 a report was published into the many thousands of cases of abuse in Australian institutions from 1950 to 2009:

'A 'stark warning of an exhaustive five-year investigation by an Australia Royal Commission into institutional child sex abuse … McClellan singled out the Roman Catholic Church in particular for often putting reputation above the safety of children in what they found to be decades of systematic sexual abuse … a familiar pattern of scandals dogging Catholic institutions globally.'[1]

In August 2018 in Pennsylvania, USA, a grand jury heard that more than 300 'predator priests' had abused more than 1,000 children over decades. The report investigated six dioceses out of eight; the other two dioceses had highlighted similar findings from an earlier report. That is 100% of the diocese from two investigations in a single state.

[1] CNN, 18th August 2015

On 5th October 2021, Sky News reported the findings of a French commission that estimated 330,000 children were sexually abused by 3,000 abusers working in the Church from 1950 to 2020, two-thirds of them priests. There are many other examples from all over the world.

In Ireland, the Magdalene Laundries took in unmarried, pregnant women, usually young and desperate. They were shunned by society, including their own families, because of the moral teachings of the time. The girls worked long hours in appalling conditions, were unpaid and underfed. Babies were removed at birth; many died and were secretly buried in the garden. One institution kept a dead baby in the fridge, to prove to the mother that her baby had died, so the sisters could sell the child for adoption at a profit. These girls were treated as sinners and therefore had no rights. Many were sexually abused during their ordeal. This practice lasted for 200 years ending in 1996. The moral standards of the preachers were maintained, whilst making huge profits for the Roman Catholic Church.

On 18th August 2018 the Pope visited Ireland to beg forgiveness for decades of abuse by members of the Roman Catholic Church. Standing next to the Pope, the Irish Prime Minister Leo Varadkar said:

'…brutal crimes perpetrated by people within the Catholic Church, and then obscured to protect the institution at the expense of innocent victims … child sexual abuse, the Magdalene Laundries, mother-and-baby homes and illegal adoptions were stains on church and state.'[1]

Varadkar called for the separation of church and state, where religion was no longer at the centre of society.

So an organisation promoting a 'God of love' protected itself in thousands of cases, in many countries over decades against the most vulnerable in society. The question is, why did the Pope come over in August 2018 to apologise, and how could the weakest in society possibly threaten such an enormously powerful organisation? The previous papal visit was thirty-nine years earlier, at a time when 90% of the Irish population described themselves as Catholic. In 2018, only 40% described themselves as Catholic. The most plausible explanation is that the Catholic Church did nothing to protect victims until these stories threatened to undermine its credibility and power amongst its worshippers. Preserving the Church's authority was more important than protecting the children.

[1] Wikipedia, Magdelene Launderies

Even when the Pope made his profuse apology, the Church was still defending itself. It is still not totally open about its past crimes, and still attempts to frustrate investigations.[1] The Irish government issued a formal state apology and set up a compensation fund of £50m for the victims. The Catholic Church has not offered any money.

This headline in huge letters also in *The Sunday Times*, summed it up:

Who knew about the abuse?

**THEY ALL DID**

It was not the Church that addressed these issues but people seeking the truth who kept digging up the facts (literally dead bodies) until they could not be denied.

Pope Benedict XVI (Joseph Ratzinger) lied during an investigation into child sexual abuse when he was Archbishop of Munich and did nothing to protect numerous victims over years[2]

Indigenous populations were treated similarly in Canada, the USA and Australia. The dominant group determined society's values and imposed them on vulnerable minorities. They justified the enormous suffering they inflicted by arguing that they were 'civilising' these minorities. America was built on migrants fleeing persecution in Europe in their quest for self-determination; this right did not extend to indigenous Native Americans.

Between 1863 and 1998, more than 150,000 indigenous children in Canada, were taken from their families and placed in schools. The children were often not allowed to speak their language or to practise their culture; this has been described as 'cultural genocide.'

In June 2021, reports of 751 unmarked graves for indigenous people at the site of a former residential school in Saskatchewan, Canada became international news. Many dozens of unmarked graves were discovered in several locations. Physical and sexual abuse at the hands of school authorities led many children to run away. In Canada, an estimated 6,000 children died, with some estimates putting the death toll

[1] Stephen Bleach Sunday Times 17th February 2019)

[2] (theconversation.com 28th Jan 2022).

considerably higher. This is a higher death rate than Canadian soldiers suffered in the Second World War, and they were children at school?

In 2008, the Canadian government formally apologised for the system. After 14 years of campaigning and dragging the Churches reputation through the mud, in July 2022, the Pope apologised for the actions of individuals within the church, but did not acknowledge that the Roman Catholic Church was responsible or open church files or offer evidence from people in the church who personally know exactly what happened or offer compensation. Why did they not offer compensation : possibly because if they had, they would have had claims from around the world that might have bankrupted the church. How commercially minded!

Karrle observes that whenever people lose control of their lives they can easily become victims of exploiters, a painful lesson he carries with him from Africa.

All this information is based on recent evidence; however, it is implausible that these practises only started recently. Has it ever been different? This gives a powerful insight into how organisations operate – and the Church is no exception.

The IICSA (Independent Inquiry into Child Sexual Abuse) examined child protection in thirty-eight religions in England and Wales, including Jehovah's Witnesses, Baptists, Methodists, Islam, Judaism, Sikhism, Hinduism, Buddhism and nonconformist Christian denominations[1]. Cases of sexual abuse were not limited to particular faiths, and incidents of abuse were rarely reported or dealt with appropriately.

Barriers included:

a) blaming the victim,
b) sex not being openly discussed,
c) deference shown to religious figures built a trust that could be exploited to perpetuate abuse,
d) many organisations were dominated by men,
e) mistrust of government bodies and external institutions emanating from fears of religious persecution,
f) the concept of forgiveness being misused, both to put pressure on victims not to report their abuse and to justify failures by religious leaders,

[1] *The Guardian*, 2nd September 2021, 16.50 BST IICSA)

g) failure to take effective action where allegations are made

'What marks religious organisations out from other institutions is the explicit purpose they have in teaching right from wrong.' (IICSA)

Richard Scorer, a specialist abuse lawyer at Slater & Gordon, said: "It is clear from the report that too many religious organisations continue to prioritise the protection, reputation and authority of religious leaders above the rights of children. In the light of today's report, the arguments for mandatory reporting and independent oversight of religious bodies are overwhelming."

In *The Sunday Times,* 20th February 2022, Matthew Syed wrote:

*'On Wednesday, a Vatican insider estimated that up to one million Italian children had been abused over seven decades... This isn't merely a story of evil hidden in plain sight within a global institution, but a glimpse into the nature of theological criminality... This was a story not merely of individual evil but of institutional complicity, not only the cardinal but also of hundreds of others who didn't want the story to leak; legal departments that sought to block journalistic enquiry into rape allegations; legions of clergy who regarded the pristine reputation of the Church as more important than the welfare of the innocents they were supposed to protect ... (the) infallibility of the Pope is taught to children as literal truth, about how cardinals are proclaimed to be conduits to the Almighty ... the inevitable consequence of placing divine authority in holy men and manuscripts ... Isn't this how criminals masquerading as priests were able to compel silence on such an astonishing scale? Isn't it how fundamentalist imams are able to inspire youngsters to commit mass murder in suicide missions, assuring them that these acts are not evil but the highest form of virtue? Isn't this – to widen the perspective – the way that religious institutions have perpetuated crimes throughout history, a story that must be understood not as an aberration but as an essential feature of any kind of fundamentalism?*

The Catholic Church, amongst many others, has protected and tolerated paedophiles for hundreds of years at the expense of the victims. As a secretive organisation they are well practiced in the art; have always resisted worldly oversight into their affaires; and used God as a higher authority to avoid responsibility for their actions.

## Rose Volunteers

Rose applies and is accepted as a hospital support worker by a local charity after disclosure barring service (DBS) checks have been completed. She becomes a 'befriender', which involves spending time with patients, helping them to access the hospital library, sometimes reading to them or just helping at mealtimes, like reading menus. The nurses are frantically busy caring for their bodies but this leaves long empty hours when their minds are desperate for human contact.

Taking the drinks trolley onto the ward is always an opportunity for conversation. Meeting different people makes every day special and opens conversations about things that had no relevance before. Although Rose only plays a minor role in the hospital, she helps people at a difficult time in their lives and forms friendships that are deeply rewarding. Nobody has depended on her since her children were young.

The most precious gift she can offer patients is her time and the simplest action, like holding their hands, can be very important. One old lady says, 'Nobody touches me anymore.'

When a frail old gentleman who can hardly talk complains of pain and cannot reach the call button, Rose alerts the nurse. Within minutes, the consultant whisks him into the operating theatre. Rose never finds out what was wrong, but she does not want to imagine what might have happened if she had not been there.

At Christmas, a choir from the local church visits the hospital to sing carols to the patients, many of whom never receive visitors. A couple of the old ladies cry as they remember their childhoods and families. Rose is deeply moved.

## The Marriage of Church and State

Karrle wants to discuss these issues when he sees Graham. Wednesday arrives and so does Graham.

'Afternoon, Karrle. I'm a little early and thought I'd pop in, if you're free?'

With a wry smile Karrle retorts, 'Until the Home Office releases me from this room, I am always free!'

'Well, I knocked on your door the other day and you were out.'

'I must have been at the library. The staff are very good. If they've not got a book I want, they order it from another library.'

'Why? Have they not got enough books for you?'

'Not the ones I want to read.'

'So what are you reading now?'

'Religion, as you instructed,' replies Karrle with a smile.

'And did it convert you?'

'Quite the opposite, it raised many questions about organised religions and their impact on the world.'

'So now you are an atheist?'

'You cannot prove or disprove the existence of God, so the debate is unresolvable. The important thing is not whether God exists, but how you live whether God exists or not. The Catholic and Protestant Churches seem merely a method of harnessing the need for humans to coalesce into teams for mutual advancement by providing a package of answers to the things some of which they cannot know. This is not heavenly, it is very worldly.'

Graham laughs. 'Nice to see you sitting on the fence, as usual.'

'OK, so apart from worldly reasons why is the Catholic Church centred on Rome?'

'No idea. Why not?'

Karrle starts to deliver his thoughts. 'The more you look at it, the more evidence comes to light of Church and state operating hand in glove. The Romans could not beat Christianity, so they adopted and controlled it. Christianity originated in the Middle East and Africa. Jesus was not British, European or even white, but that didn't stop the Europeans from establishing Christian institutions, forcing other Europeans to convert to Christianity, particularly in the Middle Ages, or using it as a justification for building their European empires. The author, Edward D. Andrews wrote, the missionaries were "ideological shock troops for colonial invasion whose zealotry blinded them"[1]. Protestants, Catholics and Jews all operate from completely separate power bases, dominated and protected by the country they are in.'

'Isn't that just like-minded people congregating together?' asks Graham.

'No. Rome has an iron grip on the Catholic Church. Since its formation, there have been more than 260 popes; more than 190 were from Italy, of which 88 came from Rome. Apart from the current Pope, the previous non-European pope was Pope Gregory lll, appointed in 741AD! This is remarkable when you consider that Christianity started in the Middle East and Africa (the Jews escaped from Egypt). So God, who created everything in the universe, favours Italian popes, and preferably from Rome. How power hungary is that!'

Graham, 'That's incredible.'

'The Church became so unassailable that even kings were legitimised by the blessing of the Pope. What better way for aspiring monarchs to protect themselves against worldly assailants than by adopting the concept of the 'divine right of kings', anointed by God (or his representative on earth, the Pope)? What better way to protect the Church than to align itself with the worldly powers of kings and their armies?

That did not prevent many power struggles over the ages. One arose in England when the personal ambitions of King Henry Vlll conflicted with Catholic teachings and resulted in the establishment of the Protestant Church by Saint King Henry Vlll.' Smiling, Karrle corrects a laughable corruption of the truth. 'No, by a lustful, self-indulgent and ultimately self-destructive king with wholly worldly desires. Henry went to Parliament and demanded that he be head of the Church; hence the Queen is 'Supreme Governor of the Church of England as well as head of state in a constitutional monarchy.'

As for Israel, they do not have a constitution, which is unusual even in the West. If there is no separation between the Jewish Church and state, how are the rights of Palestinians protected? They are not, as is evidenced every day!'

'But they all accept believers from all over the world!' replies a reflective Graham.

[1] Wikipedia

'Expansion is the driving force behind every empire. A cobweb may get bigger, but the spider remains in the centre and in control. What are the chances of the next head of the Catholic Church being a black female from Africa or the Far East, or the next head of the Protestant church coming from the Commonwealth? Absolutely ZERO!'

'I had not thought of that.'

'There are many important issues not brought into the open and therefore hardly ever discussed. When you question people on the basis of their beliefs, they cannot justify them without reciting a hand-me-down mantra, devoid of evidence. They react as if their identity depends upon their belief. In reality they exist as a marvellous life form in their own right without reference to anything else and justify their beliefs by talking about the afterlife of which they know nothing. If heaven is better than here, why don't people go there today?'

'That is exactly what suicide bombers do,' Graham replies.

'So suicide bombers need to damage others to get to heaven? How sick is that? The greatest falsehood told to people is that there is a better place than this, and you can enter it by carrying out the most appalling acts of cruelty on others. How do we know that we are not already in heaven and making a mess of it? This denies people the opportunity of realising their own potential. Life only lasts a minute. Use that minute.'

## Unworldly Belief Systems – Impregnable and Dangerous

Unworldly belief systems can produce irreconcilable differences when they conflict with alternative beliefs, resulting in damage evident to all. Superimposing another unworldly belief which is equally unprovable can produce conflict without end.

Those who demonstrate that they best represent group values are in the strongest position to lead and influence the group. Conflict can be a powerful tool in gaining supporters, and is widely used by many leaders. If those in charge wish to manipulate a group, the more unworldly the belief, the greater the opportunity for manipulation. The further the belief is removed from the realities of daily life, the less likely it is to be challenged. Conflicting unworldly beliefs can never be reconciled unless one or both change, or both sides tolerate their differences. Throughout the ages, what has been the motivation to make those changes? Not divine inspiration but practical advantage.

If the leader deludes themselves, they are even less amenable to evidence or logic. By sacrificing the last lifeboat – the evidence – the faithful are exposed to the considerable risk of manipulation by leaders who have their own agendas.

Beliefs should be based on understanding, not faith. Understanding allows people to know when beliefs need to change, but faith is blind and persists when understanding would point the way forward. Part of that understanding is an acceptance that we do not know everything, and God may exist. That is not the same as approving all the actions of religious bodies. The facts must be known, open discussion tolerated and balanced judgements made. Most religions of the world are very secretive and reject the right of mankind to make judgements, fostering inner circles and practices sometimes for deplorable motives.

It is important that leaders are not held up as gods, or claim that God speaks through them. Some followers, blinded by faith, assume the leader can determine outcomes in situations where they have no control. When faith meets failure, leaders must explain the failure, or modify the beliefs to give the impression of consistency or risk losing credibility. Too often they pretend that nothing has changed.

Many beliefs are used to harness large groups who lock horns with other groups causing appalling destruction. They justify the atrocities they commit as being for a greater good, whilst emotionally detaching themselves from the suffering their actions cause. Unworldly beliefs can introduce hate that no earthly justification can refute and create new enemies every day. It is not the gods that are at war but the leaders and followers of each faith, and all for worldly advantage that is translated into the language of their beliefs.

Absolute truths provide a psychological safety net, incorporating myths, exploiting man's need to believe in something. This provides comfort, removing the desire for change. It is a small ego trip to rise from being the dominant person over a group to inventing a god who created the universe and placed man at the centre. The very focus on self is a distraction from the wider truth that humans are insignificant specks in the universe. This lack of humility discourages humans from looking beyond themselves. Western religious paintings place nature in an ever diminishing role, from Jesus as a shepherd, instead focusing on people: Jesus on the cross, God in the clouds, the Last Supper, etc..

What greater arrogance can exist than to believe that the earth is the centre of the universe; God anointed man; He made us in his own image and provided all the other creatures in the world for our benefit?

King James Bible Genesis, Chapter 1: 26 'And God said, Let us make man in our image, after our likeness: and let them have dominion over the fish of the sea, and over the fowl of the air, and over the cattle, and over all the earth, and over every creeping thing that creepeth upon the earth.'

Placing man above nature is dangerous, wrong and only demonstrates how ignorant we are about the universe and even the world we live on. What a shock when we discover that we are mortal, extremely vulnerable, and all we have achieved is to build a glorified ants' nest. Autocrats need to build magnificent buildings to demonstrate their power, importance and longevity; are religions driven by similar motives?

All dictators and fanatical doctrinal beliefs use propaganda, particularly in wartime. They endlessly re-enforce stereotypes, attempting to intellectually and socially undermine our ability to discover what is true, even discrediting what people know they know. A useful distraction is focusing on trivia, whilst those manipulating society advantage themselves. Democracies are not above these influences although a free press and accountability to the electorate offer some checks and controls.

Man's ability to survive has always depended on nature, which is frequently been explained in terms of a creator. Craving acceptance, early man offered sacrifices to the gods, which had no impact on outcomes. Today, Christianity tries to do the same.

Religion rarely travels across location or time in an unmodified form. People clothe themselves in inherited beliefs, but those clothes may put them at a severe disadvantage in different environments. When the Crusaders invaded Jerusalem wearing armour in the desert, it was a sign that what worked at home was completely inappropriate elsewhere. They should not have been there. But they believed that anybody who thought differently from themselves was the enemy. The best way to acquire an over-riding authority is an unworldly belief system, answerable to nobody on earth. It can then be used as a gift so precious that it obligates the believer to rescue others by converting them or superimposing their beliefs by force. If they are wrong, this is doubly inappropriate.

Manipulation exists in every society and takes many forms. In the 1930s and 40s, Emperor Hirohito of Japan was the nation's highest spiritual authority. Unquestioning soldiers carried out millions of atrocities in the name of the emperor. The manipulators were the military who issued instructions in his name so that they could achieve their ambition of empire building. The emperor never got involved; he was a powerless, symbolic figurehead.

When the war turned against Japan, Japanese soldiers were expected to die for the emperor even if the sacrifice was futile. It was not until after two H-bombs were dropped on Hiroshima and Nagasaki with the country facing total destruction that the Emperor insisted Japan surrender. For the generals, the greatest calamity was the loss on honour. After the war, ordinary soldiers discovered that the generals had lied and were merely using them to fulfil their own ambitions of empire building.

Today there are many organisations where suicide bombers are indoctrinated with unworldly beliefs. Reason, evidence and discussion cannot convince them otherwise. Many suicide bombers are later described by acquaintances as friendly, civilised, educated, and often from advantaged backgrounds. They could be any one of us, which means the potential is in all of us. Osama Bin Laden was educated, moneyed and clever, which made him more dangerous.

QAnon indulges in a flawed reality inducing a medical condition, apophenia, the early stages of delusional thought as self-referential. These fictional characters are not to solve problems, but to create unreality, eventually accepting delusion as revelation. This apparent solving of a problem, like contradictory evidence, releases dopamine producing a psychological rush.

QAnon and conspiracy theorists have been given credibility by evangelical Christians without a shred of evidence.

*Religious people are particularly susceptible to conspiracy theories due to their belief in the supernatural and their endorsement of a good-versus-evil worldview.*

*Nearly 50 percent of white Protestants who attended church………believed that Trump was divinely anointed by God.*[1]

[1] Deradicalization Needed for Evangelical Christian QAnon Believers (foreignpolicy.com)

## World Wars I and II – Impressions and Reality

Reyansh returns home from the factory with a question on his mind. 'Papa, what do you know about the Second World War?'

Vishnu is surprised by the subject. 'Too much! Why?'

'A couple of English guys at work were saying that the British stood alone against Hitler for two years. Is that true?'

This is a serious question and deserves a considered reply. Vishnu is silent whilst considering how to enlighten his son. 'It is, apart from all the countries in the British Empire that fought against the Japanese, Germans and Italians in Asia, Africa and Europe in both world wars. In World War ll, two-and-a-half million Indians raised the biggest voluntary army in history. In World War 1, they raised one-and-a-half million. Several people from our village died in each war, and your grandfather was wounded. We've paid our dues.'

Rayansh is confused. 'But the British people I spoke to did not seem to know that!'

Searching for the answer, Vishnu gathers thoughts from the recesses of his memory. 'When Lord Mountbatten took command of the forces in the Far East, he told the troops, "They call you the forgotten army. You're not. They've never heard of you, but they will." World War ll gave the British a sense of being on high moral ground. After the war, British officers published hundreds of diaries and books of their experiences, and Hollywood made hundreds of films, but the millions of Indian coolies did not write anything. Independence was the big thing, and everyone forgot about the war.'

'What difference did it make to the war?'

Vishnu is not willing to offer more than he knows. 'Some military authorities believe that without the support of the British Empire, Britain would not have won the first and second world wars. I don't know about that, but I do know the sacrifices our people made. Women worked in coal mines until they gave birth; building the Ledo road across jungles and mountains from India to China. Eighty thousand people were made homeless when a ship carrying explosives blew up in Bombay harbour. India was bombed by the Japanese. The coolies were part of a major supply chain for Britain. We have been loyal to this country and you can be very proud of that.'

Leaning back as if the answer was written on the ceiling, Vishnu recalls a quote word for word from David Cameron. 'The Prime Minister said, ‘‘They fought together, they fell together, and together they defended the freedoms we enjoy today’’.’

Reyansh follows his father’s logic to ask his next question. ‘What would have happened if the British had lost the Second World War?’

His father utters a huge guffaw as his eyes fleetingly revisit the ceiling. ‘Huh! Then things would have been very ugly for them. In their desperation to escape, they might have climbed into small boats and attempted to sail to safety. If they could not land in Europe, they might have tried to reach Africa. Many would have drowned – and what reception would the survivors have expected? Would they have wanted people they had never met, to remember the exploitation by previous generations and push them back to England, irrespective of the fate that might await them? What would the British think if their country had been invaded by African empire builders who colonised parts of Britain with no regard for the lives of the inhabitants?

You see my son, in life you never know how the future will unfold. The person you offend today may be vital to your survival tomorrow. No, you can hold your head up high in this country or any other.’

Reyansh is surprised at his father’s knowledge and can tell by his authoritative tone that these are deeply held convictions. These words of wisdom carry great weight in his son’s mind and he will remember them. Clearly many attitudes in Britain are based on ignorance and a misunderstanding of their own history. This information also makes him feel more confident about his right to be in Britain and his place in British society.

## Science versus Beliefs

Karrle's research in the library is making considerable advances in his understanding, but the project is huge and far from complete. Societies that form large populations create an enormous pool of human resource that enables many to co-operate on common tasks. However, this does not explain how societies evolve to master sophisticated tasks, whether it is civil engineering by the Greeks, Romans and Egyptians, mathematics by the Persians, industrialisation by the British, or information technology by the Americans.

A big society will not evolve if everyone is a farmer. To learn how things work requires the gathering and recording of information by dedicated individuals whose skills are nurtured in centres of learning, where knowledge can be accumulated, exchanged and ideas advanced. Science provides opportunities to create greater wealth by increasing productivity, but it does not create societies. Communities must develop two broad disciplines: science (how things work) and belief systems (how we can work together).

Science starts with observation, gathering facts from our world to develop an understanding of processes that enable man to exploit the world to his advantage. The methodology can be independently tested and verified by anyone, at any time. Knowledge accumulates in centres of learning and is handed down over generations; Newton said he 'stood on the shoulders of giants'.

Science transforms opportunities. The greater the specialisation, the greater the improvements in productivity and the greater the population that can be supported. As this process gathers momentum, individuals (and even countries and continents) become ever more interdependent to the point where their survival depends on the stability of these ever-lengthening supply chains. Today, with the explosion of the world's population, any attempt at self-sufficiency would cause an implosion of all societies. This gives terrorists a powerful advantage when threatening the sophisticated infrastructure on which all modern societies depend.

Unlike science, belief systems can be many, varied and contradictory. There is only one body of physics, but there maybe a thousand religions and as many philosophies. Also, unlike science, there does not need to be independent, verifiable proof. A visionary can wander into the desert, fire people's imagination with stories and does not have to verify anything. Often the mantra is believe and you will see. The danger is that once you believe without understanding, you interpret all future events only through the prism of your belief: 'I lost my job, but God found me another one and it is what He wants me to do.'

A belief system does not have to be right; it only needs to work for people in the circumstances in which they find themselves, or offer acceptable justifications for failure.

Science and beliefs operate on fundamentally different principles. Science is based on accumulating knowledge and constantly changes as our knowledge expands. Belief systems are based on shared values and resist change to maintain stability. The combination provides the engine for societies to grow – and migration is one of the primary sources that fuels this process.

When beliefs are contradicted by science or alternative beliefs, conflict often arises because these divergences can be perceived as an attack on the identity, and therefore the existence, of the group. In extreme circumstances this conflict can lead to a fight to the death.

The strength of belief systems (religion being a common form) is the stability it allows for values to be shared amongst many people over long periods of time. Beliefs are often presented as absolute truths, even if the society is ignorant of the facts. What better way of doing this than to encourage belief in an unworldly being? It can never be disproved.

Societies would not exist unless the individual believes in something outside of themselves. It is a surprisingly small step between a belief in society and a belief in God; as Mary Beard says, 'Civilisation is an act of faith.' If facts later disprove beliefs, just modify the belief because over long periods of time the believers are a different generation facing different challenges and as long as the current belief suits the current believers – what the heck!

Well, one problem with living only in the present is that it detaches us from the past, does not explain how we got here and fails to explain what todays problems are. Offering no information on solutions, it steals our imagination. Life is a perpetual struggle to maintain continuity in the face of the ever-changing forces of nature. The narrower the basis of our existence, the more vulnerable we are when life breaks through, changing our certainties. Many species have lived for millions of years, whilst religious beliefs have existed for a few thousand years. They are substantially untested.

It is ironic that a common criticism levelled by believers against science is that science changes all the time. Scientific evidence that contradicts religious beliefs can be dismissed because believers have 'absolute truth'; and by definition, God created the universe, so 'absolute truths' will be here forever. Therefore, what one scientist has just discovered can be dismissed because later it will be contradicted by another. In the past, science did not have the evidence to refute religious certainties, which were used to control the faithful. Survival depended on these absolute certainties. The truth is that the world population is completely dependent on our use of scientific knowledge and has often been the major driving force of changes in beliefs.

Recognition that the developments of science and social norms are fundamentally irreconcilable appears self-evident, yet each cannot survive without the other for the sustainability and evolution of human society. Specialists can only spend their time bringing new knowledge to the human library in a stable society, which requires shared values that enable the group to function.

Even shared values have to evolve, and the process of change needs to be managed by enlightened individuals within the group or by new individuals entering the group. To sustain the world's current population, today's societies are dependent on both science and shared values, but conflicting unworldly belief systems can be a barrier to integration and prevent different societies working together. There seems to be no integration between religions, for example Protestants and Catholics. Neither are willing to compromise their identities or power base.

Migrants entering Britain are a challenge to the existing social order, but no change is neither desirable nor possible, and the attempt will eventually guarantee failure. History reveals that most of the beliefs we think are core to our identity were imported. Ideas come from many different sources and are utilised by leaders to create the identity we believe defines us, often with no connection to the original creators. A wonderful example is Country-and-Western music. The banjo and singing the blues came from Africa, mixing with various cultures including Costa Ricans; and slick city types from the east coast of the United States (when they realised there was money to be made out of it). This is not the popular image marketed today of 'hillbillies' and 'country-folk.'

To protect what is most important requires flexibility and accommodation.

'If you want things to stay the same, then things have got to change.' [2]

Karrle is satisfied with the development of his understanding of the grand scheme and where he fits in. Another day, another step.

[1] Deradicalization Needed for Evangelical Christian QAnon Believers (foreignpolicy.com)

[2] Giuseppi Tomasi di Lampedusa

## Evaluating the Church

To be self-righteous is to be convinced of one's own rightness. Once the concept is accepted that the Bible is the word of God and incorporates 'divine wisdom', it follows that church leaders derive their authority from God, and their pronouncements are God speaking through man. Kings were answerable only to God as interpreted by God's representative on earth, the Pope. This was the perfect explanation for the Church to present opinions as absolute truths; those that thought differently were condemned as heretics.

So why does the Bible give a wealth of insight into human society but is misleading and completely devoid of information about the universe, which allowed wrong statements to be adopted as absolute truths? One answer is time.

The Bible was written by man less than two thousand years ago, but the universe is far older. Converting time into distance, if the universe is 13,700,000,000 years old and the circumference of the earth around the equator is 24,901 miles, then one earth mile represents 550,200 years. An 80-year-old man would move nine earth inches from birth to death and Jesus's birth was less than 20 feet away from today. That is like crossing the road. How would it be possible to know about the mountains, deserts, forests, seas, North and South Poles and the Equator within 20 feet of where you were born? The statistics are so disproportionate that tinkering at the margins is immaterial. How could the Bible, written by humans, possibly describe things man had never seen, or had no knowledge of?

The Bible is a hugely important historical document which has had an enormous influence on the development of human society, but it is neither the complete nor absolute document for which it is used. It offers a wealth of stories and observations about human behaviour, with recommendations on how we should treat each other. These are frequently ignored, by all parties, including the Church, when they it conflicts with self-interest. The Bible is a reflection of how little man understood about the universe, until science started to provide some answers.

Religious organisations are still dominated by men, and embody all the strengths and weaknesses of other worldly organisations, but they do not take responsibility for their actions which are justified by unworldly beliefs. This is unacceptable. The Church must be held accountable for its' actions, like any other organisation. Religion needs to fit into the world because the world will not fit into religion. *Monotheisms (single faith beliefs) are by their nature intolerant.* [1] Calling beliefs 'absolute' truths is a powerful tool to require individuals to co-operate to achieve tasks for the benefit of the group and the leaders.

Although Karrle is focusing on his own Christian background, in many religions women are deemed the chattels of men and therefore second-class citizens. He wonders why male-dominated faiths subordinate women. Is this essential for human society to function, a reflection of the insecurity of men, or merely a historical legacy? If it is either of the last two, how much does it restrict human potential? Today there are many women in important roles in most organisations, and evidence that the top 100 companies quoted on the London Stock Exchange are more profitable when more than one woman is on the board of directors. The same observation could probably be made about minorities.

There have been many multigenerational conflicts in the world. One of the oldest came after the death of the Muslim spiritual leader Muhammed in 632AD. His followers could not agree on his successor and split into two main groups, Sunni and Shia. Their power struggle, passed down the generations, drag millions into the conflict causing unspeakable suffering of innocent people like the children in Yemen today. Why is this? It is because both groups want to become the dominant power and will use all the weapons at their disposal, including religion, to satisfy their worldly aspirations.

Not all philosophies put humans at the centre of the universe. Buddhism respects all life; Chinese philosophers believe in the harmonisation of humanity with the heavens, and in many ways were far more enlightened two thousand years ago (Analects of Confucias) than many Europeans are today. Unfortunately, this did not stop many extremely vicious wars within Chinese borders. Learning from other civilisations is greatly enhanced with a confident, tolerant and humble attitude, not always the strongest characteristics of Europeans or their offspring, the Americans.

Many religions have historically been associated with the sun (day/night), the moon (monthly cycle) and the four seasons (year). There is more evidence that the sun is the source of all life on earth than God.

---

[1] 'The Name Of God' by Selina O'Grady, The Sunday Times, 11th August 2019

Karrle reflects that the Roman Catholic Church is generally a benevolent organisation, but many others are not. The Roman Catholic Church deserves severe criticism for its actions and hypocrisy, but it is easy to use the Church as a scapegoat to avoid the reality of how similar the collective responses of all groups of humans are to preserve the team from which they derive personal benefit.

Within our lifetime, there have been many examples of UK organisations failing to protect individuals: trafficked sex slaves and workers in every major town and city; orphanages in Jersey, Telford and Rochdale; the BBC; the royal family; the music industry, etc. All organisations have the same balancing act between truth and beliefs. This can be very challenging for those in authority, who like all of us, are perfectly capable of selectively seeing only those facts that support what they want to believe.

Many people accept the religious teachings of their community without questioning their truth or relevance to their lives, becoming defensive or aggressive when challenged. A reliable sign that somebody is indoctrinated is when they reject evidence that contradicts their beliefs without listening.

Indoctrination makes evidence irrelevant. People have the ability to think and not just obey (Melvin Bragg). It flatters their ego to believe that humans are superior because they dominate other creatures and have the ability to think, yet accept unquestioningly beliefs incorporating how to think and act, even though it is their beliefs that will guide their actions throughout their lives. For many, it is more to do with social acceptance than religion

Religion has a powerful influence on the world we create for ourselves. Our prosperity depends not only on the provision of goods and services but the acceptance of ideas and shared values founded on political, philosophical or religious understandings. Being part of the inherited social fabric of human society they are usually a combination. Even if inherited religion is rejected, customs, language and social organisations invisibly mould all societies. Religion is so intertwined into the evolution of all societies that it is impossible to know the cost or benefits of alternatives. Even without religion there would still be nation building and wars, justified by alternative explanations.

Karrle is confounded. The Catholic Church has done many good things in his country including providing education and healthcare for the poor. Many Catholics have dedicated their lives to helping others according to the teachings of the Bible. Christianity has been one of the major factors in the development of the principle of equality for all and the democratic institutions we hold most precious today.

The best thing that can be said about Christianity is that it incorporates the core values of humanity. Yet all these good things are worldly benefits, inextricably controlled by Europeans, who benefit the most by the present order. It is difficult to see how these benefits have anything to do with the existence of a god.

Karrle finds these revelations extremely disturbing causing him to re-evaluate many certainties that had formed his understanding of life. None of his research disproves the existence of God (because that is impossible), but it exposes the dangers of uncritical faith which often blinds followers, shaping their identity, society and history. Karrle reflects on the extent to which white organisations determined his beliefs, and whether these have helped or hindered him.

He recognises that many countries have achieved highly sophisticated societies to the enormous benefit of their citizens. Although countries like his own have very destructive elements, many societies have made great strides and demonstrated what humans can achieve. This is something to learn from and build on, not destroy.

## Love Poem

Andy is captivated by Mohini; she is a vision almost too delicate to touch in case the world might damage perfection. Her eyes are where heaven is, a place he wants to live in forever. The gentle way he holds her hand connects them in an open display of unquestioning commitment and respect so profound that both want to believe that love's gift is absolute protection from the world.

And yet…Andy is deeply troubled that for now he has to keep his love for Mohini hidden, without knowing when it will ever be different. Nobody is like 'his Mohini', and having found his soul mate, she must never be lost. She MUST understand how important she is to him. But how?

He goes to the library and finds a line from a fusty old poetry book that nobody reads but it captures what he is trying to say, and surprisingly quickly he fills in the rest from his heart. Yes, that is what he must say. He hides the paper in his school work and returns home full of elation and trepidation; too nervous to eat or rest. The maddening hours of night are too long; precious moments are for dreaming of their future, not wasting on sleep.

At school the next day, he waits for a quiet moment and without warning coyly pushes the piece of paper face down towards the centre of his world. Words hurriedly glued together with love attempt to describe the contents of his heart. With mounting tension Andy waits. He cannot breathe.

Looking slightly puzzled, Mohini casually picks up the paper, turns it over and reads:

> Borrowed words can always say far better than can I
> Of love and dreams and wishful things that last until we die
> Of times relived and words unsaid and feelings running deep
> In life's deep ruts we chain ourselves, our paths may never meet
> And yet in all life's twists and turns things are not what they may seem
> Tread softly, Moh, tread softly, for you tread upon my dreams.

Moments hang.
Andy's life is suspended. Unbearable tension is crushing him.
She must be reading it again.

Their full significance slowly percolates and coalesces into a profound realisation as Mona Lisa awakens and slowly offers a wonderful smile, so pure and tantalizing. Her beautiful, soft brown eyes meet his and deliver the desperately needed message. Now drowning in joy, their love will last forever.

She folds the poem and puts it in her school book, a secret that must be concealed from both their families. With no solutions, they only have their total commitment to each other. It is all that is possible for now, but for the moment it is enough.

Andy's hearts' desire is to scoop Mohini up and protect her from any harm the world can devise. Surely pure love cannot fail.

Neither of them can imagine fate concocting an unspeakable cruelty of such foul malevolence that it will crush one of nature's beautiful creations and threaten Mohini's very existence?

## Birth of the Book of REB

Karrle believes that his thoughts go a long way towards explaining the causes of human conflict. Nobody goes to war disputing the laws of physics. They will use knowledge to gain an advantage over an opponent, but the motivations for war are all too rooted in the world we all know. Often all sides in a conflict believe God is on their side, but God has never manifested himself during a battle to determine the outcome of these worldly competitions. God's intentions are always interpreted by men with an agendas advancing themselves.

Karrle has condensed his thoughts down to three key strands:

Belief systems which could be the same throughout the world, but never will be because experiences mould groups to be different and ideas are too often hijacked by manipulators for their own purposes.

Rules which are specific instructions within the group as to how they should behave within and between groups, and are justified by reference to their belief systems, and

Experiences which can be similar within a group but are always unique to the individual. Even within the same family, the eldest child will have different experiences from the youngest, the mother different from the father, and so on.

Problems may arise when personal experiences expose deficiencies in the rules, putting pressure on individuals and sometimes the whole society. Where this is not sustainable, the rules change or the society is weakened, possibly to be superseded by others who do not carry this impediment. Easter Island is a perfect example where the natives cut all the trees to make religious idols until they did not have wood for fishing boats. They starved and resorted to cannibalism.

These three strands are totally interlinked, Rules…Experiences…and Beliefs and are unique to each individual. It is almost as if everybody has their own personalised book. Yes, that's it: everybody has their own book of Rules, Experiences and Beliefs (REB).

This is Karrle's eureka moment. He feels like Karl Marx must have done at the British Library having advanced human understanding on completion of his major work, *Das Kapital.*

There are things that are fundamentally true based on the world we all share, but each individual interprets the world according to their own unique Book of REB. Humans prosper by working in groups, but they must co-operate with others who each have their own Books of REB.

Karrle's research is now complete. He returns to his cacophonous furniture to rest and think about his own Book of REB. Now his life must move to whatever the future holds.

## From the Heart

Karrle can't wait to see Graham and articulate his concept of the Book of REB. At their next meeting, Graham gives him his undivided attention.

Having concluded, Karrle remains silent as Graham mulls over his response. ''In its way, it is profound … and yet…it says nothing new.''

Karrle jumps in enthusiastically. 'That's the point! All the pieces are there, but it puts them together and is very simple. Everything is complicated when you don't understand the pattern, and simple when you do. The idea is not to disrespect people's beliefs, but for people to think for themselves and not be manipulated by others. It is a cruel corruption to justify worldly destruction with unworldly philosophies.'

Graham offers one hurdle. 'The trouble is some people don't like their beliefs being questioned.'

Karrle thinks about this for a moment. 'But by definition, unworldly beliefs cannot be ''known'' to be absolute truths in any worldly sense, and therefore contradictory beliefs have inherent irreconcilable differences. It is ironic that Christians decrying "terrorists" who justify the killing of random civilians in the West with unworldly beliefs, try and superimpose their own beliefs, which they don't recognise as just as unworldly.'

Graham struggles with the concept of any alternative. 'OK, they may be being manipulated, but many need God to give life meaning. The thought of there not being a God makes life pointless and depressing.'

To Karrle, this is not a valid argument. 'Depression is an emotion built on disappointment in the past and fear of the future, all measured against expectation. The solution is to alter your expectations. If somebody says "I've lost my legs and my life is over", if they give up, they are right. If they adjust to their new reality they are also right. Some people who lose their legs lead very fulfilled lives. If the world we live in is all there is, maybe we would value other people's lives more. Those that justify terrible acts of cruelty based on rewards they expect in the afterlife would be seen as perverse and dangerous. Living in the here and now might give people a wonderful sense of liberation and a focus on tackling the problems in their life. Taking responsibility is empowering. Waiting for the afterlife can make you fatalistic and apathetic.'

‘Yes, but people rarely have all the information or personal experience on which to make decisions, so at some point they must rely on the judgement of others. As you said the other day, we are all on the spectrum of prejudice.’ This is one of Karrle’s favourite phrases to describe the concept of the Book of REB.

‘As a child brought up in a monotheistic culture, the majority accept their beliefs as the norm because there are no accessible alternatives. As people mature, the boundaries and limitations become more apparent, and it is important to evaluate how your beliefs fit in with the realities of your life and understand the organisations they came from. Every mono-culture has limitations.’

‘You know, you should write this Book of REB, but please don’t quote me in it. I am very worldly about avoiding unwanted attention.’ They both laugh.

‘I realise that many people would be offended by it, but any ‘absolute truth’ that cannot survive an open discussion is about *power* not truth. And how else do humans escape from endless revolving conflict? Aggressive reactions to perceived challenges to people’s beliefs does concern me.’

Pondering, Graham replies thoughtfully, ‘Describe what is real from your heart and it will echo in the heart of everyone who recognises the journey. Echo others’ experiences and it will be as empty as the echo.’

‘That sounds like a quote from my book: “Let your experiences formulate your beliefs, not your beliefs formulate your experiences”. The problem comes when beliefs try to answer questions on things that cannot be known.’

‘Now THAT I do believe! Is that Book of REB 2?’

Karrle cringes at the suggestion. ‘Hopefully not. My brain may burn out before then.’

These conversations are irresistible, and Graham always comes away thinking about new ideas, but as usual he has overstayed and is running late so he quickly shuffles off to his other appointments.

Karrle feels a freedom in exploring his thoughts with Graham, and the comfort of conversation is important. Confident that his thoughts are insightful he has no idea where they will lead him – if anywhere. There are still many challenges, the principle one being the Home Office decision on his right to remain in the UK. But, having discovered the Book of REB, he feels more in control of his future.

# Part Three

# Old Troubles Bring New Troubles

## For Some, Life Falls Apart

The local cat, Bungle, and Ryszard are Lech's only close friends in the house. Ryszard works for an English chicken farmer, DJ Houghton Chicken Catching Services; it is a gangmaster firm, and supplies all the main national supermarkets.[1]

The operation runs 24/7 and Ryszard works more than a hundred hours per week. He has nothing to show for his efforts apart from exhaustion, despair and failing health. Constant exposure to ammonia gives him permanent headaches, chest pains, stinging eyes and a loss of taste. Lech is not surprised because his friend's clothes always smell of the farm.

Ryszard is also from Poland. He left his girlfriend behind with the promise of bringing her to England in six months' time, when he is 'established'. That was eighteen months ago, and he has not heard from her for four months. Any future they were planning together is now a memory as acidic as the ammonia.

The two men are sitting in the kitchen, everyone else has gone to bed. Concerned for his friend, Lech asks, 'How is the chicken farm?'

Ryszard remains unmovable but eventually mutters, 'Terrible!' Silence. 'They owe me five weeks' wages. I might get some on Tuesday.'

His friend's efforts are clearly not working, so Lech suggests, 'Why don't you get another job?'

His slumped frame draped against the table for support, suggests effort equals pain. Ryszard mutters, 'I have no time, money, energy. I owe two weeks' rent. If they pay me up to date, I will leave.'

Silence. 'If they pay me up to date I will leave,' he repeats as if repetition fortifies his resolution. 'Anyway, my friend works in a warehouse for Amazon and he says it is just as bad. He's on a zero-hours contract and sometimes there's no work but he still has to be available in case they call. At least I get my hours in, even if they don't always pay me.'

Lech stares into his friend's face. 'You can't keep going like this.'

'A guy at the farm gives me speed. It keeps me going.'

Shocked by this revelation, Lech pleads, 'Ryszard, please, you MUST stop. It will kill you.'

[1] *The Guardian*, 11/04/2019

A convulsive cough precedes a lifeless reply. 'My friend, you do not understand. Inside…' And he runs out of words to describe inside. Then he suddenly starts again. 'Drugs relieve the pain of living. I don't know what normal life is any more.' Smirking, he whispers a secret to himself, 'But I know where hell is!'

Exhaustion, monotony and bullying are taking a dreadful toll on Ryszard; he is a lost soul in the crowd, living in the shadows, becoming ever more frightened of the light. It is evident to any casual observer that he is cutting the last threads to his sanity and humanity; a flawed hero in a slow-motion disaster movie, hurtling towards oblivion.

This surreal existence, where happiness is unobtainable, has become his new life, a retreat from an uncaring world where savage injustices are meted out by a faceless system. Now a chameleon, he is becoming the shadow, condemned to endure this foul refuge as it accompanies him to his end.

Many in England lose control and find escape in self-destruction. In Poland people are poor, but poverty is accepted and tolerated. In this coveted destination of England, hopes are raised and dashed, making failure more crushing. Returning home is not seen as an option. Men, cut off from family and friends, do not blame society for their failure but themselves; rather than staring misery in the face every hour, they retreat into faceless anonymity.

Lech reflects on how, in an apparently free society, open-market forces result in a permanent underclass of low-paid workers (not only foreigners) desperately trying to hold their lives together in an unfulfilled search for happiness. At the same time, consumerism is benefiting the majority, and big business is making huge profits.

Consumerism sounds like a dirty word, the engine that powers economic inequality and creates huge markets for those with power and money, all in the name of democratic choice. Everyone knows that this is exploitation, yet nobody does anything. There is an implied contract, not written anywhere that, for the privilege of being tolerated, migrants sacrifice their rights as human beings. If employers operate illegally, as long as it does not impact on the majority it is not sufficiently important to take action to protect the vulnerable. Anyway, it makes things cheap.

This same majority can relieve any guilt by simultaneously being shocked at the occasional stories of suffering and reports of employers who are caught. In this land of opportunity, for some the glass ceiling is so low they cannot stand up and survival is barely possible.

Lech wishes he had words that could move these mountains but he has none.

Ryszard is imploding into a twisted version of the person who bounded off the coach at Victoria Coach Station. He was a bright, fresh-faced, joyous youth with the skin of a Polish prince and eyes that could see the future – and it was good. One of nature's creations, so bright it was a delight to bask in the sunshine of his optimism. How could so much thirst for life come to this?

Like most men, Ryszard was cared for as a child and never grew out of the habit. He had offered himself in good faith and found he was unrequired. This boundless enthusiasm was based on hope and inexperience; now experience had crushed hope, leaving him screaming in silence. Was this Edvard Munch's vision when he painted *The Scream*? Remorselessly, agonisingly, pitifully, his dreams and identity are draining away drip by drip, replaced by nothing.

Two weeks later, Ryszard cannot get out of bed. He loses his job and lodgings and arrives drunk at the Salvation Army, where he is refused entry. He ends up on the street. Sleeping wherever he can, he quickly discovers a new circle of streetwise friends who know when and where occasional free meals are available, the location of sheltered doorways, and places to avoid maintaining invisible. These days Lech rarely sees his friend. Driven exclusively by the need to lose himself, he is imprisoned and sustained by drink and drugs.

The two meet for the last time in a café. Lech is shocked at how frail, ashen and old his friend looks. Ryszard's shabby clothes smell of street life; he has stained teeth, dirt lines on his face and dead eyes that could have been on a fishmonger's slab. Diminished and discarded, he fumbles in his breast pocket and pulls out his last remaining treasure: a worn photo of his girlfriend. He strokes the image with his grubby thumb for whatever comfort it can provide. The photo, like him, is almost unrecognisable, damaged beyond repair by English grime, but is still a cherished relic of what might have been.

The lack of control over his life now extends to his body as disobedient fingers trail four spoons of sugar from bowl to cup. To conceal his inner emptiness, Ryszard avoids eye contact, offering only occasional fleeting glances in Lech's direction. Talk is introspective, strained, and intermittent. Responses are empty, hollow, spiritless. Mumbled stuttering renders sentences over-ambitious. Silence articulates a void between them that cannot be crossed and is only broken by Lech rummaging through scattered memories to recall events and conversations from happier days, but these are now irrelevant, an unkind reminder of what Ryszard no longer has.

Remembering the pleasure Ryszard got from Polish jokes, Lech tries to recall some from his childhood. 'I heard they closed the zoo in Warsaw. The duck died.'

A faint nod of the head acknowledges receipt. Lech tries again. 'You remember the guy Jakub, who shares my room and keeps looking for my money? I have found a new place to hide it.' Silence. 'Under the soap.' No response.

Both are trapped in this horror movie, isolated by events in a scene with no dramas, just passive observers witnessing the inevitable conclusion play out in a quiet English café. Lech knows how the film ends but, as the audience, he is powerless to alter the script. Now his friend's only ambition stretches to the next disconnect from the world. Lech senses that Ryszard's mind accepts that there is no escape but has failed to inform his body.

The two men go to Sainsbury's opposite the Transport Museum where Lech buys his friend a sandwich and some milk for £3.95, including the carrier bag. This is more than an hour's pay at the carwash. It is time to leave. The two stand together on a street corner and offer a ritualised man hug. Tension suffocates breath as they each hold the other tightly for several seconds, knowing that when their grip relaxes, Lech will be complicit in releasing Ryszard's life to its fate. Neither speak, in silent acceptance that there are no plans. Any pretence would be a lie, the final capitulation.

Drifting back to the shared house, Lech realises that this inconspicuous moment conceals an earthquake that has engulfed his life. Yesterday's normalities are gone. From the moment he left his wife in Poland, he has suppressed his emotions, summoned his inner strength and faced the challenges alone, believing that, as a strong man, he could battle through, whatever. Now, witnessing the pitiless dismantling and futile destruction of a pure spirit is devastating, leaving the very foundations of his self-belief unprepared and overwhelmed.

Contorting lips disfigure his face and his heart explodes. Fresh rain fails to dilute bitter tears. As principal witness to a tragedy, try as he might he is powerless to save, grip or even touch what must be rescued. Shocked by his own impotence, this reality is unbearable and could suck him into a very dark place with no escape. This is not his self-image, nor is the abyss his intended destination.

That last image of Ryszard can never be forgotten, but only re-enforces his determination to keep strong and be the man his wife and children expect.

## Lech Phones Home

'Hi, Karolina, how are you?'

'I am good. How are you?'

'Fine. How are Julita and Zenon?'

'They are fine. Zenon starts school next week. He is so excited, but I do not have enough money for the school uniform. Can you send me a bit more this week?'

They both know this is a problem but Lech does not want to disappoint. 'I will try. How much do you need?'

'About £100.'

'It may be difficult. I might be able to send £80. Can you borrow the rest from the family?'

'I have already done that, and you have not paid your uncle back for the money you borrowed to go to England. I don't like to ask. Can't your friends in the house help?'

He is cornered. 'I will try.'

Changing the subject, Karolina asks : 'Are you still getting on with the other housemates?'

'Yes, we laugh a lot,' but his monotone words fail to mask the truth.

By making no mention of Ryzard, Lech is shielding his wife, but this deprives her access to his emotional pain. Is this kindness, cowardice or merely a symptom of their lives drifting apart on a tide of unwelcome troubles? They are both struggling to conceal their realities from the other. Powerless to help, both believe the best they can do is not to reveal the emptiness of daily living, marooning each on separate emotional islands. Today, Lech's emotional pot is full.

Karolina cannot resist asking the same question every phone call. 'When will you be coming home? The children miss you and I miss you.'

'Not yet. I need to find a proper paying job and life will be better. Maybe you could come to England.'

'You know I can't leave. Mum cannot look after dad on her own.'

With no more to say, Lech winds up the conversation. 'I have to go now.'

'Love you.'

'Love you too.' He misses his family. The children might grow up thinking he does not care. He misses his wife and the sex they enjoyed.

Lech returns to the shared house with its stale sweaty clothes and empty beer cans.

Maybe tomorrow will be better.

## Africa- Richest Resources - Poorest People

Can enlightenment of the past explain the mysteries of the present? If so, will gathering knowledge and ideas guide tomorrow's actions?

Yesterday's research predetermines today's investigations and understanding the history that has brought Karrle's life to this point is imparting a growing awareness that he is defining himself in a way he has never felt before. Despite this developing connection and the many subjects investigated, he has not improved his life or that of his countrymen. The Home Office decision on his 'right to remain' might be critical to so many futures.

As his only audience, Graham is a valuable echo-chamber for articulating and advancing his ideas. Casual chatting progressively reveals a little more of themselves, providing a solid foundation for their evolving friendship. Karrle is Graham's favourite client; he is articulate, never any trouble and always a delight to talk to. Today, Graham makes time for a cup of tea and an update. 'Hi, I have an hour to kill so I thought I'd pop in and see how you are.'

Repeating what has become a ritual, Karrle says, 'I'm good, thanks. Would you like to join me in a cup of tea?'

'I don't think there's room for the two of us,' Graham jests. Looking at the interesting selection of teas on the shelf, he sticks with the tried and tested. 'I'll have some Yorkshire tea, please.'

Shaking his head Karrle responds, 'That is so strange. The one place it is not from is Yorkshire. The tea comes from East Africa and India, is served in a China cup and the only local thing is the milk, probably to make it whiter! Typical of the English to copy something, assume ownership and then dictate to the rest of the world!'

They both smile at this mild teasing tinged with an element of truth. Boiling the kettle Karrle asks, 'How do you take your tea?'

Graham has not finished being mischievous. 'I thought I was going to drink it here. I didn't bring a receptacle.'

Karrle acknowledges Graham's banter. 'You're on form today. But thinking about it, the British are very proud of their national identity, yet your national drink is tea and the national symbol of England is the lion, neither of which have anything to do with Britain. Presumably, your native animals were not considered to have the necessary qualities.'

Graham realises he is not going to win so he changes the subject. 'How's your research progressing?'

'Very well. I am looking at the history and economics of Africa.'

Graham is always impressed with the thoroughness of his client's research. 'And what has it taught you?'

'Many things. I now understand why Africa is the poorest continent in the world.'

Searching for a possible answer Graham suggests, 'Isn't that because of wars and poor education?'

'Yes, that is part of the problem,' Karrle concedes the present-day reality, then comes back with a question, 'but why is the continent so rich in resources and the people so poor?'

Graham is not sure and hesitantly repeats, 'Because of wars and poor education?'

Having stretched the limit of Graham's knowledge, this opens the door for Karrle to divulge his insights. 'To understand Africa, firstly you have to understand how enormous it is.'

'I know, it's big' Graham replies.

Repeating the conversation he had had with Connection Man, Karrle expands. 'No, it's mind blowingly bigger than anything you can relate to in England. You can fit the twenty-seven EU countries into Africa twice, and still have room to put Greenland in four times.'

With raised eyebrows Graham admits, 'That is big!'

Karrle delivers the knock out blow, 'And still have room to put England in thirty-three times.'

Graham's quizzical expression is touching on disbelief. 'Really!? It doesn't look that big on a map.'

'That's because of the Mercator Projection. When you spread a round Earth onto a flat piece of paper, everything at the top and bottom extends to the full width of the sheet. If the earth at the equator is 24,901 miles, then the North Pole increases from a dot to 24,901 miles.'

Graham admits, 'I had not thought of that.'

'There are many truths that go unnoticed. The reason that size is important is to understand that Africa is made up of fifty-four countries and many hundreds of tribes over vast distances. Before I came here, I only thought of my family, neighbourhood, tribe and country. I only became African when I left. The continent is too gigantic ever to be a homogenous entity, any more than you think of the French, Latvians and Albanians being the same as the English. The continent contains many societies. Can I tell you about one of them you have probably never heard of, the Kuba Kingdom?'

Graham nods: 'You're right, I haven't!'

'It is not surprising, most Africans have not heard of them either. The Kuba Kingdom was established by Shyaam a-Mbul around 1625AD in what is now the Congo. He travelled around a number of tribes and learned many things. When he returned, he brought a number of the tribes together to form a kingdom with a capital as the political and trading centre. By absorbing the talents of many ethnic groups, ideas were shared and the inhabitants enjoyed economic and social mobility. The king was responsible to a council, which had a legal system with juries that operated in many ways like a modern society. This lasted until the nineteenth century.'

Graham could feel himself being drawn in. 'So what happened?'

Like Poirot, the Belgium fictional detective, Karrle delivers the masterstroke. 'The Belgians arrived![1] King Leopold II of Belgium wanted to become richer and more powerful, and decided that acquiring overseas territories was the way to do it. He commissioned Henry Stanley to investigate the potential for extracting wealth from the Congo. Stanley confirmed that it was 'ripe for the picking.' Stanley was a reporter for the *New York Herald*, and his adventures were recounted throughout the world as heroic exploits into the mysterious, dark, exotic continent.

Leopold hired ruthless mercenaries called the Force Publique and handpicked governors for each district, giving them dictatorial powers on a commission-only basis. The sovereignty of the natives ended when they were press-ganged into forced labour to plunder Congo's natural resources. They slaughtered elephants for the ivory and worked to death in mines for gold, silver, diamonds and everything of value that could be removed. When the price of rubber sky-rocketed, it was a game changer. Production quotas were imposed on everything, and any shortfall resulted in the hands and feet of the natives being cut off. If a man needed both hands to work, Force Publique would cut the hands off his wife or children. A Catholic missionary, Edmond Boelaert, was told, "From all the bodies killed in the field, you had to cut off the hands. He (the captain) wanted to see the numbers of hands cut off by each soldier, who had to bring them in baskets.'' [1]

[1] https://www.pnas.org/content/116/2/593 Leopold

Missionaries bought land from the locals and established a base which became a back door for government and commercial operations to move in. When King Kwet aMbweky refused to sell his land, soldiers destroyed several villages along the Sankura. The Kuba Kingdom was conquered by three separate attacks in July, 1900. Some of the local tribes, the Bushong and Kete, even turned to the missionaries to plead for protection from the demands of the company.

There were many uprisings, which were crushed with immense cruelty. When a medicine man invented Tongatonga, which was said to deflect militia bullets, this convinced a number of tribes to join forces and they were far more successful. It is interesting that Tongatonga served a similar purpose to belief systems, like Christianity, in uniting people in a common cause. It delivered much more power to the larger group to achieve their objectives. Unfortunately, it did not save them, much like Christianity. After many villages were burned and the inhabitants slaughtered, the king eventually surrendered on 7th February 1905.

Villages continued to be looted and women and children kidnapped until the men had collected enough rubber. Villagers could not perform their duties, like food collection and house building, and the fabric of their society decayed. The whole of the Congo was traumatised and this led to the destruction of their society. For more than thirty years these atrocities were on an industrial scale. An estimated ten million Congolese were killed, nearly twice as many as Jews killed by Hitler. Unable to match the state's firepower, migration became a necessity. Many fled to areas where there were no rubber trees, resulting in conflicts with other tribes, starvation and disease.'

Dismayed, Graham's only comment is: 'That is terrible. I never knew that.'

Karrle continues. 'It is not widely known. Systemic amnesia has meant that most of this history has been lost or ignored. In Belgium, Leopold is known as "Leopold the Builder" because of all the magnificent buildings he built from the profits of human suffering, but Belgian schoolbooks have made no mention of what truly happened until recently.' He shows Graham a picture of a magnificent Belgium building financed from the profits of exploited and murdered Africans, Cinquantenaire in Brussels.[1]

---

[1] By Redvers - https://www.flickr.com/photos/redvers/1074888992/, CC BY 2.0, https://commons.wikimedia.org/w/index.php?curid=3541509. No alterations have been made

These buildings remind Karrle of one of the laws of physics: equal and opposite forces. He wonders how much suffering was inflicted on innocent Africans to produce the wealth required to fund these tombstones to his ancestors. If King Leopold II was responsible for around ten million deaths and built a hundred buildings, each building cost ten thousand African lives, a vile testimony to the glories of empire.

Karrle shows Graham another picture, of Africans mutilated by the Force Publique. [1]

[1] Wikipedia. MutilatedChildrenFromCongo.jpg. Provided by: Wikimedia Commons Attribution-ShareAlike 4.0 International (CC BY-SA 4.0)

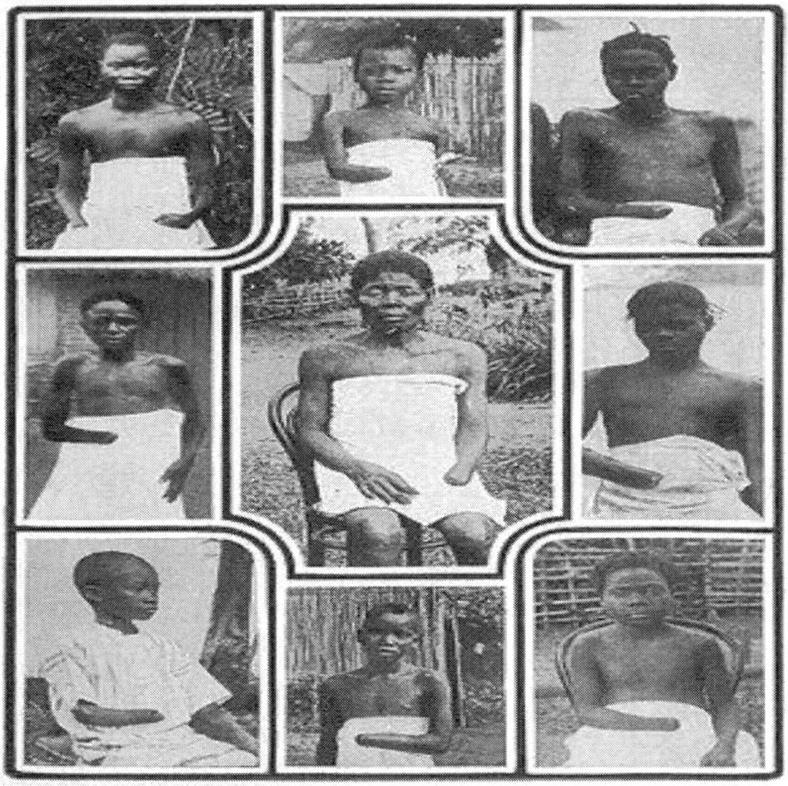

FROM PHOTOGRAPHS, CONGO STATE

"The pictures get sneaked around everywhere."— *Page 40.*

Karrle's words are grim pronouncements, reflecting the deep trauma these stories have on him. Although the events happened long ago, he knows that they created the conditions that are destroying his country today. They are the source of modern practices and what must be tackled in today's thinking.

Graham is stunned into silence as Karrle moves on. 'Those that benefited from the trade, both African and European, did not wish any official records to exist. Most stories in Africa are oral and lost to future generations, thus destroying the history and identity of Africans today.

One notable feature of empires is the requirement to create records in order to administer over vast distances. As the victor tells the story, it is often these accounts that are preserved for posterity. Very little was recorded in Africa before the Europeans came, so most of their history is lost.'

Trying to find a positive, Graham interjects, 'Well, that's one up for civilisation.'

But Karrle cannot leave this unanswered. 'Interesting word you chose – civilisation. You had the same misrepresentation in your own country long before Europeans arrived in sub-Saharan Africa.'

'Really? When was that?'

'In Britain, when the Anglo-Saxons invaded and the Roman Empire collapsed. The period 400 to 600AD is known as the Dark Ages. The accepted story, handed down for hundreds of years, is that the Romans were civilised and the invaders "barbarians", and the collapse of the Roman Empire was the end of civilisation. The reality was that the Romans had been very barbaric in dominating and destroying native tribes. The process of change after they left Britain was much more peaceful, with farming, trade, inter-marriage, music and culture thriving. It was not the end of civilisation but the end of empire and the beginning of self-determination.'

'So why do they call it the 'Dark Ages?' Graham asks.

'It is because there were hardly any written records, unlike during Roman times. It was archaeological evidence that contradicted the myths. It is a good example in your own history of how words written often centuries later had an agenda that distorted reality. The European empire builders told stories that suited their point of view. The widespread cruelty exacted on local populations was conveniently forgotten, motivated by the reality that their power derived from their wealth – and much of that came from plundering Africa. European abuse, destruction and the disastrous process of de-colonisation are still an inhibitor of Africa's development today. Without history, there is no identity. Without identity, dignity is easily destroyed.'

Graham tries to distance those actions from life today. 'That is appalling, but they were the actions of a few cruel men who died long ago.'

Again, Karrle corrects a popular misconception. 'The trading arrangements set up by the Europeans continued for decades after the Europeans left, as did the mutilations and bonus systems, and there has not been a democratic government in the country since. The population survives under appalling conditions on a tiny percentage of the average American income. When conflict exploded in the 1990s, five million

Congolese died. It was the highest death toll in any conflict since the Second World War, yet the event was barely noticed by the outside world and soon forgotten.'

Graham poses a question in the hope of some salvation. 'Those are terrible events, but surely some people went to Africa with good intentions?'

The answer is not comforting. 'The people who travelled to Africa had a range of motives. They comprised adventurers, mercenaries, military and government personnel, representatives of commercial enterprises and religious zealots. What financed this invasion and encouraged these practices were the fortunes made by pillaging Africa's natural resources.

Even by the moral standards of the time, it was considered unacceptable to treat the natives with such brutality. In 1884/85 the Europeans held a conference in Berlin, to agree the division of African land between the European powers and avoid unnecessary conflict. To gain control of the Congo, Leopold II agreed to improve the lives of the "savages," including converting them to Christianity. The fate of Africa was decided in Europe, and spreading Christianity happened to coincide with making themselves very rich. It is white Europeans who need to believe what is not true to justify their actions.'

Graham blinks at this sharp comment. Karrle continues unabated. 'But the agreement had fatal flaws. Leopold had no intention of doing anything but take out everything he could at whatever cost, which he did for another twenty-five years. These atrocities were conducted out of sight of Europeans. When the extent of the brutality became known, Leopold was forced to hand over control to the Belgian government, which actually passed a law making it illegal to kill Africans. Can you imagine that? What would you think of an African country having to pass a law stating that it was illegal to kill the British? But the organisational structures established by the Belgians still operate, and the systemic abuse of the population and extraction of resources have never stopped.'

Truly shocked, Graham says almost to himself. 'That is unimaginable,' but feels compelled to marginalise the story. 'Belgium is only one country. Surely the other European countries were better?'

Karrle broadens the picture. 'These were not the isolated actions of a rogue country gone berserk, but only one story in a pattern of events. Europe was a hotbed of competing nations looking to become more powerful than their neighbours. To achieve, this they needed to increase their wealth.

Until the mid-nineteenth century, inland sub-Saharan Africa was unknown to Europeans and was seen as a vast landmass full of natural resources. Fifteen European countries including Portugal, Holland, France, Denmark, Italy, Britain, Belgium, Spain and Germany all desired access to these resources to feed their growing empires. The first land grab was in 1415, and accelerated aggressively during the nineteenth century. By 1913, 97% of Africa was under foreign rule. Everything of value was taken – gold, diamonds, ivory, rubber, copper, oil, timber, fish – anything that could be seized and sold.

Cotton and sugar, cultivated in the West Indies and America, were very profitable but their populations were too small to satisfy European demand, so Africans were enslaved and transported across the Atlantic. Military might crushed any opposition, and the plunderers believed that controlling the land entitled them to all the continent's resources – including its people. European empire builders were thieves quarrelling over the spoils.

The territories created were administered and controlled by Europeans based on agreements made in Europe. No Africans were present. Europeans determined borders between territories, often by drawing straight lines on a map modified by natural barriers like the Sahara desert. This defined which European power controlled which natural resource. But cultural variations over large areas are graduated according to the local environment and traditions. They do not fit into neat territories, particularly for tribes that had been nomadic for hundreds of years. The Europeans had little knowledge or regard for the local inhabitants or the practicalities of their lives. Europeans did not live there, so they did not care about the devastation they left behind.

The mistreatment of the natives, although not universal, was very common. It suited European objectives to believe that Africans were children who could not administer their own affairs, a habit that too many retain to this day, and is still used as an excuse for exploitation and abuse. It is easy to de-humanise people if you do not understand their language and culture – a technique used by dictators. The question is, who were the savages?'

Graham responds, 'We had the more sophisticated society.'

Karrle snaps back at this inherent confusion of values - 'Are paedophiles celebrated in your culture?'

Visibly shocked at this rhetorical question, Graham says, 'Certainly not.'

'How about rapists, robbers and murderers?'

'Obviously not!'

'Well they are some of the heroes that built the British Empire. The celebrated British hero, Clive of India, authorised the digging up of crops in Bengal to grow more profitable crops for export, like opium. Millions starved.[1] Another hero was Cecil Rhodes, who many believe prepared South Africa for apartheid. These are the figureheads. Imagine the hundreds of people they commanded whose atrocities remain unreported.'

Graham concedes, 'I am sure that some of those things went on, but we never knowingly approved of them.'

The case is won, as 'Poirot' delivers the final verdict. 'Precisely! You never knew. All the British saw were the shiploads of contraband arriving at their ports and never asked questions. The problem is that even today you are receiving ships carrying plundered assets from Africa and are still not asking questions. You British have a saying "out of sight, out of mind". Africa was, and still is, both.'

Both men are silent as the enormity of the conversation sinks in. When they resurface, Karrle continues. 'If Hitler had won the Second World War, killed all opposition and treated Britain merely as a resource for his empire, would he have civilised you? He didn't win, so you feel safe in your answer. What if President Putin, built a weapon that could neutralise your defences? What if he conquered your country, banned all organisations including the churches; dictated that everyone had to be a member of the Communist party; started exterminating groups like military personnel, university professors, political leaders, church leaders, those who are old and sick. If his was the only story told, he would say that he had cleansed you. Who is the savage?'

Graham defends what he believes. 'The British were better than that.'

'Britain had the BIGGEST empire in history. Yes, the selling of slaves was banned – after 200 years, although slavery continued for decades after that. They also sold opium to the Chinese for 100 years. The might of the British Empire was built on exploitative trade.

[1] Dan Snow, *The Birth of Empire*, 25/02/2019

Eventually, when slavery was abolished, the British government paid huge sums of money to compensate the slave owners for the loss of their "property". That resulted in a hundred stately homes being built in the UK. British taxpayers, including migrant workers, continued to repay this debt to compensate the slave owners until 2015[1]. No compensation was ever paid to the slaves for their loss of life and liberty.

The French treated Haiti far worse. When the Haitians rebelled and won independence in 1804, the French were preoccupied with European wars and were in no position to take back the islands. In 1825 they raised a strong military force and threatened to recapture Haiti unless compensation for their loss of property was paid by the ex-slaves. The final payment of the ninety million French francs was paid in 1947. The crushing financial burden has kept the islanders desperately poor to this day and led to rampant corruption, inequality and poor health. Today many districts are run by gangs, often because it's the only way to survive. At least the British people paid the compensation themselves. Some believe that this was the only way William Wilberforce could gain the support to pass the law in the British Parliament.'

Graham is speechless for several moments. 'I had no idea. I consider myself fairly educated, but I was barely aware of these things. I knew that Europeans established empires and did some terrible things, but nothing on that scale.'

Illustrating the cultural distortions of the truth, Karrle continues. 'There is endless coverage of the glorious military battles of Britain's past – the Battle of Britain, D-Day, Waterloo – but scant coverage of darker episodes. You have only been told half a story. Sometimes half a story is so misleading that it is a lie. The tragedy is that these events still plague the lives of hundreds of millions today.

People do not realise that many public buildings and institutions in Liverpool, Glasgow, Bristol and London, including the Bank of England and Lloyds of London, were financed by the slave trade. These form an integral part of the great institutions in Britain today. What is even less understood is that the empire created the economic, political, cultural and social infrastructures of British society today. Many traditionalists want to preserve British identity as if it can be bottled,

[1] https://www.mirror.co.uk/news/uk-news/taxpayers-still-paying-british-slave-12019829

immune from foreign influences, but it was formed *because* of these foreign influences.'

Graham replies as best he can. 'The impression in England is that we also did a lot of good. Are you saying that the empire builders were evil, or a great example of change?'

Karrle offers a balanced reply. 'They are two sides of the same coin. It required enormous determination, bravery and flexibility to build the British Empire. People acted based on what they knew, not necessarily from bad motives, but many were ignorant of the consequences of their actions. We are only beginning to fully appreciate the depth of this challenge. Unless we learn from the past, the damage will continue to impact future generations.'

Graham tries to bring the conversation up to date. 'But at least we gave them their freedom. They are now independent countries and can do what they want.'

'Ah! Decolonisation!' Karrle smiles in agreement.

'Yes, if that's what you call it.' Graham looks at his watch. 'Ah! Once again, you have kept me far too long. I have to go, but I would love to hear your thoughts on de-whatever you said.'

Their conversation leaves Graham deeply unsettled and he decides to check out what he can remember of Karrle's statements. He is astonished how much information is available but how little he truly understood. It was as if the past were dead and had no relevance to today, and today's problems had no history: they are just the way things are. With no sense of connection or responsibility, this creates a sense of apathy that things will never change. He can see how intolerance is based on frustration of the present, without understanding or resolution, except resolution through conflict.

## Poem Discovered

Mohini cannot spend more than half an hour with Andy after school because she is expected to go straight home. She enters the house and drops her books on the hallway table as always. Shortly afterwards, her father moves them and a piece of paper floats to the floor. A casual glance reveals that it is not in his daughter's handwriting and stimulates his curiosity.

Reading it, Vishnu notices her abbreviated name, Moh, and realises it might be a love poem to his daughter. Such blatant disrespect cannot be tolerated. As head of the family, it is his responsibility to control her social interactions and protect her reputation so as not to impair her suitability for a future husband.

King of all he surveys, like a lion, Vishnu discharges an ear piercing, thunderous roar, 'Mohini, come here.'

Slowly descending the stairs, she spots the anger in her father's face and the fateful piece of paper up in his hand.

'WHAT is this?' he demands.

Like a rabbit caught in headlights, she is wide eyed and motionless. 'Nothing,' she murmurs.

Advancing and shaking the paper in her face, her father booms,

'Don't lie to me. WHAT …IS …THIS?'

'Just a poem,' is her flimsy reply.

'I can see that. Why have you got it? Who wrote it?'

'Somebody from school.'

'Is he a Hindu?'

'No!' The die is cast.

'You should not allow boys to write you poems. Anyway, it is rubbish. You cannot chain yourself in a rut. You are either in a rut, or you are chained. You cannot be both.'

Cornered, terrified of losing Andy but now defiant, Mohini disregards any consequences and contradicts her father. 'Yes, you can. I am in a rut and want to get out, but you are chaining me here' she blurts out.

Blood vessels appear on his neck and temples, as spiralling rage grips her father. Threatening disownment, Vishnu demands, 'I forbid you from talking to this boy EVER again. You know you will be betrothed to a respectable Hindu boy.'

Calming down slightly, he searches for an explanation for such errant behaviour against family and tradition, 'What were you thinking? Why do you not respect the family?'

With her emotions now fully out of control, Mohini unthinkingly throws the words back in her father's face. 'Why does the family not respect me?'

Fearful of the consequences of the shame his daughter could bring on the family, and particularly the attitude of his powerful cousin and employer who is a strict traditionalist, Vishnu strikes his daughter in the face with ill-considered force.

Shocked and defeated Mohini runs to her room in floods of tears. Everyone is against her.

# The New Face of Slavery

Graham is fascinated to learn about the decolonisation of the European empires. Karrle seems to explain things with a clarity and objectivity that gives real understanding. Whilst there are many sources of information, much of it is conflicting, leaving Graham unsure which ones to trust. As he knew Karrle before he started his research Graham is confident that his client did not start from a fixed opinion and then search for evidence to justify his prejudices. Karrle's analysis is the result of extensive investigation and reflection.

Unfortunately, Graham is fully booked with appointments for the rest of the week and busy with family matters over the weekend, so he has to wait until their scheduled appointment the following week. Wednesday afternoon arrives and Graham knocks decisively on the door. 'Afternoon, Karrle.'

'Hi. Good to see you.'

'I have reserved the rest of the day for your afternoon lecture.' Graham gives a cheeky smile. 'I checked out a few things when I had some time, and they seem readily supported by historical evidence, so I'm hungry to learn what else I don't know.'

They settle down over a cup of tea – not Yorkshire this time; Graham remembers the mocking comments and decides to be a bit more adventurous.

Although Karrle knows what he is going to say, he hesitates over the first sentence. Sitting straight, he clears his thoughts and draws a deep breath.

'OK! Right. So where do I begin? Firstly, you have to understand what the European empires left behind when they granted independence. Empire building, which had been all the rage in the nineteenth century, had become untenable by the mid-twentieth century. Britain and France had narrowly won the Second World War, but the herculean effort had virtually bankrupted them.

For the same reasons that the Romans built roads across their empire, the infrastructure constructed by the British – roads, railways, ports and airports – were primarily to extract and transport materials and populations, and facilitate the rapid movement of troops, if required. Nairobi, the capital of Kenya, started as a railway town with much of the workforce coming from imported India. Many Indians settled in a number of East African countries until the president, Idi Amin, expelled them from Uganda in the 1970s.

Africans lived a tribal existence in dispersed communities growing agricultural produce like cocoa, which were labour intensive but very low paid. Local tribesmen hardly benefited from any of the infrastructure built by the Europeans, who treated them merely as a cheap source of labour. They often focused on mining, which is probably the most destructive business on the planet and does substantial, permanent damage to the environment, endangering the health and sustainability of the local wildlife and population. In the Congo the mining sector accounts for ninety per cent of export revenue.'

Thinking about this, Graham interjects, 'But that was a long time ago. Since then Europeans have granted these countries independence and attitudes have changed – and not just in Africa. European ideas of citizenship and democracy have changed dramatically over the last couple of centuries. Judgements about past events have to be interpreted in the light of the understanding of those involved at the time. You can't judge history by how things end.'

'True,' Karrle acknowledges. 'But before you bestow too much credit on the Europeans, you have to understand that this was not a free gift. The Europeans had offered independence in exchange for support for their European war. After the war, many of these subjugated peoples demanded what they had been promised and could not be denied. There had been uprisings and mutinies in the past, but the Europeans had been able to suppress them. World War II was a game changer for power and ideas.

When the territories of the British Empire fought to preserve freedom and democracy for the British, it raised the unanswerable question: what about the liberty of the people who had fought for British freedom? What about the rights of all men? The Europeans tried to prevent, and later frustrate, the process but this was an intractable challenge that was often handled ineptly with appalling results, like the decolonisation of the Congo by Belgium.

France tried to preserve its empire with various attempts to create subordinate citizenship in a federation, but citizenship implies equal rights and equal living standards between the people in France and the colonies. This was impossible to deliver. And obviously, equal rights would have made the French a minority in their own empire.

Britain faced unmanageable opposition from many parts of the empire and independence soon followed. It was not until 1960 that many of these territories were decolonised, but the diversity of their histories presented more challenges than opportunities. Sometimes the outcomes were catastrophic, as demonstrated by the British failure to learn from the partition of India and Pakistan in 1947.'

'I remember that from my school lessons,' Graham says.

'Yes, but what you probably did *not* learn was that India's independence was treated as an administrative exercise by the British, with total disregard for the practicalities or the ramifications of partitioning one vast nation into two. King George V1 sent his cousin, Lord Mountbatten, to organise the division, and he appointed a British barrister who had never been to India. Mountbatten wanted to return to England as soon as possible so he brought the date for independence forward by ten months. The new borders were kept secret, locked away until two days before the partition so that the information did not interfere with the ceremonies for the transfer of power. The relocation and dislocation of tens of millions of people resulted in riots, looting, rape, murder and a million dead – it's been compared to the worst atrocities of the Nazis. Mountbatten returned to England and was promoted to Lord of the Admiralty.'

Graham had heard a thousand stories of victims of exploitation, but somehow these had washed over him. He'd never allowed himself the mental space for a deeper understanding of the root causes. What interests him now is the impact these events are having on the present day.

'So how did that leave these newly formed territories after independence?' he asks. 'I know that many are struggling as democracies, but they are making progress, aren't they?'

'India and Pakistan were left devastated and have never recovered. Since partition, they have gone to war twice and bitter arguments still remain over Kashmir. Seven decades later they are still each other's greatest enemies.

In Africa wealth-generating activities are concentrated in a few areas controlled by small, tight-knit groups of people, highly protective of their advantages. The newly independent states were not structured to support the bulk of their populations, whose aspirations had been heightened to enlist their support for the concept of independence, not unlike Brexit.

The few centres of major wealth creation involved plundering natural resources to supply the needs of mainly western markets. The two points of control were the mines and the ports – whoever controlled these had access to the lion's share of the wealth and power over the country and its people.'

'Why did they want to control the ports?' Graham asks.

'The ports are the gateway between a territory and the rest of the world. Whoever controls the gateway collects taxes and the distribution of resources that derive from the gate itself – customs revenues, foreign aid, permits to do business in the territory, entry and exit permits, and permission to move money in and out of the country. Controlling access to important export markets and revenues enables those in control to reward their followers and exclude their rivals. This single location of wealth creates a single point of power and intense rivalry in a winner-takes-all contest. The winner could only guarantee retaining control by not sharing power, thus preventing the development of democratic processes to influence decisions and demand accountability.

In Angola, Sierra Leone and parts of the Congo, civil conflict took on new dimensions when organised groups gained access to diamond-rich areas and established smuggling networks to get diamonds out and arms and consumer goods in. In Angola, oil exports pay for government armies while diamonds bankroll the rebels.'

Karrle adds, 'And remember, Sierra Leone and Angola are home to millions of innocent victims without choices.'

Graham listens intently and for the first time starts to understand how difficult these human dilemmas are. Although he had dealt with migrants for years and heard many stories, he had never been to any of these countries or had any direct experience of any of these traumas. Their pain could not be experienced second hand. His job was to deal with the practical problems of the few migrants who managed to get to the UK. He also had little awareness of how culpable many European countries still are and feels compelled to question the foundations of values he believed represented 'Britishness.'

Karrle continues his discourse. 'A cyclical pattern, started by the Ghanaian President, Kwame Nkrumah, was repeated many times: an appeal to the common citizen, promising an opportunity of participation in government, followed by fear of the exercise of citizenship and repression. There was little incentive for those in power to create a broader business community which might challenge the existing elite.

Representing only factions within the country, many governments become over-dependent on these pockets of wealth, leaving the vast majority of the population desperately impoverished. In Nigeria oil, which employed very few people – and many of them foreign – ruined cocoa as the state elite jealously guarded the national resources and turned against the power base of the cocoa producers. That resulted in Nigeria becoming more dependent on oil exports for government revenue and foreign exchange. Seventy per cent of Nigeria's total national income is derived from oil.

In the Congo, once President Mobutu exploited the democratic process to gain power, he became a dictator and ruled for thirty-two years. Despite it bing widely recognised that he was corrupt, Mobutu was given considerable financial support by the West, even against those fighting for democracy. Military assistance by the Belgians, French and Americans suppressed rebellions in order to prevent the collapse of an artificially created nation state. The fear in the West was that a power vacuum might allow communists to gain control. Some of Africa's most conflict-ridden states in the 1980s and 90s had been among the largest recipients of economic and military aid intended to foster Cold War alliances, including Angola, Zaire, Somalia and Ethiopia.

In December 2018, Doctor Denis Mukwege had treated more than 50,000 victims of war rape in the Democratic Republic of the Congo over twenty years. Many have appalling internal injuries inflicted with insane savagery. He said, "We are going backwards … what is protecting perpetrators, even here in Europe, is silence[1]. His reward has been numerous death threats, twenty-four-hour armed guard protection, removing his family from the Congo for their safety, and winning the Nobel Peace Prize for his noble efforts. The only reason it is noble is his personal stand against appalling outrages perpetrated on humans by other humans.

It is perverse that it suits corrupt African leaders for the young, talented and ambitious to escape to Europe thus diminishing internal opposition, maintaining stability for those in charge. This process is not painless for those fleeing, and many in exile experience cultural bereavement.

British imperialists had long standing plans for the development of the colonies. After independence these resources were converted into

---

[1] *The Sunday Times*, 9th December 2018.

foreign aid. This had the benefit of reaffirming the generosity of the "mother country", whilst allowing the benefactors to deny responsibility for creating a distorted economy and the social and political consequences of raising expectations with no hope of delivery. Simultaneously, Western governments and international institutions are only too willing to work with gatekeeper states.'

Graham interrupts, 'But not everyone was exploitative. Some people genuinely believed that Africans were incapable of running a modern government.'

'Yes, they did. But, as always, it was a convenient justification for self-interest. In hindsight, it was the same misguided, benevolent arrogance that wanted to believe that women were the property of men and Africans had to be "civilised" by teaching them European religious beliefs – the colonisation of the African mind.

This is no foundation for the democratic processes that took hundreds of years to evolve in the West. Europeans have had a massive impact on Africa today, and yet the ex-colonial empires have taken very little responsibility for the countries or processes they created, whilst still benefiting enormously from the exploitation of Africa's resources. Africans have no natural inheritance because it has been robbed by the West. Africa has the psychology of a rape victim, blaming themselves for their misfortune. I came across a line by an English poet from the Midlands', Edmund Blunden, that struck me: "When time makes plain the action in all parts".

For most of their history, Africans have been independent. Perhaps one day Africa's proud and noble history will be valued by the world. Seventy per cent of African art is in Europe. Repatriating art, like the looting of Benin bronzes now in British museums, would demonstrate respect and build understanding.'

Graham is truly taken aback. Grappling with the enormity of these revelations, he struggles to find words that can even attempt to address these atrocities. 'This is very, very disturbing … but where do we go from here?'

Karrle gives the best answer he can. 'I don't know the solutions yet, but understanding is the first step and I know I am on the right track. The past explains the present but offers no solutions. All parties need to work together to find those.'

## Mohini Tricked

All the girls at school are locked into a competition to look the coolest. Mohini knows she has natural physical advantages, but presentation is everything. Clothes and makeup are a requirement. She talks to her friends to find persuasive arguments that will convince her parents to allow her the freedom to express her burgeoning personality.

Her mother is the most amenable but understands their cultural traditions and fears hostility from her husband who is acutely aware of his reputation in his community, surviving at the behest of his cousin, the restaurant owner. As a wealthy businessman, he has the luxury of being able to enforce his strict traditional values on those who depend on him, yet these same values are suspended on customers whose money he needs to sustain his position in the community. Loss of employment would throw Vishnu onto the UK employment market of which he knows nothing, and for which he is very ill prepared. Even the possibility of such dishonour is beyond his imagination and cannot be contemplated for an instant.

Mother and daughter go shopping and select items which display her daughter's natural beauty. She will be a knockout on Saturday. Mohini arranges to see her friends at 7pm.

It is 6.45 pm when she walks into the front room. Vishnu's face flashes black at his daughter's outrageous display of flesh and he forbids her from leaving the house. This humiliation in front of the whole family is making her life impossible, and she rushes to her bedroom in tears, again.

Determined to do what she wants, Mohini drops from her bedroom window with minimal damage to her clothing and is only ten minutes late meeting her friends. Her wide-eyed distress is obvious.

Tracey, an occasional member of the group, immediately picks up on the new girl's disorientation. Mohini hardly knows her. Tracey is always getting into trouble, but seems friendly. She approaches Mohini. 'What's up mate?'

'Nothing!'

'How did you rip ya jacket?'

Mohini, caught off guard, answers honestly. 'I caught it on a window catch.'

'Climbin' out, I'll bet?'

Surprised Mohini replies : 'How did you know?'

‘Your dad wouldn’t let you out, I’ll bet. My dad tried that and I told him to go fuck himself.’

Showing her distress, Mohini says, ‘I’ll be in terrible trouble when I go home.’

Tracy offers a solution. ‘Don’t go. I’ve got friends where you can pop in whenever you want. No questions asked.’

‘I don’t know. Will they mind?’

‘Course not. That’s what mates are for. They’re very friendly.’

Confused and befuddled, Mohini needs time to think. She cannot go home just yet and this would give her some space. Forty minutes later, the two girls arrive at a block of flats in a part of town Mohini has never visited. The lift smells of urine. Feeling ill at ease, she sticks to Tracy. They arrive at flat number 34 and Tracy knocks on the door.

A voice inside shouts : ‘Oo is it?’

Full of banter, Tracy lifts the letterbox flap and shouts, ‘Come on, open up. It’s ya girlfriend.’

A scruffy man opens the door. He might be in his thirties but looks much older, and is instantly forgettable. Observing the new girl, he swings his arm into the hallway, inviting entry. ‘Hellllooww!!.... Who’s your friend?’

Tracy answers, ‘Just a friend! Trouble at home.’

Voice smiles, displaying poor dental hygiene. ‘Well, you’ve come to the right place. Make yourself at home. Pretty thing, in’t she?’

They enter the living room where two other men, looking overly relaxed, are drinking. Tracy introduces the new girl. ‘This is Mohini. Got trouble at home and needs somewhere to stay.’

‘Oh, I can’t stay long. I will have to go home soon,’ Mohini explains.

Settee Man straightens his crumpled clothing and sits up. ‘That’s OK. Have a drink, luv.’

Mohini has never tasted alcohol and declines politely. ‘Oh, er, I don’t drink, thank you.’

Armchair Man rejoins, ‘House rule, luv. You gotta have a drink.’

All eyes are on Mohini. She does not want to offend. ‘OK. Can I have a small one, please?’

Voice fetches a tumbler from the kitchen and instructs Settee Man, who is nearest the bottle, ‘Give ‘er some malt. It’s a ladies’ drink!’

The tumbler is half-filled with whiskey. Mohini glances around the room, which is as neglected as its occupants. This is not a side of

England she has seen before, and the unspoken tension makes her pensive. Searching for something to do, she picks up the tumbler, has her first taste of alcohol and shudders' to the great amusement of all. Laughter bounces off the walls and fills the room. It is not nice.

Settee Man tries to sweeten the offering : 'Come over here, luv. I'll put some lemonade in it. It'll taste better.' He gestures for Mohini to sit next to him on the settee. 'Try that. Better, innit?'

Mohini decides to get rid of it and drains the glass in one go.

Voice, alarmed at the disappearance of such a costly drink, says, 'Hey, steady, lass. That stuff's expensive.'

Settee Man reassures his friends : 'Don't worry. I'll get some more,' and he refills Mohini's glass.

'Oh, no, thank you,' she says. 'That was quite enough.'

Armchair Man joins in the fun. 'Nonsense. It tastes better when you get used to it. Cheers, everyone.' They raise their glasses. Mohini does the same, but only takes a token sip.

Settee Man stretches an arm towards her. 'Smoke?'

'No, thank you.' Mohini is embarrassed and shies away.

Settee Man tries to push a cigarette onto her but is rescued by Voice. 'Leave 'er alone. She don't have to smoke it she don't want to.'

'OK. Cheers, everyone.' Settee Man raises his glass and looks directly at Mohini.

All this time, Tracy has not spoken. Mohini starts to feel strange. When she looks around, her friend is nowhere to be seen. Not knowing the way home is a worry. Everything appears more fluid and uncertain. 'Where is my friend?'

Settee Man tries to reassure her. 'We're all friends here. This is a very friendly place.'

Armchair Man repeats the comment. 'Yes, very friendly.' The other men laugh and resume their slumped positions, looking even more relaxed, which only adds to the jarring, uneasy atmosphere. Something is not right, but Mohini does not know what to do.

Encouraged to drink some more, she tries to make the sips as small as possible without being rude. This strange feeling is getting worse – the room is spinning.

Settee Man says something about lying down and leads her to a bedroom. Ah, yes: lying down is good. Then she feels somebody next to her. Now she is being touched. It is Settee Man.

Rejecting whatever is happening, Mohini demands, 'No. Don't touch me. Please.'

Foraging hands are in her underwear and cupping her breasts. She tries to push him off, but he is too heavy and strong. His vile breath revolts her. She pleads with him to stop, but to no avail. His hands are around her buttocks and her short skirt offers no protection. Her father told her not to wear it. Shoulders crush her chest as she feels her bottom being raised, her knickers removed, and then a dreadful stabbing pain as Settee Man straddles and enters her.

She cries out for help. There it is by the door – the other men. Surely they will stop him.

Leering in the doorway they shout encouragement. 'Go on my son, fill ya boots.'

The other man shouts excitedly, 'I'm next.'

Settee Man is grunting, then suddenly he shudders and collapses on top of her. He is pulled off, to be replaced by Armchair Man and then Voice. Mohini's spinning, overloaded senses release her into unconsciousness.

Even escapees eventually have to return to reality. As consciousness returns, her head is still spinning and her crotch feels painful and soggy. Turning her head, she sees Voice getting dressed and a £10 note on the pillow. 'That's for you, for being a good girl. There's more where that came from,' he promises.

What is this revolting man talking about? Slowly her mind recalls the horror. 'What are you talking about? You raped me.'

In a commanding tone, Voice replies, 'Now don't start talkin' that language, young lady. You came 'ere of your own free will, got drunk and offered us sex. There are three witnesses and Tracey. Who d'you think the police are goin' to believe, the four of us or a whore?'

Mohini's head stops swimming with the realisation that her world is shattered. EVERTHING has been taken away: she can never go home, never see Andy, and never live happily in England. She has been evicted from her world to one she hates, with no chance to return. Her life is ruined.

'You had better clean yourself up. You've got a customer in two hours. Don't try leaving. The door's locked and there are no phones. We've taken ya mobile.'

A customer, a customer for what? OH MY GOD! Not a repulsive old man wanting sex? What is she to do? She must escape.

Steadying herself she slowly stands up and moves towards the window. Six floors up. If she jumps she will die. Maybe that would be for the best. She has two hours to decide.

# Part Four

# Chaos Amidst Order

## Lech in the Shared House

Working at the car wash provides little joy, satisfaction or variation apart from the weather, which is either hot, cold or wet. Hot and wet is acceptable; cold and wet is the worst.

Each day ends when the boss pays everyone from the day's takings, which is followed by the long walk to the lodgings, stopping at one of two local Polish shops for lager and minimal food shopping before the nightly ritual of cooking and eating. This routine fills the day, leaving little time for washing (which is dictated by the bath-time rota), followed by a few inconsequential conversations before taking aching limps to bed to try and dream of kinder times. This grinding routine does nothing to raise spirits and for many, surviving seems the highest attainable ambition.

This evening, several men are talking in the kitchen. One says that they need to get some women in the house, a suggestion that receives a general murmur of approval. Jakub, a round-faced, tubby Pole, grabs the attention of the group. 'I know where you can buy one for £30. My mate's been there.'

Borysko, the only Ukrainian in the house, is sceptical. '£30? You're joking. What's wrong with her?'

'Nothing,' Jakub retorts. 'She's pretty and will do anything you want. Indian girl.'

Ludwik suddenly shows considerable interest in the conversation. 'Oh yeah, where is she?' Although from the same district of Poland, as Lech they have never become friends.

Jakub supplies all the information requested. 'In that big block of flats round the corner with the green door. Number 34.'

'That's disgusting. How could you?' Lech asks to the amusement of all present.

'Easy,' says Ludwik, accompanied by smirks all round.

## Business Is Booming

Charles has sacrificed a lot to become the successful businessman he is today. He has made his mark in life, and is a shining example of what can be achieved by anyone if they have enough determination. People must help themselves and not look for hand-outs.

This endless focus on increasing his personal wealth has absorbed his life's energies but it has given him little understanding of the lives of others. He only mixes within a tight circle of friends, family and business colleagues, and hardly knows anybody who is not like himself. The nearest he comes to meeting people with different life experiences is his housekeeper and chauffeur, who are controlled by contractual agreements for the services they provide.

His decisions have a major impact on the lives of his employees, their families and many others who depend on him economically to support the lives they lead, yet they never feature in any of his thoughts or decisions apart from their cost to the business and legal rights. Charles is unaware, and has no interest in, these invisible links that allow him to accumulate his considerable wealth. In short, he has not discovered the people that form the community he depends upon.

Charles believes in the universality of his own experiences. He is normal, and therefore his are the standards by which he judges others. This process usually concludes in recognising the deficiencies in others. He is locked into a narrow world of self-belief, and does not have the time to venture out into activities that might challenge his understanding. He flies to many countries, holds meetings in air-conditioned offices, visits the best restaurants, does a deal and flies out again. The whole world looks the same. He knows, he's been there.

Being captain of a large wealth-creating organisation bestows considerable personal entitlements, privileges and freedoms to pamper his ego, and is completely consistent with his belief that he is an example that anyone can follow. Whilst on a Caribbean holiday, he buys a house on a whim. On returning he exclaims with obvious pride 'everything is so cheap and a housekeeper is only £60 per month, hardly a round of drinks. This display of wealth is visible proof of how successful and worthwhile everything he does is.

As an upstanding UK citizen he would love to help those less fortunate, but what can he do? He has to be practical. Any problems in society are issues beyond his control and therefore not his responsibility.

He does everything he can, and could not do any more. He knows because every minute is fully occupied.

## White Privilege: Myth Vindicates Abuse

Karrle starts to investigate the psychology of racism, why it started and why it persists today. Knowing Graham is due to visit, he can conduct a survey of one and bounce ideas off his only close friend.

Graham is a few minutes late as usual. The kettle has already boiled. 'Hi Karrle. I've brought both ears. What would you like to talk about today?'

'Racism!'

'Well, I like to start light before we get heavy.'

'There seems to be a lot of progress towards equality in the law, certainly in the West, but social progress is far slower. Do you agree?'

Graham ponders a little. 'Yes, absolutely. I would go further. People do not recognise their own racism because it is so deeply rooted in their culture.'

'Interesting! We are all on the spectrum of prejudice. So with regard to race, where on the spectrum are *you*?'

Graham's reflects a little longer before answering. 'Well, I grew up in Littlehampton in Sussex. In our neighbourhood there were no foreigners – not just non-whites, I mean NO foreigners. Once a French boy came to our town on a school-exchange scheme and was attacked in the street and lost two front teeth. Everyone was shocked. I remember thinking that our whole community had been tainted by this one incident. As for people from different continents, well, I saw pictures in books like I saw pictures of rhinos, but I've never seen a rhino, apart from in a zoo. To me, people with curly hair looked odd and different, but that was a long time ago.'

With a twinkle in his eye he adds, 'These days, I would say that I AM colour prejudiced. I THINK COLOURED WOMEN ARE GREAT – it's all that chocolate flesh!' and he waves his arms in the air in a ridiculous representation of uncontrollable ecstasy. 'I don't know what's wrong with me, I just don't fancy the blokes.'

Karrle smiles and slowly shakes his head. This light relief is needed, but he can't be offended because he asked the question. 'So were you prejudiced before?'

'No, I never met any non-whites, so it was never an issue. I was ignorant through inexperience. Now I have met people from many countries, I appreciate their beauty for what it is. It always amuses me that people with pale skin travel thousands of miles to get a tan. Now I know more, I understand and value the differences.'

'Precisely,' Karrle interjects. 'Everything has its own beauty without reference to anything else. Snowflakes, lions, sunsets and fish are all beautiful. Nobody assesses their beauty in relation to the other. Non-white skin does not need to reference itself to white skin to prove it is as good or nearly as good. It diminishes potential because it lowers expectation, and is always wrong. Trying to do so is to apologise for who you are, and the attempt implies an acknowledgement of inferiority. It is important not to diminish ones-self by focusing on our limitations compared with those around us. The truth is the opposite: differences should be celebrated as an expression of individuality and our unique contribution to the world.'

Graham agrees. 'What you say seems so obvious, but it needs to be said to combat ignorance. It was only a few generations ago it was commonly believed that people of colour could NOT be beautiful.'

'Their brains blind their eyes.' Karrle agrees. 'Stereotyping dehumanises people into two-dimensional figures and is used by those that want to control others. If black people are judged purely by their skin colour, you become blind to the person. Decisions are simpler, but suppressing problems will eventually emerge in divergent, destructive forms.'

'Sadly, it is very common,' Graham concurs.

Karrle has also studied the sociological impact of stereotyping which he can relate to his own experiences. 'These prejudices infect so many people that they become social norms. If everybody around you thinks the same, the influences that make up your culture are imperceptible, creating structural forms of privilege and unconscious bias. It is only when you experience different cultures that you can understand your own, including things you have been taught are wrong. In many social structures, personal relationships develop and make a nonsense of beliefs. I have even heard someone say, ''I don't normally like black people, but you're alright.'' The evidence of their own eyes contradicts the stereotypes they have accepted.'

'I had a Somalian client who used to say, ''The man who has not travelled does not have eyes''. '

'Very wise. I did not understand the values of my society until I came to this country. 'Africa' is so huge that back home it did not define anything because everybody was from 'Africa.' Now I am here, nobody knows where my country is so I am just labelled 'African.' Any difficulties with the language or customs are interpreted as evidence of inferiority, because Englishness is perceived as the 'norm.'

These attitudes are so embedded that they are invisible to the English. White supremacy can be seen as a fringe minority, but it is so pervasive it is barely noticeable to most people apart from those it is directed towards.

I believe that racism is the survival strategy of systemic power, and white privilege is essential for the disempowerment of non-whites. It provides a comfortable justification for exploitation, whilst avoiding responsibility. Whiteness is the norm and holds the centre ground – it is the occupying force in the mind. Black British history was invisible because it was ignored. In the sixteenth century, Queen Elizabeth 1 complained that there were too many black people in the royal court and during the Roman Empire, York had a bigger proportion of black people than it has today.'

Following this train of thought Graham asks, 'I didn't know those things. And how do you describe yourself now? Do you identify with your colour, religion, country or continent?'

'None of them. My home is the planet I live on. I am a citizen of the world, an Earthling. Anything else seems to define limits, which then become barriers to anybody perceived as beyond those limits.'

'An Earthling! Hmm, that sounds strange. I have never thought of myself as an Earthling.'

Karrle explains, 'Defining yourself differentiates you from others and makes understanding easier. Creating a stereotype defines everyone in terms of your pre-conceptions. Right from the early days of cinema Hollywood used simple, undemanding plot formulae, always with a happy ending and always with a white hero, whether they were cowboys, Snow White, angels, whatever. Even Tarzan in the Brazilian jungle had to be white. If the story required black people, they had to be either bad or simple.'

'That's true,' muses Graham. 'I cannot remember seeing an old cowboy film with a black hero.'

'That is because there weren't any. Art, be it paintings of kings, early Hollywood films or city buildings, reflects the values of the society that produced it. The absence of black figures in European art extended to painting black women white, like the Queen of Sheba who was from Ethiopia, and Andromeda who was a Greek mythological figure. In many churches, Jesus is white, sometimes with blue eyes, and God is painted 'in our image' – always white. Conscious or not, it is a lie. Art is frequently used by those in power as a statement of supremacy, a weapon of war through propaganda, and is used very effectively by many dictators. They particularly have a weakness for statues of themselves. They can't have too many.'

'I remember seeing crowds toppling statues of Mussolini and Sadam Hussein after they were deposed,' reflects Graham.

Continuing, Karrle explains, 'In Hollywood, this misrepresentation was because the financiers, filmmakers and audiences were overwhelmingly white, which perpetuated an enormous cultural injustice as the norm. The same is true of Premier League football. Winning is highly visible and fortunes ride on success, so many of the best players are non-white, but appointments to the board rooms are decided by groups of like-minded individuals behind closed doors. Barely any non-white people hold top positions in football management. This subliminal indoctrination pervades the collective subconscious of our culture, resulting in destructive outcomes where white people have defined the identity of black people. If black people accept this, they will continue to be suppressed. Africans are still being represented by the opinions of white Westerners, and sadly, many Africans accept the myths. Even degrees of blackness carry a social stigma.'

Karrle picks up an article that he has been reading about the American writer Dream McClinton and quotes, ' ''American colorism was born out of slavery. As slave masters raped enslaved women, their lighter-skinned illegitimate offspring were given preferential treatment over their darker counterparts, often working in the house as opposed to the fields''.'[1]

He recounts a story. 'I knew a five year old who asked her mum when she would turn white. She knew she was not bad, so she assumed that she would change colour when she got older. These deeply entrenched patterns cannot be removed from our minds, but they can be overwritten by experience and understanding.'

'Yes. I was much older before I understood,' confirms Graham.

'Not everything people learn is right,' replies Karrle. 'Sometimes you have to unlearn. The effect on the suppressed is to reduce people's

---

[1] https://www.theguardian.com/lifeandstyle/2019/apr/08/dark-skinned-black-girls-dont-get-married.

confidence and expectations, which feeds through to lower educational results, lower income opportunities, cheaper housing, restricted social interaction, poorer health and shorter life expectancy. These outcomes are passed down through the generations and create deprived communities within communities, which evolve into ghettos, robbing the next generation of opportunity.

Trevor Phillips, who was chair of the Commission for Racial Equality, calls it ''sunset segregation.'' You may work in the same company, but residential segregation means that in the evening the poor go back to their own community, often on the bus. This is very corrosive to the human spirit and diminishes the individual and society. These abandoned communities become breeding grounds for deep resentment, which can turn into radical and destructive attitudes.'

Graham tries to lighten the conversation. 'There you go again. I make a joke and you make it serious.'

Karrle does not want to trivialise the subject. 'Yes, you can laugh and forget, but you have never walked in black skin. I do – every minute of every day. I only have to ask a stranger for directions and, before I can complete the sentence, they have made assumptions about my social status, employment, intelligence, cleanliness and attractiveness. This is not only wrong and inappropriate but insulting.'

Venturing into history, Karrle continues. 'Early man came from Central Africa so nobody was white, not Jesus, not Mohammed, nobody. As our ancestors moved northwards, dark skin did not absorb enough vitamin D from sunlight and so skin had to become paler. White people are only coloured people who have lost their colour.'

'Ah, so you're saying White is the New Black' muses Graham. 'Well, there's a turn up.'

'No, White is the OLD Black.'

Graham smiles at another challenging concept, as Karrle moves on. 'White skin does not make different types of human being. White is not the centre of anything, apart from itself. To listen to such ignorance is as annoying as white people owning Christianity.'

Challenged again, Graham asks, 'What do you mean?'

'White people have no innate superiority because they are Christian. They act as if England was the birthplace of Christianity and a gift generously bestowed on the poor unfortunates in the British Empire. None of the first Christians were white: they were from the Middle East and Africa. The Church of the East was based in Baghdad, Iraq. Northern

Europeans adopted Christianity rather late, in the seventh century, about the same time as it spread to China. The Christian institutions that organise the faithful are typical of white Europeans – they adopt Christianity, establish the religious organisations that represent God on Earth, and dictate to the rest of the world, thus maintaining control for themselves. Europeans are not blameless or saints. Any sense of moral superiority is misplaced. Their smug arrogance is based on their history of using military might to subjugate other peoples, and plunder their resources for their own benefit. Hardly conducive to a modern Christian attitude, is it? If I did that in this neighbourhood, they would call me a thief and throw me in jail.

European empire builders inflicted great humiliations on other nations that still damage relations today. China's attitude to foreigners is deeply affected by the opium wars with the British. The same is true of the Russians – they are paranoid about being cut off from the world by enemies on their southern borders, which makes it easy for Putin to play on those fears for his own ends. And what crystallised those fears? It was the brutal attacks on Russia by ambitious and greedy Europeans, like Napoleon and Hitler. In World War II, there were 450,000 UK civilian and military deaths. Russia lost 26 million :

**26,000,000** dead in a war they did not start.

The same happened in WW1 and Russia did not start that either.

The British are 1% of the world's population with 0.04% of the world's land. They have a lot to learn if they want to continue benefiting from what the world has to offer. Or maybe "Johnny Foreigner" needs to teach them a few more lessons.'

Graham recoils at this outburst. 'Wow! That was both barrels. Excuse me for existing.'

Karrle has been winding himself up, pauses and collects himself. 'OK, OK, I accept that. Nothing is all good or all bad. All empire builders have used force to dominate others for their own advantage, including kingdoms in Africa, but it is hypocritical to pretend that past actions can be justified as benevolent acts. Any vestiges of old imperial attitudes put the British at a severe disadvantage in working with the rest of the world to address today's problems.'

Curious to know his thoughts, Graham asks, 'So why were the British first to industrialise?'

Graham is impressed by Karrle's immediate answer. 'The Industrial Revolution started in Britain because they had the good fortune to have natural resources like coal and iron ore, and flat land that facilitated the movement of goods, people and ideas, unlike many parts of Africa. Victoria Falls may be attractive for tourists but they are huge natural barriers for trading up and down the river.

Britain also had an open society where the rights of the individual were enshrined in law. Ideas were exchanged; merchants could capitalise on the discoveries of scientists and both were left to focus on their different specialisms. This was a productive breeding ground for the birth of democracy, which is the most common constitutional structure in the world today.'

Knowing that there will be a counter argument Graham quips, 'It sounds like a superior society to me.'

'Britain prides itself that it has not been invaded since 1066. Your country has not suffered hundreds of years of the raping of your resources, people and environment.'

'Fair point!' he concedes.

'This is not a battle over present-day moral judgements on past events, it is recognising what are the challenges of today and working together to solve them for the benefit of all. Unreconciled divisions weaken all of us and today's challenges are no less than in the past.' Karrle has now finished and sits calmly.

Graham is deeply moved by Karrle's passion and awareness of the causes of injustice that are often unwittingly imposed by societies and individuals. It is only now that Graham has an emotional understanding of the challenges faced by migrants wrenched from their homeland, and the alienation of not being accepted where they must make their new home. Humans are social creatures and isolation is a deprivation of their basic need for companionship and respect within the community, wherever it is.

Graham appreciates another stimulating dialogue on important matters, but is always running late and rushes off to his next appointment. By expressing what is important, Karrle is increasingly optimistic that this path of discovery will lead to something of value.

Little do either of them know that Karrle's life is about to change forever.

## Flat 34

This is not the life he had planned for himself or his family. Lech knows he can do a worthwhile job, earn good money and make a profit for anyone who employs him, but when he tries to convince an employment agency to put him forward, he is met with polite justifications as to why there are more suitable candidates. He suspects it is not because he is Polish, it is probably because he has no employment record in this country. Why would an employer take the risk on an unknown when there are so many other good candidates? This is where working at the carwash is a disadvantage because it implies that he has accepted less and may not be capable of more.

Ryszard is no longer at the shared house and has not been seen for weeks; this only emphasises Lech's increasing isolation and growing intolerance towards the other housemates. Estrangement from his family, and the constant daily effort whilst living on survival money in such bleak surroundings, are draining his spirit. He thinks of himself as a good man deserving of respect and, unlike some of his housemates, he respects women. Prostitution is something he is deeply opposed to, but relentless isolation is unbearable.

It is the end of another working day. Although he is tired, he has to get out of the house; anywhere will do, as long as there is space, fresh air and people doing normal things.

Looking through the railings of a local park he sees children laughing and playing, running around with not a worry in the world and wonders what his own children are doing. Meandering aimlessly around, he inexplicably ends up outside the block of flats with the green door.

He stops and stares for several minutes before looking around; all is quiet and there is nobody in sight. He knows he should not be here, but there is nowhere else to go.

Moving towards the, door he tries to open it. It is locked. Good! He is saved from his demons. At that moment, a figure appears on the other side and upon exiting, holds the door open inviting entry. Lech acknowledges the stranger's politeness and walks through, giving an involuntarily, 'Cheers.'

The stranger rejoins, 'See you, mate.'

Now inside, Lech has passed the threshold. What should he do next? Maybe the stranger was a customer and has just left. She might be alone; he does not want to meet anybody else.

Lech takes the stairs; there is a lift, but he does not want to feel trapped. Flat 34 is on the sixth floor. He climbs slowly; he can hear his heart beating. Eventually he arrives at the sixth floor and reads the numbers on the doors. There it is: number 34. The door looks a bit tatty, with boot marks near the bottom. That is not a good sign.

He waits. There is no music, no shouting, no voices. Nothing. Does he want to risk he knows not what, entering the unknowable? Maybe the flat is empty.

Hesitantly, he gently taps on the door, half-hoping but not hoping that it is empty. Then, he would have tried and failed; he has done his best and can go away. Mission accomplished.

An occupant, wearing socks, approaches the door. Lech has no warning until the door suddenly opens, jolting him and creating a huge cavernous invitation into what?

A lethargic, slovenly man, about forty years old, blocks entry. He greets Lech with a puzzled stare. Without an ounce of grace he grunts 'Yeah?' No answer. 'Ave you come to see the girl?'

Lech nods.

'That will be £30. In advance! She's in the end room,' the man says, dictating the rules.

The garage boss has paid £36, cash in hand for today's labour, so Lech has enough to pay the man. The rent is not due until Friday, so that is not a problem for today.

Transaction complete, Lech slowly walks to the end room. Now behind him, and beyond Lech's focus, the man says: 'You got thirty minutes. An hour's fifty quid.'

Lech does not have £50, so that is not an option. So far so good. He has not said anything – apart from 'cheers' to the man downstairs.

The end room is a gauntlet that stretches beyond safety. The corridor is poorly lit, shedding minimal light on shady secrets. Small steps edge Lech ever nearer the door. Stretching for the handle, his hand is unaccountably shaking. He turns and opens it. The door moves too slowly, as if a dark secret is about to be revealed.

The furniture is tatty, neglected and uninviting, confirmation of the humiliating activities and endless indignities it is condemned to witness. This is their last refuge before being thrown on the scrap heap. Like the occupants, they would never be welcome in any respectable household. More of the room is exposed. Ah! There is the obligatory bed and sitting on it, a girl. She looks shockingly nice, a vision of beauty in a den of iniquity.

'Hello,' she says in a quiet voice.

'Hello,' Lech replies in a quieter voice.

'Do you want to close the door?' she suggests.

'Er, yes.' Lech obediently complies. Door closed, they are truly alone. He stands in the middle of the room like a candle.

The girl says, 'You have thirty minutes. What do you want?'

Lech has never been asked such a question. 'I don't know.'

'You must be pleased, or it will be very bad for me.'

'I will be pleased,' he says politely.

Mechanically the girl starts to remove her clothes without any emotion or recognition that he is in the room. He could just as easily be a peeping tom, viewing from another building.

She lays on the bed, covered only by a sheet. Talking to the frozen statue, she directs the next part of the process. 'You had better take your clothes off.'

Without further conversation, Lech meekly does as instructed, standing with his back to the girl to hide his modesty. This is awful, but it is undeniable.

He lays beside the girl. With no eye contact, she touches him. It is totally impersonal and horribly, horribly, wrong, and weird … like exposing something long hidden, but not unwelcome.

Lech feels panicky and unresponsive. What is wrong with him? There is nothing wrong with the girl. Suddenly the physical over-rides the mental. He is caught in the moment, and the girl knows he is about to come.

'Do you want to put it inside me?'

'Yes, please.'

She leans back stretching towards the stained bedside cabinet for a condom, but Lech can no longer contain himself. With a shudder and audible gasp, as if fighting for air, he explodes over the sheets.

His head swims with relief before guilt gradually returns. 'Sorry.'

The girl starts to clean up. 'That's OK.'

'It's been a long time,' he says apologetically.

'Yes, I can tell.'

Lech has been there only minutes and he has bought thirty, but there is no conversation, no point in staying. She has done her job and he is not wanted. Lech gets dressed in stony silence and leaves. As he opens the door, he hesitates for a moment, turns and asks, 'What's your name?'

'Chrystal.'

'Bye, Chrystal. Thank you.' She does not answer.

He returns to the street.

Outside Lech, feels more human and ashamed. What has he done? What has he become?

The girl's deafening silence made it clear what she thought of him, but if she thought so little of him, why was she there? Maybe, like him, she had nowhere else to go.

Both are depressed, and recognising each other's isolation only re-enforces their own. These thoughts are trapped in his head. They cannot be forgotten, nor can they be shared.

## Alex Mugs a Black Man

Football is not the greatest sport in the world. It is the *only* sport.

Football is Alex's life, as it was with his father and his father before him. His son, Andy, plays for the school team; Alex's dream is to see his son play for the club he has devoted his life to. Today is an end-of-season, must-win local derby. All his mates could not be anywhere else but supporting their team.

Tension makes everyone anxious and intolerant. The battle rages end to end, in a desperate struggle to avoid relegation. The home team might survive with a draw, but in the dying seconds an inspirational goal by the away team seals their fate. It is scored by a black player with an unpronounceable name.

The home supporters are sick. And angry. Pouring through the gates of the football ground, they dive into the nearest pub to drown their sorrows in an ocean of lager. All are silent, wallowing in private misery. Eventually words are needed.

Gary invites an explanation. 'How the fuck couldn't they find the net? We had 60% possession!'

'If you can't score, you can't win,' Jim answers with impeccable logic. Although not too bright, everyone has known him since school. He is tolerated like old family furniture, but not today.

'No shit, Sherlock,' snaps Alex, glaring into his pint.

John always says the right thing. 'It's all these bloody foreign players. The leagues are overrun with them, like the country.'

Grinding his teeth, Alex talks into his lager. 'When my dad used to take me, it was local lads playing in front of local supporters. Some of the players even lived within a couple of streets from us. I used to see them in the local chip shop. Now I can't even pronounce half these buggers' names, and we still don't win nothin'.

Jim ventures another comment. 'Some of these minorities are OK, just misunderstood.'

Alex deliberately twists the comment. 'I have the greatest respect for misunderstood minorities, like white, Caucasian, male lager louts. It's not them, your honour, it's the lager.' They all laugh obediently.

At that moment, Gary spots an isolated figure across the road. 'Hey, look at that blackie over there. He looks like the twat who scored the winning goal. Don't look like a millionaire, does he?'

'Another tosser who shouldn't be here!' John is still saying the right things.

Provoked into action, Alex shouts from the pub entrance, 'Oi, twat! Fuck off where you came from.'

The black man ignores the taunts and continues walking on the other side of the road.

'Shithead's still here!' Gary's statement of the obvious prods the group.

Alex rises to the challenge. 'Why don't you go home you fucking black bastard?'

The black man looks isolated and jobless. He does not answer.

Alex , now enflamed, shouts each word slowly above all competing noises: 'I ... SAID... WHY ... THE ... FUCK ... DON'T ... YOU ... PLAY ... THE ... WHITE ... MAN ... AND... FUCK ... OFF ... BACK ... TO ... BONGO-BONGO ... LAND!'

The black man stops and slowly turns fully facing his hecklers. This is the final straw. Sick to death of diplomatic retreats, his mind snaps and a red mist descends. Now someone else, this is one verbal battle he is not going to lose.

'May I enquire which white man is that? The one who conquered our lands, raped our women and stole our resources, or the one who believes in tolerance, democracy and equal rights?'

This is a challenge that Alex does not know how to answer. He can only retort, 'Say that again, blackie.'

The lone pedestrian surveys England's finest: a bunch of drunk morons. 'You're too full of self-importance to understand your own insignificance.'

All eyes move to Alex as the pub falls silent. Provoked and the centre of attention Alex cannot back down. 'Look, shithead, you're in my country. Fuck off home.'

The verbal superiority of the black man is designed to highlight the inferiority of the unthinking. 'Ah, I forgot. You believe you are the centre of the universe. Sorry to break the news, but you are a miniscule irrelevance. When you depart this earth, the tiny splash and infinitesimal ripples will fade to nothing as if you had never existed. You will remain somewhere out of sight, re-joining the earth from whence you came.'

Stunned, blinking in disbelief, John still manages to find the right words for the audience. 'Alex, you're not taking that shit off a nigger, are you?'

Venting his rage, confrontation is inevitable and Alex has the only army. He slams his pint down and strides menacingly towards his target, followed by the pack. The black man stands motionless in disbelief as this short, thick-set man spins his body and lands his clenched knuckles squarely in the face of his defenceless victim.

As he staggers back, the mob attacks, raining blows with fists and feet. In trying to avoid one blow, a delicious boot from behind crashes into his midriff, producing an exquisite, agonising contortion.

The team are spurred on by whooping cries of encouragement and self-congratulation. All resistance is quickly extinguished; as the earth spins and voices fade, the victim retreats beyond reach into darkness.

As the severity of the assault becomes evident one gang member exclaims, 'Alex, that's enough. We gotta go. We got form round 'ere.'

Alex gives one last kick, targeting his victim's head which whips back with a sickening thud on the pavement. 'Now, THAT's enough!' he declares with obvious glee.

Tension released, the group run off and disperse, satisfied with a job well done. The limp body caresses the pavement as red submits to gravity and trickles into the gutter. A girl attempts to go to the victim's aid and is restrained by a stranger. 'Don't get involved, luv. Let the police handle it.'

The pub staff are informed and an ambulance is called. Left half-dead, the victim is taken to Coventry University Hospital. His condition is serious.

Two hours later, the police arrive. Despite there being dozens of people present, there are no witnesses. The officers believe it might be a football hate crime, but they do not know whether it is the home or away supporters. The victim does not appear to be a football fan.

Despite the seriousness of the assault, with no leads this is a low priority crime. At the police station the investigation is concluded with the completion of a dozen forms and filed under 'unsolved crimes'.

## Lure of 34

Nothing is as it should be. Lech is exhausting himself, risking everything and achieving nothing. Endangering all his links to decency, he contemplates a path that is as perilous as it is inexplicable. Against all logic, he decides to try and see the girl again, if only to make things right in his own head.

After work, he has a shower and knocks on the door of flat 34. A different man opens it. Lech stretches his arm out, offering £30. 'I've come to see Chrystal.'

'Who?... Oh.' The Minder laughs and takes the money. 'She's in there.'

'Is it the same Indian girl who was here last week?'

'Yes. We only have one Indian girl. Very popular.'

This time Lech walks straight in. The room and the girl are unchanged. That is a relief. He announces himself. 'Hello again.'

The girl offers nothing but an uncaring glance. 'What do you want me to do?' she says without any eye contact. She had used the same words before. This is obviously the standard line to every 'john' (customer) and Chrystal is not her name.

This is not what he came for. 'Can we talk?'

'Yes, as long as you like. I prefer talking, but you only have thirty minutes.'

'My name is Lech. What is your real name?'

'Chrystal.'

'I don't think it is. Why won't you tell me?'

'This is my life now, and my name is Chrystal.'

He can see how unwelcome his prying questions are. 'OK Chrystal. I did not mean to upset you. I just want to be your friend.'

Anger flashes across her face at this obvious perversion of friendship: 'What? By fucking me?' She never speaks like this, but this isn't her and it seems right.

'No,' Lech says. 'I was lonely. Don't you get lonely?'

'No. Every day I have friends come and fuck me!'

'Sorry.' Failing to respond meaningfully, the conversation is lost and he remains silent.

Irritated beyond words, and having no desire to talk any more, she instructs her naïve abuser, 'Just do it and go!'

Not knowing what to say, the actions follow the normal routine. She takes her clothes off and lies on the bed. Lech does as he is told. No words are exchanged and he leaves.

What a disaster. That is not why he went there. Now he feels worse; he has spent the money that was meant for his family. In Poland, he is respected; in England people do not respect him and now he is losing self-respect.

He does not phone his wife that week.

## Karrle Meets Rose

Rose does her rounds as a volunteer at the hospital, usually Monday, Wednesday and Friday, with occasional extra days covering for absentees. Today there is a new patient, heavily bandaged with numerous visible injuries. He has so many bandages he is almost mummified. Rose approaches the bed and, projecting professional jolliness, tries to initiate a conversation. 'Hello, dear. Would you like a cup of tea?'

Karrle does not answer.

'Would you like a newspaper?'

Karrle does not answer.

'Can I get you anything else?'

'No.'

Rose can see that he is deeply traumatised. She does not know what to say. 'OK, dear. I will be here Wednesday in case you want anything.'

## Rose's Hospital Round

Wednesday arrives and Rose follows her usual hospital rounds. Approaching the new patient, she tries to engage him in conversation, offering her best cheery smile. 'Good morning.'

'Not for me,' replies the motionless occupant.

Maintaining her buoyant tone, Rose continues, 'The doctors are very good here. I am sure you will feel better when you are well again.'

Karrle does not answer. Seeing how depressed he is, Rose tries to address the issue. 'You're going to be here a long time. I always believe it is good to talk. Can I get you anything? We have a very good library. Would you like a book to read?

'Yes. The Book of REB.'

'I don't know that one. Who wrote it?.

'No one. I've not written it yet.'

'Oh … right.' Rose is not sure if he is being deliberately provocative, but she decides to give him the benefit of the doubt. 'What's it about?'

'It's about why I am here and nobody cares.'

Knocked back, Rose flounders for something to say. After several moments she continues, 'I'm sorry to hear that. I care.'

'But what can you do about it?' returns the uncooperative patient.

'I don't know.' And accepting defeat for today, Rose leaves.

## Lech Decides Never to Return ... Until

Lech resolves to write off flat 34 as a terrible experience. It has achieved nothing, wasted precious money, and the stress is awful. He sends money home the following week and tells his wife that he has been too ill to work, but it was nothing serious and he is better now.

His wife says she has sold his bike to pay for the school uniform. It is the best bike Lech has ever owned, but what can he say? Just life ratcheting down another notch to a new low.

Two weeks later, the girl's conversation is still in his head; it was all wrong, and cannot be lef like that. He decides to return to the flat to make things better, or at least try. This time he is not nervous; he is on a mission.

Lech pays the man £30, strides down the hall and opens the bedroom door. The girl looks worn out and defeated, a look he recognises all too well. 'Hello.'

The girl stares at him momentarily but does not answer. She starts to take her clothes off. Lech sits on the bed. 'Sit down please. Look! I'm not going to touch you. I just want to talk.'

For the first time she is startled by the comment and focuses her attention on Lech.

'Can you tell me a little about yourself, please?' he asks.

The girl blocks any discourse. 'There's nothing to say.'

'Please?'

She can see that he is lonely and doesn't mean any harm, but she wants to forget her past and her present, so what is there to talk about? Sighing, she offers the most superficial summary she can muster. 'I lived in India until I was fifteen and came over here with my family. I liked England until I met these people.'

'Can't you leave?'

'And go where? My father would not have me back. I have disgraced the family. He said I should stick with my own kind, and he was right. That's all I want you to know. What about you? Where is your family?'

'In Poland. I came here for work, but I cannot earn enough to live a decent life. I came to see you because I am lonely.'

Studying him with fresh eyes, she realises he is not a bad man, just in a bad place. 'We can have sex if you like?'

He is deeply touched by the sincerity of her offer and smiles into her eyes. 'No, thank you. I would rather have your friendship.'

To offer herself because she thought it would make him happy means so much to him. She felt that the only thing she has to offer was her body for his physical gratification, but she has something more unobtainable that Lech needs: friendship.

Unearthing forgotten memories, they talk about their private thoughts, both shielding from a hostile world. As he leaves, they put their arms around each other. Her worn face softens and delivers a genuine smile that will warm Lech's heart for a long time. They have shared themselves, re-affirming their humanity if only for a fleeting moment.

As Lech returns to the shared house, there is a discernible skip in his step.

## Not All Wounds Heal

Rose is aware that Karrle is not only physically damaged but has serious issues in his life. This troubles her; she wants to help, but what can she do?

By chance, her suggestion of books from the library seems to have struck gold, and Karrle immediately becomes her most avid reader. He requests books about politics, history and economics, all of which are of no interest to her, and with incomprehensible titles. If they are highly specialised or on waiting lists, they often take a long time to arrive, which Karrle finds very frustrating, but it creates opportunities for chatting.

As their conversations progress, a natural warmth grows between them. Rose finds herself staying a little longer each time and so, like Graham, she starts to make Karrle the last visit of the day.

Despite his troubles, which she is mindful not to probe into, she can see Karrle is highly intelligent. Her genuine interest and tactful questions are polite and unchallenging, and Karrle looks forward to their talks. When kindness is a rarity, it is appreciated more and Graham is the only other person since he left Africa more than two years ago who has listened to his thoughts.

Rose asks why he is in England and he starts to tell of the events leading up to him fleeing his country. These stories shock Rose who cannot believe that anybody would behave like that. Posing the obvious question she asks, 'Couldn't you go to the police?'

'They are the ones carrying out the atrocities. The police were the biggest gang on the streets.'

Rose does not know how to react. She has no experiences that she can relate to these events. 'But you are safe now. Has seeing these awful things made you stronger?'

'No,' Karrle says emphatically. Deliberating thoughtfully he continues, 'Inside … something … died. At the time there were no tears. My paralysed emotions did not return until I learnt about the loss of my friend. It was then that I realised the scarring was permanent.'

Following his own thoughts he continues. 'The lowest point was realising that I was powerless to protect those I love most. Now I understand the suffering of others it reminds me of the pain I caused the people I love. Even innocent comments trigger flashbacks; I will never escape. Distance and time are not a cure, they just make me feel more isolated and angry.'

He pauses and thinks for a minute. 'I want to free myself from the past. Now I speak my mind, I feel freer. That is why I will write *The Book of REB*. It is my defence and the nearest I will get to repairing the damage.'

They are both silent, each in their own thoughts. Eventually Rose says supportively, 'Well, I think you are very brave.'

'I am not brave. My actions caused the death of a very courageous and dear friend and brought needless danger to my family and his. Now he is with me every step I take, there is no escape from thinking about the events that led to his death. I ran away to save myself and deserted my friend, who was captured and brutally tortured to death.'

'What could you have done?'

'I should have let him leave, and escaped when he was safe. They were not after him and he risked his life to save me. That body in the ditch should have been mine. Whenever I see unnecessary suffering, it reminds me of what he suffered and I did not.'

Rose feels compelled as ask the next question. 'Why did you not do that?'

'It happened so fast. I had no time to think.'

Considering the evidence she offers words of comfort. 'Your friend would not blame you, and nor should you.'

Karrle is grateful for Rose's sympathy but cannot be consoled. 'Rationalising does not remove the burden that I will always carry. Inside I am weak, barely holding myself together. I can sit alone, remember events in my life and cry. It is less painful to keep my emotions locked away. I would do anything to stop the pain, but I cannot because I have a responsibility to those I deserted.'

She offers reassurance as best she can. 'Well, I think you are strong.'

'I don't want to be strong, I want to be me. I lost touch with who I was. I was searching for myself… I was not well. It took life to hurt me really badly before I learnt to fight back, uncovering aspects of myself I did not recognise. Failure gave me the freedom to discover myself. It is the environment you live in that determines what you are. I am a different person and have to live life with who I am now. The damage I sustained has taught me what is important, making it easier to recognise what is important in the lives of others. It has given me new targets that would not have been possible without these experiences. Now I believe that the more I share, the richer I am.'

'You still stand up for what you believe in.'

'The bad things that I have seen have not changed my belief in what is right, they just provide more evidence of the damage caused by what is wrong.'

'You are a good man. I am sure you will do the right things.'

Leaving his mother in danger, crossing Africa, his uncertain status in England, and lying in hospital having been attacked, Karrle's faint reply, acknowledges the daunting challenge. 'I will try.'

'Thank you for sharing those stories. I hope it did not upset you too much.'

Karrle shrugs. 'These thoughts are in my head. I live with them every day, but I feel better for putting them into words and I have nobody else to talk to. Thank you for listening.'

'I will see you Friday. Goodbye, dear.'

Rose collects the empty cups and biscuit packet, leaving Karrle with the remnants of their conversation. She thinks about Karrle, how damaged he is, and wonders what more she can do to help. By the following day she has thought something.

## Coveted Employment For Lech

The spring on the tinny letterbox cracks shut, followed by the dull thud of newspaper on the hallway floor. A Polish housemate pads to the door and gathers it up and, as always, thumbs through the jobs section. One advert catches his eye: a local factory is hiring sixty workers.

Mentioning this opportunity to a couple of housemates generates little enthusiasm; only Lech and the Ukrainian decide to apply, and the two of them go together. The job is skill specific and his friend fails the interview. Lech starts nervously, but as they get deeper into the job specification the interviewer is impressed by his technical knowledge and attitude and offers him a job: full-time, permanent, tax-paying employment.

After two harsh years of struggle, continuous disillusionment and suppressed emotions, the door that Lech has desperately been waiting to open finally obliges, and he joins the English. Like the re-appearance of a long absent friend, control of his life is returning and the permanent anxiety that he never learnt to live with subsides, as if gravity has been banished.

Rediscovering himself, escapism becomes less important and the nightly drinking stops. With the higher wages, he focuses on planning for the future, sending more money to his wife each week, returning home at Christmas with presents and starting to repair the damage that his long absence has caused every member of the family.

Lech learns that his employment is with a long-established family business, now run by the son of the founder, a man called Charles. People say Charles is bright and ambitious, and is always looking for opportunities to expand the business. Lech is only part of the latest wave of recruitment. One cloud on the horizon is a rumour that the boss is looking to cut costs through automation; the only thing stopping him is the inability to find reliable machines without jeopardising quality. This dark cloud gives many workers a constant sense of insecurity.

A strange comment from one of the older men who apparently has been there for years sticks in Lech's mind: 'He's not a patch on his old man. 'is life was a fuck up until the old man retired. His problem is he's like Donald Trump, has to be seen to be better than his dad.' Most strange!

To Lech, Charles sounds like a fine businessman and anyway, he is just grateful to have a job.

## Food for Thought

Rose polishes off her round at the hospital with a visit to Karrle. 'Morning dear. I have brought you some fruit. I didn't know what to get, so I chose a few different types. I hope they are what you like.'

'You did not need to bother, but thank you. I will enjoy eating them.'

'That's OK. I wanted to.'

Karrle eyes open wide as he spots an Irvingia Gabonensis, African mango. 'You managed to get an African mango. How brilliant of you! They are so difficult to find in this country. I will enjoy that after my supper tonight.' He selects a banana. 'It is a welcome relief from hospital food. It is not very nice. I am not surprised they throw away over 4,000 meals a week.'

Banana finished, Rose broaches the subject she had thought of earlier. 'You mentioned that you wanted to write a book. Can I ask what it is about?'

Karrle dismisses his work as frivolous. 'Nothing. It's just an idea.'

Knowing that he never does anything trivial, Rose persists. 'I am interested, if you would like to tell me.'

There is a significant pause. Karrle puts down the orange he was about to peel. 'It's trying to explain why people have beliefs that they think are universal truths, and yet there is so much misunderstanding, division and conflict in the world.'

'Yes, I sometimes wonder about that. What do you think it is?'

'It's complicated and I'm tired. Can we talk about it tomorrow?'

'I don't work Thursdays, but I will be in Friday. I would like to know what you think, if you would like to tell me. Goodbye, dear. Enjoy your fruit. See you Friday.'

Karrle wonders how he is going to explain his thoughts. He is tired and not sure if he can explain it in a way that this lady will understand.

## No Plan for Planet A and No Planet B

The police inform Graham's office that one of his clients is in hospital having been assaulted. He decides he must see his friend and makes enquires about visiting hours. Wandering through the hospital corridors, he eventually finds the ward, but cannot conceal his shock at Karrle's visible injuries.

'Oh my God, Karrle. Sorry I have taken so long to visit. The police were very slow at informing the office. What on earth happened?'

Recounting the events, Karrle displays surprising objectivity and remarkable inner strength. Graham is greatly relieved that his friend appears to have suffered little psychological damage, but can't escape the thought that the rationalisation of these events may be evidence that he is in emotional denial. That does not prevent the two men renewing their friendship, with the usual banter, almost wallowing in each other's company.

An inquisitive insect appears from nowhere and settles on the bed. Karrle stops talking and focuses on the visitor. Transforming a piece of paper into a magic carpet, he slides the modified transport under the unintroduced guest and, despite his personal discomfort, he climbs out of his bed to an open window, and gently lowers then shakes the paper. Not understanding the opportunity offered, the insect clings onto what it knows before slipping into the garden for a soft landing.

Graham had expected a terminal solution. 'My wife kills creepy-crawlies on sight.'

'Fear comes from what we don't understand. "Creepy-crawlies" were on this planet millions of years before us, and created the world that enabled humans to evolve. They are vital to our survival today.'

'My wife can survive without them. Maybe that is proof she is not human. I've always had my suspicions.'

Karrle elevates the conversation on an extremely important issue. 'That is because we don't understand the processes that created and sustain life. These relationships are invisible to us, even though they are vital to our survival.'

Graham looks uncomprehending but curious on concepts that are obviously unfamiliar. Karrle expounds further. 'The first life forms evolved in the sea three billion years ago. The earliest life forms on land that we are aware of, were mushrooms around 500 million years ago. They eat rock, extracting minerals producing surplus food which allowed plants and insects to evolve. But mushrooms are not plants, they have a cell structure similar to humans because we share a common ancestry.'[1]

Graham's eyes open like shop windows. 'Get away!'

Karrle continues. 'Spines developed from fish, as did skulls, muscles, fins and jaws. Millions of years later, lungs and limbs evolved which we inherited from amphibians – water-based animals with a spine, like frogs and toads. The first land animals appeared 450 million years ago. Insects developed wings to access the air. Reptiles dominated the land but were cold blooded and could only be active in sunlight, the opposite of Dracula (he quips). Later still, mammals[2] developed warm blood but were very small, which enabled them to move around at night when the retiles were not active and hide during the day. Then, sixty-five million years ago, a six-mile-wide asteroid struck the earth off the coast of Mexico, killing most of the dinosaurs and allowing the evolution of warm-blooded, hairy, intelligent mammals like whales, meerkats and apes, of which we are a very recent variation. Some smaller reptiles survived and evolved into birds.[3]'

Remaining silent, Graham is interested, but cannot see what the point is.

'All life forms on earth are carbon based, but when the Earth formed there was no oxygen. It was released by biological organisms absorbing carbon forming carbohydrates – photosynthesis – and releasing the oxygen back into the air. The main providers of oxygen were plankton, and later trees, which today accounts for around 80% of the oxygen produced. Plants and insects created the environment in which man exists today, from the air we breathe to the food we eat, the clothes we wear and the water we drink. Tell me, Graham, do you ever think about the other creatures we share the planet with?'

'Every time I have dinner,' Graham retorts, smiling at his own humour.

Undeterred, Karrle pursues the point. 'I was looking at a photo of the world taken from space. Earth is a ball on its own, which barely interacts with the wider universe apart from receiving energy from the

---

[1] Paul Stamets

[2] *Rise of Animals,* David Attenborough

[3] *Rise of the Mammals,* PBS America

sun and being held in its orbit by the gravitational pull of the solar system.'

Sitting back, Graham observes, 'I feel this is going to take me on a long journey.'

Karrle develops his thoughts: 'From a distance, the Earth appears very simple, but in reality everything is immeasurably complicated. Every living organism depends on a global eco-system, a web of delicately balanced, inter-dependences, connected by the universal struggle for survival. Insects form an infinite number of tiny architects that create the world into which man evolved. They are more important to the world than humans. Mankind cannot survive without the activities of insects, but insects will survive and prosper without man. Humans delude themselves that they are masters of their own destiny, ignoring the reality of their total dependence on things they do not understand and take for granted. In the world of complex interdependence, there is no hierarchy among the issues.[1]

Graham looks perplexed. 'Excuse me for interrupting, professor, but what does that mean?'

'It means that if the predator cannot survive without the prey, then they are both equally dependent on the stability of the environment that sustains them both. We understand very little about the creatures on whose activities we are totally dependent. That is dangerous because we cannot assess risk if it is not visible to us until destruction occurs.

Many people think that because to date we are the most advanced creature on the planet, this confers entitlement. Unless it is of use for us, like race horses, anybody who forms a relationship with another species is inadequate, compensating for their inability to relate to other humans. I think the opposite.'

'Why am I not surprised?' agrees Graham with a smile.

Settling into a steady rhythm Karrle presents his analysis. 'Many life forms have appeared and disappeared. Synapsids were creatures similar to mammals and dominated the land until they were wiped out 251 million years ago by volcanic eruptions in Russia, which covered one million square miles. Dinosaurs then became the dominant land animal until an asteroid destroyed their environment. We relate to mammals because we evolved together and have much in common. Communicating

---

[1] http://ijbssnet.com/journals/Vol_6_No_2_February_2015/33.pdf

across species is an evolutionary development, not a regression. Not to be able to relate to something because it is different is a limitation.

The more we learn, the more we observe how universal are the intimate relationships of animal to animal, animal to plant, and plant to plant, and vital for the eco-system on which all life depends. We believe that what we see is everything is there, but there are colours, light and sounds that exist that our senses cannot receive. Research shows that mice sing as beautifully as birds but the sound is pitched beyond our hearing range, so we hear nothing. There are billions of interactions in nature of which we are completely unaware. So, Graham, why is it that many British old ladies have cats?'

Graham bounces back, 'Because their horizons are shrinking and they don't go out of the house to meet other people.'

'It is partly because of isolation which is one of the biggest social problems for British citizens and migrants alike, but also because the elderly have the time and make the effort to form relationships. Children have a natural affinity with animals, but modern society shields us from so many experiences of the natural world that it's no wonder that over time we lose connection with our instincts. For many people, nature is what we stare at through double-glazed windows. We are conditioned to think that everything unfamiliar is threatening. The movie industry has made multiple fortunes by projecting danger as something unknown that is sneaking up to do us harm.

The truth is that cooperation between species enriches the lives of both. Christianity has done a lot of damage by propagating the idea that all the animals were put on earth for man's use, entitling us to do what we want with them. This is arrogant, dangerous nonsense. Man came very late to the party and has learnt to use what he has found. As long as mankind deludes themselves that man is the most important thing in the universe, they will not look beyond themselves.

Some of the Far Eastern philosophies have far more respect for nature and our place within it. As the most intelligent creatures on the planet, mankind has the unique opportunity to learn how the world works. This is a privilege accessible now that should be acknowledged with wonderment, not a calculation as to how we can exploit it for our personal gain whilst taking no responsibility for our actions. We are murdering the natural world that we are utterly dependent on without knowledge, respect or gratitude. We should have the deepest veneration for all life on the planet.'

Graham butts in with a light-weight contribution, 'It's a bit late to befriend the chicken on my plate.' Karrle is not impressed. Lifting his hand in recognition that his frivolity is trivialising important issues, Graham recants. 'OK, OK, I hear what you're saying! But you must admit that animal welfare is given increasing importance, and there are loads of nature programmes on the television, so we are learning more about other creatures.'

Karrle nods his head, acknowledging the point, then responds, 'There is accumulating evidence that factory farming inflicts enormous cruelty on animals. As for nature programmes, the documentaries provide information but the world is seen through a lens which removes any meaningful human experience and diminishes everything to an intellectualised, sterile entertainment, alongside Disney and the latest films. Early man must have been much nearer nature, but now even Africans are losing touch. I am always amazed watching documentaries about some of the remotest peoples in the world and the natives wear T-shirts probably made in China.'

Graham thinks of an example where man is venturing beyond the Earth. 'Elon Musk wants to go to Mars by 2040.'

'That is only possible within the laws of nature. The more we damage the environment, the more we diminish our children's heritance.'

Graham listens quietly following the flow of ideas, not feeling that he can disagree with any of the statements as they unfold like waves on a rising tide, imperceptibly but remorselessly edging a little higher up the beach. He wonders where the high-tide mark will be and decides to go with the flow, but not before defending the status quo. 'The dangers of global warming are widely recognised and governments are taking action.'

Karrle puts these efforts into context. 'The majority of the public do not want their lifestyles to change, and governments don't believe they have the support of the public for the drastic actions required, despite evidence from the world's academics. The impact of global warming on sea levels, the threat of rising temperatures on corals, sea life, land creatures and plants is well known, but there is another danger where we understand very little, which means the risks cannot be calculated and might be even higher.'

Graham looks surprised. 'Really. What is that?'

'Biodiversity. We are losing up to ten thousand species a year and the rate is accelerating[1]. Two out of five plants are facing extinction[2]. In the UK, farmland birds have declined 58% since 1970; in Germany, the biomass of insects has dropped 76% since 1989, and in Puerto Rico rainforest insects have declined up to 98% in thirty-five years. The natural balance of the oceans are being destroyed as large predatory fish are being stripped from oceans that have become 30% more acidic since the Industrial Revolution.[3] Even the ocean currents are changing, on which the balance of all life depends.

Man selected plants with the properties to become food in an exclusive partnership, poisoning their competitors and sterilising the land. Mono-agriculture, like monotheism (single-belief systems), takes vast areas of land for the cultivation of a single crop – 80% of the world's cultivated land is used to produce meat for us to eat. Mono-cultures exhaust the soil and create fragile environments where small changes can have catastrophic results, making the planet uninhabitable. Bio-diversity is bio-security. By reducing diversity, it diminishes a species' ability to adjust to change, increasing the probability of extinction. This goes against the history of life on earth. It is projected that one million creatures are in danger of extinction, the sixth mass extinction, and the first caused by animals – us![4]

Mankind is behaving as if the actions that benefit us as individuals get lost in the vastness of the world and have no cumulative consequences. Outcomes appear increasingly distant from our day-to-day existence. The longer the supply chain, the more complex the connections become, and the less visibility we have on the things on which our survival depends. The more the bubble becomes artificial, the more the natural world is treated as 'unnatural' and threatening. Living in denial is not a solution because all life forms are interconnected within the same eco-system in a finite world.

We may be top of the food chain for now, but focusing exclusively on ourselves without recognising our dependence on the pyramid of life will cause our own destruction. Man will die out before insects do, yet we have dangerously little understanding of the impact of

---

[1] The Garden Jungle by Dave Goulson

[2] David Attenborough

[3] Mark Carney, ex-governor of the Bank of England

[4] David Attenborough

the extinction of any species on the delicate relationships of the eco-system. There are projections forecasting a 40% extinction of insects within a few decades, and virtually all insects within a hundred years.[1] "One of the biggest impacts of insect loss is on the many birds, reptiles, amphibians and fish that eat insects … If this food source is taken away, all these animals starve to death."

A UN report suggests that 30% of the world's agricultural land is already degraded and the world has only 60 harvests left.[2] It takes a thousand years to produce three centimetres of soil. You cannot exhaust the soil and whack in a few chemicals and pretend that everything will be alright. That is playing Russian roulette with many species including humanity. Respecting people's freedom does not extend to the right to kill the rest of us. What sort of lunatic logic allows actions that will kill the planet? This questions our fondly held notion that we are intelligent, civilised, superior creatures. Humans are taking what they want by destroying what we *need*, vandalising beauty and burning the book of knowledge before they have read it. The climatologist Jane Goodall believes the loss of bio-diversity could spell the end of humans on earth – and factory farming is a major step in that direction.'

Graham is shaken out of his comfort zone. 'What can be done about it?'

'We need to downgrade our lifestyle. The good life needs to be culturally driven, not consumption driven. Not being part of the rat race is a journey of exploration of self and the world. Being close to nature, including animals, is good for diffusing stress, mental health and happiness. What is required is a total rethink and immediate, drastic action.'

'Such as?'

'I don't know,' Karrle admits. 'Mankind knows how to take what has been laid down over millions of years, but does not know how the world works and therefore how to live sustainably. The media dominate with news about minor changes to the entitlement of sectors of society, and then select examples of vulnerable people which is a total distraction from the important issues. Consumption in the West is 20% to 50% too

---

[1] https://www.theguardian.com/environment/2019/feb/10/plummeting-insect-numbers-threaten-collapse-of-nature

[2] https://www.scientificamerican.com/article/only-60-years-of-farming-left-if-soil-degradation-continues/

high. It is not only inequitable in terms of wealth distribution throughout the world, but also completely unsustainable. There needs to be a total rethink about how societies function.'

'So we are screwed,' Graham concludes.

'No, there is always a solution, but not necessarily the one you want.'

'You always say that. I can't see any.'

'Some immediate actions are obvious,' says Karrle. 'Stop using fossil fuels and use natural energy – wind, waves, solar and volcanic.

Net-zero carbon emissions is an imperative, and well before 2050. By destroying the processes that store carbon, $CO_2$ levels are the highest for 800,000 years[1].

One hundred per cent cessation of deforestation. Reforestation should be a minimum of 110% of current usage. Timber should not be sold on the international market without authorisation from an international body that can enforce quotas and penalties. Wetlands (peatbogs) store twice as much carbon as the world's forests and are easy to bring back, like the London Wetlands Centre. Since 1900, 64% of the world's wetlands have disappeared.

Existing soil should be nurtured and re-used. More wild flowers, a greater range of pollinators, more forest and grassland. Even degraded land can be used for wild plants. Weeds are pioneers, and animals return naturally.

Legal protection of plants, insects, animals, birds and fish incorporated into international law. It should be a criminal offense to destroy them, with severe punishments.

Drastically reduce food waste. Buy locally produced food. The longer the food chain, the higher the proportion of food that is wasted and the more vulnerable all societies become.

Single-use plastics should be banned unless essential and there are no substitutes. Britain exports 457,000 tonnes [2] (www.letsrecycle.com) of plastic every year. It is not biodegradable and enters the land, sea and air, damaging all creatures. Most clothes contain plastic, and every wash releases millions of fibres into the environment[3].

---

[1] Mark Carney

[2] Mark Carney

[3] BBC, War on Plastic

Pesticides should be banned, and man should be prepared for the reduction in yields per acre. One way to sharply reduce the consumption is to tax all high-polluting meats, including beef.'

Graham protests, 'The British love their meat. They will never agree to that.'

'Attitudes change rapidly when driven by necessity. Look at Covid and mask wearing, or attitudes to smoking. Initially the reaction to restrictions on where people could smoke was seen as an invasion of civil liberties. Now it is considered extremely anti-social to impose smoke fumes on others because we know the health risks. Similarly, with income tax. In 1799 it was introduced as a temporary measure to pay for the Napoleonic wars, and now the British accept heavy taxes on alcohol, tobacco and fuel, all of which damage humans. Why eat meat and expect somebody else to pay for the damage caused?

What we are talking about is lowering our standard of living, raising the quality of life and enriching our future. We don't know how to do that yet, but if we want to survive we will have to learn.

The public can improve the environment in their own gardens by growing plants that are natural to the environment and attract insects, birds and animals. The best thing for a garden is to build a pond, even two square metres, and put in a few water lilies. It will be a magnet for wildlife. Domestic gardens should have 10% of their land completely untouched to allow nature to take its own course, with its location written into the deeds of the property.'

Graham can only see problems in all of these suggestions. 'Think of the weeds that would drift to the rest of the garden. People would hate that.'

Refusing to accept that argument, Karrle counters, 'As soon as man stops altering the land, nature starts returning it to its natural state. Death is merely nature reclaiming us. What you call weeds are natural to the local environment, and are part of the ecology that is vital to our existence. Plants from different parts of the world may look pretty to human eyes, but they produce deserts as far as indigenous species are concerned. If nothing is done, people will have far worse forced upon them, including global conflicts between the "haves" and the "have nots". Remember, the British have economic wealth at the moment, but are "have nots" in terms of the food and materials they need for their population and factories.

Despite the blindness of mankind's self-belief, humans are of very little significance beyond themselves. Man is only a temporary interlude. If we disappear, other life forms will not stop evolving and the gap we leave will be filled by something else. Humans are a net negative for the world. If each species in the world had one vote, humans would probably be the most hated creatures of all time. Indeed, David Attenborough has described humans as "a plague on Earth".'

Graham admires Karrle's ideas but is sceptical that they can be achieved. 'I see the points you are making, but they are very drastic. What are the chances that they will happen?'

Karrle does not need time to reflect. 'Very slim!'

'If that is true, doesn't it make all your ideas pointless?'

This time Karrle pauses before commenting. 'There is not the political will. The countries of the world deal with each other as independent states, frequently requiring unanimity before decisions are agreed. Even then, they often do not carry them out. Look at the 2010 Copenhagen Agreement where the rich nations promised $100 billion a year to support the developing countries with the costs of climate change. By 2020, only a tiny fraction of that had been delivered. Why would countries like Russia, Saudi Arabia, Australia and Brazil, which are heavily dependent on fossil-fuel exports, cut off most of their national income? COP 26 in November 2021 reaffirmed the commitment to restricting the rise in temperature to 1.5C, but based on current actions, forecasters predict that we are heading for 2.7C. You come from a country where life is comfortable but cannot sustain itself. Britain is living off the resources of the rest of the world. Catastrophe may not be visible until it is unavoidable.'

'So we are doomed,' Graham repeats, finding this outcome more credible.

'Not if there is a fundamental change of attitude.'

Graham cannot see a solution. 'So what will change attitudes?'

'*The Book of REB*!' Karrle answers with confidence.

'Huh! Best of luck with that one!'

Karrle is not offended by Graham's laughter, it just illustrates the scale of the attitude problem. 'We are slowly recognising our inter-connections, but massively ignorant of our inter-dependence. If ever there was a time for shared values and collective intelligence, it is now.'

Graham responds, 'I'm glad I came to cheer you up. Maybe you'll do the same for me sometime!' When he leaves, his head is spinning from these challenging ideas. He is more broad minded than many, but still has a lot to absorb before he accepts how much his lifestyle impacts the planet, and how urgently he needs to act. Still, today is a small step.

## Rose Is Introduced to *The Book of REB*

On Friday, Rose arrives at the hospital and completes her rounds. As usual, she makes Karrle her last visit; she is in no hurry to go home and enjoys their talks. 'Morning Karrle. You are looking better today. How are you feeling?'

'I am improving, thank you.'

Wasting no time, she broaches the subject on her mind. 'Can I ask you about your book?'

Karrle does not really know where to begin. His deliberations suggest that this is going to take a long time, so Rose decides to sit on the bedside chair. Focusing on something not in the room, but with affirmative glances towards Rose, he starts to explain the role of belief systems as the linchpin holding societies together, re-enforced with rules. Pausing, he checks that he has explained it clearly, 'Does that make sense?'

'I think so. Everybody needs rules.'

Moving on he explains how rules deal with specific circumstances and as circumstances change, the old rules may be inappropriate for the new challenges. This can cause conflict for individuals, within and between groups. He continues, 'The original story will be defended as the group acts to isolate or destroy any dissenters, unless the position becomes untenable. Then history will be re-written and a seamless change will be presented as if it has always been so. This is normal and healthy for the group to realign with present reality and happens all the time.

Everyone makes judgements about their place in the world viewed through the porthole of their own experiences. Each person's *Book of REB* is unique to them, so there is a constant battle to interpret their experiences within what they are told to believe. Migrants arriving in this country can find this particularly challenging as can the local population.'

'Yes I see. Er … thank you. That has given me a lot to think about. Would you like another cup of tea?' She only partly understands. Karrle is a clever man and it sounds important but heavy.

She gives Karrle's comments little thought. She does not think she has a *Book of REB* and yet she is curious to know more.

## Alex Hospitalises a Prostitute

Saturday is the best day of the week, especially when Alex's team are playing at home. When they win he is in heaven, losing makes life abysmal.

They have been losing a lot recently. Today is the worst: beaten 5–0; he leaves the football stadium seething with rage. The manager selected the wrong strategy. The players looked lost on the pitch performing like buffoons, making basic school boy errors. Two players were sent off, and given the way the team performed, 10–0 would not have been unexpected. Alex is as sick as a pig.

As a faithful season ticket holder since his dad first took him as a little boy, this is too painful to bear. If they get relegated again he will not buy a season ticket next year just to watch crap teams like Coventry City. Empty Saturdays would be an unbearable hole in his life, but pride and anger would not let him witness the endless humiliation of the team he has loved.

It is now early evening and he needs to be alone. Alex does not want to drink with his mates, and definitely does not want to go home. Passing Fishy Moores, the old fish and chip shop where his dad used to take him on the way home after a match, is now the Shop Front Theatre and even that has closed. Coventry is unrecognizable, only blocks of student accommodation everywhere full of foreigners. There is no sense of belonging. Somebody needs to do something.

Wandering off, he decides to visit a local brothel he went to last year. Upon arrival he has to wait. This annoys him further, but it is cheap and he does not have much spare cash. Eventually he pays, enters the bedroom and is dismayed to find a dark-skinned girl. Standing in the hallway he shouts, 'Is this all you've got? I don't like darkies.'

'Sorry, mate,' the minder replies. 'The others are busy. One's visiting a customer, and the other is paid for the evening.'

Alex scowls and vents his anger. 'Bollocks! I can't wait. She'll have to do.' Back in the room, he barks at the girl, 'On the bed.' He goes over to her and rips off her knickers, throwing them across the floor.

Alarmed Mohini cowers, but he holds her down roughly with one arm as he thrusts his fingers inside her. She winces at the harsh treatment. 'Ow! Please stop, you're hurting me.'

He likes that. 'I've bought you and I will do what the fuck I like.' His actions become rougher.

Mohini cries out, 'Stop! Stop!'

Alex is angered by her resistance and delivers a stinging slap across her face. She screams and the minder rushes into the room. Seeing how frightened she is, he quotes the rules, 'You're not allowed to hurt the girls.'

Alex advises the minder, 'If you don't want worse, you'd better piss off.'

As a young man, the minder was never a sporty type; now, in later years, his chubby, under-developed body is no match for the aggressor. Paralysed by apprehension, the minder remains motionless, but his lack of movement is interpreted as an insufferable challenge to the demon in the room.

Robotically rotating his head, Alex locks the minder in the cross hairs of an evil stare and with sinister intent, leaves no doubt that the final warning has already been delivered. 'Fuck off, twat.'

The minder willingly accepts the recommendation and immediately leaves the room.

Directing his aggression to Mohini, he growls, 'Trying to stop me enjoying myself, are you? I'll teach you not to cross me, you slut.'

His mind gushes uncontrolled violence as his body locks into his speciality, whipping round delivery of a fist fully in the face of his defenceless prey, breaking her jaw and hurling her backwards against the headboard. This is only the beginning of an ordeal that will change her life forever. Keeping up a torrent of abuse, Alex's sandpaper chin harshly scrapes against her rapidly swelling face as his mouth is pressed against her ear, drowning her mind with vitriolic venom.

No client had ever treated her like this. This is as deeply humiliating as it is meant to be. Mohini closes her eyes but that makes it worse as the words drown her remaining senses.

Years of anger and frustration surge through his body as he pours hate into this 'filthy, black whore.' Relishing absolute control, he turns her small frame onto her front and buggers her. His wife would never allow him to do that so he is going to make the most of it. He hasn't had this much carnal satisfaction for a long time.

Smelling the fear and intense intimacy of every breath, murmur and wail only deepens the purity of Alex's satisfaction, as if this act is retribution for a lifetime of disadvantage. This defenceless victim is paying for the sins of his world. What he will never understand is that his desire to totally devour and extinguish his victim will fail, but in the attempt, it is he who will be consumed by hate and destroyed.

When he has finished, she lifts her head from the pillow. Through a severely swollen jaw, she mutters almost inaudibly, 'You bastard.'

With eyes possessed and vice-like jaw he utters a thunderous snarl, 'Yoouuu what!' Grabbing her hair Alex drags her small frame onto the floor, landing heavy boot marks from head to toe kicking out all of her senses leaving her small body deformed and motionless. With the pressure released, the football match is forgotten; a mere emotional memory. Alex casually dresses and saunters off to complete the rest of his evening.

The minder enters the room and stares at the bloodied figure kicked under the bed with only her twisted legs visible. He does not touch her but phones the boss, who asks if the girl is alive. Mohini moans as she re-joins a very different world from the one she was evicted from.

Having never left the flat from the day she entered, she has no idea of the address. Now she is too disorientated and weak to focus on anything. She can no longer service customers and therefore is of no value. There must be no connection with the flat, she must be disposed of without attracting attention. They wait until it is dark, wrap her up in a blanket and drive several miles, where she is dumped in a quiet side street.

Her small frame rolls from the packaging and drops to the floor without movement. Sometime later, a local dog walker sees something heaped by the roadside – not fly tippers again!!! The object stirs – bloody, bloody hell. It's a human!

Immediately, he calls the ambulance and police. She is in a dreadful state. Has she been run over, mugged or what? Drying blood glues the hair, partially obscuring the face of what she appears to be a young girl. What a horrible scene, the police will have to sort it out.

Mohini is admitted to Coventry University Hospital.

# Part Five

# From Disorder Emerging Patterns

## Britain's Invisibles

Rose enjoys the stimulating conversations with Karrle and always comes away rejuvenated. She changes her routines so that she visits Karrle every day, bringing his favourite West African fruit: papaya, pawpaw and mango. Her usual shop rarely sells them, so searching in unfamiliar places is in itself a small adventure. Other practical gifts include pens, paper and the occasional cake, which she bakes herself. Getting out the old cake tins reminds her of when the children were young and family cake time was quite an occasion. Karrle appreciates these moments, dividing the cake and sharing with the other patients; grudgingly even the chocolate cake, which is a particular weakness. These moments become the focal point of the day for Karrle and are increasingly treasured.

'Hello, Karrle. I have brought you a notepad and pen, as you asked. You get through them so quickly, you must be creating your own library. How are you feeling today?'

'Getting stronger.'

'Good, I'm so pleased. You will be out of here soon. They need the hospital beds.'

'Then you will have a new patient to befriend. Tell me, Rose, what is it that you like about your hospital rounds?'

'Well, I met you!'

'And I am glad we met, but you worked here before I arrived. What made you do that?'

'I love coming here. The patients really appreciate the little things we do for them. It is easy to make new friends, and they value having somebody to talk to. At home, the house is empty. The children have grown up, married and moved away. They lead busy lives, so I only see them occasionally and visiting them is a major effort.' Rose sighs rather heavily. 'My husband still works. He hates his job but can't afford to retire.'

'What about friends?' Karrle asks.

'I used to meet other mothers for coffee, but their lives moved on and we drifted apart. Life was passing me by and I was bored to tears. Outside the hospital, nobody cares. When you reach a certain age you become invisible, as if you don't exist or it doesn't matter if you do. It's a disgrace how society treats old people.'

With exaggerated sympathy Karrle responds, 'It sounds awful! It must be like waking up one day and discovering that overnight you have turned black.'

Rose suppresses an involuntary giggle, but knows there is an edge to the comment. She says thoughtfully, 'Sometimes it takes your whole life to learn who you are.'

'When I left Africa, I lost everything that was familiar to me – including myself. It has taken a long time to reconcile myself to the failure of my dreams, and rediscovering who I am and what is important. I am beginning to accept that other things have value and I look for joy in different places.'

Rose can see many admirable qualities in Karrle, and that heightens her curiosity. 'You have no visitors. How do you keep going?'

'This feeling of isolation is new to me and not easy to deal with. I get by living inside my head. I have the memories of my life before, and the responsibility of what I must do. Searching for the truth is my way of taking control, freeing my mind and re-affirming my identity. If I believe I am only a victim, I accept bad outcomes and have no hope.'

'Well, I wish you would teach me,' she says rather dolefully.

Karrle acknowledges the scale of the problem. 'I find social isolation here is a major problem, and not just for immigrants. On the radio the other day, it said that nine million people in Britain experience social isolation and they have a 30% chance of dying prematurely. And that was before Covid. I suspect when we look back there will be many stories of silent suffering behind closed doors. Already they say domestic violence has increased. I notice many old people in hospital have no visitors and they are so grateful to have you to talk to. Nobody should have nobody to turn to. It is one of the major problems in your society.'

Rose agrees. 'You see things with fresh eyes that we accept.' This seems an appropriate moment to ask a question that has been on her mind for some time. 'You know this *Book of REB* thing you were talking about the other day? You said that societies make up explanations about things they do not understand. Why would they do that?'

Karrle adopts lecture mode. 'In order to gain the support of the group they represent, leaders – political or religious– need to have explanations which are presented as complete in order to give confidence to others that they can solve any challenge the group faces. All faiths are based on assertions, some of which may *never* be provable or disproved. You can believe something forever if it cannot be proven wrong.

Where beliefs butt up against reality, the final option is to revise the belief system. The early Christians believed that the Earth was the centre of the universe and the sun went round the Earth. Questioning this 'absolute truth' was to attack the faith, so the Church treated this as heresy, punishable by death. We are now told to marvel at God's creation of the universe.

Those early Christians were not bad people, but they formed explanations from what they knew and filled in the gaps for what they did not know. But maintaining their beliefs proved very destructive, as Galileo found out. He could see through his telescope that the Earth went round the sun, but the evidence was suppressed and he was tried for heresy.'

'You said your book explains why you are here. What did you mean?'

Karrle recounts the circumstances of the gang that attacked him and explains why it happened. 'All humans form groups for companionship, protection and prosperity. Other groups are seen as competition. If a group feels under threat, instinct dictates the members defend themselves, often by attacking the other party. If the two groups can work together then both may enjoy enhanced protection and prosperity, but there are dangers. Differences can be misunderstood and exploited by those with their own agendas, which can lead to conflict and weaken one or both societies. Some individuals use conflict to strengthen their position within the group, even at the cost of diminishing the society they live in. That is how gangs form.

Africa is weak because people don't have the shared values and social mechanisms to resolve disputes peacefully and too often resort to violence. America is strong because the individual is allowed to prosper and most conflicts are resolved peacefully. An exception to the rule is Donald Trump, whose strategy is divide and conquer, even at the expense of making the whole country weaker. If he is on the top of the sandcastle he is better off than before, so he doesn't care if his actions make the sandcastle smaller. Similarly, the mafia destroy wealth. The regions in Italy where they are strongest are the poorest, but they are the top dogs.'

Rose does not fully understand. 'So how does that explain why you are here?'

'A group of men saw me as threatening their social order, and the only way they understood to preserve their values was to attack me. I did not fit in with their Book of REB.'

Rose's face displays deep disapproval. 'How awful! I am so sorry to hear that.'

Resuming his train of thought, Karrle reflects, 'It's a sad truth that the more unequal the society, the more nationalistic and divided it is. In many of the most impoverished ghettos in the world, gangs with nothing fight over the one thing they do have – the territory they live in. They will kill members of other gangs on sight if they wander into an area they control, even if there is no gain to either side. The reality is that the more they isolate themselves, the more they become detached from the synergies of living in a wider society. The more prejudiced a person is, the smaller they make their world.'

Rose nods in agreement. 'Yes, I'm sure you are right.' Trying to think of activities that might offer Karrle some comfort, she asks about his interests. 'Do you listen to music?'

'Occasionally. The music I like reminds me of home. Some I cannot listen to.'

'Why is that?'

'Music is a soundtrack to our lives and opens the emotions. I like the words from a Leonard Cohen song:

Ring the bells that still ring
Forget your perfect offering,
There's a crack in everything,
That's how the light gets in.'

The words are lost on Rose. 'What does that mean?'

'I don't know, but it resonates with me, (ha ha). I believe the songwriter meant the more perfectly you try to present yourself to others, the more anonymous you become and the more difficult it is for others to relate to you. The cracks reveal the real you. Here's another one.' With an imperfect voice, Karrle sings a verse from another song. ' Don't destroy the land and make it desert sand. Who sang that?'

'I don't know.'

'The Yardbirds, 1965.'

'You know a lot about old British music.'

'Hospital radio. I even know some of the regular presenters. They ask for requests, but they don't have music from my country.'

Rose asks, 'Do you like things other than music?'

'I like various forms of art because it communicates across cultures and can travel anywhere. It plays to the heart rather than the mind.' Reminiscing, Karrle reflects on warmer memories. 'My favourite musicians are Jose Carlos Schwartz and Ze Manel. One was killed and the other banned.'

They are both silent, not knowing how to progress the conversation. Finally, Rose remembers her library duties. 'Those are very sad memories. Do you ever relax by reading fiction?'

'No.'

'It can be good for the imagination.'

'Reality is far more unbelievable than fiction. Fiction is what comes out of people's heads; reality includes everything else. The things that have happened to me are unbelievable.'

'I read fiction to escape from reality.'

'I cannot escape my realities.'

'It sounds as if you need some escapism.'

'Later, maybe. For now, I need to change my realities.'

She says goodbye, collects the cups and leaves. Rose reflects on what a very serious and troubled young man Karrle is. His ideas give her many new things to think about and she can feel herself being increasingly drawn into his world and involved in life; but it is becoming more complicated and judgements that appeared simple before are becoming cloudy.

## A New Patient For Rose

Some patients are too ill for conversation, or are asleep when Rose does her rounds, but many are grateful to meet a friendly face. Having overcome her initial inhibitions, Rose's improving confidence makes it easier to respond to patient's needs. Social differences and preconceptions that ruled her life in the outside world, melt away as irrelevant barriers. Almost effortlessly, she learns the pleasure of meeting new people, appreciating the richness of their characters and enjoying their company. It feels so natural now, but it is strange to think that before she became a volunteer, she would never have let such a varied mix of people into her life.

A new patient is admitted, a small Asian girl who is in a pitiful condition. She has several broken ribs, a grotesquely swollen face, wired jaw and cuts and bruises from head to toe. Breathing, moving, drinking and talking cause considerable discomfort, and pain killers are only partially effective. The poor girl makes a tragic sight.

Each day Rose talks in bright and breezy tones, trying to engage her in conversation but the girl knows that the pain would be a poor reward for the effort. The old lady may be well-meaning but she would not understand Mohini's problems and Mohini has no intention of sharing them.

## Lost After Loss

Andy does not know why Mohini disappeared. There is no information from the school, and the hostility of both families makes any enquiries impossible. His greatest fear is that she has been taken to India for an arranged marriage and he will never see her again.

Such an agonising thought is beyond pain and imagination. She has captured his heart and unleashed an uncontrollable craving for love that only 'his Mohini' can satisfy. Without her there is no hope, no future, no point in anything! Life is blacker than black. Every empty minute carries an ache that knows no kindness.

His father, Alex, cannot understand why his son is moody and withdrawn. 'Cheer up, son, you look as if you've lost a tenner and found a quid. I know it's not the football season, but you'll be back in the team come September.'

'I know, Dad.'

Andy's only hope of happiness is to find Mohini. If he could find out which part of India she had gone to, he could bring her back. He has no money, but maybe he can get a job on a ship. Yes, he can make enquiries. He does not want to hurt his father, but nothing must stand in the way of true love. Whatever happens, his dad must never know.

He *will* make enquiries!

## In The Hospital Garden

The mid-afternoon sun is warm and welcoming. Looking through the window, Karrle decides to escape from the bustling routines of the hospital and sit in the small, enclosed garden. He discovers an old but sturdy wooden bench and sits down. The backrest has a solid brass plaque neatly screwed in the centre. Karrle reads the engraved words:

*In Memory of Margaret Toothill, Born 15th June 1915, Died 14th February 1995. A Mother, Nurse and Friend, Much Loved and Missed.*

The plaque is polished, so somebody still cares. Karrle cannot help thinking that if he died right now what evidence would he leave that he had ever existed or had any impact on the world. These sombre reflections are interrupted by the arrival of his one regular contact with the human race. 'Morning, Karrle. I wondered where you were hiding. It is good to see you outside on such a lovely day.'

'Morning, Rose. I thought I would find some space and clear my thoughts.'

'You're always thinking.'

'Yes. Poverty and inactivity have created the perfect conditions for unlimited thinking, but the compensation is that the slower I go in life, the more life I see.'

'What were you thinking about this time?'

Karrle's head tilts slightly as if trying to summarise an off-beat thought. 'Oh, er, life on earth.'

'Yes. It is a wonder to behold God's creations!'

Pondering on Rose's comment, Karrle rises to his feet and walking to a flower bed collects a handful of soil. Returning to Rose, he unfurls his fingers displaying the contents and asks a question, 'Which is more important, God or this soil?'

'God, of course. He created everything.'

'That is one possibility. Can we examine another?

Without soil there would be no plants
Without the plants there would be no herbivores.
Without herbivores there would be no carnivores.
Without carnivores there would be no humans.
Without humans there would be no God.
God needs the soil, the soil does not need God.'

Rose is taken aback and does not know what to say. Scrambling for a response she replies, 'You don't sound very grateful. It was the Europeans that brought Christianity to Africa.'

'After 600 years of suppression and exploitation, it is the Africans who need protection from the Christians. There is a saying in Africa that when the white man arrived in Africa, he had the Bible and the Africans had the land. Now the Africans have the Bible and the white man has the land.'

Surprised, Rose states, 'The Bible contains God's words for everyone.'

'The bible is a collection of stories not written by God but by people who were not there at the time of the events they describe. It is a story which has man as the centre of the universe. In the same way, new-born babies focus purely on themselves until they learn that they have to fit into a wider world. The Bible barely mentions the universe. If these are the words of God, where does the Bible mention the dinosaurs who inhabited every continent for more than 150 million years, far longer than man has existed. Did He forget?

If God does exist and is everywhere, then you cannot be in a place where he is not. Sacred locations are merely historical sites, like the Tower of London. Religion has produced wars like the Crusades, which still set the pattern for conflict a thousand years later, destroying the lives of countless millions. There are future generations who will learn to hate people they will never meet. This is not the product of a god of love, or individuals basing their ideas on personal experience, but indoctrination by a group whose values are based on unprovable assertions, who come into conflict with other groups' unprovable assertions.

If God does NOT exist, then it does not matter which bit of the rock you live on as long as you can sustain yourself. Any conflict that ensues is due to worldly conflict over resources. God is being invoked as an instrument of power. It also means that no group has a "divine" right over any location or other group.'

Rose is confused: 'But what about the teachings, the miracles and the churches all over the world?'

'What is the greater wonder of the world, cutting stones into blocks and mounting one on top of the other to form a church building that might have stood for a thousand years, or the stone they used which may be a hundred million or five-hundred million years old?'

Looking around the garden Karrle carries on. 'Try and find any stone that is less than 100,000 years old and it will have existed longer than modern man. See that ring on your finger? I assume it is made of gold. How old is it?'

Rose says with pride, 'My husband bought it for me thirty-two years ago. It was brand new from the jewellers.'

Unusually, Karrle contradicts her. 'That gold is older than the sun. We know this because we know how elements are made and how to make new ones. The sun is made of hydrogen and helium and does not produce enough energy to create gold. That happens at the end of a star's life, when it burns out and becomes a supernova, so your gold was created by a previous star. What is the greatest wonder, the fact that your gold is billions of years old or the fact that a human found it in the ground and shaped it into a circle and you wear it on your finger? Humans did not make anything in the world, we just found the materials and learnt how to use them.'

Stunned, Rose can only say, 'I did not know that about gold.'

'God has kept his people ignorant for thousands of years on many things, but because His existence cannot be disproved, he is invincible.'

Rose retorts, 'Anyway, you cannot possibly know what will happen to the sun. That is in the future.'

Karrle answers with an example. 'If you had never seen a leaf before and I showed you one, you would not know how it was created or what its purpose was. If I took you to a forest, you would see billions of leaves on thousands of trees in all the varieties. Over two years, you would understand the seasons. The universe has more stars than there are leaves in the world, all in different stages of their life cycle. There are many examples of dying suns.'

Rose protests, 'But God loves us and will protect us.'

'That sounds pretty hollow if you come from my country. When there is a natural disaster like a tsunami or earthquake, which religious group does God spare over the others or the disbelievers? None of them.'

'So you are saying that God does not exist.'

'The beauty of a belief in God is that his existence cannot be disproven so…'

'…so he is invincible.' She says, completing the sentence, but not believing.

'Right. Why accept unproven and unprovable statements. Just because it cannot be disproven is no reason to believe it. That is like saying, "I cannot see round the corner, it must be an elephant." The ancients believed the sun was God because it gave energy to create life. That it enables life is true, so there is more evidence to support that theory than that there is a Christian God.'

'Is that true? I read that there is a deep trench in the ocean where they have found life not dependent on the sun.'

'Yes, the Mariana Trench off the coast of Japan. That hardly disproves the point, because the Earth came from the sun and therefore is part of the same energy source. The real point is that any belief system that makes you destroy earthly things, like killing innocents on religious grounds or believing that the world and all the animals were given to man by God, is contrary to all the evidence. Man is far less important than he would like to imagine. A humbler awareness of our place in the universe would be far more in keeping with reality.'

Rose is bemused. After all her kindness, to challenge the beliefs that she has accepted unquestioningly seems ungentlemanly.

Karrle decides to qualify his comments. 'Remember that all beliefs have gaps to make them coherent to the human mind, including anything I say. The gaps are not always self-evident, but the next time you hear of an atrocity carried out in the name of God you can be sure it is done for earthly, not heavenly, reasons. The ones who believe otherwise are the most deluded. We are only insects on a rock.'

'I don't feel like an insect.'

'That is because each of us look at the universe through our own porthole. I am sure the insect does not feel like a human.'

These are challenging thoughts, but Rose does not have arguments to counter Karrle's observations. Although she is beginning to look at things differently, she cannot agree with everything Karrle says.

## Vishnu's Family Guilt?

At the insistence of her father, the family make no enquiries about their daughter's disappearance, much to her mother's distress. Vishnu does not want any attention drawn to an event that risks bringing public shame on the family. Mohini has not contacted her family, which Vishnu takes as further evidence of disrespect.

When Mohini is taken to hospital, the medical authorities report to the police that a patient has been badly assaulted. A member of the crime squad visits Mohini, who gives her name and address, but refuses to supply any further details.

An officer knocks on the door of the address supplied. 'Good evening, sir. May I speak to the parents of Mohini Chakraborty?'

'I am the father. What can I do for you, officer?'

'Have you seen your daughter recently, sir?'

'No. She left home three months ago and has not been in contact. I was worried. Has something happened to her?'

Maintaining a formal manner, the officer continues with his enquiries. 'Did you report her missing to the police, sir?'

'No. I was afraid that she would bring disgrace on our family. Where is she, officer?'

Persisting with his line of enquiry the policeman continues, 'You weren't worried enough to report a missing person?' He looks at Vishnu with palpable disapproval, but there is no response.

'I am sorry to inform you that your daughter is in hospital. She seems to have been severely beaten. Do you know where she has been for the last three months?'

'No. I disapproved of the people she was mixing with and she left suddenly.'

'Do you know who these people are?'

Maintaining an uncompromising posture Vishnu replies, 'No, I never met them.'

'On what basis did you disapprove…sir?' asks the officer with undisguised disapproval.

Without a hint of embarrassment Vishnu tells the officer, 'They were not from our community. They were locals.'

Barely finding the words to maintain a courteous manner whilst suppressing his anger the officer replies, 'It is difficult to live in England and not meet local people…sir!'

Vishnu is not going to be lectured to by a young Englishman with no understanding of Hindu culture and he closes the conversation. 'Thank you, officer. I will not detain you any longer.'

The officer leaves and Vishnu's son, Reyansh, rushes into the room. 'I heard every word. This is terrible news. I must go and see her.'

'No, you will not!' his father instructs vehemently. 'She has brought enough shame on this family.'

'You should not have been so strict. Mohini is a good girl.'

Vishnu corrects his son. 'She has been behaving badly ever since she came to this country. I warned her but she would not listen. This is what happens when you move to a degenerate country with no standards. We should never have come.'

Reyansh realises that it is no use arguing. It is disrespectful to challenge the decisions of the head of the family, and useless to point out that corruption is far worse in their home country. Poor Mohini.

The police officer suspects the family are involved in the attack on the girl, which was extremely vicious and must have involved considerable aggression and emotion. Maybe this was an 'honour beating', which would explain why they never reported it. He will include this in his report.

## Mohini Must Rebuild Her Life

Mohini listens to Rose chatting and laughing with another patient and thinks it would be nice to talk. After six weeks, the wiring is removed from her jaw. The doctors are pleased with her progress; the jaw has set in the correct position and mobility is good, although Mohini's bite feels slightly different. As her spirits improve, she engages in light conversation.

Rose realises that this girl has a warm, caring nature but no confidence at all, and she never mentions her past. Rose thinks it is such a pity that an obviously lovely girl arrived at the hospital in such an appalling state. Clearly there are dark episodes in her life that Mohini does not want to revisit, and as Rose never pries into these untold stories, their conversations have a comfortable freedom on which to build a friendship, which the girl desperately needs and Rose values.

'I don't know what I will do when I leave here,' Mohini confides to Rose. 'I can't go back.'

She does not say where 'back' is. Rose wants to offer some hope. The only thing she can think of are the words of the African about understanding the influences in your life and taking control to make the changes you want. Her explanation is muddled and Rose recognizes it sounds foolish. The only thing Rose can think of is for Mohini to talk to Karrle and she offers to introduce them.

# Mohini Meets Karrle

Mohini has no intention of sharing her experiences with a well-meaning stranger. Not wishing to appear ungrateful, she says she will think about it. What she thinks about is how to say no. Eventually, having no ideas of her own, she unenthusiastically agrees.

'Karrle, this is the girl I was telling you about,' Rose says. 'Her name is Mohini.'

'Hi, Mohini.'

She looks at the tall, thin, good-looking black man lying on the bed. 'Pleased to meet you,' she says politely but without sincerity.

'I'll leave you two to talk,' and Rose continues her rounds. The two strangers are alone.

Mohini busies herself looking round the room, avoiding eye contact. Karrle breaks the silence: 'Pleased to meet you too. How can I help?'

'Rose told me about you. She said I should talk to you.'

'What about?'

'I don't know.'

'Well, why don't you start by telling me about yourself.'

'OK.' Mohini will keep this impersonal and superficial. 'My family came from India and we thought we would be safe in England.'

'Huh.' Karrle interrupts. 'Ain't that the truth? You've got to be English to be safe in England. See, we have something in common already.'

His strong but gentle voice and fireside manner, sprinkled with delicate humour, is disarming. It is as if they have known each other for ages, and reminds her of Barack Obama.

Mohini relaxes a little and smiles back at him. Beginning her story, describing the circumstances of the move from India, it soon becomes difficult to tell half a story and for it to make sense. Unwittingly her inner thoughts surface with a momentum of their own. For the first time she addresses her feelings towards her father, Andy and the circumstances of her arrival in hospital. Unloading things she had tried to forget propels the story forward, as if it is news to her and she cannot wait to hear more. Focusing increasingly on how she feels about the events that have left her like discarded rubbish releases a strange lighter, freer self, as if a window in a long-abandoned house has just been opened.

Karrle listens attentively without further interruption, his eyes closely observing her. He can sense her vulnerability, and believes that she has good instincts and needs help.

Having said far more than she had planned, Mohini falls silent looking a little apprehensive.

Karrle does not respond for several moments and then sympathetically delivers an answer as if a great secret is about to be shared. 'I know a person who can help you tackle all of your problems. A really wonderful person, who will support you for the rest of your life. Would you like me to tell you who it is?'

'Yes, please.'

'You!'

Recoiling from this rebuff, Mohini realises she has said too much, humiliated herself and wasted her time. Rejecting the impossible, she states the problem that is so obvious it should not need saying. 'I can't do anything. The bad things that have happened to me are not what I ever wanted.'

'Why did they happen?' Karrle's soft tones illicit a response.

'Because we moved from India and don't fit in in this country.'

'Do you like it here?'

'I did,' Mohini replies positively.

'So apart from your recent experience, you fit in. So what does not?'

'My father wants me to live as if I were in India, but I can't.'

'Why?'

Annoyed and defensive Mohini again states the obvious. 'Because everything is different here.'

Karrle persists with his line of enquiry. 'So you have changed, but your father has not. Will England ever change to be like India?'

Mohini's frustration with the stupidity of these questions starts to show. 'No! Of course not!'

'So your father will never fit in unless he makes some changes, and you will never fit in if you blindly follow your father's wishes.'

Finally Mohini can state the inevitable conclusion. 'So there is no solution!'

For the first time, Karrle disagrees. 'There is always a solution. It may not be the one you want, but in the end the situation always resolves itself.' He pauses before proceeding.

'You know, we often believe that the past is set in concrete and the future is uncertain but the past was never certain, nor is the future. The only thing concrete about the past is that it is over and we know the outcomes. We delude ourselves that they were certainties based on fundamental truths and therefore will never change in the future. But they are only a single outcome based on specific circumstances that may never recur. Our knowledge of those circumstances is always imperfect; and often we only select those aspects that fit the story we want to believe. The past that is remembered is only a reconstruction and becomes part of a mythology.'

Mohini looks perplexed.

'All the tallest buildings in the world are built to be flexible.' Karrle asks, 'Why is that?'

'I don't know?' says Mohini, not seeing the point of the question.

'What would happen if they were completely rigid?'

'I don't know. Maybe they would snap?' she offers, lost and not caring.

'Correct,' says Karrle. 'All the pressure would be inside the building and it would be more likely to break. If the building bends, the pressure inside is a lot less. It is the same with people. The more you adapt to your environment, the less internal pressure you will feel, and the happier and healthier you will be. Does that make sense?'

'Sort of,' she admits. 'But I can't make my dad change.'

'You are young and have the rest of your life before you. If you stay in this country, you will only be happy and prosper if you accommodate to life here. You come from one community, and your inexperience may make you believe that there are no alternatives, but if that community represents only 1% of humanity, then 99% of people live different lives. It is a mistake to think that you can move continents and not have to adapt, or that there are no alternatives to what you have known. Creatures that have existed for millions of years have had to adapt to their environment or they eventually die. All empires and belief systems throughout history have changed with time and location, or they perish. Without that flexibility, they would not have grown in the first place. Better to live in harmony with your environment than to fight a losing battle until it destroys you. Flexibility is a strength, not a weakness.'

'But I am a Hindu, not a Christian.'

'Don't let society define who you are, neither British, Indian or any other. That does not mean you give up all your beliefs, but where they conflict with present reality you must be objective enough to re-evaluate their relevance to you and adapt them where necessary. The person ultimately responsible for you is *you*. If you don't value yourself, no-one else will. If you accept everything you are taught without question, you are indoctrinated, whether you are Christian, Communist, Fascist, Muslim, Buddhist or whatever.

'The mantra of "believe and you will know" is indoctrination and the foundation for eternal conflict, be it against the environment or other beliefs. This makes you very vulnerable if the organisation is destructive or just plain wrong.

I call it your *Book of REB*. You cannot make your father change, because his *Book of REB* is not the same as yours. It may be similar but it cannot be the same because his solutions to life will never be identical to yours. That is a fundamental truth which is normal and healthy. What is always wrong is the belief that things will never change. It is a big challenge but you can learn to accept that it is your father's choice to adapt or not, and you may have to accept the consequences if he doesn't. You can only help him understand if you understand. That is difficult but it allows you to start taking responsibility for your own destiny, make decisions that are right for you and learn to live with the outcomes.'

Mohini listens with interest. His words are thought-provoking but she does not know how to apply them to herself.

After an hour and a half Karrle needs to rest. 'I am rather tired. We can talk about this tomorrow if you wish.'

'OK. Thank you for your time.'

Karrle has given Mohini a number of things to think about but they raise questions without answers, and she has no idea what her solutions might be.

## Chicken Tikka Masala – an Unlikely Solution

Karrle has an optimism that sees through problems with a clarity that Mohini finds uplifting. Somehow he seems to instinctively understand many issues that she had not considered and puts them in simple terms which offer her choices. At the moment coping with day-to-day challenges is as much as she can manage. Chatting daily, they are often together when Rose enters the ward. She is delighted they get on so well and gradually the three of them form an inner circle of friends.

Mohini is grateful to Karrle, but unsure how to move her life forward. 'I appreciate the time you have spent talking to me. It has made me think differently about things – but I am not sure how it helps me.'

Always reassuring Karrle replies, 'That's OK. Solutions usually take time and are rarely obvious, but there is ALWAYS a solution.'

Her youthful spirit seems burdened with a weight that cannot be carried. 'I can't see how things will change for me.'

'Things cannot stay the same, so they will change. You are young, you don't see alternatives, but there are always alternatives. The important thing is to deal with what is real, take responsibility for changing those things that are important to you, and deal with things if they get worse. Failure is not about not succeeding, failure is not trying. Martin Luther King said, "I never fail. I succeed or I learn something." Searching may open doors later, that are not visible now.'

Mohini is interested but still confused.

'Do you know the most popular meal in this country?' Another strange question from this unusual man.

'No,' she smiles.

'Chicken tikka masala. Do you know where it was invented?'

Mohini offers a logical guess, 'In the Punjab?'

'No In the UK. Glasgow. Do you know how?'

'No idea.' She laughs at the absurdity of the conversation. This might be silly but it is fun, and there must be a point somewhere.

Karrle develops the tale. 'A customer went to an Indian restaurant and ordered a chicken tikka. When the waiter brought the meal it was dry, and the customer said, "Where's the gravy?" '

'I don't understand. What's that got to do with me?'

Karrle continues, 'The chef then opened a tin of tomatoes and added seasoning to create the customer's "gravy".'

Completely perplexed, Mohini looks at Karrle. 'So?'

'So, when the customer went into the restaurant do you think that he, the waiter or the chef thought of a sauce? No. The customer entered the restaurant with certain expectations and the restaurant offered what they knew. This created a problem and the solution was something new, that none of them could have known. You have a problem and there is always a solution – and who is the best person to find your solution…?'

'Me?' The young apprentice is rewarded with an affirmative smile.

Over the next few days, Karrle goes into more detail about Mohini's *Book of REB* which helps her understand how all societies have values that vary between groups. Many of these values are far more subjective than the society believes. Mohini has moved from a society dominated by one set of beliefs to a society with many different beliefs. In a multi-cultural society, you don't have to change your beliefs but you have to work with others who think and behave differently. Understanding and tolerating the differences, without suppressing what is important to Mohini is the only way she will be happy. Coming from a culture that discourages females from expressing themselves in public, she feels inhibited by the judgement of others. Karrle has to address equip her to deal with this conditioning.

'Do you feel guilty about being Indian?'

'No!'

'Do you feel guilty about your skin colour?'

'No!'

'If you stole from a shop would you feel guilty?'

'Yes.'

'Why? It is because of what YOU did. You did neither of the other things. Never feel guilty for being you. Taking responsibility creates opportunities but also potential dangers. You must be aware of these influences and not be bullied into following rules that damage you.'

Gradually these conversations open up new ways for her to look at herself and offering opportunities to take control and make decisions about her future. This is progress. She has defined her problem and recognises that she is the best person to find a solution. This gives her something specific to focus on. But what is her solution and will it be better or worse?

Karrle says that building a skill develops the person. He advises Mohini not to be limited by the expectations of others, or diminish the possibility of all the things she could become. Noting her natural empathy, he suggests that she offers this talent by helping those around her. 'They are real people with real problems who need real help.'

Social services fear that when she is eventually discharged from hospital she might be in danger if she returns home They take responsibility for her safeguarding, and provide her with a flat and support. This newly discovered independence allows her to start a new life – and time to discover her own *Book of REB*.

# Unguarded Words Reveal a Deep Wound

Despite Karrle's best efforts, Mohini cannot see a future for herself. She has lost her family and the love of her life; however, she is spirited, responsive to people and wants to improve her life. Rose suggests that she becomes a volunteer at the hospital like herself. The experience can be used as a reference for future employers.

Embracing the opportunity takes Mohini's mind off her own problems, and she quickly learns the routines. Being brought up to respect her elders as wise and nearly always right, she soon learns that everyone is vulnerable at points in their life, and she can offer real help that is cherished by most of the patients. Meeting men and women, young and old, from many countries, introduces her to a fascinating variety of people.

She also discovers she has a natural instinct for caring, and thrives on being appreciated, something she desperately needs at the moment. For the first time in her life she feels respected *and* in control.

Karrle is struck by the transformation in her. 'Do you like working as a volunteer in the hospital?'

'I love it!' she glows. 'People are so grateful. I have made many new friends.'

'They appreciate help at a difficult time.'

'I do feel sorry for some of the old people, particularly the English. Many dread going home and being on their own. It seems wrong in a society with so much wealth. It makes me sad.'

Karrle confirms her observation. 'Yes, it's called "British urban isolation". I have already been introduced to it. Your neighbour can be having terrible problems, or just be chronically lonely, and you would never know. People habitually select friends from the same economic background; change your financial circumstances and you change your friends. What sort of society is that?

In Africa, and I am sure in Asia as well, we saw our neighbours every day. There was always somebody around if you needed. There are many things that the British could learn from our cultures and a lot more to discover than just the food.'

Mohini reminisces. 'I miss the life we had back home. There was always somebody doing something interesting. Over here people seem to finish their job, go home, close the door and watch television.'

'Yes. We were money poor but family rich. In Britain, it is the other way round.' He cannot help noticing how Mohini's health and beauty are returning. Teasing her, he says, 'You *are* looking well these days. You'll be attracting a boyfriend soon.'

The happy mask is instantly ripped away, revealing a deep raw chasm. Her little light is extinguished, and Karrle realises his blunder. 'Oh Mohini, I am *so* sorry, I did not mean—'

She cuts him off, her voice trembling. 'It's OK… I … lost…' She fails to complete the sentence, her head sinks and her voice trails to nothing as she tries to shrink physically from the pain she's worked so hard to control. '…I shall never love again.'

Both are frozen in shock. Finally, Karrle says gently, 'That is not true. You have a lot of love in you, and people can see that. That is why everyone likes you. Someone will see the love in you, and hopefully you will let them share their love for you.'

In a shaky voice Mohini replies, 'My heart is broken. Memories are too much for me.' An involuntary tear wells up, as her chest heaves a convulsive sob. She looks so small and vulnerable, a crushed angel disappearing before Karrle's eyes. He understands too well, and offers words of comfort. 'Sometimes your heart has to be broken to recognise the suffering of others. You recognise their pain and want to help. That is what they see in you.'

'Didn't you say that terrorists want people to suffer pain so they will understand the pain of others?'

'Yes, but that is driven by hate, not love. Hate wants to cause pain, love wants to stop it. Unnecessary pain never makes anything better. Someone will see your love and love you for it.'

'I hope so. I doubt it.'

'Believe me, I am right. To quote Martin Luther King, "Stick with love. Hate is too great a burden to bear".'

Karrle hopes he is right. To see this delicate flower damaged and tortured by the brutality of others weighs heavily on his heart. Although she has recovered physically, the mental scars are still raw. It would be tragic if this treasure, capable of so much love, does not find the happiness she so richly deserves. He finds some consolation in the thought that happiness is natural to her, and she is young and has a strong spirit.

## Chance Meeting

It is Lech's only day off in the week and he needs to shop for food. Crossing the road, he catches sight of a girl that reminds him of somebody. 'Chrystal?'

The voice sounds familiar but it can't be directed at her, so Mohini ignores it.

'Chrystal!' This time it is louder and nearer. A petrifying thought jellifies her mind: please don't let this be an ex-customer. She is frightened to look round. When she does, recognition is instant for both. She turns and walks away.

'Chrystal, can we talk?'

Swivelling momentarily towards her pursuer, she snaps, 'Go away,' before abruptly walking away and quickening her pace. He continues to close in. 'Go away, I don't want to talk. GO AWAY!'

'Please, please. We used to talk and I am glad to see you.'

'I had no choice then, I do now. Go away!'

Lech gently holds her arm. 'Please,' he implores.

Mohini's words are abrupt. 'I am alright. Now we have talked, goodbye.' She goes to turn away but does not move, as if requesting consent.

Seeing her hesitation, Lech makes a humble request. 'Our conversations were important to me and I know you enjoyed them. You are still my friend. Please. Just a minute.'

She had found it easy to talk when Lech was a stranger and she believed she would not see him again. He had been good to her, but her past must not destroy her future. The Bean and Leaf Coffee House is across the road so Mohini nervously acquiesces. 'All right. One minute.'

They sit at the back of the café, hidden from the street. Old memories flood back, drowning Mohini in a sea of turmoil, anger and trepidation.

'You are looking well. I am so glad,' Lech says warmly. 'What happened to you? I went back and they said you had left. I never returned.'

Mohini does not want to delve into detail. 'They did not treat me right so I left. I met somebody and my life is much better now.'

'You have a boyfriend?'

'NO! I had a boyfriend once, but he is lost forever. I met a wise man who told me things that helped me understand who I am and gave me a sense of direction in my life.'

'What sort of things?'

'It's difficult to explain. He calls it his *Book of REB*. He says we are all conditioned by our experiences, rules we live by and beliefs, and those who cannot see themselves are the most conditioned.'

'Everybody knows that,' says Lech unimpressed.

'Yes, but each person, even in the same family, has their own book because each individual's experiences are personal to them. He says we all look at the universe through our own porthole. Projecting our values onto others causes conflict.'

'You're right, that sounds complicated. What's that got to do with you?'

Taking charge of the conversation Mohini continues. 'My dad and I have different perspectives on life. How we respond depends on our experiences and values, and my experiences will never be the same as his. I can never live his life and he can never live mine.

When he imposed his *Book of REB*, it caused conflict and I left home. I lost the protection of my group and was exploited by people who pursued their own *Books of REB*, which was very destructive for me. Individuals survive by being in a group, so there are constant adjustments between the individual and the pressure to abide by common rules. Now I understand my own REB, it is easier to understand other people's.'

'You never talked like this before.'

'I was trying to live somebody else's *Book of REB*. Now I am living my own,' she explains.

'You're different, but still the same person I recognise.' Lech is so glad that they have met and wants to talk some more. 'Would you like another coffee?'

He can see the change in her, but struggles to understand why. They talk for three hours over four cups of coffee. She tells him that, as a friend, he must never let her past be known.

Lech comes away thinking if this young Indian girl can find herself then as a man and head of the family he should be able to do the same. *Book of REB*? Strange! Lech tries to work out what his *Book of REB* is and wonders if it will help.

## Lech Challenges Charles

The increasing profitability of Charles' businesses fuels his confidence and ambitions. Markets are changing and he can see new opportunities to expand. If he could sweat the assets a bit more, he could make super-profits and be recognised as an international player.

A team of consultants are brought in to analyse the company's operations and make recommendations. Their report compares the man hours paid with the labour content of the output from the factory and reveals that 30% of employees time is non-productive. If 50% of the non-productive hours could be recovered, then output could increase by 21% and profits by 40%.

The consultants recommend that all shop-floor employees clock in and out of every job and wear electronic tags so their output can be monitored and analysed every second of the day to discover where the inefficiencies lay. Charles is impressed, and announces his plan to the workforce who are horrified, but feel powerless to do anything about it.

Lech remembers Ryszard and how he had done nothing whilst his friend slowly deteriorated, and determines not to make the same mistake even if it risks his job. By chance, he sees Charles in the car park and, against his natural instincts, he strides purposefully towards the boss. But what to say?

'Excuse me sir, you do not know me, but I must speak with you.'

Surprised Charles asks, 'Who are you?'

'My name is Lech. I work in your factory. It's about these employee monitors you want everyone to wear. You cannot do it.'

'I think I can. It's my factory.'

Lech grabs at half-digested ideas that he can remember from the *Book of REB*. 'This is a bad rule. It will create bad experiences and undermine beliefs.'

'What are you talking about. Go away. I am busy.'

Lech persists. What he must say suddenly becomes clear. 'If you treat people like machines, they will have no respect for you and all your money will mean nothing. A man who makes money without regard for the people who work for him will be no more respected than Fred Goodwin, Mike Ashley or Sir Philip Green. I have read your British press. We workers are not stupid.'

'This will make more money, which secures everyone's jobs. Don't you want that?'

'Not at the expense of my dignity and sanity,' Lech says and storms off.

Charles is shocked and bemused by this unsolicited verbal assault. He is appalled by any association with successful businessmen who have been pilloried in the press.

He asks the factory manager who this man is. Once Lech has been identified, the manager asks if Charles wants him sacked. Charles says no. There are delicate negotiations with the unions, and this is exactly the sort of bad publicity that he does not need. Lech is obviously a fool and Charles is the resourceful entrepreneur. He must think.

With a heavy heart, he ditches his consultants' report. The business must expand; the only way is to hire more labour, but how to turn a negative into a positive? Charles places an advertisement in the local press to recruit 120 additional workers and issues several press releases demonstrating how local business is keeping jobs in the UK (even though 60% of his workforce are non-British). There are even a couple of articles in the national press, and the Employment Secretary refers to it in the House of Commons as an example of a successful enterprise in Britain. It will recorded in Hansard, as a permanent record in a British Parliamentary debate.

Charles is glowing. The cream on the cake is his introduction of bonus and suggestion schemes, so that if the workers achieve some of the productivity increases his consultants have targeted, they could be paid over the minimum wage from the additional profits without costing Charles a penny. Yet again, this reaffirms why he is so successful and a great asset to society.

## Karrle Leaves Hospital

Today is the day Karrle will be discharged from hospital and Rose comes to say goodbye. She finds him sitting in a chair, reading as usual. 'Morning, Karrle. The doctors say you are leaving us to convalesce. I am so glad that you are getting better, but I will miss our talks.'

'Yes, as a member of the permanently unemployed, convalescence comes naturally.'

'I am sure a clever man like you will find something.'

'I hope so, but I don't feel optimistic.'

'You will.'

'Thank you, Rose. I will miss our conversations, too.'

Good news floods in, Karrle is released from hospital and shortly afterwards is granted a 'right to remain' for eighteen months, quickly followed by a national insurance number. The Job Centre expect him to find work, but nothing is offered. Is it because of his colour, the fact that he has no UK employment history or something else he does not understand?

Weeks go by and he continues his studies at the library. Contrary to expectations, the more information he digests, the less confusing are the pieces and the clearer the integration of ideas. Developing an understanding of who he is and the environment he must navigate, his confidence is growing that it will move him nearer his mission of establishing justice in his homeland. He also acknowledges that his financial security and independence depend upon gaining employment and, although helpful, the Job Centre are increasingly aggressive in their expectations of rapid self-help.

One day at the library, he wanders over to peruse the newspapers and notices an article in the Coventry Telegraph about a local employer recruiting workers. He finds the address and applies. The interviewer is pleased that he speaks good English, is articulate and can understand instructions, but is worried that an obviously intelligent man will not stay in the job for long. On balance, he is one of the best candidates and a job is offered.

Is this the start of a new life? He will follow this path and see where it leads. Certainly his first taste of economic freedom will be a breath of fresh air and provide an opportunity to learn what British 'normal' is.

# Part Six

# To Build the Future Address the Past

## Karrle's First Job

It is Monday morning and Karrle is uncharacteristically nervous. Today is the first day of his employment in the UK. The daily chores of washing, shaving, dressing and eating a small breakfast offer little distraction before he catches the number 18 bus to Tile Hill, reaching the factory twenty-five minutes early.

Surveying the tired and unimpressive building, he surmises that any glories the structure has hosted are lost in the mists of time and its future is merely acceptance of gentle decay. But no, on entering the reception what a surprise! It is bright, spacious and airy, implying rebirth from within and aspiration for the future.

Registering his presence, it is forty-five minutes before he is collected by a member of the Human Resources department to be given the obligatory basic induction course. This largely entails explanations of health and safety regulations and procedures, and the location of the fire exits. The job content training could be compressed into five uninteresting minutes, but is padded out to half a day because of some legal requirement; after which he signs a form to say that he has received the mandatory training and understands and agrees to abide by the company rules.

The national minimum wage is also the maximum. It is evident that opportunities for promotion from the shop-floor are negligible because of the lack of training and a hierarchical, elitist management structure. Being low paid also means low status. The inherent inefficiency of the tasks are so profoundly boring, the only people who will do the work are poorly motivated employees with few alternatives, thus validating their low status in the eyes of senior management. With nobody investing the time to improve this backwater, Karrle can feel his brain eating itself from the inside and is convinced that the job should command a premium for mental torture. His ability to sustain this much-needed employment demands that his imagination changes the crushing tedium into something that can be endured.

Searching for escape, his mind takes a slow walk around the task he is chained to, and soon realises that simple changes could make the process much more efficient. With no expectation of a response, he decides to enter the idea in the company's new suggestion scheme. The accountant evaluates the proposal using cost / benefit analysis and confirms the idea will reduce production times and stock levels.

The plan is implemented and quickly saves the company £100,000 a year. Charles, the managing director and owner, is delighted that his idea of a suggestion scheme is producing fruit so quickly and resolves to encourage others to offer improvements by rewarding the employee publicly with a cheque for £500. Come the appointed hour, the work force assemble on the factory floor for a presentation by the managing director.

Charles waits for the employees to fall silent, then begins his speech, 'I am delighted to present this award and a cheque for £500 to one of our newest employees, who has put forward an idea through our company suggestion scheme that will save thousands of pounds a year. This will help the company to be more competitive and secure all our jobs for the future. This is a wonderful example of the opportunities for improvement that exist in every job in the company. Well done, Carl.'

Surprised and embarrassed by the unsolicited attention, Karrle coyly averts his gaze from those assembled as he accepts the cheque. The employees dutifully applaud before drifting back to their work stations, leaving Karrle alone with the managing director. Unable to walk away, he stands like a shop-window dummy.

'Well done again … er … Carl.'

'It is Karrle…K…A…R…R…L…E. It is African, not European.'

'Oh, sorry.'

'That's OK.'

Charles's mood is still jolly and cannot avoid an element of curiousity regarding his new employee. 'Your idea was brilliant. What made you think of it?'

'It was simple, once you understand the process. We all see the same things but make different observations.'

'Very true.'

'I only seek the truth. Not to do so is a waste of life,' Karrle says earnestly.

'Yes, indeed! You are a deep chap,' Charles observes. He finds himself slightly in awe of the other man, and does not know why. He rarely makes spontaneous decisions but his instinct tells him that this is an opportunity. Uncharacteristically, he makes an impulsive offer. 'You know, Karrle, it occurs to me that you could look at other parts of my business and suggest improvements. How would you like to be the Cost Reduction Officer?'

‘I would like that very much. Thank you. What would you like me to look at?’

‘I don’t know – whatever you want. I get the impression that you will recognise the potential for improvement when you see it. How about doing that for a week and reporting back?’

At last, there is something worthwhile for Karrle to focus his mind on. Is he starting to be seen as a human? If so, it is a good feeling.

## The Suit

Leaving the shop floor, Karrle joins a new team in the offices. Memories of the target-driven, remorseless grind of the old job quickly fade and are replaced by new anxieties that are less visible but just as stressful in completely different ways.

'Office world' rules are assumed, often unwritten or articulated. Oblique references are all that is required because it is assumed that everybody knows their place. The British class system is so ingrained into the fabric of the organisation that business is conducted through role play, by threads so thin they are undetectable to the casual observer. Even people from different countries are infected, suppressing their identity as a prerequisite for admission to the world of opportunity, respectability and career advancement.

The first challenge is to acquire a uniform to convey the message you want others to see, either for peacocking or camouflage; a uniform to give the appearance that everything is the same, and camouflage to disguise the differences. Karrle needs both.

The £500 suggestion-scheme money facilitates this ambition, and he ventures into West Orchards Shopping Centre to investigate men's clothing shops with a list of requirements:

Suit: he discovers a dapper little number that feels like it should belong to somebody else.

Shirt: white would not be flamboyant and unchallenging (very important as a newcomer) and will pass unnoticed, ticking one of the unwritten rules.

Ties: more than one because you cannot wear the same tie two days running, it implies poverty. Many offerings are entertaining but inappropriate, so he settles for three, plain and dull. Another box ticked.

Socks but what colour? Black, of course, to go with the shoes.

Shoes: they have to be black.

In total he spends £350, and tries to convince himself that this is an investment. In his previous world this is a fortune, and for what? To join a club whose membership is of no interest. Still, the suit fits well and the mirror reflects a sharp-suited, dynamic 'businessman.' Any African chubbiness has long since drained away, gifting him a slim athletic build from his travels and English diet. Time to fool the masses.

The impact is instant and electrifying. By signalling his compliance to social norms, he could not avoid the conclusion that in the eyes of his new colleagues the suit had created a different person – competent, serious, well organised and purposeful. This is a tremendous boost to his confidence, and reminds him of a quote from Albert Einstein: 'Small is the number of people who see with their eyes and think with their minds.'

Shallow though it is, there is a secret pleasure in being accredited with virtues instead of summarily dismissed with disdain. The suit has transported him to the land of plenty where abundance is assumed and subtly displayed or its absence concealed.

His life's experiences to date leave him ill-equipped and initially disorientated in his dealings with the formal administrative departments and expectations of the status-conscious employees that make up a modern commercial organisation. This is a challenging psychological journey, but one that he is committed to completing.

Focusing on issues raised, evidence available and actions implemented, Karrle gradually notices that an initial display of positivity is a cardinal requirement to demonstrate commitment to the team – but when the words stop, so do the actions. It is as if the words are only the official version for the naïve and those avoiding responsibility. It's not that people say no, it's just that things do not happen.

The ambitious, who want to survive and prosper, tune their antennae to managing threats, which manifests as supporting suggestions that benefit themselves, whilst avoiding responsibility and risk. The response involves accepting the worthiness of new ideas whilst presenting the benefits of the status quo and dangers of change during later discussions.

Office jealousies create an undercurrent that masquerades as the Freudian subconscious controlling the conscious; in truth, motives and actions are deliberate and calculating. It is only when lines are crossed that articulation exposes the subterfuge. Karrle is a raw recruit whose suit has allowed him entry into this world, but he has another suit and it is made of armour: everyone knows that the new arrival has the ear of the boss and so, for the moment, he is untouchable. Subversion is the order of the day, as invisible defensive poses are maintained by all whilst displaying another of their strengths: patience.

Much later, Karrle will ruminate on the similarities between the unspoken truths that explain how the commercial world really works and the actions of the empire builders, both political and economic, where self-interest determines actions which are later rationalised away in order to extol virtue and consistency. His move from factory to office is almost a metaphor for the two worlds of Africa and Europe.

This is certainly true of the ethnicity of the employees. Although the employees on the shop floor are overwhelmingly East European, African and Asian, when Karrle moves into the offices he is immediately struck by the absence of non-white senior managers or directors, with only a smattering of non-white employees in junior or minor supervisory roles. As a traditional British engineering company, everyone accepts that this is 'normal.'

A few of these ethnic minorities behave as if they were trying to outdo the British for Britishness. Is this class, history or racism? It dawns on Karrle that it was none of them because it is all of them! Strange and unhealthy!

## Admission to the World of Western Business

For the first time Karrle feels recognised and respected for the person he is and not just an African, black man or refugee.

At the end of the week, he writes a report with several recommendations and a couple of days later he is called into the office to discuss his findings with the boss. He knocks on the door and enters Charles' world. Looking up from his computer, Charles smiles across his presidential desk and motions Karrle to sit down. Obligingly, he sits in the visitor's chair, a sumptuous, leather experience that immediately puts him ill at ease. Charles initiates the conversation, 'Thank you for your report. It was very interesting. There were several things about my company that I did not know. Are purchasing and stores really so disconnected?'

Confident in what he knows, Karrle is straight to the point: 'Worse! As the new guy, I was trying not to offend people I hardly know. The Purchasing Department order drills that are too long for the job. They are the only ones in stock, so production have to cut them to the right size in order to use them. Purchasing see what is being used and re-order more of the wrong drills. The bigger ones are more expensive and reduce production capacity wasting time cutting them down to size.'

'Madness. Why doesn't somebody say something?'

'They do, but the people who can do something about it are too busy fighting bigger fires.'

'But you saw the answer!' Charles looks for affirmation.

'It's called "Management By Walking About". You should do it. The day-to-day tasks should have support systems that run themselves so senior management only need to get involved when there is a problem. It is not dynamic or productive to fill every minute with pre-planned jobs. They are based on what you already know. Unless you ask the right questions, how do you learn what you don't know? You lose flexibility and miss opportunities to adapt and improve. You have far more opportunity to change internal things that are generally within your control than things outside the organisation, which are usually beyond your control. Ninety-nine per cent of change is slow, incremental and organic.'

Perplexed Charles asks, 'How do you know so much about business?'

'I don't. I try and understand the whole. Business functions within an environment, it is not something in addition. It produces a few internal mechanisms, but if you only focus on those, you may lose sight of the big picture and fail to recognise opportunities or dangers until it is too late. It's called the Black Swan effect.'

'OK. Yes, I see what you mean… You know, Karrle, you certainly look at things differently and that can have its advantages. I believe that your talents could be used in other areas of my organisation. How do you feel about taking on a bigger role?'

'I would like that very much' and Karrle smiles appreciatively.

## Improbable Friendship

Karrle's analysis of problems is inspirational, energizing the stale management processes continually retreading the familiar, which stultify initiative and challenge nothing. He has an innate instinct for understanding process, and exposes critical flaws in several projects, avoiding expensive mistakes. As Karrle intuitively points out, it is cheaper to fail early. Who knows where they might lead? After all, his insights had simplified a production process that had been running for years, and relatively painless changes have already boosted profits. As Karrle explained, change is a process, rarely an event, and '99% of changes are small incremental steps inside an organisation that are within your control'. The same is true in life.

Charles and Karrle enjoy each other's company. Their very different life experiences create a fascination that propels conversations forward in ever freer, franker and wider discussions forming a strong bond based on belief in the other. And sometimes, it is just good to talk.

During one conversation after business hours, Karrle recounts the time the river near his village overflowed and a neighbour's house was washed away. He saved the lives of two family members and some of the livestock. They stayed in his home for three months whilst theirs was rebuilt.

'That was very good of you,' says Charles approvingly.

'In my village everybody knows everybody. If you know them, they are your friends. When they have a problem, it is expected that you will help them.'

'Still, it was good that you did it.'

'When life is hard, you depend on the help of others. If somebody dies, everybody in the village attends the funeral to pay their respects. It is similar in other communities. Velena, a Bulgarian friend of mine, told me of a tradition in her country where they pin a picture of the person who has died on a tree in the town to inform the community that they have passed away. You can walk down an avenue of trees and many of them display pictures. I thought how respectful sharing an important memory with the community.'

'You know, you'd make a good Christian.'

Karrle is taken aback. 'I was hoping to be more than that.'

'What, you want to be God?'

'No, I was hoping to be a good human being. There are many good people who are not Christians.'

Charles acknowledges the observation. 'True. Sorry. And there are many Christians who are not good,' he says, thinking aloud. 'There are things your society could teach the British.'

'It is very different here,' Karrle observes. 'People focus on their jobs, go home and close the door. Many only mix with their families. It makes it very difficult for migrants to adjust and make friends. Velena says the British are so reserved it is difficult to judge what they really think. If they ask questions, you don't know if they are interested in your problems and will help or are just nosey.'

Karrle recognises these observations as a dehumanising experience on an societal scale. He quotes George Bernard Shaw. ' "Two things define us: our patience when we have nothing and our attitude when we have everything" .'

Charles picks up on the implication. 'That sounds like migrants are patient, and the British have everything.' Karrle thinks that some people have too much of too much, but says nothing and the conversation moves on.

These exchanges are extremely important to Charles. He has to be very discreet about voicing controversial opinions, but how else does he learn unless he breaks new ground? He is convinced that if he is to ever achieve his ambition of becoming much richer, he must tackle and overcome bigger challenges in the future and can only do this by thinking differently ('thinking outside of the box' is one of his favourite, uninspiring phrases).

His managers refuse any opportunity that may risk the security and smooth progression of their mapped-out careers and comfortable lives. Charles senses this but cannot get them to break out and offer more. His fear is that remaining in his comfort zone will result in settling for what he already has, and missing opportunities is a precursor to failure. However seductive, he must learn to be less habitual.

Karrle's reasoning is the same as Charles' but with very different aspirations. When the mould is not fit for purpose, nothing of any importance can be achieved without breaking the mould. He has no time for political correctness. Not talking about issues that affect everyone preserves what needs to change, suffocating any open discussion of ideas, allowing inequalities to remain unaddressed under the facade of showing respect. A person's race is part of their identity. Not talking about race may be perceived as polite, but it implies that talking about identity is impolite, allowing racism to go unchallenged, keeping the poor, poor. Karrle is the only person who is not deferential to the boss, frequently challenging Charles' pronouncements.

Stepping into this new world has transformed his life. There must be connections with the world he left behind, but he struggles to understand how these two worlds co-exist when they seem like different planets. By being close to the mechanisms of the commercial world, he is learning how capitalism produces great wealth, but cannot avoid the evidence that its uneven distribution is one of the root causes of many of the problems in his country. He realises he has walked into the privileged existence of the other planet, subsidised by the suffering in the one he has left, but these human divides mask the reality that there is only one planet.

Like Charles, Karrle also fears the seductive cosiness of comfort. However good these times are, his personal journey is not at an end. Remembering the words of the revolutionaries in the café, he accepts it is his moral duty to help his countrymen. Pulled between success in England and the dreadful troubles in his native land, his unexpected good fortune does not relieve him of his obligations.

He needs a plan of action, but first it is important to learn more about how this new world works and what opportunities England may offer in discharging his responsibilities. Right now, he is recovering, learning and enjoying the new challenges afforded by his relationship with Charles. Carrying the dreams of those dearest to him in his heart, his commitment remains undiminished; yet time is slipping away. Karrle recalls the writing of John Milton:

*''How soon hath Time, the subtle thief of youth, stol'n on his wing.''*

## Football Dream Dies

Autumn arrives, and once again Andy is picked to play on the right wing for the school team. He has race horse speed, but neither a footballing brain nor finesse and always disappoints. Failing to capitalise on the opportunities his speed implies is a source of continuous frustration.

His father is a dedicated supporter and attends all school matches, continually shouting advice from the side line. This burden of expectation is a source of considerable resentment, which Andy hides as best he can.

During a match against a posh, local team, he sprints down the wing attempting to intercept what should not be a fifty-fifty ball. His sliding tackle reaches the ball a fraction before the lumbering defender, who is upended and half-somersaults onto Andy's knee. The resulting, dull crack can be heard fifty feet away.

Excruciating pain instantly morphs Andy's face a ghostly white, his eyes roll and he vomits. Alex rushes to his son and has to be restrained from hitting the frightened defender, settling instead for a torrent of expletives. The match is abandoned.

The hospital X-ray reveals multiple fractures that will require several operations. Doctors advise Andy to avoid all contact sports; at best the reconstructed knee will always be a weakness. Alex is devastated. In a flash, *his* dreams of watching *his* son play for *his* club are destroyed.

Andy's pain is real but the hidden reward is relief that the inevitable dashing of his father's deepest desires have been taken out of his hands. After all, everyone apart from his dad knew that Andy was not even the best player in the school team. With the burden of expectation removed he is now free from what would inevitably have been inescapable failure.

## Economic Slavery

How does the Africa of today fit in with the new world Karrle is experiencing in Britain? This challenge absorbs all his spare thinking time. He understands the historical events that created the exploitation that is so pervasive, but how is it sustained. If the faults are so obvious, why are there as many setbacks as advances?

The debating chamber that he has formed with Charles offers valuable feedback to understand British attitudes to the increasingly visible evidence that Karrle is uncovering. His analysis may be correct, but it does not reveal the extent of the ignorance or hostility that must be addressed to rescue his countrymen or save the planet, which is rapidly becoming the overriding issue for everyone.

It is late afternoon and the day's duties are winding down. Allowing space for open conversation, the two men relax over a cup of tea. Strolling to the office window, Karrle glances across the street where a grossly overweight woman is struggling to board a bus with two small children. He comments that in Africa only the rich are fat but in Britain it is the opposite.

Charles asks what he feels when he sees pictures of starving African children on the television.

'Anger.'

'It is very sad,' agrees Charles.

Karrle's responds darkly, 'It is very unnecessary. They are all victims.'

Puzzled, Charles asks, 'Why unnecessary? Is it all the wars?'

'No. Africa is portrayed as poor, dying and surviving on charity thanks to the images constantly displayed on television by Oxfam, the Red Cross and others paid for by well-meaning Western donors.'

'But surely you cannot be against people giving money to those who may die without it?'

Karrle's eyes flash. 'Charity soothes the symptoms and ignores the disease. If a charity saves one child, that is good, but it is morally indefensible if millions in society benefit from the economic exploitation of hundreds of millions and their conscience is alleviated by small charitable donations. Leaving the system unchanged to condemn the next generation of economic slaves in morally bankrupt. The reality is that Africa is a rich continent subsidising the rest of the world.'

'Surely not. What makes you say that?'

Convictions are decanted into words. 'Africa is rich, it is the Africans that are poor. If Africa is poor, how do you explain the billions of pounds of resources that have been exported to the rest of the world for centuries? How can an African work full time extracting materials from the country where he was born and be part of a supply chain feeding multi-billion, multi-national corporations, selling his nations resources to the richest countries in the world, and not earn enough to feed, educate or properly house his family? How is it that most of the gold that man has ever extracted from the earth has come from Africa of which the Africans own virtually none? The number of people living on $1.25 a day or less in Africa is estimated by the United Nations to have increased from 290 million in 1990 to 414 million in 2010 – and that report is nine years old.'[1]

Charles grapples with these ideas. 'The world economy is expanding and Africa's revenues are increasing. Developing countries should be getting richer.'

'The population growth outweighs the number of people rising out of poverty. A shocking truth is that the twelve countries with the lowest income per head in the world are all in Africa. The eleven countries most dependent on agriculture are all in Africa, and the countries with the highest proportion of their population starving are in Africa. The lesson is, grow food and starve. What is that if not the product of a corrupt system? Check it out on Google.

The impact on the health of the population is appalling. Life expectancy is slowly rising, but at the present rate of progress some African countries will take more than 200 years to reduce their child death rate to five times the current UK death rate. Tell me, Charles, what is the difference between free-market forces and slavery?'

Charles believes he is on strong ground on economic issues. 'In a free-market economy, the labour is free to move. As slaves they are not. Anyway, we abolished slavery on moral grounds.'

'Do economic slaves have more freedom? Some slave owners were paternalistic, some employers are not.'

Charles becomes defensive. 'There is a limit to how much responsibility Britain has for situations in independent countries.'

This is a thin veil concealing the truth and must be uncovered. 'Because the West purchase from independent legal entities, it suits them

[1] United Nations, 2013

to believe that these are free-market forces, so they have no legal or 'moral' responsibility even though everybody knows that in these countries adults and children are employed on subsistence wages with virtually no employee or human rights. If it were truly an open market, Africans would not work for $1.25 a day. What opportunities do they have to improve their lives? If the only alternative is starvation, it is not an open market.

In earlier times, you owned what you made. Today's sophisticated world economy transfers control away from the individual. Africa is owned by remote, anonymous people, many of whom are not even in Africa. The chain of ownership has become ever longer, disempowering those who produce the goods and services that sustain the rest of the world.'

Charles listens but does not relate any of this to his life. 'What can one business or one country do? They operate in the same markets as their competitors.'

'The slave traders could have said the same until it became illegal. So Charles, if the criteria is merely personal economic gain and you had the power, would you re-introduce slavery?'

'Of course not!'

'In answering that, you have to bring in other values. Surely one of the benefits of human civilisation is that people have the freedom to make choices based on their values. What does it say about Western society that allows these practices to continue in our midst? "Open-market forces" are not a justification for abusing other humans, and the facade that we are powerless to interfere whilst funding these corrupt practices is an immoral, abdication of responsibility. The question is not whether slavery is unacceptable, but how much of our economic structures and attitudes today were formed by the exploitative trading and social patterns established when the trading of slaves was legal. Western commercial companies take nearly all the added value for the products that come from developing countries. They are very happy to take the profit and avoid the responsibility.'

Thinking logically Charles asks, 'So why don't the producers process and sell it themselves?'

'Because national governments and the EU work very closely to protect their corporations from open competition and the West own the means to process, transport and control the markets that these products are sold into. In many cases the economic logic would be to process the raw materials at source and send the finished product to market, reducing transport costs and environmental damage. This is deliberately uneconomic because of import tariffs, regulations and vested interests, which make building the necessary infrastructure uneconomic. For example, where is the world trading centre for coffee?'

Bemused, Charles guesses. 'I don't know! Kenya?'

'Switzerland.'

Astonished, Charles can see the irony: 'Switzerland!! Well, they've got the climate.'

'Over sixty per cent of the entire world trade is transacted there, and half of the rest is in Hamburg. How can millions of desperately poor subsistence farmers compete with a few multinational conglomerates who have the money and power to make the laws, write the contracts and run institutions all skewed for the benefit of the West?'

'Yes, but now they are independent, so they are free to do as they wish.'

'This might appear true,' agrees Karrle, 'but the only infrastructure – roads, railways, ports, airports, energy and water – were not to support the local populations, but to export food and materials out of Africa for the West. Social infrastructure, including health, education and the environment were – and still are – grossly underfunded. Gold, diamonds, copper, oil, etc. concentrate wealth in isolated pockets, owned by foreigners or a few elite Africans, who maintain control by suppressing their people. The local population grow food which is labour intensive, keeping producers desperately poor. The poverty in Africa today is a direct consequence of the unfair practices which were established by the European empires in the nineteenth century.'

Dismayed, the only thing Charles can think of saying is, 'That is a very harsh environment to grow up in.'

'What would the cost of resources be if Africa had a welfare state and high taxation? Africa has twice the population of Europe and would become a larger market, attracting investment from all over the world; asset prices would rise, and the developed countries would be considerably poorer. Today Africans are tenants in their own country. Don't talk about open markets.'

'Why don't they change the rules, they're independent?'

Karrle has to correct this comforting misconception. 'Sadly, this is another popular myth.'

'Please explain.'

'Western commercial enterprises used their influence to continue trading on similar terms to the empires. Europe knew that political independence was of little value without economic independence. The beauty of this arrangement is that exploitation is continued by their African business partners, whilst the sham of political independence supports the lie that the West are in no way accountable. Exploitation, suppression, rebellion and starvation are not their problem, a very cold-blooded attitude.

This myth is widely accepted by the electorate in many of the old imperialist countries, thus avoiding guilt for the incalculable human suffering of past, present and future generations. Some British now feel themselves the victims of immigration, whilst simultaneously blind to the fact that over generations they continue to be the beneficiaries of massively under-priced resources that have destabilised Africa and artificially raised Western living standards. Endless negative news supports the myth that Africans are incapable of managing their own affairs. Africans are still not in control of their own destiny.

By adapting to more a more "enlightened" environment, the exploiters appease their consciences with charitable donations, respect for the democratic freedoms of other countries; detaching any sense of responsibility by feelings of superiority: "look at how they behave". The concept of free-market forces completes the entrapment, sanctioning the full range of prejudices, relieving guilt and inducing a sense of disconnection and apathy. The West have the same dilemma today that confronted them in the nineteenth century. They banned slavery, to their own economic disadvantage, because of its inherent inhumanity. What action are they going to take to stop economic slavery?

So when you ask me what I feel about starving children in Africa, I say I feel angry.'

Charles is silent.

Karrle is shining a light into the world economy that even as a businessman Charles has accepted unquestioningly. His business world starts when materials arrive in the UK, and he has remarkably little concept of what happens overseas. He knows that poverty is widespread in many parts of the world, and had assumed it was due to these countries being incompetently run by scheming, ill-educated and (as per the constant drip of press articles) corrupt people in their own countries.

He had heard some of these things before, but they were easily forgotten as irrelevant to his life and nothing to do with him? Being told explicitly by somebody he respects that, even today, Western capitalism may have considerable responsibility for these injustices is sobering indeed!

Karrle is a jewel, who had had to deal with problems for which he has no responsibility, and until now, Charles felt no connection.

## Rich Africa, Poor Africans, Western Robbers

Charles cannot stop thinking about his conversation with Karrle and feels compelled to come to a conclusion for his own peace of mind. The next day he continues the discussion. 'I understand some of what you are saying, but why are these workers paid so little?'

Karrle relishes articulating his thoughts and enjoys the practice. 'The most widely traded tropical agricultural product in the world is coffee. Twenty-five million smallholders grow 80% of the world's coffee. How can they compete with a cartel of multinationals?

'As with all African exports, small African nations are impoverished and disadvantaged at every stage in their dealings with major corporations, who have the money to retain the best professional, legal, accounting and banking expertise. They use many techniques, from contract negotiations and legal dispute procedures to self-reporting (and massively understating) the volume and quality of what they remove, all designed with the intention of obtaining the lowest price by whatever means. The bulk of the wealth taken from developing countries is due to trade mispricing, of which false invoicing is responsible for the greatest loss. This immoral strategy is deliberate embezzlement, and is practised every day by Western commerce.'

Charles interrupts, 'Why are people treated like this? Surely it is against the law.'

This is easy to answer. 'Because they are vulnerable and the law is not enforced. There are even reports of commercial companies avoiding prosecution by poaching bright, local government investigators with offers of high salaries and enhanced career prospects.

These highly targeted strategies did not evolve by accident, and neither party are innocent. The more corrupt the institution, the more entrenched and destructive these forces are. The wealth allows the African dealmakers to control their own countrymen, which gives the West what they seek most – low-cost stability of supply, with little or no taxes over years, even decades.'

Charles lights up at the last comment. 'I am not surprised. We have the same problems in the UK.' Turning to his laptop he Googles 'company tax avoidance UK' and 13,400,000 results appear in 0.46 seconds. He selects one.

'Look, the *Daily Mail*, 11th March 2017. Vodafone UK sales of £6.7 billion, corporation tax paid nil. EE, UK sales £6.3 billion, corporation tax nil. There are loads of them: Amazon, Apple, Starbucks, Thomas Cook, Microsoft, YouTube. Even home-grown entrepreneurs like Richard Branson's companies are offshore and pay no UK tax[1]. So who pays for the education, healthcare, roads, police and pensions for the people they employ in Britain? My cleaner pays more tax. When I think of what my business pays because it is UK registered, it makes my blood boil.'

Karrle is glad that Charles feels a sense of outrage, although his perspective is different. 'It is true these multinationals adopt the same strategy in many countries, but there is one major difference. Although these companies employ many workers on the minimum wage, often doing soul-destroying jobs, they operate in a high-cost economy and pay in many other ways through VAT, rent, rates, fuel duty, income tax and national insurance on the people they employ in the UK, as well as the money their employees spend on housing, consumer products, restaurants, etc.

Even including all the thousands of UK companies paying corporation tax like yours, it represents only 7% of UK government revenues. But the big payoff is that London is probably the biggest tax haven in the world receiving countless billions from legal as well as illicit funds, with few questions asked. As one writer described it: "the financial city of London levitates on black money".

The Office for Budget Responsibility[2] for 2022–23 forecast the government will spend £168m on health; education £77m; public services £130m; defence £32m; pensions, universal credit and welfare £250m and £373m on other expenditure – a total of £38,000 per household. How much of these other forms of government revenue can African governments collect from a company paying no company tax and a population earning $1.25 a day, whilst considerable national income disappears into private hands? There is not the money to develop a sophisticated prosperous economy, and pitiful tax collections deprive African countries of desperately needed funds to create a safety net for their people. Do you know the definition of a tax haven?'

Charles answers confidently, 'Where you don't pay tax.'

It's Karrle's turn to move to the laptop and he Googles 'tax havens' and reads: ' "A tax haven is a country that offers foreign

[1] Diane Abbot, member of Parliament, Bloomberg, 21/04/2020

[2] (Home - Office for Budget Responsibility (obr.uk)

individuals and businesses little or no tax liability in a politically and economically static environment. Tax havens also share limited or no financial information with foreign tax authorities".[1]

Where are many of the greatest tax havens in the world? I will tell you: the Channel Islands, Isle of Man, British Virgin Islands, London, Cayman Islands, Singapore. Do you see a pattern here?' The question is rhetorical.

'Britain,' Charles answers obligingly.

'How many African countries have passed laws in any of these territories?'

'Obviously none,' Charles responds obediently.

'It is national governments that pass the laws in their own territories, creating secrecy jurisdictions where legal and illegal money can be hidden. Corporations extract, process and sell Africa's resources, defrauding Africa in the process. National governments around the world create the tax havens for the profits to be hidden, and the banking system facilitates the transfer and concealment of the proceeds avoiding disclosure and taxation. The West establishes, regulates and runs all these operations. Africa cannot change the rules, but they get the blame.'

Until now, Charles had not connected these processes to appreciate the iron grip the West held around Africa's throat; naively believing these were the same market forces in which he operated. His only comment is, 'That is morally indefensible.'

Karrle is now in full flow. 'It is even worse when you analyse the long-term impact. The UN has calculated the illicit flow of money out of Africa is running at over $50 billion annually and rising rapidly. Since 1980, illicit outflows are estimated to have been three times today's total African debt. Some countries pay more than 20% of their national income in debt repayments. There are loans dating back to the 1980s that have been repaid multiple times, the original loan often embezzled by the leaders of the time, with the cash now sitting in offshore tax havens, protected by the Western financial system.'

Charles wants to know if this is the full picture. 'Yes, but what about the drugs, trafficking and corruption that is rampant in many African countries?'

---

[1] http://www.investopedia.com/terms/t/taxhaven.asp

'Supplying Western markets you mean?' Karrle bounces back. 'I wondered when you were going to mention that! The illicit outflows from criminal gangs is only a third of the total. The largest volume comes from western business, but the criminals utilise the same avenues the West created, operate and protect for their own corrupt purposes. Are Africans the criminals or the victims? Who suffers the most? This environment funds conflict, war and destruction, and the West benefits enormously.'

'You make the West sound very corrupt, but they operate within the law.'

Karrle tries to broaden the context. 'All societies have laws. Just because actions are within the law does not make them moral. Slavery was legal once. This Western conspiracy robs the poor of what they do have. African governments are permanently impoverished with desperate populations, often survival depends on working within corrupt environments. As long as these injustices exist, escaping extreme poverty will cause uncontrollable immigration for generations; some dying in their attempt to reach sanctuaries like Europe. The disapproval of those not in danger will change nothing.'

Charles listens to all this in silence. His only comment is, 'What a bleak picture.'

Undeterred, Karrle resumes. 'Inadequate income and huge debts owed to a subsidised West deplete already deficient funds. It is the opposite of how the West run their own economies, where over-spending is financed simply by printing trillions in various currencies and pumping the cash into the system in countries like USA, UK, Japan, Germany, Italy, China and others.

Europe was treated differently after the devastation of the Second World War. The USA created the Marshall Plan, a $15 billion fund (at 1948 prices) for reconstruction. The world had seen the injustice and suffering the Germans experienced after the First World War that gave rise to Hitler, and they believed it was the only way to stop Europe falling into anarchy. The West need to adopt the same approach with desperately poor populations. A sensible deal could be struck. Buying Africa's resources at fair prices could be the way to pay back the West. There is a solution if people look for it.

Charles looks worried but unconvinced. Karrle offers another example. 'Look at the response to coronavirus. The rich countries conjured up trillions of dollars of debt to sustain their economies, with no plan or idea as to how to repay it. Africa is totally exposed to the ravages of the virus and has utterly inadequate access to finance to sort out its own problems.'

Charles responds, 'Help is being offered to developing countries.'

'It is completely inadequate. A cynic might conclude that this is an attempt by the West to respond to international pressure but, more importantly, to avoid re-infection.'

'It cannot be right that all the blame falls on the West,' Charles protests.

'No, but only the West has the power to change it. The question you must ask is: at what point did Europeans cease to be responsible for present-day Africa?

a) When they conquered the territory taking "ownership" of the land, resources and the people? Or
b) When they extracted the resources from Africa for their European industries, taking absolute control of their conquered territories, transporting twelve million slaves across the Atlantic and killing multiple more millions in Africa? Or
c) When they de-colonised, creating countries with artificial borders based on European ownership boundaries, with unsustainable economies and superimposed political systems for their own convenience without regard for the lives of the people who lived there? Or
d) Now, when they employ millions directly and indirectly, working in conditions that would be illegal in the West? Or
e) Now when they defraud African countries of their resources by legal construction, false documentation and embezzlement? Or
f) Now, when they have irrefutable evidence that their commercial activities are destroying the environment and damaging the entire world for their personal short-term financial gain?

Europeans have had more influence on Africa than any other continent, and after 600 years Africa has the richest resources in the world and the poorest people. So the question is, how much will the West sacrifice to create a more equitable world? If the answer is nothing, then all our futures are already sealed.'

'How is it that people know so little about these things?'

'Secrecy.'

Charles looks puzzled. 'Secrecy?'

'Secrecy!' emphasises Karrle. 'Which countries are the most secretive about disclosing personal financial information?'[1]

'I don't know. China?'

'The top three are Switzerland, Hong Kong and the USA. Of the fifty-four countries in Africa, only one is in the top sixty.

It is the secretive financially sophisticated countries that attract illegal funds managed in all respects by the West. Roughly $1 trillion flows illegally out of developing countries annually[2], about ten times the amount of all the foreign aid flowing into these same economies. Charity is just small change to appease the conscience of the West, not paid for by the commercial companies making their profits out of Africa.'

'They can't keep it a secret forever, can they? I mean, you found out.'

'It is available, but I had to do a lot of research,' replies Karrle. 'Despite the efforts of companies and countries to keep their operations covert, pioneering individuals, social organisations and legislative authorities are increasingly demanding transparency. US Justice Louis Brandeis said "sunlight is the best disinfectant". The EU is demanding public companies to disclose the tax they pay in each country they operate in, and the results are very embarrassing. Check it out on Google.[3]

Political weakness and public ignorance have allowed business to ruthlessly run amok. In nature, where a species is overhunted natural selection sooner or later takes out the predator. These exploitative practices are unacceptable and public exposure must change attitudes, or the West will become a legitimate target.'

Charles is shell-shocked, not by his friend's frankness, but the facts he has revealed, shaking the foundations of his own beliefs.

---

[1] Tax Justice Network publish the Financial Secrecy Index, a table based on objective criteria

[2] Global Financial Integrity (GFI)

[3] ECA Track It Stop It Get It

## Karrle's Eureka Moment

There is widespread astonishment throughout the company that the managing director has promoted Karrle so quickly; after all, he only made one suggestion and now he lives in the boss's pocket.

This unlimited access to the managing director causes resentment amongst a number of the managers, particularly those who had worked for his father and who now feel their input is ignored. Most dare not refuse to co-operate, and decide to wait for Karrle to make a mistake, but a few see that he is bright and worth talking to.

Charles' endless drive to improve profitability provides opportunities for Karrle to investigate a number of departments, which he tackles with his usual forensic analytical intensity. Despite the risk of exposing his lack of experience that many is see as assumed knowledge, his rationale often takes the conversation to places that many long-serving employees have overlooked.

An ambitious young manager called Tom sees Karrle as a conduit for getting his pet ideas to the boss. The two men brainstorm potential areas of improvement. Reasoning that, as materials make up 40% of the sales price, purchasing must have opportunities to make savings. Tom suggests Karrle investigates how the buyers determine the economic order quantity with a view to reducing costs and stock levels, freeing up cash.

'Go and see Lech. He places the orders,' Tom suggests.

Karrle enters the stores office. 'Hi, I'm looking for Lech.'

'That's me. How can I help?'

'I would like to understand the criteria used for ordering critical and high-value production items. I wondered if you could explain how the system works.'

As they discuss the basis on which materials are re-ordered, evidence comes to light of inappropriate authority levels, lack of integration of the purchasing function and the habitual nature of the decision-making process. Karrle comments how short sighted some people are.

'I agree,' Lech says. 'We all see the universe through our own porthole.'

Karrle picks up on a phrase that is familiar. 'That's an unusual saying.'

'It's from *The Book of REB*.'

Incredulous, Karrle's body and gaze freezes. Staring directly at the storeman, Lech is unnerved by such a powerful response to a casual comment. Are his ears deceiving him? Now both are motionless.

'Where did you hear that?'

Apprehensively, the storeman replies, 'A young girl told me. She said she had been badly damaged by other people who used her for their own purposes, but discovering her own *Book of REB* enabled her to understand other people's. It gave her the confidence to take control of her life. *The Book of REB* made that possible.'

With bated breath Karrle asks, 'Was this a girl in University Hospital Coventry?'

'Not when I met her.' Lech had promised not to reveal how they met.

'Oh! It probably wasn't her then. I did speak to an Indian girl once. Maybe they were friends. I did not know that anybody had taken any notice of my ideas.'

It is now Lech's turn to look astonished: 'They were *your* ideas?' he says with wonderment. He grabs Karrle's hand and with considerable enthusiasm shakes it vigorously. 'Dear sir, dear sir, it is a great, great honour to meet you. You must tell me more. It has changed my life already.'

This is becoming ridiculous. 'Really? How?'

'When the boss wanted to put electronic tags on all the workers, it gave me the confidence to challenge him. He changed his mind and recruited over a hundred people.'

Now the circle is complete. So this was the event that triggered Karrle's employment, his meeting with Charles and the opportunities that had been invisible before. He had told Mohini that solutions appear if you search for them, and now his own life had been changed by the very path he had been describing.

Three revelations are too much to be contained. Karrle's eyes ignite as his face bursts with rapturous delight, hot on the heels of a booming laugh that he thought had been lost in the sands of the Sahara Desert.

What ludicrous, delicious irony is this? And what a profound revelation! Cut off from everyone that was precious to him, isolated and empty, he grasped at straws to understand what had brought him to this point, and unwittingly addressed the fundamental challenges of the lives of others, laying a path they had followed with glorious results. This is his moment in the sun.

At critical moments in life, feelings of utter isolation are a normal response to seemingly impossible challenges. *The Book of REB*, through a process of comprehension of self and the world, had unlocked understanding, giving strength and direction to navigate life's injustices in what appeared unwinnable situations. Here was evidence that *The Book of REB* contained truths that had impacted the lives of this Polish man and at least two Indian girls, and created the circumstances for his own rescue.

How many others may have heard of his ideas? Who could have guessed where it would lead, or where it might lead. This truly is a Karl Marx moment.

He recalls Graham's words: 'Describe what is real from your heart and it will echo in the heart of everyone who recognises the journey. Echo others' experiences and it will be as hollow as the echo.'

## Mohini's Hospital Rounds

Mohini misses her talks with Karrle. Pouring her energies into volunteering is an essential distraction allowing precious time to repair her life. Some patients love to tell this young girl about their past lives and she seems genuinely interested, remembering what they said with remarkable detail. A few stories seem a little embellished, but this is all part of the richness of life, offering new insights into people's lives; how varied and yet how similar. Most revolve around the family; career achievements seem to fade and become less important years after the events. Mohini realises how important families are, and reflects on her own loss. The hospital rounds become slower and the time flies.

The orthopaedic ward is always fascinating because the patients are more varied, anything from the fragile elderly breaking hips, to injured athletes playing exciting but dangerous sports. Entering the ward, a cursory glance reveals a vision she is completely unprepared for: the bed by the window is occupied by Andy.

It has taken every ounce of her strength to hide a broken heart and create the fragile world that is now her existence. The burden of her shame instantly crushes any optimism that was trickling back into her life. Staring in petrified horror, the poor girl is paralysed by disbelief.

Andy turns his head and the recognition is instant. 'Mohini?' He is stunned beyond words. She seems different, but she still owns his heart.

Brought back to life, Mohini awakens from the nightmare. Shaking and unable to suppress her tears, she flees the scene. Exposed and defenceless, she has nowhere to hide and nowhere else to go.

Rose sees her abandoned trolley, but where is Mohini? Her disappearance is out of character. Hoping it is nothing serious, she covers Mohini's wards and does not report her absence. Arriving at Andy's bed, the patient is clearly agitated. They have met before and he has always been polite, if reserved. This behaviour is very different, and the cause is quickly revealed. 'Where is that Indian girl that does your job?' he asks.

'Pretty, isn't she?' Rose replies, surprised at the directness of the question.

'Yes, but what is she doing here?'

'Same as me, serving the patients. Why, do you know her?'

The lovers had promised each other that their relationship would remain secret, and even in his desperation Andy does not want to break his word. He does not know what to say, so he says nothing.

Rose remembers how appallingly damaged Mohini was when she arrived at the hospital. The girl must be protected, yet she is curious to know more. Neither Rose nor Andy know how to handle the situation and the silence is awkward. Conversation suspended; all questions remain unanswered.

Andy is deeply troubled. When the love of his life suddenly disappeared, he assumed that her father had sent her to India for an arranged marriage. She had spoken of this several times, and he knew that this was not what she wanted. Maybe the marriage had failed and she had been sent back in England in disgrac. This could be his opportunity to come to her rescue. He would talk to the old woman if she came round again.

Rose finishes her rounds on the wards but is troubled by Mohini's disappearance and the tense questioning of the boy. They obviously have a history. The girl needs help, but is Andy the saviour or the villain? His leg injury was very severe. Was there a connection?

# Independent Britain: No EU or Migrants

Charles is following his daily routine of skimming the newspaper before starting work, when Karrle enters the office. 'Just reading all the excitement about the number of immigrants entering the UK. Net migration seems to be going up and up.'

'I wouldn't worry about that. Brexit will solve all the problems!'

'You think the government will get a grip?' Charles asks.

'Not a chance! The restrictions on the free movement of labour will damage the UK economy and encourage illegal migration as the only alternative. The illusions swirling around this polarised debate allows opportunists like Priti Patel to further her career as the mouthpiece of British prejudice.'

Charles looks at Karrle. 'Good morning. Did you get out of the wrong side of the bed?'

'Morning!' Karrle replies, the conversation clearly tickling his emotions.

'You're obviously not a fan of Priti Patel. How can you not be a fan of somebody called Priti?' observes Charles.

'She refuses to address the issues, offers no solutions and will fail on all fronts. The French received £55m to stop immigration across the channel and Britain are about to throw another load at the problem. Then there is the £120m for this Rwandan fiasco; all the while the relentless underlying pressure on migration will continue, irrespective of decisions made in the UK. Brexit is merely the UK shooting itself in the foot.'

'What do you mean?'

'The Brexiteers appeal is based on invoking memories of a past that never existed, and promising the undeliverable.'

'What is undeliverable?'

'Independence!' Karrle explains his statement. 'The world is consolidating into power blocks and what does the UK do? Leave the biggest free-trade area in the world. The UK is smaller and weaker than any of the major players they will be negotiating with for the vast majority of their international trade and yet David Davis, Secretary of State for Exiting the EU said, "The free trade agreement … should be one of the easiest in human history"[1], as did Liam Fox, Boris Johnson, Michael Gove and other Brexiteer opportunists. Where's that? Planet

[1] 20th July 2017

Zog! Six years after the referendum, just look at how tough the EU negotiations have been. Brexiteers pedalled criminal misrepresentations, like the fantasy that the £350m UK weekly contribution to the EU would go straight to the NHS, ignoring all the EU funding that comes back and the benefits of a free trade zone. All their arguments were dishonest or delusional. Brexit is so divisive, and Boris Johnson is such a maverick that he deskilled his government, compounding the errors. Tories, like Liz Truss, are saddled with the burden of defending the indefensible.'

'What about the argument that we buy more from them than they buy from us and this gives us the upper hand in the negotiations?'

'Garbage! Just because something is a fact, does not make it objective evidence. Forty-five per cent of UK exports go to the EU, 6% of their exports come to us. Who will lose the most in a dispute? Are they going to sacrifice the EU dream for us? Not a chance! We walked away.'

Charles raises a commonly-held opinion. 'Some people like the feeling of being independent.'

'But not the reality of poverty! The whole concept of independence is a dangerous illusion. Do you use a mobile phone?'

'You know I do!'

'Then it is certain that it contains cobalt, and a good chance that cobalt was mined in the Congo by desperately poor workers digging deep holes into soft ground that frequently collapses, burying the diggers. This is completely unregulated. How about using wood, oil, plastic, chocolate, wool, sugar, cotton, fruit, nuts, corn, copper, gold, diamonds, etc?'

'Of course, everyone does,' retorts Charles.

'Then the same "everyones" are being subsidised by Africa. The people who dig it out of the ground benefit far less than the British. This inequality causes conflict and, because it is vital to your lifestyle, it makes you vulnerable. If the Chinese realise their ambitions and gain control of the sources of raw materials, do you think they will allow grossly under-priced raw materials to flow to the West indefinitely? They will supply the finished product at prices they decide, or refuse to supply, like rare earth materials. How will the UK support their industry or pay for these goods?'

These ideas seemed too radical and stark to have occurred to Charles.

'If people want to be truly independent,' Karrle goes on, 'take all your clothes off and stand in the middle of a field. Within hours you will want are clothes, food, shelter and companionship. Oh, and by the way, as you do not own the field, you will be trespassing!'

'That's ridiculous.'

'Is it? Let's start with food. Britain has not been able to feed itself for generations. Hitler tried to starve Britain, Kaiser Bill attempted the same in World War I, and more than 200 years ago Napoleon did a deal with Russia to stop supplying wheat. British cities would not survive two meals after the fridges emptied, and society would implode within days. None of this has anything to do with the recent influx of migrants.'

'But those things are not going to happen,' Charles assures himself.

'You are correct, provided we have allies we can depend on, i.e. we are part of something bigger.'

'Which we have.'

'Really? Well let's look at that. In the last hundred years, Britain narrowly won two world wars with the help of the Americans, Indians and the rest of what was then the British Empire, almost bankrupting itself in the process. Britain will need the help of others in the next hundred years, be it from disease like Covid, natural disasters resulting from global warming, or war – Russia in Ukraine and next China in Taiwan. Britain today has the smallest army in 200 years – 74,000 in July 2019 – and is not in the top thirty largest armies in the world. Enemies don't need to invade Britain, they can just cut off supplies. What support will Britain be able to depend on in the future?

Both world wars started in Europe, and Russia and the Chinese were on our side in both. When the next war comes, will India, Pakistan, South Africa, Singapore and Hong Kong, amongst many others, be involved? and if so, which side will they be on? India and Pakistan see each other as their greatest enemies and are more likely to be fighting each other. Britain could be dragged into their war.

You would have to be on medication to believe that our future is safe based on the past. And what is Britain doing? Walking away from the group that has been the centre of conflict throughout history to retain the mythical concept of "independence". Nigel Farage may cause more damage to the UK than any politician in generations.'

An ironic smile flickers across Charles' face as he replies, 'Sitting on the fence has never been your strong point. In an uncertain world, people feel that independence gives them the freedom to react to the unexpected.'

'Even inside the country, Britain cannot collect the crops it grows, run the NHS, care homes or construction industry. We don't even have enough HGV drivers. Even *you* cannot run your factories without foreign workers. Weakening the ties with those you depend on does not give you independence, it diminishes your options and freedom of action!'

'On that basis, I assume you do not agree with the Scottish National Party's ambition of independence from Britain?'

'The SNP are overdosing on wishful thinking. Scotland exports more to Britain than the rest of the world put together, so leaving a free-trade market that takes the majority of their exports is idiotic. In addition, the Barnett formula gives direct payments from the English tax payer to the Scottish government at a rate per head higher than any other part of the UK.

As for an independent voice, if Scotland joined the EU they would be 1% of the population of Europe. How could they compete for European funding, against Eastern European countries like Bulgaria with a similar population but on 25% of the income per head when Scotland is in the top twenty wealthiest countries in the world?

'The idea that the EU will support countries breaking up into smaller factions to be re-admitted as independents into the European Union shows zero understanding of the realities. You need unanimity to become an EU member – and Spain, for one, with Catalonia demanding independence, would not agree.'

Charles mentions an oft-quoted argument. 'The Scots have oil…'

Karrle cuts him short. '…that will run to almost nothing within a generation, and which is heavily dependent on violently fluctuating world oil prices. In 2020, the price fell from $68 a barrel to below $20. It has gone up recently, but the world is moving away from fossil fuels and, as extraction becomes more expensive, profits will dwindle. That is no basis on which to plan a nation's future.

There are still too many people reminiscing about perceived past glories and injustices, which is a very poor psychological framework for dealing with the challenges of the future. Brexit is a seductive illusion, and recent good fortune is no guarantee of immunity in the future. Relying on luck makes the UK a hostage to fortune.'

'The loss of privilege is hard to adjust to sometimes,' says Charles feebly.

Karrle cannot supress some emotion in his response. 'The British are still privileged and have a lot more adjusting to do, like the delusion that white people can continue to control the world. What proportion of the world's population do you think are white?'

Charles guesses. 'I don't know – 35%?'

'Today they are around 16% and falling every year. People with white skin have always been a minority in the world. A thousand years ago, there were more Chinese than Europeans, and early man lived in Africa and was black – yet white people control the world economic system.

The number of black people is increasing rapidly, and the whites are not even replacing themselves. They need young immigrants to provide the labour to support their economies. The proportion of white people will continue to diminish for several generations. Within two generations white people will be in the minority in the United States and some European countries. In 1950, Europeans were 22% of the world's population, in 2017 they were 10%, and are forecast to reduce to 6%. In some continents white people are in tiny numbers, yet they still control most of the world's wealth. This is unsustainable.'

Karrle shows Charles a graph projecting population growth [1]

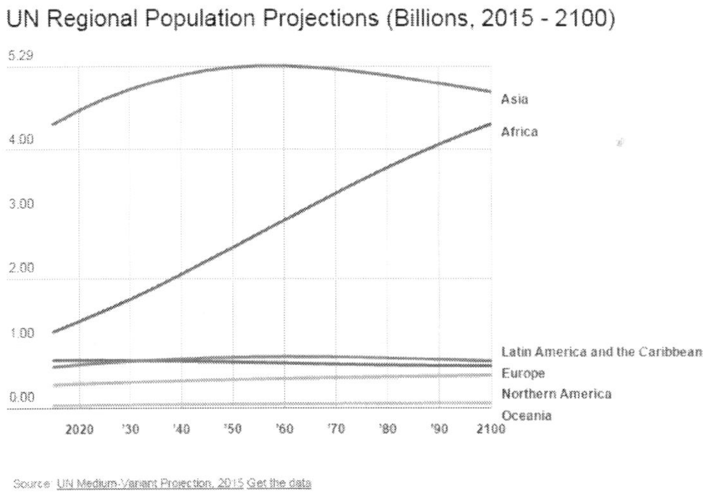


[1] https://www.businessinsider.com/africas-population-explosion-will-change-humanity-2015-8?r=US&IR=T

‘Are you saying that the days of white supremacy are over.’

‘It is inevitable, and a good thing, too; but not yet. But like the Russian Revolution, just because there are problems with the current system does not mean that what replaces it will be better. The problems ahead cannot be avoided. They offer huge opportunities but also risk catastrophic failure. Solving these challenges requires a team solution, and not all the team members are in Britain.’

## George Wright

George Wright was production manager under Charles' father and can remember Charles as a young schoolboy, visiting the factory during his holidays. After a lifetime of service George is due to retire in a couple of years, but Charles needs to make changes now if he is going to keep ahead of his competitors, and George resists everything new.

A different approach might crack an old nut. Charles suggests a few ideas for productivity improvements he would like Karrle to discuss with the production manager, adding with a wry smile, 'This will challenge even you.' The comment raises Karrle's curiosity

Knocking on the production manager's door and entering, Karrle is greeted by a scowling, raisin-skinned, heavily-jowled face that resembles a disapproving frog; it is decorated by a substantial moustache, crowning an over-proportioned body. Maybe he is more like the descendent of a now-extinct walrus.

Karrle's intrusion is not welcome. 'Yes!' the walrus growls.

'Hello. My name is Karrle. Charles suggested that I come and talk to you about opportunities for improvement.'

'I know who you are! What do you know about the industry?'

'Not much.'

'Well, don't you think you should find out before you come here wasting my time? I'm a very busy man.'

This defensive approach seemed to imply that it is impossible for anybody to understand the issues without specialist knowledge. Karrle is surprised how easy he has found it to identify problems which, once defined, generally suggest their own solutions. 'If you could spare fifteen minutes, that would be a start.'

'I have to finish this production schedule. Come back at 3.45.' Since the boss has requested the meeting, this appears to be active obstruction.

Karrle is dismissed and the production manager's eyes return to the papers strewn over his desk, the confused expression on his face reminding Karrle of an old man he had seen at the library, trying to send an email, but frightened of the keyboard.

George certainly lived up to his reputation. Charles has described him as a man who gets things done, but his way, and 'as solid as a rock.' Certainly Karrle had witnessed the granite, but he is also convinced that the production scheduling could be handled more efficiently by a simple computer programme.

George Wright is a rather limited man who has always craved respect, clinging to everything that he believes reflects his status and entitlement. He has never been afflicted with self-doubt, or humility; his supercilious manner is that of a butler to a great lord, assuming all the pomp of somebody he knows with the authority of a self-appointed defender of the unwritten rules.

The price, not visible to him, entraps him in a role defending what nobody else wants. In George's mind, this merely confirms the need to 'maintain standards', but the effect is to re-enforce his isolation, turning a bad habit into a siege mentality and making any alternatives seem too risky.

He is riddled with Britishness, a royalist to the core, always standing on higher moral ground. He once overheard himself being referred to as 'PLS'. When the subordinate was questioned about the remark his quick wit explained it stood for 'Production Leads Sales.' This reaffirmed his self-belief, for as he always says, 'If I don't make it, they can't sell it.' To everyone else PLS stands for 'Pompous Little Shit'.

It is 3.45pm and Karrle knocks on the door and enters. 'Excuse me. Are you free?'

Without ceremony or grace, George snaps, 'Sit down! What do you want?'

'Charles asked me to look at the possibility of moving towards Just-in-Time production.'

George's eyes stare daggers as he hurls back his response. 'What!! Not that old chestnut!' Exhaling fire and smoke, maybe he is an extinct dragon, not a walrus, but he is still unknown to science. 'I've told Charles it's a waste of time but he won't listen. Investing in expensive systems will be uneconomic as long as he keeps employing cheap foreign labour, impoverishing our economy, and keeping the British unemployed.'

Karrle is shocked by this obvious frontal assault on a non-white, non-British member of the company. Defending himself, he answers: 'Foreign workers do not cause unemployment. They create wealth in the communities they work in, and support many key parts of the economy like agriculture, construction and health care.'

'Balderdash! Of course they do. Big companies are always announcing mass redundancies, and British people who have worked for years find themselves on the scrap heap. They only get offered low-paid jobs competing with foreigners.'

Karrle is forced to correct this misrepresentation. 'You are confusing immigration with automation. America lost five million manufacturing jobs in ten years, but 85% were due to automation, only 15% to factories moving overseas. When multinationals announce thousands of redundancies, it is not to hire immigrants. You can do all your banking without meeting a bank clerk and all your shopping without meeting a shop assistant. In the UK, low-paid foreigners create more jobs by increasing demand. They help maintain UK competitiveness in export markets, pay PAYE and fill the jobs that the British don't want. It is the young foreign workers who care for the retired British.'

'You make them sound like bloody saints. You obviously haven't been in England long.'

'Long enough to know the facts. Migration has always brought enormous benefits. America was built on immigration, and it is not only people that migrate but ideas, culture, science – everything that drives civilisation forward.'

George growls, 'Drives it into the ground, more like. You can't deny that the low paid are suffering because of the numbers of foreigners willing to work for nothing, and many of the middle classes are being pushed into low paid jobs because they can't get better.'

'As I said, that is caused by automation. It's undeniable that the recent high volumes of immigrants have caused a social reaction to the practical problems in the short term, and sometimes they are not always handled very well, but it is an illusion to think that things will get better if migration stops. During the Industrial Revolution, many thousands lost their jobs – but who wants to go back to Victorian times? Migration offers new challenges and produces new solutions. These changes will not always benefit the individual, but they will enrich the society on which all individuals depend. It is the same gift to future generations that parents sacrifice for their children in the hope that their lives will be better.'

George has been silent longer than his patience can tolerate. 'Yes, we sacrifice for our own children, not everybody else's. If you lot ran your countries properly, you wouldn't need to come over here.'

Karrle wants to say, 'Let us put our minds together to see what future we can create for our children,' but knows the effort would be fruitless. Angered by listening to empty words and shit moral judgements without solutions, he endeavours to sound reasonable. 'The British felt they had the right to go anywhere in the world.'

With unwitting irony George bites back, 'Well, we didn't expect you to follow us home. There are too many of you for this small island. We've given you freedom, developed your economies and are still your biggest customers. What more do you want?' His jaw is set solid as he glares at his adversary.

'You judge me by your impression of the country I am from. I doubt if you have been there and probably could not find it on a map.'

George silently agrees. He has no interest in where it is, and no intention of finding out.

Karrle continues. 'In which country are all individuals good or all bad? If you decide the person you think I am when you don't know me, you deny me my humanity. If you act on your prejudices, you may make some very poor judgements that damage both of us.'

Although he has run out of arguments, George is not a believer. Just because this uninvited intruder can come up with some smart-arse comments does not mean the man is of any standing. He's from bloody Africa, for God's sake. The bloody man's lucky to be here, without spouting all this ungrateful claptrap. All he can think of saying is, 'Well I am a traditionalist and proud of Britain.'

On the wall there is a picture of the Queen and, unmistakably, only a few places behind is George as a younger man.

'Ah, yes tradition. It is important. I assume that you are a royalist.'

'I certainly am. George, like the kings of England.'

'Quite so.' Karrle pauses, then says, 'You know that King George I was born in Germany.'

'Maybe so, but that was a long time ago.'

'And King George II was born in Germany.'

The silent hostility is worth its weight in gold, and Karrle cannot resist maximising his verbal supremacy as he continues. 'And King George III was also king of Hanover, as was King George IV. And King George V changed the name of the House of Saxe-Coburg to the House of Windsor. It is good to see that you are upholding the British tradition of adapting to foreign influences.'

George sits in sullen silence.

Now motoring, this is no time for Karrle to stop. 'By the way, congratulations on the Industrial Revolution.'

'What do you mean?'

'You seem to be taking personal credit for it. And well done on winning the Second World War. Remind me, what exactly was your part in it?'

'Don't be bloody stupid. I was not even born then.'

'Ah, that's a relief. So you won't be taking the blame for the Kenyan detention centres of the 1950s, or complicity in the Bengal famine of 1943, or the rape and murder of many indigenous peoples in the process of building an empire? I am a bit confused. What have any of these events got to do with you or your assumed superiority?'

The silence is now deafening. Eventually George launches his reply, 'They are the successes of the society of which I am a member.'

Karrle gives a deep sigh of regret. 'Oh dear! Oh dear! So you are taking responsibility for the atrocities perpetrated by the empire builders, which have appalling consequences on the lives of hundreds of millions today. In which case, what are you going to do about it?'

With a face of stone, George replies, 'Nothing. It's not my problem.'

'Then it is others who will have to deal with the consequences, and you will be a bystander, clinging to your hand-me-down values and cursing the world as events pass you by.'

This is not the sort of conversation that George is used to, and confirms that Karrle is an enemy. He always has been, but now George had something specific to focus his dislike on.

The meeting has achieved nothing, apart from baiting a walrus. George is stuck in a time warp of unquestioning acceptance of the stories of the glory and superiority of the British Empire, sustained by the rose-tinted glasses of famous leaders, military victories often against other European pirates, and extravagant displays of power and wealth, epitomised by huge, exalted buildings constructed all over the empire.

Pride and the assumption that the British Empire was a good thing is now tainted with the evidence of the crushing of local cultures by the invader's superior technology, industrial power and arrogant self-belief. This myth was portrayed as public duty, benevolence and civilising the savage native.

'Amnesia is the privilege of the powerful; but one way or another, we all live, and die, with the consequences.'[1]

[1] Gary Younge, *The Guardian*, 31st May 2019

George fails to understand that nearly everything that makes up the fabric of his life and demonstrates continuity was created before he was born by people he has never met and from places he will never visit, all gifted by nature. He is equally unaware that today will not last forever, nor that his inability to recognise the inevitability of change will condemn him to the dustbin of history.

What he is desperate to hold onto is impossible to preserve. His rigid resistance will guarantee failure, not necessarily in his lifetime but in the attitudes he might successfully pass on. It has as much chance of success as wishing a glorious summer's day would last forever without realising that this beauty would not exist without the other seasons.

These simplified myths create a mind-set that is completely ill-equipped to deal with evolving challenges. As Gary Younge wrote: 'Only the whole truth about the past can heal the present', and George's universe has shrunk to the size of his head and become a prison.

Karrle reflects on Charles' comment. George is indeed solid as a rock; he is igneous that cannot metamorphose.

## No News for Andy

Andy is desperate to know what happened to Mohini and why she is working in the hospital. Nothing else occupies his thoughts. The old lady is the only one he can talk to. He must persuade her to tell him.

It is two days before Rose appears again. 'Good morning. How are you today?'

'OK. Excuse me for asking, but where is the Indian girl?'

'You seem to know her?' Rose says cautiously. Her eyes focus intently on Andy's reaction.

'Yes, we went to the same school but then she disappeared.'

'Well, she is here now,' Rose says, trying to defuse the intensity of the questioning.

'But why is she working in the hospital?'

'She had an accident and came into the hospital, and now she helps others. She is a good girl.'

'I know, she was my girlfriend. What accident?' The wild distress in his eyes is profound and sincere.

'I don't know, but I will see if I can find out anything for you.'

Andy seems unaware of whatever terrible experience Mohini had had and Rose can see that his shock is genuine. Maybe he can help this troubled little girl, but it has to come from her. Rose will have to think about this with great care!

# Part Seven

# Nowhere to Hide

## Charles' Wealth

Charles enters the office where Karrle is already at his desk. 'Morning, Karrle. How did you get on with George?'

'I thought dinosaurs were extinct. He's old enough to remember the stories of the empire, and young enough not to know the facts.'

'Sounds like the full blast.'

'George is certainly a man with an opinion, and generous enough to share it. He doesn't know any of the people he judges, and uses his ignorance as evidence of their inferiority.'

Charles smiles and moves on to discuss the business of the day, the practicalities and cost saving of consolidating two administration functions. Business concluded, the conversation moves to families. Charles has two children; both go to public school where sport is a high priority, much to their father's approval.

Charles' dearest wish is that his children will follow in their father's footsteps and join the family business, creating a third-generation dynasty. He would like them to gain a business education, which neither have shown any inclination to pursue.

'If you want to give your children an education as to how business operates, send them to my country to work in filthy, dangerous conditions for $1.25 per day supplying materials for the West. They can have a wide choice of careers, from agriculture to mining to deforestation, and the job will last them all their lives, which might not be very long. One of the things they will learn is what it's like to be looked down on as a lesser human being through no fault of their own.'

'You know that's not going to happen,' says Charles indignantly.

Unwavering, Karrle responds, 'It happens every day to millions of children throughout the world.'

'It will not happen to mine because they have better opportunities. However, I accept many do not.'

Karrle understands how outrageous it sounds but believes the connection between the two worlds should not be dismissed. 'You can go to bed in the certain knowledge that there is nothing you have to do tomorrow merely to survive, but all life is a struggle. If your life is easy, it is because somebody else is struggling to provide what you enjoy and take for granted. Because you make no personal effort and see nothing of their struggles, it is invisible to you.

Millions of children will wake up tomorrow to perform tasks, like carry drinking water contaminated by the demands of European industry. They will search in streams for semi-precious stones that are of no practical use to them, or look after siblings because their parents have failing health. You have no apparent immediate pressures, but the sands of time are running against you.

The comfortable life you lead now is an opportunity to address the inevitable, mend the roof while the sun is shining, as your politicians like saying. If you make no effort to change outcomes, what will you hand to your children and what will they hand to theirs? We must learn how to become good ancestors.'

'It is not something I have given much thought to.'

'That is easy and comfortable, but the reality is that life in the UK is supported by a series of almost invisible but vital links. They run so dependably that they do not impact on the daily lives of the British, who are blind to the appalling reality that in various links in the chain there is enormous exploitation, deprivation, cruelty and suffering. You are a guest on the bridge of a ship viewing the magnificent horizon, unaware of the lives of the galley slaves below who keep the ship going on which you are utterly dependent. Because none of your actions are directly responsible for anything outside of your immediate comfort zone, you feel no sense of responsibility.'

Charles cannot refute the point and acknowledges the reality. 'That is a journey I never wanted.'

'You are only just beginning to realise it is a journey you are already on. If an economic migrant is desperately poor supplying resources for the West, is it unreasonable that they want to move to the community that disproportionately benefits from their labour? What does it say about those who benefit and do nothing?'

Charles is silent and Karrle moves on to ask a rare personal question. 'Tell me, Charles, why do you pour your life's energies into accumulating wealth beyond your needs?'

This is a serious question and demands some thought. Slowly and hesitatingly, Charles constructs an answer. 'I suppose … it is to protect myself and to leave some mark on the world.'

'It is impossible to protect yourself from life. You can conquer the world at a moment in time, and control nothing that lasts.'

'I don't know what else to do. These are the targets that I was brought up with.'

'Ah-ha!' exclaims Karrle triumphantly. 'That is EXACTLY the point. These are the values of your society, and they have served you well, but they have caused many of today's problems and will be responsible for a catastrophic future unless they change.'

'Maybe I fear that anything else would risk too much of me.'

'Your wealth allows you to build walls to protect yourself from life around you. The greater your wealth, the more isolated you become. Living in a gated community in an unstable world will not make you safe. As the world economy integrates, polarised attitudes based on short-term benefits for the individual increase dependency on people we never meet, understand or have empathy for. The longer the supply chain, the more certain it is to break, probably in a way not foreseeable, as it has in Ukraine. The next generation will start where we finish and the threats to the future are already with us.

Today's privileged are the lucky recipients of the achievements of the past, whether it be from earlier societies advancing man's knowledge, or the evolution of life forms over hundreds of millions of years, or geological resources formed over billions of years. The personal contribution of any individual alive today is at most tiny and usually nil. Arrogant displays of self-worth are gravely misplaced, and a mind-set of entitlement without responsibility makes us ignorant victims.'

An unnerving realisation is dawning on Charles, that he is unwittingly doing the very thing that he criticises his managers for – living in his own comfort zone.

# Is Capitalism a Spanner in the Works?

It is his day off, and Karrle is sitting in the library thinking about capitalism. He has learnt a lot and seen first-hand the great benefits enjoyed by the society of which he is now a member. He also has personal experience of the widespread poverty trap that the majority of his countrymen endure and understands the anger of some who want to tear down the whole system.

Karrle fears that the global population has exploded to such a level that survival depends on the progressively integrating world supply chain which itself is destroying the planet making humans perilously vulnerable. Any breakdown in the system risks the implosion of civilisation and the possible destruction of humanity.

The only way forward is to build on and modify man's achievements to date, to reduce income inequality and create a lifestyle that is sustainable for the planet. Solutions may make capitalism an unaffordable luxury. What is required are bold, open discussions, agreeing common truths and working together as a single world tribe.

Karrle understands the gigantean challenge, but maybe his most important contribution is to write *The Book of REB*. In order to have any measurable impact, the message must be simple and clear; so how does capitalism contribute to the problem and can it contribute to the solution.

The present system benefits one half at the expense of the other half. Solutions will require agreement and sacrifices from both. How do you describe capitalism in a way that acknowledges the colossal achievements of which many are rightly proud, *and* drastically modify behaviour to secure a sustainable future? To clarify his thoughts he decides to write himself a letter.

*Dear Karrle,*

*Capitalism has done an outstanding job and achieved what it was designed for. It has made many societies unimaginably richer by providing populations with an ever-improving quantity and quality of goods and services, whilst rewarding individuals by allowing the provider to retain any profit for their personal use.*

*This system worked wonderfully well by allowing merchants to trade freely in a range of goods across wide geographical areas, making those in charge richer and therefore more powerful. London and the UK became the world trading and financial centres they are today by enshrining the rights of individuals in law and introducing the concept of limited liability enabling the raising of capital for a wide range of high-risk ventures.*

*The Industrial Revolution really transformed the opportunities for capitalism by utilising new inventions from a range of eccentric, and usually aristocratic, individuals who dedicated their lives to research and were willing to make their findings freely available, thereby advancing the pool of human knowledge. The Royal Society, formed in 1660, is the world's oldest national scientific academy and quickly became 'an international network for the practical and philosophical investigation of the physical world.' Entrepreneurs used these discoveries to learn more efficient methods to develop new, improved and cheaper products. Human ant nests developed the organisational structures to exploit the world's resources, fashioning methods and processes to exploit the natural resources of the planet for the benefit of the exploiters. Consumption exploded as capitalism raised the standard of living of hundreds of millions of people throughout the world, advancing civilisations at an astounding speed, and propelling our collective knowledge at an ever-accelerating pace.*

*The vision, perseverance, courage and scale of the challenges for scientists, inventors and entrepreneurs should not be underestimated or disrespected. Their achievements created the life we enjoy today, but the inventors are not responsible for how later generations exploited opportunities far beyond the perceptions of the scientists. Alexander Graham Bell hoped his invention of the telephone might eventually result in there being one phone in every town! The British can rightly be proud that they were the first nation to industrialise, but not where we are today.*

*The benefits of capitalism are shared by everyone in the West, even asylum seekers. When anyone can shop seven days a week at Primark and buy a six-pack pair of pants for £4.50, i.e. 75p each, and the designs, materials, dyes, packaging, transport, retailing and finance come from different continents, you are benefiting from capitalism. This is taken for granted which illustrates how far we are removed from reality.*

*Public schools demonstrated superiority, churning out inspired pupils to support the empire via the Army, Navy, Foreign Office and Church, replicating institutions throughout the world, particularly in education, thereby moulding the next generation. These organisations taught people to administer an empire, not to invent. It was the industrialists and technologists who created the financial backbone that made the British Empire the biggest in history. To be respected by the 'Establishment' was seen as a noble aspiration, and the empire funded by capitalism was conclusive evidence of superiority.*

*The English public school may have bred the spirit of adventure which ran the British Empire, but the rewards of empire were not shared with the English working class or Wales. Wales had the biggest lime and slate mines, and Cardiff had the biggest coal port in the world, not to service the needs of the Welsh, but as a piece in the British Empire jigsaw.*

*Capitalism has shaped many societies, including the UK. The Industrial Revolution created regional communities: the industrial working classes mining coal, iron ore, etc.; factories employing armies of people living in overcrowded back-to-back houses; ports transporting people and materials across the world; railways connecting industrial cities; the middle classes and the financial City of London. This created clearly defined social and economic divisions and evolving philosophies, usually based on experiences within each economic community.*

*Capitalism is like a spanner: it is extremely useful for the right job, but if you need a saw or a screwdriver, it is useless. It is undeniable that capitalism has been a roaring success, but today and every day, capitalism's limitations are being glaringly exposed and failure to learn the lessons will guarantee disaster.*

*Some people have a myopic, almost religious, faith that capitalism is invincible. The financial City of London is staffed with armies of young, dedicated and talented people, driven by the need to make huge fortunes quickly. Markets are too often controlled by people focusing on the mechanisms of wealth creation. Insiders enrich themselves at the expense of outsiders, masquerading as 'free-market forces,' rigging the system and legalising the robbery of millions of people from around the world, many of whom are desperately poor. Through third parties, the West employs more economic slaves in Africa today and reaps greater benefit from exploitation than at any time in history – today – now – this minute!!! They accumulate vast monopolistic profits at the same time as contributing almost nothing to many of the communities from where their wealth is generated.*

*In 2020, during the first year of the Covid 19 epidemic, the wealth of the world's billionaires increased 60% because governments pumped vast quantities of cash into the world economy at the same time as millions struggled to survive and many have not (there are seven million Covid 'reported' deaths and rising). This was achieved by ingenious techniques of borrowing from the future. Private debt became public debt and the economic crisis became invisible to those in charge. The stock market is disconnected from the economy and society.*

*The logic of open market forces suggests that when sales volume goes down, profits will fall, but for monopolies when supply falls, prices spiral (look at energy costs in 2022). The resulting inequitable distribution of wealth is a powerful argument for increasing taxes so that those who benefit the most contribute the most to the society from which they derive their wealth.*

*So how is capitalism, which has brought so many benefits, destroying the world?*

*Capitalism is a man-made concept to allocate the world's resources between humans. Money as a means of exchange, is easy to measure and compare. £2 is more than £1, and £1.51 is more than £1.49. To make more money the object*

*ive is to standardise demand and scale up supply forever. Capitalism's attempt to eliminate diversity by standardising nature is the opposite to how the world evolved and functions. This is a process of wanton devastation.*

*Many aspects of nature are invisible to capitalism until scarcity is translated into money, generating a market price. Until then, it is free. In reality, nature provides the opportunity to make short-term profit by plundering the world's resources, whilst offering no education about how to sustain life. Everything we believe we own was created before man existed and is not being replaced. The West is living off the fat of the past, and today's profits are robbing the future.*

*Capitalism glorifies the individual by servicing their needs and desires, providing a mechanism to make the rich, richer. Humans are addicted to consumption, needing ever larger fixes to satisfy their needs in an insane dash to self-destruct. Modern marketing's principal purpose is to stimulate desire to consume ever more by creating envy in a must-have-now mind-set. When did you last see a television advertisement that gave price and performance above desirability?*

*This is reinforced by Christianity, which has elevated man above nature, asserting that God made man in his own image (why?), and provided the animals for man's use. Really? Animals were here hundreds of millions of years before humanity existed and created the environment that mankind evolved into. This appalling arrogance could be fatal for man's ability to come to terms with reality and do what is necessary to survive.*

*When society's core values gravitate towards wealth creation it encourages people to trade planet for profit, devaluing health and happiness. Deaf and blind to the consequences of man's greed, we are too busy destroying the world with ever-greater efficiency to worry about the future. This is dangerous. Life cannot exist without many things we do not understand, cannot measure and cannot be traded. Losses to the environment are unseen and cannot be calculated, ignoring systemic risk. This is like running with your eyes shut. You will not understand the danger until after the collision. This is not a sign of applied intelligence or civilisation.*

*The world's wetlands are essential to life on earth but are being destroyed at a frightening rate. Re-establishing them will come at a financial cost – but where are the financial returns? Who is going to raise the money and who is going to repay the lenders. The burden will fall on future generations sacrificed on the altar of short-term individual advantage. Mark Carney (ex-Governor of the Bank of England) recommends a carbon tax and investment incentives for emerging technologies. He believes the market is a vital part of the solution but also requires public understanding and the political will.*

*Who are the trailblazers? Western industrial society and capitalism's drive for ever increasing profit. The British led the way in the standardisation of everything and the destruction of the world. A sustainable economy cannot exist without a healthy ecology.*

*We can adopt any belief system we like: capitalism, communism, Christianity, whatever, but if it entails the destruction of our world it is not only useless, it is an attack on nature that will eventually destroy us. There are numerous examples of societies that died out because they self-destructed or failed to harmonise with their environments. The collapse of Easter Island is a microcosm of the world today.*

*Capitalism prides itself on finding solutions to make more money. Whatever the stated policies of any society, there will always be people who try to find ways to circumvent the rules to satisfy any demand. Not only the rules but the practices which are not written down and often invisible. Organisations, structured on national lines, are poorly equipped to tackle the destruction of the eco-system. That is why man needs to learn that, whatever our history has taught us to date, the next lesson is how to become one global tribe. If we do not redress the balance then nature will. And if we destroy the planet, do we even deserve to exist?*

*Yours faithfully,*

*Karrle*

Karrle looks at this letter to himself and is surprised how critical and pessimistic it sounds, but the logic makes sense even though it rips apart conventional understandings.

# Is Democracy Legalising the Right to Kill the Planet

Satisfied with his letter to himself on capitalism, Karrle's thoughts move onto a consideration of democracy: '…today we venerate it as the cornerstone of Western civilisation'[1]. How 'normal' is democracy in human history, and what of today?

*Dear Karrle,*

*Individuals work together for the benefits they gain from being a member of a group. A human is like an atom, complete in itself but able to join others to make something bigger. Humanity has advanced because immigrants are other atoms that join existing atoms to make molecules for the benefit of all the atoms.*

*The larger and wider the team, the greater its ability to adapt to changes in the environment and competition from other groups. The team usually has one leader creating opportunities for the ambitious to build kingdoms and empires. Autocracy is an uncomplicated organisational structure, common amongst most mammals throughout evolution. It could be argued that totalitarianism is the natural order, and democracy is a man-made imposition. It is far more fragile than we like to imagine.*

*Today, democracy is built into the fabric of the belief system of the West. We breathe it as if it were a law of nature, but it is yet another man-made concept that we take for granted. There is no automatic right of freedom of the individual. How individuals and societies relate to each other is determined by the perceptions of the group.*

*The Greek concept of democracy, 2,500 years ago, was for the poor to make all the political decisions, giving them power over the rich. People would assemble in public places, orators debated the issues of the day and decisions were made by a show of hands. Equality and fair play were central. This very open forum was accessible to everyone who was a 'citizen', but their definition of democracy was very different from today. Being a 'citizen' excluded slaves, who were conquered peoples, neutered, with no civil rights. Women were the property of men and could not vote*[2]*. These practices only lasted 150 years, but remained a concept in Greek philosophy.*

---

[1] Bettany Hughes, *Athens, The Truth About Democracy*

[2] Bettany Hughes, Athens – *The Truth About Democracy*

*In the UK, democracy is a modern and moving target. By 1780 in England and Wales, it is estimated that less than 3% of the population were eligible to vote and even fewer in Scotland. By 1831 there were no Members of Parliament for Leeds, Manchester or Birmingham. Not until 1918 was the franchise extended to all men aged twenty-one, whilst women were not considered responsible enough to vote until the age of thirty, provided they had property. By 1969 the voting age was lowered to eighteen for men and women.*

*This European concept of democratisation is culturally alien to many societies, and the liberty evolving in Britain often stopped at Dover. Hong Kong was ruled by the British for 150 years before the first election was held in 1991, and then only to hurriedly establish a democracy before returning the territory to the Chinese in 1997. Despite this, the trend was clear: democratisation was becoming increasingly aspirational in many parts of the world, e.g. the Arab Uprising (2011) and Hong Kong protests against Chinese autocracy (2019–20).*

*The principles enshrined in the Western perception of democracy raise many questions regarding historical events that have shaped today's social and economic structures. The West have been happy to trade democracy for security when it suited them, subverting a number of newly forming democracies in South America and Africa. In many countries leaders play lip service to the principle of democracy whilst advantaging themselves, controlling information and silencing opposition. In times of uncertainty, people look for strong leaders with radical solutions like Donald Trump, who say they have the answers, but rarely do. When anyone criticises Trump, he attacks the character of the person, not the statement and attempts to undermine their credibility by suggesting they have ulterior motives. If you say it enough times, people will begin to believe it. This undermines the democratic process and institutions.*

*Science and logic do not always win against resourceful communicators, because they are restrained by what can be proven. Doubt is the best weapon in defeating a body of facts. Truth has little to do with winning the argument. This was the tactic used by the tobacco industry for decades.*

*In 1979, the board of the oil company, Exxon, were presented with a research paper from their own scientists, the Exxon Research and Engineering Company, stating that man's activities were causing global warming. In 1988 at an open, televised hearing in the United States*

*Senate, scientists stated that extreme summer temperatures would become increasingly common. What did Exxon, Shell, BP, Chevron and other oil companies do? They funded the GCC and hired highly paid and very clever specialists in denial.*[1]

'The Global Climate Coalition (GCC) (1989–2001) was an international lobbyist group of businesses that opposed action to reduce greenhouse gas emissions and publicly challenged the science behind global warming.' [2]

*None of what is happening today is a surprise to the scientists who predicted climate change decades ago with disturbing accuracy. This is unethical, utterly lacking in integrity and is where big business undermines democracy.*

*'America's democracy may be holding on by a few threads.'*[3]

*There is a direct connection between raping the world's resources, destroying the planet and economic inequality. The European Empire builders established the international economic systems that operate today. Africa was the weakest and most vulnerable continent because of its instability, including hundreds of years of slavery. Economic inequality fuels political inequality. When it is legitimised by the law, it maintains injustice. If the laws are merely a legal construct to deprive people of what is theirs, and wealth distribution is seen as unfair, the entire philosophy of the Western world is undermined and in danger of corroding from within. This feeling of powerlessness is not only in Africa but is infecting many societies throughout the world, including Western democracies.*

*Shared values are breaking down; extremist views are gaining credibility and respectability, and there are many legitimate injustices for them to focus on. These strategies polarise wealth and power, with opinions barricaded behind fixed positions drowning out debate and the democratic process. If the masses lose faith in the values of Western society and the democratic process is ineffective in resolving these issues, then democracy will be supplanted by undemocratic forces. 'The growth of rejectionism across the political spectrum.'*[4] *One man, one vote democracies can become unstable when the majority feel dispossessed.*

---

[1] *Big Oil v The World*, BBC2, 21/07/2022

[2] *Wikipedia*

[3] Steve Clemons, *The Bottom Line*, Aljazeera, 22/07/2022.

[4] Nigel Farage, *Europe's Forbidden Colony*, Aljazeera

*Populism is a crowd response to perceived injustice, and can spark destruction of the established order and revolution, with those seen to benefit under the present system becoming the main target. The consequences of losing the democratic structure would jeopardise the rights of every individual.*

*One of the democratic principles is that no one is above the law and no-one is below it. The present system treats those at the bottom as cheap labour, or merely consumers, for those at the top who control the wealth-creating industries. People are increasingly questioning the moral basis for many laws whose historical motivation has too often been the protection of the advantaged. Not to respect future generations or those with whom we share the planet, sacrifices the values we will need in the future.*

*Africa has no inheritance. Its independence has been taken away. It is not credible to believe that its people have control over events that disadvantage their lives, or that starving is the choice of the individual. Extremes of poverty and inequality need to be a burning moral issue for the world. Africa and Europe are neighbours; one is enormously rich, the other has enormous riches, which the enormously rich neighbour uses to increase its own wealth, but they pay the leaders of their neighbour who are drunk on power and spend the money on themselves. As long as this corruption exists, migration into Europe by any means will continue.*

*Democracy respects the freedom of individuals and nations, but humans are so interdependent that actions in one location impact on the world – yet the mechanisms for resolution are limited by democratic entitlement. These rights have been elevated above nature. The United Nations is almost powerless unless there is unanimity, even where evidence of loss of life and the destruction of the planet is overwhelming. One of thousands of examples is Russia's invasion of Ukraine blocking supplies of grain for the Middle East and Africa, threatening the lives of millions – even that huge problem is dwarfed compared to global warming.*

*Another fond illusion cherished by many is that Britain is an island whose unique identity must be preserved at all costs. Apart from the reality that we all came from Central Africa, Britain has always absorbed invading populations, including Romans, Picts, Teutonic Angles, Saxons, Jutes, Vikings, Normans, French, and Dutch (Frisians) – and this was before the British roamed the entire world. Nearly everything that we use today did not originate here. Britain has been very good at adjusting to changing circumstances, which is how the empire was originally built. Today Britain is one of the most diverse countries in the world and an international centre, completely dependent on those connections.*

*Isolation is not an option, yet recent debates have focused on short-term issues. What is independence if Britain cannot feed and clothe its people, run its factories, avoid climate disaster, or defend itself? Isolation brings impoverishment and a reduced ability to manage challenges in the future, which are already visible on many fronts. Small tribes get taken over by ambitious bigger tribes. Attempting to freeze the present, guarantees long-term failure. Risking short-term failure is part of long-term success.*

*Democracy in practice today : In the recent competition to replace the UK prime minister, Boris Johnson, the last eight candidates all emphasised the imperative of economic growth to support increased expenditure (ie consumption) for defence, NHS, education, HS2, levelling up, pet projects, etc. The current level of consumption and needless waste is far too high and rarely leads to increased happiness. Humans are killing themselves and the planet.*

*All the interest groups are conspiring to ignore the looming catastrophe: the politicians want to be elected; business wants ever-increasing profits, and the public want to pretend that life will go on improving forever. All would prefer to ignore the evidence that academics are increasingly understanding and those on the margins are already experiencing. When resources run out, the disorderly plunge in consumption will leave societies shattered, competing for what remains, with the strongest taking what they can and the weakest returning to primitive self-sufficiency. Starvation will become the new norm.*

*If these challenges to democracy are not addressed by the people who have democratic rights today then without shared values and internal checks on power, totalitarianism will continue to chip away at the democratic principles we take for granted, as is happening on every continent today. Society may revert back to autocracy as the 'natural order' and humanity will have lost one of the great achievements of civilisation.*

*Yours faithfully,*

*Karrle*

Reviewing his letter he is reasonably satisfied that it reflects his thoughts on democracy: admiration for the principle and concern about the practice.

## Charles Rethinks

As the conversations between Charles and Karrle continue to advance, the open dialogue both need and enjoy gradually becomes more complicated. Almost imperceptibly, it begins to define their identities and crystallise their differences. Increasingly undeniable to both, the system Charles has lived by all his life is not open to everyone and has inherent inequalities and unquantifiable injustices. With mounting trepidation, Charles is forced to confront his inner fear that maybe he is not the glowing example to the rest of society that he had always believed himself to be. Through the systems that support his lifestyle, he is indirectly part of a society that exploits the disadvantaged. Is he going to defend privilege in the face of truth?

Is Karrle biting the hand that feeds him? Ideas proffered by the disadvantaged can be interpreted as an asset grab from the advantaged for the sole purpose of taking what does not belong to them. Has a line been drawn that neither can cross? Their strong relationship, like tectonic plates, is being prised apart by unstoppable, but invisible forces. The relationship slowly morphs from mutual curiosity into creeping apprehension questioning the old certainties. Their daily lives are unchanged, but what of their futures?

The boss is becoming increasingly aware how few answers he has, and recognises the need to evaluate opportunities and assess risk. There is only one person he knows who may have the answers, and he turns for guidance to his employee. 'What can Africans do to improve their lot?'

'Not much. It must come from those that control the system, and that will not happen without a fundamental rethink about the foundations of our history. To move forward we need to turn the page, but we cannot if the page is only half-written. Black Lives Matter does not invalidate history, but it needs to be incorporated into an objective understanding of the past, to know how to improve the future.

Living with problems today created by the past will not improve the future. Building the British Empire was a great achievement, but it incorporated exploitation and injustice. Today we have the information and social values to understand the damage this still causes, but many attitudes have become absorbed into our culture and handed down through the generations, which makes it difficult to recognise in ourselves.

When these unthinking habits are challenged, we often ignore the evidence and react instinctively, rationalising explanations to justify the past to ourselves. But the evidence keeps gnawing away and the problem will remain until it is addressed. Over time, the original causes get twisted as injustices mount on both sides, which are frequently real and provide ammunition to validate entrenched positions. This educates the next generation in the problem but not the solution. Understanding this will make agreement and implementation of the necessary changes easier.'

'What sort of changes?' Charles asks rather tentatively.

'Stop killing the planet. Pay an economic price for the resources purchased, enabling developing countries to enjoy a reasonable standard of living. Rebalancing will reduce inequality, poverty and make the world a safer place.'

Forever the businessman, Charles is hyper-sensitive about paying more for anything if there is an alternative. 'Why would the West pay higher prices for the resources they purchase?'

'Because they need the resources. Why should anybody work for $1.25 a day and the West receive all the profit?'

Charles' understanding of economics raises a problem. 'If the wages rise, say by 600%, the price of the finished product will rise sharply and demand will go down, making many Africans unemployed.'

Karrle dismisses this point as one-sided. 'Good! That will release many people to do more productive work and those on higher wages will boost the local economy, creating local employment in new industries. Why should a community be stripped of alternatives just to supply Western economies. And if consumption falls in the West, that is exactly what the environment needs. It is a win-win situation.'

Charles disagrees. 'Not exactly. The West will be significantly poorer.'

'The West is on an unsustainable trajectory that will destroy many societies, including affluent ones. The West should support Africa becoming more self-sufficient.'

'OK, good point on sustainability,' Charles concedes. 'But how can Africa become more self-sufficient?'

'They must produce more finished goods from the materials they already have, and increase domestic consumption, the same as the Chinese have been doing for years. As for carbon footprint, sending raw materials around the world for processing and round the world again to market is insane. The economics defy common sense.

Take Nigeria as an example. Crude oil is 95% of Nigeria's exports[1] but they buy back refined oil from Western refineries at ten times the price, spending billions on imports and placing huge sums in the hands of the very few. It's a wonderful scheme for robbing the country and depriving the people. It also prevents the local population from developing the organisational and people skills necessary to become independent. One ray of light is Nigerian businessman Aliko Dangote, who is building an oil refinery to enable Nigeria to become self-sufficient.'

Charles is doubtful. 'You are asking the wealthy countries to voluntarily reduce their standard of living. And there are other considerations. Reduced wealth means less to spend on military security at a time when international tensions are increasing. I can't see the West agreeing to that.'

'When the facts are freely known, public opinion will change. The legislators will bring in new laws and business will adapt, as occurred with smoking and is starting to happen with the ubiquitous availability of single-use plastics. This is the democratic process, but it is vital that it is not controlled by interest groups, as has happened in Africa, Russia and China and the West with tobacco and oil.'

Charles is looking for positives. 'The West has brought stability in international relations. There are fewer wars now than ever.'

'Maybe amongst the wealthy countries at the moment, but don't tell that to the tens of millions trapped in war zones right now as their countries are being torn apart. Much of this conflict is driven by poverty and inequality, and the major powers either look on, do nothing or play power games fighting proxy wars.'

Protesting, Charles replies, 'Yes, but Western capitalism has not caused all the problems. It has improved the wealth, health, life expectancy and quality of life for hundreds of millions. That is something to be proud of.'

'I agree. The effort and achievements are huge and sometimes noble, but time exposes all the parts, including inequitable wealth distribution and environmental catastrophe. We need to put our minds

[1] Wikipedia

together with good thinking and new imagination. Change is inevitable, the question is who controls it.[1]

Charles looks puzzled. 'Changing public opinion, international law and business practices could take decades.'

'We haven't got decades. Imagine the human race is in a plane flying at 30,000 feet with enough fuel to land safely if the descent begins now. Flying until the plane falls from the sky is the ultimate stupidity. It is imperative to get out of the thought mode of good guy, bad guy. It is merely a statement of where we are as a human race. If the poor hate the rich and the rich fear the poor, it will end in conflict and the outcome could be unimaginably ugly. Doing nothing will guarantee the demise of humanity.'

Charles protests his innocence. 'But if I tried to do something, I might lose everything and change nothing. I cannot change things in isolation.'

'Then don't be isolated. It is not acceptable to benefit from an unfair system and do nothing to change it when the information is evident to anyone who looks.'

Staring this moral dilemma in the face makes Charles very uncomfortable. Disturbing thoughts run through his mind but he remains silent.

'So now you are becoming more aware, as a prominent businessman, you can start to put pressure on your government. Being too busy making money in an unfair system makes you part of the problem.'

'How can I be responsible for atrocities that occurred before I was born.'

Karrle agrees. 'You can't, but where historical events established social norms incorporating injustices impacting lives today, and your actions maintain those practices through habit and ignorance in the face of available evidence, you have a duty to re-examine your behaviour or expect to be the target of those suffering the consequences of your actions. Clinging to damaging beliefs will lose control of our fate and diminish our future.'

'You sound very bitter.' Charles studies Karrle's face to gauge his reaction.

[1] Kumi Naidoo and Winona LaDuke, Aljazeera 28/12/2021

'No, I'm not bitter – but I am pointing out unacceptable abuse and suffering that is happening now. Individuals have to take responsibility or acknowledge their own moral dilemma and make up their own minds about what, if anything, they are going to do about it.'

'I was more comfortable when I knew less.' Charles' deflated tone acknowledges uncharacteristic hopelessness.

Karrle understands. 'That's how I had a happy childhood.'

Recalling his childhood, Charles reminisces, 'As a little boy, I felt pride as I looked at a world map with all the pink representing the British Empire. It is only recently that I have learned about the cost in innocent lives.'

'If the only changes are the rules dictated by governments and business, without social acceptance, it will have little impact. Tell me, Charles, how many non-white people do you know?'

'My cleaner is from the West Indies, and I deal with a couple of non-white businessmen.'

'That hardly qualifies as integration. Those are contractual relationships. Social integration is the best protection against the future. Some communities are almost exclusively from the same ethnic groups and are forming economic, social and cultural ghettos and elites.'

'And I know you!' Charles interjects.

'Yes, but our relationship was formed on a contractual basis, too. We have both moved beyond that and are learning from each other in ways that would be impossible within the confines of politically correct, role play. It is vital that people retain their identity but also make contact with the wider community. If we only see others as two-dimensional caricatures, defined by a rigid, pre-ordained structure, we classify individuals into simplistic groups and fail to make meaningful connections. Differences can be interpreted as irreconcilable, eventually leading to conflict, weakening the whole society.'

'Why do you want a fight?' Charles offers teasingly.

Karrle smiles. 'You had the protection of ignorance to preserve your misplaced sense of superiority. Unfortunately, that ship has sailed and isn't coming back. You have the opportunity to go on a thousand-mile mental journey. If you decide not to take it, do not deceive yourself that your life will remain unchanged, you will just be swept along by events you are not part of. Not to think of the galley slaves makes you complicit. "These are the barbarities in the period in which we live"[1].'

'Well, you have exposed me to ideas which I never entertained before. People say I have become more unconventional since we met.'

Karrle agrees. 'I would say that you are thinking for yourself. Certainly as I get older, I rely on convention less. The key is to welcome everyone's talents as the best chance for a healthy society, and not be limited by convention.

These are not comfortable thoughts and Charles remains silent as Karrle moves on. 'Charles, neither you nor I are guilty of events before we were born. Are we so imprisoned by our histories that we have lost the ability to agree what is right and wrong? As intelligent people can we not look at the same things and recognise common ground? Why, because you are British, do you feel responsible for things that you had nothing to do with?

With sombre deliberation Charles forms his thoughts. 'I suppose… it is because I now recognise that many of these past events have shaped where we are today. They explain why I was born in a privileged society and you were born in an impoverished one. It is guilt about my unfair advantages and fear of losing them. Many of the attitudes that orchestrated those events still resonate today.'

Karrle's face lights up. 'Charles, I am very proud of you. See, we can agree on many things.'

'But can we agree on what to do about them?'

'We have already made an excellent start. The key is to maintain an open dialogue based on trust and work towards agreed goals. That will move things in the right direction.'

For the first time, Charles starts to truly realise just how stark these differences are and fragile many of his core beliefs. His eyes are now open to previously unseen dangers as he starts to realise the reality that he sits on top of an economic pyramid which does create wealth. He comes from a society that controls the mechanisms that enable him to cream off a disproportionate share of the wealth created, which enables him to live a lifestyle that offers choices and protection. However, that privileged position depends on there being a pyramid with him at the top and many at the bottom facing challenges and deprivations in what we

[1] *For Whom The Bell Tolls*, Ernest Hemingway, 1940

like to believe are civilised societies. The system depends on inequality and therefore, by definition, cannot be a choice available to everyone. Part of the protection Charles benefits from is isolation from many of the realities that others face in the same society. His awakening to these issues and people outside his immediate circle are becoming rooted into his thinking, where previously he never gave himself mental space.

This new understanding challenges his desire to get richer and the outcomes and sustainability of that desire. The world looks different. He feels himself becoming slightly more appreciative and empathetic but also defensive and less confident. This was not an aspect that he had considered when he took Karrle on board to look for new opportunities. He also feels that this new thinking gives him responsibilities that he never wanted. Charles had always prided himself on seeing opportunities in the darkest of situations, but at the moment he sees far more threats than opportunities.

Thomas Paine, founding father of America, said, 'The mind, once enlightened, cannot become dark.'

In spite of this, these glaring truths have resulted in a shared understanding on many issues. They leave both Charles and Karrle better equipped to understand the challenges in their search for a better future. This is half way towards a solution, but neither man knows how to achieve the second half.

# Business Benefits Society – But Which One

Even at public school, Henry was a maverick, like the time he put weed killer on the school lawn outside the headmaster's office in the shape of a rude word. Everyone knew, apart from the teachers, until the lettering could not be denied, but as always, Henry never got the blame.

A larger-than-life character, he has grown more outrageous with age. After several years enjoying the best that London had to offer, he moved to Africa and became the third generation to run the family business, an ambition Charles wanted to replicate with his children.

As Charles and Henry pursued their separate careers, reunions became increasingly problematic, but when they occurred, Henry was always bursting with amazing stories. Out of the blue, Charles receives a message from his old friend who is back in England, suggesting they get together over lunch. It is an offer he cannot refuse.

'Hello, Henry. Good to see you. How many years has it been?'

'Too many, too many, old man! When I realised I was coming to England I thought I must look up my old friend, Charlie. How's business, dear chap? I hear you are doing rather well in old Blighty[1].' (old fashioned expression for Britain).

'I'm making ends meet,' Charles says modestly. 'Is the family business still in Africa.'

'Damn right, it is. Best place in the world. You should try it sometime, but it's not for girls. You have to be tough to survive.'

'I seem to remember that your family knew how to turn a profit from difficult situations. What's it like these days?'

With a beaming expression and hearty chuckle, Henry booms, 'Better than ever, better than ever! Timber in Mozambique, copper in the Congo, couple of situations in Nigeria.'

'What about agriculture?'

'What? And deal with all those farmers, crop failures, climate change and God knows what? Too difficult to control. I like businesses that are concentrated into a small area and deal with as few people as possible. The labour is plentiful and dirt cheap. The blacks work for nothing.'

'I hear that many are on starvation wages.'

[1] Old-fashioned expression for England

Henry's expression morphs at this surprising challenge and his tone becomes defensive / aggressive. 'I pay what I have to, and not a penny more. If they don't like it, I can get plenty more *and* they know it!' Like a cancerous growth, a tight, malevolent smirk spreads across his face as he basks in this parade of verbal strength.

Charles is not satisfied to let these stories float harmlessly passed him, and probes a little further. 'Some would call that slave labour.'

Henry is now a little rattled. 'No it's not! They are in their own country and free to do what they want. I just offer them a job – they don't have to take it. Anyway, the slave trade was a big mistake.'

'On moral grounds?' Charles asks hopefully.

'Good God, NO, my boy.' Henry laughs at his friends naivety. 'Bad business.'

Charles is not enjoying this conversation but with his recently acquired perspective, his questions are venturing into new territory and he is curious to learn how his friend thinks.

Henry continues, now relishing educating a British businessman. 'We transported twelve million slaves a quarter of the way around the world, and look at the trouble it has caused. One and a half million died on the journey, and more than 200 years conflict. America even had a civil war over it, and for what? Endless civil unrest. And today African Americans cost well over twenty times more than a Congolese miner. Once they are in your country, they are endless trouble. You probably don't know, but in 1900 the total population of Africa was 120 million. Now there are over 400 million workers in Sub-Saharan Africa alone and they cost me $2 a day.'

Charles interjects, 'I know – 414 million by 2010. A friend told me.'

Henry looks surprised, but continues. 'Er, right – and they are increasing by over twenty million a year. It's like running a salmon farm where the stock gets bigger and bigger all by itself. I blame all these medical innovations keeping babies alive and the adults live longer too. No, it's far better to keep them in Africa.'

'Those conditions would be illegal in England. I would never get away with it.'

Henry's arguments have won the day. Sensing total victory he adds, '*That's* the beauty of it! In Africa you have no responsibilities, barely any taxation and nobody bothers you. You have to work with the local officials, which costs a bit, but it's cheaper than the alternative. I could not stomach the regulations that you have here, they'd send me round the bend. I bet if somebody has an accident in England there's hell to pay. We just get another one.'

Disturbed by the brazen heartlessness of these revelations, Charles asks, 'What about the population? Don't they understand and resent white people?'

'Some do,' Henry concedes. 'But we make sure the chappies are always respectful. Some are even grateful.'

'What about public opinion over here?'

'Charles, do me a favour. The British don't know because they don't want to know. As long as Tesco's has everything they want and that German company, Aldi, is cheaper if money is tight, they are happy. If the news bothers them, they can always donate their change to Oxfam. No, they are more concerned about how many immigrants you let into Britain. But your factories are full, Charles, so everyone is happy.'

'Not everyone!' Charles contradicts.

'The ones who vote and the ones that matter are. If the government and the public are bothered about war, famine and disease they can give money to the charities or use the United Nations as a talking shop. Either way, it is not a cost of doing business in Africa. I am very grateful that NGO's (non-government organisations) and government foreign aid programmes subsidising business; and the chaos that everybody complains about is a godsend.'

Charles is stunned by Henry's cold-blooded righteousness. The silence that follows requires Henry to clarify the obvious confusion in his friend's mind. 'The disruptions mean that nobody knows what is really going on. And even if they do, there's nothing they can do about it.'

Charles continues to sit in silence, trying to conceal his bubbling outrage.

'You know Charles, secretly the British public are very grateful. They can maintain their standards and somebody else does all the dirty work. They are prisoners of their own beliefs. It feels like an open prison, but they understand where they should not go. A few wander off, have bad experiences, and are a lesson to the others. Public pressure focuses on governments increasing foreign aid, whilst secretly, the government protect business interests. Television fills in the gaps. It works a treat.' Henry's verbal dominance oozes self-satisfaction.

'Surely it can't stay like this?' Charles protests.

'Why not? As long as we have the money and the technological advantage. God forbid they ever catch up, or they will want to use what we take for themselves, and then where would we be?'

Charles is revolted by this open display of inhumane cynicism, and shocked that Henry's heart is black beyond imagination. Barely maintaining his normal polished politeness, he invents another appointment and hurriedly leaves.

His assumption that civilised values were universal throughout the British Empire is shattered. Staring him in the face is clear evidence of the widespread suffering of unknown millions being callously inflicted by people purporting to share the values Charles has taken for granted all his life. His acceptance of Britain as a beacon of excellence to the rest of the world is shredded. Was Henry right? Had the foundations of the British Empire, that Charles had been brought up to be so proud of, only flourished because there were people like Henry creating the wealth, glories and myths that those in England believed reflected the evidence of their greatness? Were 'British values' part of the myth? Was it only British industrial and military domination of so many nations that imposed a self-justifying story that many British still believe is real.

By accepting the status quo without question Charles had been blind to this hypocrisy and vile sickness. It had always been in plain sight, but he had never asked the questions. Africa was run for the convenience of the West and in the process the West empowered, legitimised and facilitated despots suppressing their own populations. The West feels righteous indignation and moral superiority when Africans escape the horrors of their own countries and become uninvited guests in the havens that benefit from the corruption they are fleeing from.

Henry perpetuated these misrepresentations on a diet of greed, myopia and self-interest, running organisations that inflict incalculable suffering. Whilst Henry is a very old friend, Charles has no appetite to meet him again, EVER.

Karrle's words had seemed radical at the time, but in the face of these brutal truths they are far more solid than the beliefs that Charles had accepted all his life. This new knowledge has given him an even greater respect for his new friend.

The endless pursuit of personal wealth is irreconcilable with the values Charles had always accepted. In a strange way, he has been liberated from the shackles of his old pre-occupations. It is not that he doesn't want to be richer, but only now does he understand that it is not the only, or even the most important thing in life. It is not a requirement to be driven by insatiable ambition and only now does he understand that he is OK as he is. Imperceptibly a burden had been removed and the relief is strangely empowering. As Karrle said, sometimes you have to unlearn things you have accepted in the past as true. Charles' *Book of REB* had undergone a seismic and permanent shift. Now he must grapple with the consequences.

## The Confession

Karrle's disturbing ideas are playing on Charles' mind. At their next meeting, and without reference to his disastrous meeting with Henry, he observes, 'You are not like anybody I have met before.'

Karrle smiles and replies, 'I am no different. I am the product of my life experiences. It is those experiences that are not like other peoples. The British do not understand the challenges that face most asylum seekers because they have no experience of trauma or dislocation of their lives. The invisible fabric that formed the tapestry of migrant's lives has been shattered; the memories of what they had and the pain of what they have lost. Without family, friends or understanding, they have to learn how British society functions in a new environment that even leaves many British isolated. For many migrants it causes lasting mental damage. Not everybody gets through.'

'I cannot imagine what it is like to be an asylum seeker,' Charles acknowledges.

'The main difference between us is due to luck and circumstance. The life I knew has been destroyed, yours has not. My life was disadvantaged from birth due to circumstances that go back generations. Unless you have experienced injustice, you cannot understand.

Charles' expression becomes unsmiling. 'In 1805 when the British Parliament made the slave trade illegal, my family lived in Manchester, spinning the cotton picked by negro slaves in the southern states of America. There were no labour laws protecting my family. Children as young as seven worked up to fourteen hours a day, six days a week, crawling under moving machinery and frequently losing hands and limbs, even being decapitated. The air was thick with dust that damaged their lungs and discipline was brutal.'

Surprised by the vehemence in Charles' tone, Karrle responds, 'That is appalling, but your society evolved to offer legal protections to improve the quality of life of your citizens. In my country this level of exploitation still exists, supplying what you in the West buy for peanuts. The injustice is that the West is still indifferent to this abuse. You have not experienced personal injustice to that degree.'

'I may not know what it is like to be an asylum seeker, but that does not mean I have no understanding of injustice. If you don't mind me saying so, you are talking like a "black man".'

Karrle is shaken into silence; a black hole has appeared and Charles has disappeared into it.

Charles confirms his declaration with passion, taking on the persona of a stranger. 'Believing that white people cannot understand injustice is judging me on racial grounds – precisely what you accuse the British of doing.' His body is now tense and he does not continue.

Disorientated, Karrle is merely an onlooker for whatever follows.

The absence of words intensifies the moment. An explanation is needed, and Charles battles with the task. 'I… er … do not talk about this…'

Trapped in the moment, he struggles to move forward. 'I was married very, very young. I made a girl pregnant. I did not love her, but marriage seemed the honourable thing. My mother was a nurse and she became pregnant by a businessman. He never married her, and she brought me up on her own. The rest of her life was a struggle, and she sacrificed a lot for me. I could not be responsible for repeating that.

I did not understand at the time, but my wife was a serial mother. I had four children by the time I was twenty-seven. She divorced me. I gave up my job to contest custody because I realised she was not a good mother. Her childhood had been appalling, but I had been loved and did not understand how different families can be.

I contested custody but, because I was male and a wage earner and she was the mother, the court dismissed my application for custody with barely any investigation of the facts. She intimidated the children mercilessly, so that they were frightened to see me. Richard, the second eldest, sneaked out to meet me and was horse-whipped and shut under the stairs. I found out years later in a conversation with my daughter.

Contact ceased. I thought that trying to see my children whilst she had custody would only add to their punishment, and that it was kinder not to provoke a situation where I had no control. I poured myself into work to preoccupy my mind, but it denied them protection when they needed it most. That was the worst decision of my life and I will never forgive myself.'

The mood is deathly silent. Charles continues slowly, struggling to find the words. 'When contact was resumed, I was devastated to discover their childhoods had been destroyed and they were unrecognisable. Social services were worse than useless. I had no legal rights that were enforced. They had the authority, but did nothing to protect the children or keep me informed.

The two eldest used alcohol to relieve their turmoil, then Brett, the eldest, got into bad company and started taking drugs. Richard worshipped his big brother and followed. They both left home at sixteen, by which time contact had been resumed. I discovered they were both paranoid schizophrenics and were being admitted regularly to the Caludon Centre, a psychiatric unit in Coventry.

Social services had not only been incompetent but legitimised the mother at every stage, even though I supplied them with evidence of mistreatment and they could see the deterioration in my children. They did nothing. I visited the Caludon Centre every day for weeks. When I left one ward, I went to another to see my other son. That shear unrelenting trauma destroyed me.

By then I had a new family and responsibilities. I did everything I could to keep my new family stable and try to offer support to my other children, bottling up my emotions. That was another mistake. I was too busy earning money to support everyone, thinking that was the solution and burying myself in work, whilst maintaining jolly external appearances. I became an emotionally absent father with my new family at the same time as failing to protect my other family.'

Charles stops, and Karrle wonders what to say next. 'Where are they now?'

'Dead.'

This is too shocking to know how to respond. He remains silent, waiting to see if Charles is going to say anything.

'Brett started to believe that food was evil and died from a burst stomach ulcer. Richard discovered his body a few days later but, as a paranoid schizophrenic, he could not deal with it. Two days after he found his brother, he informed the police who found Brett in bed covered in blood. He was slumped forward, compressing his nose sideways, which had become rigid through rigor mortis. It looked like it had been broken. The police arrested Richard. He was released shortly afterwards, but never spoke about it and committed suicide two years later.'

Stunned, Karrle is disorientated, stumbling in disbelief, eventually asking, 'You said there were four children. What happened to the other two?'

'The daughter escaped from the mother into the arms of a drug dealer, got pregnant and became a Jehovah Witness. I presume she was searching for the stability she could not find in her family. She needed affirmation from her abusive mother, so it was easier to blame me. The mother has said the youngest one was not mine.'

'Forgive me for asking, but you now run the family business. What about your father?'

I grew up not knowing him. When we finally met, we did not get on. He could not be seen with an illegitimate son. Later, when his health was failing and he wanted to make up for his neglect, he brought me into the business and realised that I had some of his qualities, so it became natural for me to take over.'

'That is so dreadful. I am sorry.' How inadequate, but what else can he say?

Gone is the suit, the polished manner. Charles stands there emotionally naked, deeply damaged. Reflecting on his own situation, Karrle realises that Charles had not made his fortune but inherited it, not unlike the country.

It had never sat well with Karrle that Charles refers to himself as a self-made multimillionaire, yet his father started the business. Karrle has to ask the question. 'So you inherited your father's business, yet you refer to yourself as a self-made man?

Charles' mind drifts back to the question. 'The old man had lost it by the time I joined. His failing health had driven the company into the ground and it was worthless. I had to make some difficult decisions, which is why some of the old managers resent me, but I built what we have today.'

The explanation sounded credible, but is still a misrepresentation. Charles did not start with nothing; he was gifted a business. Karrle cannot fail to recognise that this is much like people in Britain today, who were gifted the British Empire by previous generations. That is why his countrymen still have to battle against cultural practices that are stacked against them.

Charles' revelation gives Karrle a completely different understanding of the man. He can see the damage he has suffered, for which there is no compensation, but it might also explain his need for independence and his idiosyncratic resentment of officialdom.

Karrle also reflected that it might shed light on Charles' curiosity about the injustices he himself has suffered. Certainly he seemed unusually interested for a businessman.

Neither man ever mentions the matter again.

## Rose Tricks Mohini

Mohini is terrified that meeting Andy again will force her to confront her past and destroy the life she is so desperately trying to build. It would be unbearable to see the contempt and hurt in Andy's eyes if he learns the truth. They must not meet again; at least that way, she can preserve the memories of what they had.

She loves her hospital rounds. To the outside world, she is still the bright cheery girl that all the patients love, but inside the shell hides a lost soul. However desperate her needs, she cannot risk another meeting and she refuses to visit Andy's ward.

After another operation on his knee, he is moved to the convalescence ward for monitoring and therapy. Sensing Mohini's reluctance to visit, Rose decides to orchestrate an accidental meeting. 'Hello, Mohini. Can you do me a favour?'

'Certainly, if I can. What is it?'

'I have to leave early today, and haven't visited the convalescent ward. Would you be a poppet and cover for me?'

'Happy to,' says Mohini as obliging as ever.

Starting the rounds, she reaches the convalescent ward. This time Andy sees her first, and instinctively blurts her name before he realises he has spoken. 'Mohini.' It is loud and clear and undeniable.

Immediate recognition traps her in the moment. Paralysed, she is unable to escape. Both are silent. Andy MUST talk, but seeing her blocks everything, leaving only turmoil and panic. Desperate for anything…he has to speak, he cannot lose her again … but … but what, for mercy's sake. The only thing that means anything are the words from his heart:

> 'Borrowed … words… can … always say..far better than can I,
> of love and dreams and wishful things that last until we die.
> Of times relived…'

Mohini's whisper takes over, but builds on every word.

> …and things unsaid, and feelings running deep
> in life's deep ruts, we chain ourselves.
> Our paths may never meet.'

Then their voices merge:

> 'And yet, in all life's twists and turns,
> things are not what they may seem,
> Tread softly, love, tread softly, for you tread upon my dreams.'

Disappearing in a hug, they are together again. Their unbreakable bond is renewed and must be openly acknowledged to the world forever. Without words, both know that they will have to face unknowable challenges, with nothing but love, total commitment and blind faith.

## There Is Always a Solution?

The wheels of industry keep turning, occupying the working hours of both men, but being somebody who is used to answers and not indecision, Charles is deeply disorientated. It is a feeling that is as unwelcome as it is unfamiliar. He suggests to Karrle that they have an evening meal away from the office in a swanky restaurant. Charles will pay, of course. This will not be to discuss routine matters. Karrle wonders if he has said too much and is about to be fired. Evaluating his options he concludes that this is not about him. If he cannot speak the truth in England, how can he ever hope to address injustice in Africa? He must pursue what is true wherever it may lie and whatever the cost to himself.

Entering the restaurant, piped background music plays 'Money, Money, Money' by Abba. The words 'in a rich man's world' drift across the room as if requested for the occasion. Seated in a corner, Charles is as sharp-suited and dapper as always, but today his usual gloss looks scuffed and his manner pensive. This is going to be difficult.

After the customary civilities, the elephant in the room crashes the conversation. 'I find a lot of your ideas very disturbing. I can't see that there is a solution.'

'There is *always* a solution,' replies Karrle, 'but not necessarily the one you want.'

'Well, what solutions can you suggest?'

'Why are you a very successful businessman?'

Pausing for reflection, Charles ruminates for most of a minute. 'Well, let me see. I understand how business works. I can recognise opportunities that others can't, and I know what needs to be done to satisfy a market – and make a profit.'

Karrle pursues his line of enquiry. 'And where is the biggest opportunity in the world?'

Charles considers the possibilities, 'Um…maybe China?'

Karrle delivers the unlikiest answer with certainty: 'Africa!'

Charles gapes, open mouthed. 'Africa! Please! Which millennia are you talking about?'

'Your instant dismissal confirms why it is overlooked and therefore an opportunity. Here are a few facts:

1) China's population is 1.4 billion and rising by seven million a year. Africa's population is over 1.3 billion and rising by thirty-plus

million a year. Before 2025 the population of Africa will be higher than that of China. That is a vast pool of under-utilised labour.

2) The average wage in industrialised China is ten times higher than the average wage in Africa, and China's costs are rising rapidly. The challenge is to raise productivity in Africa, and the unit costs will be far lower.

3) Africa has vast quantities of many of the raw materials that the world cannot do without.

4) Many of these raw materials are extracted from Africa and transported to China for processing before exporting to the biggest markets in the world, Europe and America. That's around a 30,000 kilometre trip with a huge carbon footprint. Global warming would be dramatically reduced if finished goods were manufactured close to where the resources are extracted, and supplied directly to the markets. Africa has the materials, the location and the people. Why is it not the manufacturing centre of the world?'

Charles stares at the other man in astonishment. This is a shock too far, and he dismisses the idea out of hand. 'For the very reason you are here. You know better than I, the conflicts raging over many parts of Africa. It is the military forces that keep resources flowing that produce the income for many of these countries, and the technical knowhow, capital and markets in the West that create those incomes. As you have said, Africa has massively underdeveloped infrastructure for processing materials into finished products, and a massively untrained population required for sophisticated industrial processes – never mind the huge political instability.'

Karrle interjects, '5) You have articulated the problems, and overcoming them is the opportunity. What is the alternative? If the West pays the dictators, and the dictators suppress the population then you will have people like me fleeing to Europe for generations. Remember that white people are only about 16% of the world's population, and falling. You had better get used to Africans because in less than a hundred years, some forecasts predict that they will be 40% of the world's population, which is more than the present population of China, India and Europe put together. Africans will outnumber white people by at least three to one. The present is not sustainable, and the West will improve their own future security if they embrace change.

And wouldn't the many Western countries prefer to deal with fifty-four independent African countries than a single communist ideological opponent? If Africa sides with China, where will that leave Europe; very vulnerable indeed. Europeans will still need the materials, and China will try to close the supply of vital raw materials to the West and only supply finished products at prices they determine.'

Charles retorts, 'The Chinese are already in Africa'.

Dismissing Charles' point, Karrle explains why. 'The Chinese are not very popular in Africa. With a humble, constructive approach, Europeans would find that many Africans would prefer to deal with Europe than China. But many things are changing, including China and Africa. Europe will not have this opportunity forever.

The actions of the West are destroying the philosophical foundations on which their society is built, unleashing forces that they may not understand and will not be able to control, which could destroy democracy. The exploitation, abuse and suffering in Africa will maintain instability, and the outcomes may be very much to the disadvantage of Europe. The reality is that, in the long term, to maintain its advantages, Europe needs Africa more than Africa needs Europe.'

Charles butts in. '6) You have already pointed out that Africa has been badly mistreated by Europe for 600 years. Wouldn't they see this as back door re-colonisation by economic means?'

Again, Karrle refutes this idea immediately. 'Africa is economically colonised now. That's the problem. There are more economic slaves in Africa today than at any point in its entire history, and the numbers are rising.

Don't think of the present human divisions, think about the fundamentals. Breaking down the barriers will open doors to opportunities that cannot yet be imagined. In essence, nothing has changed from when the first Europeans started to explore Sub-Saharan Africa 600 years ago. Africa is a huge continent with enormous natural resources, some of which could support life in a sustainable way. Europe has the same need for resources that drove them to investigate Africa in the first place. If Europe continues its ruinous exploitation of developing countries, and tolerates an ever-rising level of suffering, how can this possibly end well for anybody?

As a businessman, you have already acknowledged that you have the skills to recognise the problems and find the right people who can make this work. That is a noble contribution of inestimable value, and deserves your attention.

Think of Europe's strengths. Unlike China, Europe has 600 years of relations with Africa and now forms part of African culture. Millions have been brought up as Christians, speaking many European languages, with an education system modelled on European institutions. Many white people live in Africa and many Africans are in Europe. That is not true of China.'

The frown on Charles' face displays his struggle with the concept. 'That requires a huge mental shift for everyone, incorporating many dangers.'

'True. Don't be fooled by the present apparent stability. The West is burning opportunity. Europe needs a complete rethink, not based on historic prejudices, religion or short-term self-interest but on a shared humanity, working with partners for a common purpose.

What would a marriage be like if neither partner ever did anything for the other unless that specific action benefited themselves? A very poor marriage indeed! Partners do things for each other because it benefits the partner and strengthens the partnership. They know their benefit will come in the future when *they* need help. As sociable creatures, humans gain enormous satisfaction by working together with others on common tasks.

This is not a marriage for life, it is a marriage for many lifetimes. Europe needs therapy to acknowledge the problems and articulate the pain, so that both parties understand and take responsibility and work on solutions, a bit like Jeremy Kyle and Graham.'

Chuckling, Charles cannot restrain himself. 'Jeremy Kyle? You've been watching too much UK television – and even he has been banned now.'

Not deflected, Karrle resumes. 'I think Jeremy Kyle would do a fine job. Europe needs to come to terms with its past before it can move forward.'

Charles is still unconvinced. 'The more you articulate the advantages that the West enjoys today, the greater the sacrifice you are asking the advantaged to give up voluntarily. Why would they agree to disadvantage themselves?'

'Yes, I accept that point. As we say in Africa, you cannot expect a man to cut the branch he is sitting on. But I have two answers. First, the risks are already there, and avoiding them is not an option. Doing nothing will make failure certain. Second, George Floyd was only one man, and a sub-issue compared with the hundreds of millions exploited throughout the world today, but if you change the status of the hundreds of millions you will make George Floyd incidents far less common.

America is a symbol of the principles of freedom on which the West was built and the East observes. Africa is an opportunity to validate the West's beliefs, put them into practice, make humanity stronger and learn to live in harmony with our environment.

It is vital that man understands our place in the universe without enlisting gods to resolve earthly power struggles. Man has become so dependent on the flow of goods and services that our survival now depends on others outside our like-minded friends, social class, country or even continent. There has never been a greater need for shared values and tolerance of differences.

The growing world population will not survive on narrow belief systems. Conflict and self-destruction will eventually become inevitable, and the solution will be the diminution of mankind.'

Shaking his head Charles articulates his fears. 'What you are suggesting would entail huge risks.'

'Taking action is less risky than the dangers faced by the first European adventurers who set off around the world in small wooden boats with sails and no map. The empires of Europe were built on that spirit. As a businessman, you have great skill in recognising opportunities and finding solutions.'

Charles asserts an unqualified truth dear to his heart. 'I have made my money by avoiding fatal mistakes, and I plan to continue doing so. I have never seen myself as an economic martyr.'

Confirming the challenge, Karrle replies, 'It is credible that you will not explore these economic opportunities, but it's not credible that you could *not* find any. You have to decide whether you are a businessman creating wealth, or a parasite living off the efforts and misfortune of others.'

'I am an entrepreneur and wealth creator,' Charles protests.

'You are, but you operate in a parasitic system and take a disproportionate share of the wealth created by being close to those who make the rules and run the system.'

Charles now accepts this, but is apprehensive about risking everything to try to change the system 'Many of these issues are not within the control of the business community. It would need governments, Europeans and Africans to change their attitudes.'

'Then that is your opportunity. Massive inequality of wealth is a major driver of these destructive forces, and the distribution of wealth is something that the business community can do something about. But I agree with you: attitudes have to change dramatically and the Western public have to know the facts. Maybe my *Book of REB* could help to open people's minds to the possibilities.'

Almost taunting, Charles replies, 'If you believe that, you had better write it. That is your challenge.'

'If I wrote it, would you buy a copy?'

'Certainly.'

'If you bought it would you read it?'

'Probably.'

'And if you read it, would you do anything about it?'

'I don't know!' Charles replies honestly.

Karrle says rather pointedly, 'Then that is your challenge.'

# Head-To-Head Defending Territories

When news breaks of the intended marriage of Andy and Mohini, all hell breaks loose.

Alex demands to know Mohini's parents' home number and phones to speak to the head of the household. 'Is that Mohini's house? Can I speak to the man of the house? Hello, is that Mohini's father?'

'It is. Who is this?' Vishnu asks.

'You don't know me. My name is Alex. I am Andy's dad. My son is planning to marry your daughter. You and I need a *serious* talk. It's important.'

'I agree. When do you want to meet?'

'As soon as possible. Tonight? Do you drink?'

Vishnu chuckles 'Do I drink? I can drink you under the table.'

Unimpressed, Alex responds, 'Good. Do you know the City Arms in Earlsdon? It's on the corner by the roundabout.'

'They do a lovely real ale,' says Vishnu, flaunting his knowledge.

'OK. Are you free this evening, around seven o'clock? I'll be at the bar wearing a brown jacket.'

'I'll be there.'

Vishnu puts the phone down. He is clear in his mind what needs to be done. This is going to be a very difficult meeting, but no way is this wedding going to take place, and this Englishman must be made to understand. Strange that he asked to meet; maybe he wants to check out the other side. That might be a good start. It suggests that he had some standards, however low. If it gets ugly, Vishnu is not afraid; he can handle himself.

Arriving at 7pm on the dot, Vishnu enters the pub, surveys the room and spots the only person in a rather grubby, brown jacket. Striding purposely towards the man draining his pint, he enquires, 'Are you Alex?'

'I am. Now about this wedding—'

Vishnu immediately cuts across Alex. 'There will be no wedding!'

Alex blinks and warms to his task. 'Good. I agree. They're too young to know their minds and this is a big, big mistake. It must not go ahead.'

'That is what I tell my daughter, but she is headstrong and will not listen.'

'Yeah, so's my son! He was doing great until he broke his leg and was in hospital for weeks. I know he was upset that his football career was ruined, but he got very moody – and now he wants to marry an Indian girl!' Expressing uncomprehending astonishment he proclaims, 'nobody in my family does that. The kid's lost his mind and won't talk to me. I told him "shake ya head, son", but it doesn't make any difference. I could give the stupid kid a good slap.'

Picking up on the comment, Vishnu tentatively asks, 'You say he went to hospital. Which one?'

'Coventry University Hospital in Walsgrave. Why do you know it?'

'My daughter works there as a volunteer. She does not get any money. Maybe that's where they met. I thought it was someone from her school. I found a poem once that a boy from there wrote – it was rubbish, about ruts and chains or something. I told her it was stupid, but she would not listen. Somebody said that boy played football, but it can't have been your boy.'

'Really! Which school?' Alex stares intently at Vishnu, hoping he is wrong.

'Sidney Stringer.'

With heightened concern, Alex confirms, 'That's where Andy went.'

Putting the pieces together Vishnu concludes, 'This is more serious than I thought. These things would never happen in my country. I don't understand it, and I don't approve.'

'Where I live has been ruined by you lot coming over here. We would both have been better off if you'd all stayed where you were. When my dad was alive, you knew what's what. These days nothing's the same.'

Both men grind their teeth in silence, occupying their hands by drinking beer. Grappling to understand, for a fleeting moment each has a glimmer of insight into the other and almost a fragment of sympathy – but what to do?

'This may take some time. Look, I came straight from work and I'm starvin'. How about goin' for some grub?'

Vishnu can see the need to talk and agrees. 'Good idea. Where do you want to eat?'

'How about an Indian?' Alex loves foreign food; it's the people he hates.

Vishnu is delighted. His eyes brighten and his voice sings in self-congratulation. 'My cousin has the best Indian restaurant in Coventry. We can go there.'

'Only if it is hot,' Alex replies adopting his alpha-male persona.

'I will order a special curry. It will make you sweat like a pig and cry like a baby.'

Slipping into auto-friendly repartee, Alex replies, 'Bring it on, my son.'

He is surprised by Vishnu. He drinks, swears and seems reasonable 'for an Indian', Alex thinks but does not say. Maybe they can sort things out together. The two wander off, chatting. 'You know I am glad you seem to understand. I think we can bring these kids to their senses.'

'Yes, indeed! I must confess I was a bit worried that tonight might go badly, but you're OK,' for an Englishman, Vishnu thinks, but does not say.

As they approach the restaurant Alex sees three of his mates. They cannot believe that he is with a non-white. One of them shouts across the street as the group get closer, 'Alex, what you doing with a darky? Do you want us to sort him out for you?'

Alex replies with unaccustomed firmness 'No, it's OK. I'm dealing with it!'

'You're dealing with a darky. Have you lost your fucking mind?' John asks incredulously.

Alex does not understand what he says next; it instinctively comes out of his mouth before reaching his brain. 'Leave him alone. I said I'll deal with it!!'

John cannot let this flouting of group rules pass. 'You've gone fuckin' soft. You've swopped sides, you fuckin' traitor. Fuck off with your new friend, you're not one of us.'

The gang walk off, spitting venom and seething aggression. Alex goes pale in shock at his betrayal of lifelong friends.

With some relief Vishnu expresses his gratitude. 'Thank you. Those men looked dangerous.'

Alex goes limp as the energy drains from his body. What has he done and why? Through clenched teeth he says, 'I … I'm losing everything.'

In a rare moment of enlightenment Vishnu says, 'No, my friend. I think you have just found yourself.'

The two men enter the restaurant, where Alex and Vishnu each face the challenge of preserving what is most precious to them whilst attempting to hold on to the beliefs they have held all their lives.

---

This is not the end, it is the beginning!

Firstly, a huge thank you to Bryony Gawne for her hand drawing of the front cover with such inspired brilliance. My infantile efforts were embarrassing, but she captured the essence of what I was trying to achieve.

A big thank you to my wife who has kept me going throughout my illness.

There are so many people who have made this book possible on this voyage of discovery and offered open friendship, many from the Coventry Refugee and Migrant Centre and many special people throughout the community. Their gift has been wonderfully enriching and will always be treasured. It has allowed time for reflection to understand my life.

To discover more author events, interviews, discussions and more

VISIT OUR WEBSITE
**prisonersofbeliefs.co.uk**

LIKE US ON FACEBOOK
**facebook.com/prisonersofbeliefsbyrichardroe**

FOLLOW US ON INSTAGRAM
**@prisoners_of_beliefs**

FOLLOW US ON TWITTER
**@beliefs_prison**

************

Connect with the author and leave your feedback

EMAIL
**readerfeedback@prisonerofbeliefs.co.uk**

CONNECT ON LINKEDIN
**inkedin.com/in/richard-roe-8b2637250**

Richard
07876572699

Page 252

King George 1st, 2nd, 3rd, 4th & 5th all born in Germany? George V changed the name of the House of Saxe-Coburg to the House of Windsor

"only the whole truth about the past can heal the present" Gary Younge

Capitalism - p. 260. Independance p.269

Self-sufficient - P272

Richard Roe has lived in England all his life. After volunteering at the Coventry Refugee and Migrant Centre, he became passionate to learn about the lives of refugees, the homeless and asylum seekers. The issues that produce these appalling outcomes are visible to all and impact everyone.

It has taken 6 years sharing time with hundreds of people and organizations to start to understand the experiences and traumas faced by those seeking refuge in the UK. The experience has changed his life and values.

His hobbies include swimming, sport (only watching these days), chess and current affaires.

Printed in Great Britain
by Amazon

86378198R00176